BLIND TRUST

BLIND TRUST

CELESTE DONOVAN SERIES
BOOK 3

RACHAEL ECKLES

APHRODITE
BOOKS

Published in the United States by Aphrodite Books LLC, New York. APHRODITE and the Aphrodite logo are trademarks of Aphrodite Books LLC.

https://aphrodite-books.com/.

Library of Congress Control Number: 2025917458

eBook ISBN: 979-8-9990647-2-1

Paperback ISBN: 979-8-9990647-0-7

Hardcover ISBN: 979-8-9990647-1-4

9 8 7 6 5 4 3 2 1

First Edition

Cover design by Anna Dorfman

The book's epigraph is from *Love Her Wild*, by Atticus, and is used by permission from the author and the publisher, Atria Books.

In loving memory of two extraordinary trailblazing women—my Grandma Sheila, who placed my very first book in my hands and stirred a lifelong love of storytelling, and my Grandma Ellie, who graciously shared all the magical stories from her overflowing bookshelves that first lit the spark within me to become a writer. Their fierce hearts, gentle strength, and unwavering belief in possibility shaped my path and live on in every word I write.

Love
   could
   be
   labeled
   poison
   and we'd
   drink
   it
   anyways.

— ATTICUS

PROLOGUE

Queenpin or Lone Wolf?
Mysterious Femme Fatale Linked to
Murder of Scorned FBI Director

Washington, DC
By Avery Quinn | August 12

The famed Riggs Hotel, reminiscent of the glamorous art deco era, was the scene of a deadly stabbing in the early morning hours, according to local police. Authorities were called to the scene around 2:30 a.m., after a hotel employee on a cigarette break saw a woman covered in blood fleeing down a back alley. During a search of the hotel premises, the body of slain FBI Director Stephen Lockwood was found in a sublevel storage room.

"There was so much blood," said the employee, who spoke on condition of anonymity. "It was everywhere—on the floors, on the walls, even on the light fixtures. Something really terrible must have happened there."

Later this morning, the US Attorney General's Office released a statement that Director Lockwood had been under investigation for his ties to vast drug-, arms-, and human-trafficking organizations, and his termination was in process.

A spokesperson for the Metropolitan Police Department confirmed that one suspect—a woman who has not yet been identified—is being actively pursued in connection with the murder. Authorities have not determined whether she acted alone or is linked to a broader network of international crimes. No arrests have been made. The incident is still being assessed, and the investigation is ongoing. This is a developing story, and more information will be provided as it becomes available.#

The Previous Day

Celeste Donovan was certain the pounding of her heart would be detectable to the men chasing her. A successful hedge fund manager with global recognition as an industry magnate, she was adept at performing under pressure. But being hunted by some of the world's most dangerous hit men, as she likely was at the moment, was on another level.

The voice of Zed, the massive former Special Forces marine and her combat instructor, boomed in her mind: "*No time for self-pity now... They will hunt you and capture you. Your only shot at survival is yourself and your training. How committed are you?*"

Very. She was certain of that—she wanted to see this through.

Finally, she reached the end of the tunnel, where she slammed into the door with all her might. It opened easily onto a street several blocks away from the J. Edgar Hoover FBI Building. She nearly fell over from her force.

Celeste squinted, her eyes attempting to adjust to the sunshine blazing down on her.

Run your heart out.

Only a few more blocks and then she could rest.

Her breathing was heavy, and she was aware she probably stuck out like a sore thumb, flustered and sweaty while clad in DC attire, sprinting through mobs of people during work hours. She could only hope they were all too wrapped up in their little inside-the-Beltway bubble to notice.

Putting her fate in someone else's hands had never been Celeste's style. While she trusted Vivienne, a retired member of the intelligence community and a cybersecurity expert turned underground hacker, she had realized she needed a Plan C in case their first two went belly-up. She had stashed her own flight fund and a change of clothes in an alley with no CCTV. When she arrived at the spot, she dove behind the dumpster, scrambling for her bag.

It was still there.

If the FBI put out an APB, her hair color, height, race, and outfit would be the top descriptors. She shed the gray suit and put on a casual ivory tracksuit, with baggy pants that concealed her weapons, along with sneakers. Pulling her wig back in a ponytail, she topped off the casual look with a burgundy-and-gold Commanders hat.

Everything else she might need was still in the bag.

Time to disappear for a few hours.

Walking briskly and taking a nonsensical route to ensure she wasn't followed, she headed for M Street, where there were bustling shops and crowds she could weave in and out of.

Slow down. Be unmemorable.

After several more miles, she was alone on a Georgetown side street about five minutes away from the shops and crowds. Despite a stitch in her side, she had to push on. *No rest for the weary.*

Then came the sound of heavy footsteps running about a block away. She guessed three sets.

"You're making a habit of allowing her to slip through your fingers," scolded a man whose voice she didn't recognize. "Find her and bring her to me. Move!"

The footsteps sounded as though they were heading in her direction. Fast.

That's my cue.

It wasn't a stretch to assume the men were armed. She raced off, staying on the desolate street. There had been enough casualties.

Still no word from Vivienne. Celeste could've used some eyes on CCTV to home in on the men's whereabouts and direct her path.

Stopping behind a tree, she pulled a Glock 9-millimeter from its ankle holster and tucked it into the waistband of her pants. Tears threatened to fall, and she squeezed her eyes shut for one moment.

You've got this.

A gunshot rang out.

Move!

She took off sprinting.

Another shot and then another. One bullet whizzed past her left ear.

She moved back and forth to make it more difficult for the shooters to aim, as Zed had taught her. The men were within shooting range, and there didn't appear to be any innocent bystanders around. She held her Glock behind her, aiming her index finger knuckle toward one of the men and firing. He wasn't hit, but at least they were now aware she was prepared to put up a fight.

She ran as though her life depended on it—because it did. She was down to a five-minute mile and had been embodying Zed's philosophy, "Stay ready so you don't have to get ready," as he always said during her street-fighting lessons. She was faster than they were, and try as they might, they couldn't shrink the distance between her and them.

A small smile broke out. She could keep going comfortably at that pace for some time.

Thank you, Zed, for pushing me to prioritize those boring hours on the treadmill.

More men could be waiting for her somewhere ahead. She cut over to M Street, where she hoped the large number of people would deter the men from firing, lest they call attention to themselves. Moving through the crowd, she feigned a casual afternoon jog, all the while mindful of the heavily breathing henchmen behind her. She strained to hear them through the other sounds around her.

"Let's get out of here before we're made," a gruff voice muttered.

And then they were gone, or at least that's what they'd want her to believe, expecting her to emerge when the sun went down. She circled back a few blocks away toward a behemoth Gothic church and flattened her body against the wall on the shadowed side.

It'll be nightfall soon.

She waited and waited until the bustling crowds shopping on M Street had dissipated, though it still felt too dangerous to be out in the open with no backup. She had lost those men earlier, but they wouldn't let that happen twice. They'd return with more muscle and bigger guns.

Before she could go anywhere, she needed to transform her appearance a bit. She didn't have a new disguise with her, but she could at least put on different clothes—her third outfit of the day. *If they didn't keep catching up to me, things would've gone a little more smoothly.* She reached into the bag, pulled out a pair of black leggings, a matching zippered jacket, and a white T-shirt, and changed in the shadows. *Now, I need to get the fuck out of here.*

Swallowing her pride, she reached into her pocket for that week's burner phone and begrudgingly dialed the one person who could extract her. *Plan D at this point?*

"What mess have you gotten yourself into this time, Mizz Donovan?" CIA Agent Gabriel Gutiérrez whispered by way of greeting.

The way he pronounced "miss" as "mizz" grated on her nerves. "It's *Celeste*," she corrected him. For the thousandth time.

"I warned you that there might be a time when we couldn't protect you anymore. Have Omar's cronies come after you? You can't expect to murder a US asset and get away scot-free."

"I didn't murder anyone," she hissed into the phone, "and now is hardly the ideal time for a lecture." She remembered then that he was her only way out.

Tread lightly.

"I have what you've been looking for," she told him. "But in exchange, I need a favor."

"What is it then?"

"I need you"—she paused and sighed heavily—"to pick me up. I'm in DC. At Thirty-Sixth and M Street Northwest."

"You're what?!" Gabe erupted. "There's a camera on every corner," he said, lowering his voice, "and the place is swarming with plainclothes Feds. With your track record, I'm not naive enough to think that your motives are innocent."

"Well? I don't have much time here. Are you coming or not? I promise it will be worth your while."

"I'm five minutes away. Hold tight."

Exactly five minutes later, a shiny black Chevy Malibu came barreling toward the Gothic Washington National Cathedral's front lawn and screeched to a halt. The passenger door swung open. It took her mere seconds to dash across the lawn and dive into the car. She'd barely settled in with her bag when Gabe sped away.

"I can't even imagine what you were thinking, having a shoot-out in front of Georgetown Cupcake! Of all the stupid, reckless, insane stunts you've pulled in the short time I've known you, this... this tops them all! You could've been killed, but since you hardly seem concerned about that part, a civilian could've gotten hurt! And then what? Selfish, arrogant—you literally think of no one but yourself!"

Ugh, maybe calling Chet would've been the better option.

Anger rose in her throat as she read his judgmental expression. He was the same buttoned-up prick who'd accosted her with accusations during her Capri honeymoon. Sometimes, like in that moment, she wanted to smudge his eyeglasses or ruffle his hair.

She had met Agents Gabriel Gutiérrez and Chet Connolly a year or so prior when they approached Celeste and her powerful financier friends to partner with clandestine units in the CIA and FBI, with a shared goal of taking down international crime syndicates. Agent Connolly—or Clit, as Celeste referred to him to amuse herself—was an FBI agent whose wife, also an agent, was killed in the line of duty by Celeste's ex, Omar Santos, while busting a weapons-trafficking ring in Miami. Chet was nice enough, but it was hard to overlook how disheveled he was in every way, the perfect foil to Gabe, who was fit, still had a full head of medium-brown hair in his mid-forties, and was polished and well-spoken. Chet, on the other hand, had a pudgy abdomen and was balding with flecks of dandruff on the collars of his wrinkled button-downs. His whole vibe was fidgety, with nubby nails bitten down to the quick.

Gabe was a first-generation American whose parents had emigrated from Guatemala. He joined the CIA counterterrorism unit after a crime ring—Omar's organization—had sold automatic weapons to rebel militants in his parents' former village. The rebels killed hundreds of people and overthrew the leaders of what had been a stable community, resulting in the rise of a far-right autocrat who remained in power. In another life, Celeste would have considered Gabe handsome, passionate, maybe even fuckable. *He's an overbearing little shit in this one, though.* He often—perhaps unwittingly, but Celeste could never be sure—derailed her plans.

"Before you jump to conclusions—" she began.

"Oh, I know all about what you've been up to. A complaint of three men waving guns around and an unidentified woman fleeing was called in... of course, it didn't occur to me that it was you until I found out you're here in DC. It wasn't a huge intellectual leap to figure out that, as usual, you were attempting to jeopardize our entire mission on some childish vigilante suicide—"

"I wasn't made, and besides, I'd have been hard to recognize." Chet had unknowingly walked right past her earlier and was none the wiser.

Her heart slowed to its normal rhythm and her breathing evened out, while she processed all that had transpired. She unzipped her jacket pocket and fingered the tiny flash drive to make sure it was real.

Celeste Fucking Donovan saves the day—yet again. She wasn't as buoyant as she'd anticipated. The heaviness was back, albeit for new reasons.

Gabe slowed to a stop when the traffic light changed. He turned to her and narrowed his eyes. "What did you do?" he accused.

When she didn't reply immediately, he continued his railing. "It's going to take me all night to clean up this mess, what with the coverage all over CCTV and all. Your carelessness is costing me a lot, Mizz—"

"Stop right there. You'll be thanking me, if you'd only listen."

The agent shot her a withering look.

"Buckle up, Gabe, because your mind is about to be blown." She summarized what she'd been up to the past few days, omitting the details that he couldn't know, that no one could know. Pushing the sorrow down, she awaited his reaction.

"I have to say, it's not quite what I expected." He drove in silence for a moment before speaking again, this time with admiration and excitement in his voice.

"I can't believe you figured out a way to hack into the system... it's... none of it makes sense... it's impenetrable... the possibilities, though, if we could get this information to the president. Do you know what this means? We could shut down the Senate's meddling... prevent the attack... but is it enough? Are we too late?" he rambled.

What I wouldn't give to distance myself from all this.

Gabe was referring to the joint briefing of the president of the United States and the US Senate Select Committee on Intelligence scheduled for two days later. If classified information about the cyberattack got into the wrong hands, the damage would be catastrophic. Celeste shared Gabe's concern about timing and hoped the information she'd found would at least delay the hearing. *He doesn't need to know about the rest of it.*

"But how did you... there's... no, it's not possible to pull off," Gabe said, shaking his head. "You surely would've... no security breach has even been reported, though. Only the shoot-out."

"The guns and the Georgetown chaos obviously weren't part of the original plan," Celeste told him. "I still got what I needed, though." *And more than I bargained for—or could've lived a lifetime without knowing.*

It occurred to her then that it could have been a mistake to have him pick her up. "Wait, does the agency use GPS on your car?"

Gabe dismissed her concern with a shrug.

"Ohh, it's a dupe fleet car, isn't it?" She noticed the windows had a 5 percent tint—illegal nearly everywhere in the United States. Monty had them on his vehicles for complete privacy. "Hmm, not bad. Fake plates too?"

He nodded. "Chet and I have to stay two steps ahead of our bosses," he explained.

Celeste, by hacking the secure FBI servers, could now confirm that not one, but two members of the US president's cabinet plus three members of Congress had been compromised and were essentially committing treason by working for a nefarious oligarch—the double agent who, as it turned out, was Omar's boss.

"You're in for some unpleasant surprises—they've also turned a few members of Congress. But I think you have at least a day or two to put a stop to this."

Strategically leaking the information she'd obtained would be explosive and damning. It would help Gabe and Chet immensely and prevent disaster in her home country. She only hoped that bringing in Gabe wouldn't cause Vivienne's plan to backfire.

I had no choice.

She wasn't even sure Vivienne was alive.

"You're not safe. They'll be looking for you. Where are you staying?" Gabe asked. "They" could be any number of awful people, though she knew he meant the three men pursuing her earlier.

"Don't worry, I have everything backed up on the cloud, and I took your advice—no big-box hotels. I'm staying at the Riggs in Penn Quarter under an alias. I confirmed they have few to no security measures in place—and it's quite luxurious," she added, knowing it would annoy Gabe. "Maybe I have a career in espionage ahead of me."

"You're staying two blocks away from the FBI, the same agency where you just pulled a heist by yourself, with no protection? No, you absolutely did not miss your calling." He didn't say so, but she knew he would have someone watching her that evening.

In her hotel room, Celeste got to work. Time was of the essence to get the information she had uploaded onto the cloud into the right hands. Even without Vivienne, who still hadn't resurfaced, Celeste had ways to ensure the cyberattack was stopped before it began. Though she'd never asked for the responsibility, she realized that with Vivienne unavailable, it was solely up to Celeste to save her country from these traitorous, corrupt men and women.

Yes, the plan had morphed a bit. *The bamboo that bends is stronger than the oak that resists.* She'd complete the mission no matter what it took. But in the meantime, she sent Gabe and Chet the evidence they'd need to reveal that there were traitors acting from within the administration. *I'll let them get a few brownie points from the powers that be while I handle the situation in the background.*

Logging in to the secret corners of the dark web, she found the person who could execute her plan. There was no time for panic over having to act alone—there was only time for action. As she'd learned from watching Ace over the years, strategically placing news stories in the right outlets was sometimes the most effective way to get things done. Now the most urgent of situations—stopping the cyberattack spearheaded by Omar's boss—was being handled.

PART I

DARK NIGHT OF THE SOUL

1

SKULKING IN THE SHADOWS

Nine Months Earlier

Burying her brother was not how Celeste Donovan had planned to spend her one-month wedding anniversary. Yet there she was, sitting in a cemetery somewhere in flyover country—what she called Middle America—listening to a pastor carry on about how her only sibling, his wife, and their daughter had met an untimely death. She hadn't mourned since the Italian *polizia* had recovered the remains two weeks prior, interrupting her Capri honeymoon with the news. Instead, she was angry. Leave it to Keith to make her special day a dark memory of him driving his family right off a cliff in the peaceful Tuscan countryside after consuming too much vodka with his cereal that morning. Sadness would hit her at some point. *But who has time for grieving amid all the chaos?*

Her husband, Theodore, squeezed her hand. He was the fairy-tale rock of support, looking picture perfect in a black Tom Ford suit and black shirt. He was so handsome—dark hair, ice-blue eyes, and a dazzling smile—that it took her breath away at times. They'd met at a Tribeca penthouse party hosted by Savin, who was not only her business partner—the Clarke in Donovan & Clarke—but also her best friend. Celeste and Theodore had had an unusual courtship— Theodore had disappeared for months, presumed to be dead, before they were even engaged. She had believed he'd been murdered by her extremely volatile ex, Omar Santos, in a blaze of jealous anger. In her grief and rage for all Omar had taken from her, Celeste had left in a whirlwind to hunt him down.

But the game of cat and mouse was much more complex than her grief-stricken mind had grasped at the time. Through an unfortunate turn of events, Omar had kidnapped her from her Paris apartment, then held her captive on his yacht in the Mediterranean. In a coke-fueled rage one night, drunk with power and more dangerous than she'd ever imagined, Omar had nearly beaten her to death.

At the moment when she was sure her life was over, Theodore had showed up out of nowhere, shooting Omar and saving her. The aftermath was intense. Her injuries required several surgeries, and it had taken her and Theodore many months to move on from the trauma. And then the couple finally got their fairy tale, marrying in the breathtaking Tuscan region in Italy. But her past had a way of following her, her brother's death a case in point, so she could never let her guard down.

Now she glanced sideways at Theodore with a limp smile and noticed the droplets of perspiration gathered on his brow. She too was damp from the humid Missouri heat and was glad it wasn't noticeable on her ebony shift dress.

The service was sparsely attended, with a handful of her brother's high school classmates, a couple of coworkers, and his wife's family, whom Celeste had met only once years before and spoken to briefly by phone to plan the memorial service.

Suddenly, she was transported back to her twenty-two-year-old self decades earlier, on the day that changed her life forever. She was sitting for her advanced mathematics final her senior year in college, racing through an exam on which she was sure she would get an A+. Engrossed in the problem-solving, she didn't notice her professor repeatedly calling her name until Savin tapped her arm. She jerked her head up to see her classmates watching, and Professor Maynard sounded exasperated at the delay.

"Miss Donovan, you have a phone call. Report to the dean's office immediately."

Interrupting an exam to send me to the dean's office?

Confused, Celeste gathered her Bluebook and exam, along with her pencils and scientific calculator, and approached her professor's desk. "What should I—?"

Professor Maynard tapped her desk. "Leave it right here. I'm sure you did fine. Now, go see—" She didn't finish her sentence, so Celeste completed it in her head. "...*what's the matter.*" She rushed out of the room and across the courtyard, breathless when she opened the office door.

"Hi, the dean requested to see me."

The receptionist looked at her quizzically. "Name, please."

"Oh, sorry. I'm Celeste Donovan, here to see the dean."

The energy shifted in the small entryway, as the receptionist's smile turned downward. "Oh, yes, yes, right this way," she said, shuffling Celeste to the adjacent room.

Dean Whitefield was nearly bald, showed early signs of dementia, and relied on a cane to get around. Despite his age, he was still a powerhouse fundraiser—the university had the largest endowment in the country—and he maintained the vigor and air of authority of a much younger man. He was at his desk and peered at her over the top of his reading glasses. "Have a seat."

She took the chair across from his desk and looked at him expectantly.

"There's no good way to say this, Miss Donovan. Your parents are no longer with us," he had said sternly. "Apparently, they were in a car accident, and the police would like to speak with you."

Stunned, she sprang out of her seat and backed away from the old man, as though physical distance from the messenger would reverse what had happened. "No, no, no... that can't be possible," she said. "I just spoke with them... last night..." They'd wished her luck on her exams, and she'd thanked her mom for the care package she'd received that day. No, there must've been a mistake. Her breath wasn't reaching her lungs. She was being strangled from within.

That was the first time she'd fainted.

Those days after her parents' death passed by in a blur. Celeste, who then had no living relatives besides her brother, had made all their funeral arrangements herself while Keith waltzed in ten minutes late to the showing, high as a kite and reeking of his favorite vice—whiskey. Her older sibling had always been a party guy, but he had crossed over into addict territory at the ripe old age of nineteen. It had been devastating in those moments to realize that not only was she an orphan, but her single remaining family member was more of a burden than an ally.

She was jolted back to the present when Theodore reached over and kissed her cheek. He nodded at her, and she realized it was her turn to speak. She smoothed her sleek ponytail and hoped her makeup had stayed put in the damp heat. Patting his knee, she rose and walked to the podium.

"We've gathered here today in memory of my brother, his beloved wife, and their sweet little girl so that we may share in the joy they brought us and acknowledge the pain in our hearts after losing them so tragically in a senseless accident." She paused for effect and touched a tissue to the corner of one of her eyes, feigning tears. As a seasoned public speaker, she knew how to invoke emotion, even when she wasn't feeling it herself.

"Their time with us was cut short, but we'll always remember how baby Evelyn could light up a room and how much Keith and Dawn loved being parents." Celeste delivered the remainder of the four-minute speech on autopilot and was surprised to see many heads bowed, wiping away tears, when she looked up. She noticed Savin and his fiancée, Rani, standing in the back, having arrived moments before.

The pastor ended the service with a prayer, and then the group gathered around the freshly dug graves to watch their loved ones being lowered into the ground. Savin and Rani walked over and hugged her. Her brother's grieving in-laws greeted her with expressions of sorrow. And Theodore, ever steady by her side with his hand on her lower back, shepherded her to the front. Was she imagining them judging her apathy? Could they sense that her mind was in fact elsewhere? Why did the memory of her parents' death have to come right then, just as she was feeling strong enough to handle the day?

To distract herself, she looked around the cemetery at the trees, the headstones, the vast rolling hills. Cars lined the drive nearby, a black Cadillac hearse in the lead. A movement caught her attention. In the distance, she could see a silver car, with a man leaning against it and smoking a cigarette. She narrowed her eyes and frowned. *Michel?* Michel Lemoine was an old friend, who had extracted Celeste from more than one sticky situation. He'd proven to be a solid voice of reason, a confidant, with whom she could trust her life. More recently, though, he seemed a bit unstable. She shook her head in disbelief.

"Everything OK, honey?" Theodore murmured in her ear. She nodded and tried to turn her attention back to the moment. *Michel showing up here? What the hell?*

The tiny silver casket with blush-pink roses arranged on top descended into the earth. She pictured her niece giggling in the videos her brother sent her every couple of months when he guilt-tripped Celeste into sending money. A laugh stifled much too soon, reminding her of the daughter she would never have. A sob unexpectedly escaped her lips. She took a deep breath and willed her racing heart to slow. *So much death around me. Will it ever end?*

After the service concluded, the two dozen or so guests made a sort of receiving line for her and the in-laws. She begrudgingly shook hands with, accepted embraces from, and made small talk with people she'd never met or hadn't seen in decades. She half listened while Theodore made plans to meet Savin and Rani for dinner in downtown St. Louis at their hotel and waved goodbye as her friends walked to their car. The most awkward exchange was last—Evelyn's grandparents offering their own words of encouragement, though they were clearly more broken up than she was. Soon only she and Theodore remained.

"How are you holding up, baby?" he asked. "You must have whiplash from the last few weeks."

"I'll be OK," she said and shrugged nonchalantly. Theodore looked disappointed, as he always did when she made light of her emotions. *In times like this, I'd appreciate it if he'd act in alignment with his British roots and gloss over unpleasantness.* To appease him, she laid her head on his shoulder. "Thanks for being here for me."

"Of course, honey. You're my wife now; you'll never experience loss without me right by your side." Theodore pulled Celeste closer. "I hate that you've had so much to deal with in such a short time."

If you only knew, my darling. If you only knew.

She kissed his cheek and replied, "I'll use the restroom in the chapel to freshen up and then meet you at the car."

"Take all the time you need. I'll be waiting."

She walked toward the small stone structure, pausing briefly at the graves. It was hard to believe her brother was gone forever. But hadn't she always known he'd meet an untimely death with his reckless and addictive behaviors? Everyone at the service lamented that he had died so young. Could the converse instead be true—that it was more astonishing he had made it so far, all the way into his forties, after chasing death for so long? Either way, it was a tragedy that his wife and child had such little time to enjoy life. Dawn and Evelyn were innocent casualties on her brother's path to nowhere. Celeste could only hope that they'd all passed quickly on impact, not suffering from pain.

She preferred the tomblike chill in the chapel air over the Midwestern summer heat. Her sweat evaporated quickly as she walked to the altar and took a seat in the front row. Maybe it was time to repent.

No. I did what needed to be done. There had been no other options, and she knew it. But she still suffered from the nightmares—violent, bloody—even if they weren't as frequent as before. They disturbed her sleep and, in turn, her husband's, with enough regularity that he looked at her sometimes with pity, as though she were a fragile, wounded doe. It was humiliating.

She'd hoped the memories would dissipate after all that had happened. *Perhaps forgiveness by some goddess or god is necessary to move on.* She silently pleaded her case, and when she was satisfied, she stood. And then she nearly jumped out of her most conservative shoes, 105-millimeter black Manolo Blahnik pumps, when Michel appeared out of nowhere.

"I thought I saw you earlier. What the fuck are you doing here?"

His eyes were red around the rims, and he appeared disheveled. He was usually stylish and put together, commanding any situation.

"It couldn't wait," Michel replied, as though they had casually run into each other in the elevator in Manhattan, where she lived and Michel frequented, instead of at her brother's funeral hundreds of miles away. Back when Celeste was an undergrad studying abroad in Europe, Michel had pursued her relentlessly. He was good-looking, sophisticated, wealthy—and the accent!—so she finally acquiesced. They had dated only briefly, though, because she soon found out he was married with small children. Being a mistress wasn't her vibe, so she'd ended things. Then, like a chivalrous hero, he'd come back into her life after so many years and had saved her in more than one unsavory situation. They got under each other's skin as only old friends could.

"What couldn't possibly wait until after I buried my only family?" Truth be told, Celeste preferred he brought her news in real time, but she wanted to draw the boundary because Michel was taking too many chances of late. Theodore was going to catch him lurking around, and that would be difficult to explain, since Theodore didn't know he existed.

"Nico's phone pinged a cell tower in lower Manhattan a day *after* he was supposedly on one of their private jets back to Dubai or Italy or wherever his brother said he was going."

Celeste noticed Michel's speech was off. *Is he drunk?* "How is that possible? We destroyed the phone."

"I don't know. But it's a problem."

Donovan & Clarke Capital, or D&C for short, where Celeste was the managing director, had made two major acquisitions before her wedding—TA Capital and the Ricci Fund. Celeste herself had sought out the procurement of the Ricci Fund from brothers Nico and Enzo after she learned of Nico's true colors and that he'd been an associate of Omar's. She was satisfied she'd gotten rid of him for good—until now. *Not today. Does it have to be today?*

"You're always bragging about your ability to clean up messes. Get rid of it."

"There's something else."

Celeste raised her eyebrows. "Well then? Don't hold me in suspense."

"Your favorite federal agents have proven they are the turncoats I've always suspected."

Michel was referring to CIA Agent Gabriel Gutiérrez and FBI Agent Chet Connolly. The agents were part of a collaborative called the illuminati (not to be confused with the storied Illuminati associated with the Eye of Providence), which she had joined—under duress—the year before. Celeste was perpetually annoyed that the Feds chose the name illuminati, as though a pair of federal agents and some financiers were operating at the same level of effectiveness and conspiracy as the Eye of Providence Illuminati. Other members included Savin; Roberto, D&C's most important client, and his wife, Samantha; Fred Warren, an archrival turned ally; and their friend Mark. *We never should've gotten into bed with them in the first place.* But no one had wanted to listen to Celeste when she repeatedly raised concerns.

"What is it this time?"

"They're inserting themselves into—"

Just then, Theodore called her name from right outside the chapel, not even one hundred feet away. She turned to face the back of the grand room, a sheepish expression on her face as her mind raced, trying to come up with an explanation.

"Disappear. Now," she hissed at Michel.

"Darling? Darling? Are you OK?" Theodore prompted, his voice getting nearer.

By the time she turned back around, Michel was gone.

"I'm in here, honey," she responded, plopping down on the nearest pew.

Theodore approached and sat down beside her. "I was worried you'd gotten lost," he joked, though his expression was one of concern.

"No, no. I needed a little time. It's all so much." *The truest thing I've ever said, though you'll never know the particulars, sweet husband of mine.*

"I'm sorry that you've lost your brother, my dear," he said, mistakenly thinking she was upset about that instead of the news Michel had delivered—that Gabe and Chet were up to no good and Nico was haunting her from the grave.

She slumped against her husband, needing his strength for a moment, authentic for once. "Do we have time for a nap at the hotel before we meet Rani and Savin?"

"Yes, as a matter of fact, we can squeeze in a quick snooze," he said, his baritone voice bouncing off the walls in the empty room.

Michel showing up, rogue federal agents crashing her honeymoon only days before—she couldn't, wouldn't keep living a life skulking in the shadows.

AT DINNER THAT EVENING, she and Theodore sat with their good friends.

"I'm grateful the two of you made the trek to my hometown," Celeste said with a nod to Savin and Rani, who was also the office manager at D&C. Savin, a Lebanese refugee who had fled to the UK as an adolescent, was the most sensitive of her friends. Broad-shouldered and checking the tall-dark-and-handsome box, he'd never had trouble attracting women. But he was notorious for latching on too quickly and usually scared off even the most smitten of them. Until Rani. Perhaps it was because she'd had a front seat to all his heartbreak, but Rani was the perfect partner for him. In addition to being kind, patient, and just the right amount of sarcastic to fit in with the D&C team, she was beautiful. She, too, had dark hair and had been blessed with the enviable Eastern European bone structure that so many women chased after with plastic surgery and injectables. In a word, Rani was stunning. Impeccably dressed and always knowing the right thing to say, she navigated life like a royal.

"Well, I wish we were here visiting under better circumstances, Celly. I can't believe he's really gone. I noticed his absence on your big day, but I really thought he was pulling his usual—" Savin stopped himself, and a panicked look came across his face.

"It's OK, Sav," Celeste offered. "Just because he died doesn't mean we can't talk about the person Keith really was. He was a fuckup. I loved him, and he didn't deserve to die, but that's what he was. He used people, and he was an addict.

"Today I marveled that he made it into his forties. How was it even possible with his reckless living and disregard for anyone other than himself?" She took a sip of Sancerre and continued, "It's devastating that Dawn and Evelyn met such a sad set of circumstances. I truly hope they didn't suffer. The kid was cute." Tears welled in her eyes. She'd never had children, writing off the idea after a miscarriage in her twenties, but the image of that miniature casket kept crossing her mind.

"No one should have to bury a child, as my mother always says," Theodore chimed in.

"How is Poppy?" Savin asked. "She and ol' Teddy appeared to be having a grand time at the wedding." His affection for Theodore's parents was apparent in his tone. Best friends when they were growing up in England, they had known each other's families well since they were small. Everyone seemed grateful for the change of topic.

"She's certainly forgotten that I exist now that she has the perfect daughter," Theodore said, and they all laughed together.

Celeste noticed Rani's smile didn't reach her eyes. She'd been quiet all evening.

"Seriously, though, Mum has never, ever forgotten to call me on a Sunday to check in since I went away to uni. Until I married this lovely lady. Now I'm lucky if I get a call once every few weeks. Poppy's always chatting with my wife instead. I've been replaced!" Theodore feigned a frown, then shared a chuckle with Savin.

"Rani, darling, thanks again for making this trek. I know we don't give you much time off from work, so I hate that you had to spend your weekend in St. Louis of all places. How have you been while we've been away?" Celeste hoped to get the other woman talking to figure out what was weighing on her mind.

"Oh, Celly, c'mon. It's no bother at all. We wanted to be here for you. What a terrible tragedy. I nearly lost it when I saw that tiny—"

"Ugh, the casket, I know. I can't unsee it," Celeste remarked.

Rani reached across the table and squeezed Celeste's hand. "You've had so much to deal with lately. You manage it all with such poise and grace."

"You're at least fifty percent responsible for me being able to get anything done. Even with building out our IT capabilities and hiring a team, you're still running the day-to-day at the office, planning a wedding, and keeping this one in line. You're amazing!" Celeste meant it.

"My lady is incredible in every way. And now that you two," Savin said, pointing to Celeste and Theodore, "have finally gotten hitched and the most *extra* bridezilla of all time has moved on to whatever you're getting into next, Celly, Rani and I can start talking about our pending union."

"You're such a nerd. 'Pending union,'" Celeste retorted, laughing. She didn't object to the "bridezilla" remark because she recognized it was likely accurate, and it didn't bother her in the slightest. She demanded perfection unapologetically, and the details of her wedding had been no exception.

"I remember that someone other than myself was reticent to use the word 'wedding' at all in any way leading up to ours, so you may want to tread lightly on calling out someone else's terminology, my love," Theodore said, his light-blue eyes crinkling with mischief. She reached over and tousled his jet-black hair.

"Touché," she admitted.

They teased each other and shared funny stories through the rest of dinner. Michel, Rani's earlier behavior—*my brother's funeral*—Celeste let it all go for the evening and enjoyed herself.

"Anyone care for a nightcap on the rooftop terrace?" Rani inquired after they'd settled the check. "I could use a little fresh air."

"Sure, I'd love to join," Celeste replied. "What's it called again?"

"RK Bar," Savin answered.

"Great, let's do it." As they walked out of the restaurant and made their way upstairs, Celeste looked appreciatively at the decor and noted the ambience. The hotel was not new, and she realized that it was the first time she'd returned to St. Louis since her parents' funeral so many years earlier.

"It's nice to see that St. Louis has leveled up a bit since my day. This Four Seasons passes muster."

The friends ordered a round of drinks from the rooftop bartender and seated themselves at a table. They marveled at how small the downtown area seemed compared with their city, where thirty-story high-rises were dwarfed by Manhattan skyscrapers. The tallest building in their view was perhaps fifteen floors.

Theodore casually slid his arm around Celeste and kissed her forehead. "How did I get so lucky?" he murmured. She rested her head on his shoulder and wondered the same.

"Excuse me, I need to go to the ladies'," Rani said abruptly. She scurried away.

"Is she OK? She seems a little distracted tonight," Celeste remarked.

"I think the death talk is bringing up old issues for her. Maybe she'll open up to you a bit about it someday soon," Savin said.

Celeste was undeterred. "I'll go check on her. I could use some fresh lip gloss anyway." She winked and walked to the restroom. Once inside, she heard Rani whispering frantically inside a stall.

"I can tell you're up to something." Silence. Then, "No. No. Don't do that—don't act like I'm crazy. Whatever you've been lying to me about, whatever it is that you're not telling me, whatever insane situation you've gotten yourself wrapped up in this time—end it. Soon." Rani fell quiet, and it sounded as though she put her phone in her bag. She let out a heavy sigh and flushed the toilet. As the stall door opened, Celeste pretended to have just walked in.

"Are you all right, darling?" she asked Rani, whose eyes had widened briefly in alarm, seemingly wondering if Celeste had overheard. "You rushed off so quickly—I wanted to make sure you weren't ill."

Rani recovered, visibly relieved that Celeste hadn't inquired about her words. "Ugh, I'm fine. A little disagreement with my sister Lani, that's all. That, the heat, and the travel on top of everything going on with the wedding have worn me out. Look, I didn't mean to burden you with this. I'm fine, really. It's nothing compared to what you're going through."

To shift the topic, Celeste thanked Rani again for coming to the funeral, though her guard remained up. Quite recently, a security check had identified Rani as a potential threat. To circumvent the safeguards that had rendered Rani's devices impenetrable, Celeste pivoted. She created a position for Rani as their chief technology officer, knowing that one of her hackers would then be able to gain access to Rani's files. *I need to follow up with Michel on that.* Though it wasn't the first time Celeste had suspected Rani was mixed up in something unsavory, she had never witnessed questionable situations firsthand before.

Back at the table, Celeste asked, "How are the arrangements coming along for the engagement party?"

"Believe it or not, it's been smooth sailing. Meredith is a goddess!" Rani said. She seemed to come alive then. Her face shone with excitement, her past discomfort well hidden.

Meredith had started out as Celeste's personal stylist, and as the years passed, she became so much more—her life manager, party planner, and close friend. Jack, one of Celeste's best friends, had offered up his Tuscan villa for the wedding, and Mere had transformed it for Celeste's wedding into a scene fit only for fairy tales. Now Celeste had lent Mere's services to Rani for her own bridal festivities.

"It will be the chicest event to hit Gin Lane," Savin remarked, referring to the road in Southampton, New York, lined with enviable beachfront estates complete with manicured lawns, full-time staff, and guesthouses. The Hamptons were collectively a Long Island playground out east where Manhattanites fled in the summer months.

"I have no doubt. Meredith always brings the glamour and magic," Celeste agreed.

"Mere may bring the magic, but you, Celly, always turn up the glam," Rani said. *Can't argue with that, I suppose.*

"Flattery will get you everywhere," Celeste said, and they all laughed.

"How many people are you expecting?" Theodore inquired.

"Only our closest friends, your parents, and of course, Savin's mum. My family is so spread out, and they don't really like traveling to America," Rani replied.

"Our wedding was the perfect size—no one sneaking in random dates, no paps selling unflattering photos to *Page Six*, no unkempt relatives causing a stir," Celeste said. *Though if my brother had cared to grace us with his presence, there's no telling what he would've done.*

They chatted a bit more about the wedding and their summer travel plans. Celeste was grateful to everyone for keeping the conversation light. Finally, she was ready to call it a night to have some alone time with her love. She could tell by Theodore's hooded stare that he was as aroused as she was, so she sped up the end-of-evening chat, and the newlyweds escaped to their suite.

"Darling, what a long day," Celeste said as Theodore closed the suite door behind them. She kicked off her heels and strode over to the minibar, where the decanter of red wine that they'd requested with their turndown service was aerating. She poured each of them a glass while Theodore went to the bathroom.

Celeste sat on the sofa and fully exhaled for what felt like the first time in weeks, maybe months. From the moment she'd found out about her brother's death, things had been chaotic. The US embassy had refused to release the bodies for the funeral because the Italian authorities suspected foul play. Once that was cleared up, transport of the bodies was held up when the flight they were supposed to be on was rerouted because of a tropical storm. This was followed by another delay from an oversold flight that had no room for the caskets. The funeral service had been rescheduled three times as a result of all this. Finally, at the point when Celeste couldn't tolerate one more setback, there was room on a plane and the bodies had arrived.

She snapped out of her reverie when Theodore returned, dressed in a white terry robe, and sat down next to her. "How are you holding up, babe?" he asked.

But she didn't feel like talking. She leaned into him and kissed him passionately, then slipped off her dress. She was wearing only a Fleur du Mal thong. His body immediately responded as he took in her naked beauty. He opened his robe to reveal his hard-on and then suckled her neck, making her wetter by the second.

"It's always like the first time with us, isn't it?" he said gruffly. The soft streetlight seeped in through a slit in the curtains, casting a glow on his broad shoulders and sculpted abs. He was gorgeous, yes. But his looks weren't why she stayed—it was because of how she felt at peace with him, the now-daily crises melting away whenever she was in his embrace.

"Mm-hmm," she purred in between kisses.

Theodore was right—their passion remained raw and exciting even as time went by. In the past, she'd never understood the meaning of making love. With him, she knew. He generously pleasured her, not to satisfy his own ego, as lovers had in the past, but because her delight was his end game. He bent down to his knees, slipped off her thong, and kissed the triangle between her legs while simultaneously fingering her G-spot. He was methodical and consistently brought her to orgasm within moments. Tonight was no exception, and she threw her head back in ecstasy.

"Oh my God, oh my God. I need... need you inside of me... right fucking now," she murmured. He didn't stop right away, savoring her twitching legs. As she came down from the orgasm high, he picked her up, her legs straddling his waist, and carried her to the bed.

He gently laid her down, and her body melted into the mattress. Then he stood above her with a glaze of her fluid on his lips, his erect cock teasing her while he admired her naked body. She knew in moments like this that the magic between them was powerful and that their connection kept growing. They'd evolved so much since that fateful first night when he had approached her on Savin's terrace.

I love you. I will always choose you.

To her dismay, Michel and his frightening messages flashed in her mind. How could she care so deeply for Theodore while continuing to keep secrets from him?

She was afraid that things were about to become much more complicated again. *I'll come clean to him. Soon. For real this time.* "When? You've had years to do so," she imagined her therapist pressing. *Don't forget that he has secrets too*, she reminded herself.

She shooed away the thoughts and focused on her husband.

After more teasing, he entered her, and she yelped with pleasure. He brought her to the edge over and over, then slowed his rhythm.

"Oh, baby, please, it's time for me again." She couldn't bear to wait another second.

He chuckled devilishly, and with one final thrust, they came together. Her body went limp against his, and she savored the momentary stillness in her mind. She closed her eyes and tuned in to her breath. When it slowed to normal, she stretched through her fingers and toes, then curled up next to Theodore, resting her head on his chest. His heartbeat was like a lullaby after the trying day. He caressed her cheek and ran his fingers through her hair.

This. This is why I did what I did. No man had ever loved her so openly. *Whatever Chet and Gabe are up to, I'll put a stop to it. And I'll tell Theodore, I will,* she tried to convince herself. *Maybe we could be stronger together with more honesty.*

When Theodore was softly snoring, she tiptoed to her luggage and reached into the concealed pocket for a burner phone. It seemed almost laughable now that she had thought the lifestyle of sneaking around had died with Omar in Rome.

Would it ever be over? She desperately longed for a peaceful life with her love and best friend. *But first, more messes.*

She walked into the bathroom and locked the door behind her. After she turned on the faucet of the enormous tub to drown out her phone call, she dialed the number Michel was using that week.

He answered on the first ring. Referring to Gabe and Chet, she hissed, "Inserting themselves into what?"

"I have to see you. I'm downstairs."

"You what? No, I can't risk waking Theodore, and Savin and Rani are here as well. No, you can tell me over the phone."

"It's important. I'm at the bar."

Click.

Jesus Christ. She tiptoed across the room and dressed in a jog suit, tucking her hair into a cashmere ball cap. Theodore stirred but did not awake. She grabbed a room key and left.

Michel was sitting alone at the end of the bar. There were a few other patrons, all men, each with his head down staring into a malt Scotch as Michel was. Not uncommon at hotels like the Four Seasons, meant to attract business jet-setters, but entirely out of character for Michel. She pulled her cap down and avoided eye contact. After making sure Savin and Rani were nowhere in sight, she sat next to Michel in the shadowy corner.

"What the fuck are you doing here? This is not OK."

He turned to look at her, and she noticed that he was drunk, extremely drunk. His eyes were bloodshot (*Again? Still?*), and his nose was red. *Is he crying?* She sighed and decided to tread lightly.

"Why don't you tell me what's going on?" she asked more gently.

"I didn't stop it. I could've intervened, you know."

"What the hell are you talking about, Michel?"

"They begged me not to tell. Forced me, really. I shouldn't have listened. And now this. I failed. I failed everyone. Twice."

Her patience with him—showing up here, speaking cryptically—was wearing thin. She looked around again cautiously, silently urging him to hurry so she could return to her room.

"I'm sure you didn't fail anyone. Why don't you give me a little more context?"

He looked at her sheepishly, as though he had said too much and regretted it. Shaking his head, he said, "It's nothing, don't worry about it." He sniffled and then straightened up in his seat, plastering a more sober expression on his face. "I looked at their call logs—the Feds. They're nosing around about... Rome."

"But the *polizia* said it was an open-and-shut case, ruled it an overdose."

"Apparently, some of the spooks there raised red flags, and their bosses wanted to take him out in their own way and on their timeline—"

"The Americans?" She laughed quietly. "'Their own way,' my ass. They let him ruin countless lives and then only get rid of him when it benefits them? Those clowns let Omar turn state's fucking witness, *protected* him when—"

"Celeste, what do you think the big bad FBI and CIA bosses will do when they find out their star informant, Omar Santos, died not by overdose but rather was brutally murdered—by an American?"

"Keep your voice down," Celeste whispered, furious.

This was a mistake. She'd never seen him drunk before. Her eyes widened as she considered a new angle she hadn't planned for. "Do you think they've made the connection of me to Omar and to my brother and his family dying the following day? Is that why the embassy wouldn't release their bodies?" *Oh my God.* How had she missed something so monumental?

Michel clumsily put his index finger on the tip of his nose. "Ladies and gentlemen, we've finally gotten through to her," he slurred sarcastically.

Panic rose, but she pushed it down as quickly. "No, no, it's too much of a stretch. They aren't going to find out about our master-piece. That murdering, rapist psychopath got exactly what he deserved."

"You don't know what information he was providing. Could've been Russian nuclear codes for all we know."

She shook her head. "Bullshit. What person could he have possibly been rolling over on that was more valuable than putting him behind bars? No one, that's who. They should be *thanking* us. On top of everything else, Omar was biding his time to reveal to his syndicate that Gabe and Chet were part of the illuminati, along with us, and we both know what danger they would have been in then. We couldn't risk it, and you know it.

"As for my brother, his wife, and the baby—don't you think they would've already brought me in if they thought something was awry?" Gabe's many cease-and-desist warnings made it clear he was on to her, and he had certainly been fishing when he showed up in Italy a few weeks prior while Celeste was on her honeymoon to tell her Omar was dead. But there had been no mention of her brother's fatal car crash until she was stateside after her honeymoon. Once she'd received that shocking news, Gabe had eased up on his accusatory tone about Omar.

Michel flagged down the bartender and ordered two shots of Jack Daniel's. When Celeste declined, he slammed both and put his head in his hands. His distress was deeply concerning.

"They'd never forgive me for this," he said, more to himself than to her.

"Who are 'they'? Your daughter is recovering well, isn't she? Why are you acting so strange?"

He caught her eye and straightened in his seat. "Has it occurred to you that they are building a case against you, against us?"

She shook her head in dissent. "For what? Not going to happen."

What she didn't say out loud was that she would disappear if it ever got to that point. But she didn't want it to come to that. She couldn't bear the thought of leaving Theodore and their life together.

No, she would stay and get it sorted if what Michel was saying had any truth to it. Nothing—and no one—would scare her off. She would leave if and only if she wanted to.

"Look, I appreciate you coming all the way here and passing along this information," she continued, mostly to convince herself. "But maybe..." She trailed off in disbelief as she watched Michel gesture to the bartender for another round. "Michel, pay attention." He looked at her again, and this time she was certain he was close to blacking out. *What the hell am I going to do with him? Fuck.* She would have to get him to his room, assuming he had one. She sighed. When the bartender returned with another Scotch for Michel, Celeste stopped him from placing it on the bar.

"Actually, we're going to go. Can you... did he open a tab?"

The bartender nodded.

"We'll take the check, then." They were the last ones remaining, so the man returned promptly with the bill—keen to clear them out, Celeste imagined.

Thank God. Michel's room number was listed on the tab. She signed and added a $100 tip.

"I'd appreciate your discretion," she said. After glancing at the amount she'd left, the bartender gave her a single nod and turned back to his cleaning.

"Michel, we need to get you up to your room. Where's your key?" He reached into his pants pocket and produced a key card. She guided him toward the lobby elevators, all the while imagining Theodore or Savin catching her escorting a strange, drunk man to his hotel room. Her heart was pounding.

"But I could've done something. I did nothing. I couldn't keep her safe... or anyone safe," Michel was murmuring on their way up to his floor.

"Don't go down that road. You've done a great job of keeping everyone out of harm's way. We did the right thing. We are *doing* the right thing. And you're a great father—you protected your daughter and prevented so many other people from getting hurt." Reminding him that Omar had ordered one of his henchmen to assault Michel's college-age daughter was a gamble, but she hoped it would make him snap out of it.

"But I promised I'd keep *them* safe..." Michel trailed off as tears fell. "That's all they asked me to do, and I failed." He dropped his head in shame. Celeste, frustrated, tuned out his babbling.

OK, now it's really time for bed.

The elevator arrived on his floor, and Michel slumped against her as she led him to his room. She looked furtively up and down the hallway, fully expecting Theodore to pop out of one of the doorways.

"Of course, I haven't *forgotten* what he put my daughter through, and I'm glad Omar's gone. I promised them, though, and I failed. But you—you're the worst of all. Entirely unconcerned that someone could be mounting an insider-trading or RICO case against you as we speak."

She tried to lighten the mood. "Imagine! So cliché if, after all this, we went down for dumping the body of a mafioso in the Hudson," she said, laughing at the thought of being dragged away in an orange jumpsuit because of Nico's cell phone. *Orange isn't a good look for me.*

"Clearly, I haven't been persuasive at all," he said, suddenly sober.

"It's onward and upward from here, Michel," she remarked.

He sighed heavily. "I've got to sleep. You've become a modern-day Medusa," he said, referring to the mythological Greek Gorgon who turned men to stone who set their gaze on her to protect herself, "and I can say nothing to deter you."

"I'll take that as a compliment. Night." She turned to leave.

"Wait—I'm, uh, I'm sorry for your loss. I know you and Keith weren't close, but I'm sure he'd want you to know he loved you."

"Uh, thanks for that," she replied awkwardly. Their relationship had no room for tenderness. "Good night."

∼

"It's been a trying month for you. How has your meditation been going since we last spoke?" Swami Maharajananda, her longtime guru, asked. Celeste sat in her New York home office on Sunday night, staring at him on the large monitor. She'd prepared herself on the flight home that day for the inevitable disappointment when Swami learned she'd abandoned her spiritual practice for the time being.

"I can see something is weighing heavily on you."

Celeste admitted it had not been going well, then recounted the wedding and the funeral. She omitted the parts she couldn't share.

"I suppose it's a combination of things. I had hoped that putting the wedding behind us would... relieve some of my angst." *Stop the nightmares and the looking over my shoulder, in other words.* "I thought I'd feel calm... calmer, I guess, after all I've been through. But I still sometimes have trouble sleeping, and my meditation, my demeanor —I don't feel stable like I used to." *In other words, I was a better version of myself when I was only concerned with fashion, food, fucking, and making money.*

"Don't abandon your practice when things are tough. You need it now more than ever."

There was truth in his words beyond what Swami realized. The danger wasn't behind her yet—it would be devastating if the Feds went sniffing around too much on top of it all—but she couldn't, wouldn't stop until she knew Theodore and the others were safe. Her vigilante justice was costing her a lot—peace of mind, sleep, and the ability to live in the present.

"I'll do my best to get back to my morning practices."

"Focus on exploring your shadow, your dark side, your past. That's when the real work begins." He recommended two books on the topic for her to read before their next session and signed off.

How would Theodore react when he discovered what she'd done, what she planned to do? Would he, the self-professed modern-day Robin Hood, the man who found good in everyone, even her, love *this* Celeste?

He'd gone earlier to shop for groceries and pick up carryout at Don Angie, Celeste's favorite Italian place. Her husband rather enjoyed plebeian tasks Celeste had previously outsourced to her hired staff, but she wasn't complaining. She took advantage of the free time to catch up on all that had transpired recently. She opened a file—*the* file—containing a grid that she used to keep track of people, events, and theories, formatted as a digital version of a prosecutor's suspect wall or murder board, like those commonly used on *CSI* and *Law & Order*. It had a graphic representation of everything suspicious, unusual, and criminal she believed people around her to be involved in, along with their names and faces, and she regularly added updates.

A smile spread across her face, and she beamed with pride. After all, she'd acted as judge, jury, and executioner, solving crimes that still had law enforcement baffled and then carrying out suitable punishment. She always strove to be exceptional, and she'd proven time and again that she accomplished more with a small team of computer nerds and mathematicians than dozens, if not hundreds, of agents and officers could do together.

She took inventory of everyone she was monitoring. Omar's and Nico's photos had large *X*s through them. But maybe she had been premature to think she'd move on so easily from those. Evaluating her potential next steps, she focused on Matthew, TA Capital's COO, for a beat. She'd have to bide her time, with NYPD and the Feds breathing down her neck. But how could she ignore the fact that Matthew was receiving millions of dollars every month from a skeleton LLC, RH Global? Why was Matthew being paid? Extortion? Was he blackmailing someone? Providing sensitive information? Who was behind RH Global? Was it someone connected to her?

The money was tainted and connected to a nefarious purpose, of that much she was sure. Arms dealing, intelligence sharing, bribery, trafficking, money laundering—it was the typical oligarch playbook. *But please, please, not more trafficking of young girls.* However, her research had already revealed that Matthew was part of the same organization as Omar and Nico, both of whom had been involved in sex trade. *Matthew, your number will be up soon.* She would make good on her promise to stop Omar's syndicate, no matter the stakes.

She added Rani's phone conversation and Michel's warnings, meltdowns, and worsening instability to her accounting of the latest

events. The demise of those on her list had to be far removed from
her life in New York and could in no way point to her. Maybe she
needed to rethink her timing, since Chet and Gabe may be poking
around more regularly. Replacing Michel was a must—he was certain
to land them in prison—but pre-breakdown, he had been invaluable.
He left big shoes to fill.

"Darling, dinner's ready," Theodore called from the dining room.
She hit the Save button and shut down her Mac. *Domestic bliss, here I
come.*

MONDAY WAS an important day at D&C. Celeste and Savin planned to
sit down with Roberto to discuss his portfolio and some new opportunities, while their senior staff would hobnob with other ultra-high-
net-worth clients that afternoon. In addition to back-to-back meetings with several key members of her team, she had to find a window
of time to break away to her secret basement apartment in the West
Village. Her go bag needed a refresh—new ID, more cash, SIM cards.
This wasn't the time to reuse aliases or otherwise get sloppy.

Celeste had rented the sublevel place around the time Theodore
moved into her penthouse. She had been in full disguise and paid for
a year in cash. She couldn't have him or their building staff apprised
of all her extracurricular activities, like her combat training, so
having an off-the-radar place was the perfect solution. She kept wigs,
disguises, and identities there—her alias treasure chest—complete
with flight funds to disappear if it ever became necessary. There was
no doorman, and in fact, she'd never run into anyone else coming or
going. The downside was that it was a bit of a dump. When climbing
through the window months before, a piece of broken glass had
pierced her abdomen, leaving a nasty gash and later a scar—another
battle wound as a physical manifestation and reminder of her clandestine life.

Now, promptly at 7:55 a.m., Celeste began her weekly staff meeting. "Good morning, everyone. Thanks for coming in a bit early today

to rehearse our latest pitches for our most important clients. As you know, we're considering a bigger presence in tech and continuing to grow our investments in infrastructure here and abroad."

She and Savin reminded the team of their key focus areas for the year and then the teams went through their pitches over the course of the next hour. Once the two managing directors felt confident the team was fully prepared, they dismissed them. Everyone gathered their things and shuffled out the door. Except Lorraine.

Lorraine was Celeste's favorite employee. She was incredibly bright, entrepreneurial, proactive, hard-working, kind—the list went on. But more than that, she was discreet. She had helped Celeste track down Omar, his holding companies, and many of his associates when Celeste had needed someone like her, and no one was any wiser at the time. To repay Lorraine for her loyalty, Celeste had persuaded Savin to launch D&C Philanthropies, and they promoted Lorraine to president of the nonprofit foundation, which aligned more with Lorraine's passion than tracking down criminal oligarchs. Though she had done it to retain Lorraine, the goodwill they'd received for being "a hedge fund with a conscience" had paid off in spades.

"Celeste—do you have five minutes?"

Celeste glanced at her gold Hermès watch. "I have exactly five. See ya later, Sav."

"Well, I didn't want to be invited to your little party anyway, Lorraine," Savin said, pretending to pout. He left and closed the door to the enormous conference room behind him.

"I'm not going to beat around the bush. I think that someone on your leadership team is—"

"This sounds like a conversation for the war room," Celeste interrupted, referring to the secure room where she and Savin discussed confidential and proprietary information and made delicate phone calls to Ace and others on their security team.

They walked down the hall. Celeste scanned her thumbprint on the reader to gain access. Once the two were settled, she nodded to Lorraine to carry on.

"Someone must be sharing our files—I can't find any other way that business-critical information is getting leaked. Messing with the Shu deal and accompanying files was the person's way of demonstrating that they can get inside." Lorraine was referring to an investment gone awry when she and her colleague Brett (also her lover, Celeste had confirmed on a recent business trip with the two of them) discovered that someone had modified figures on financials. Not only was the person manipulating files, but it had caused the Shu team to reverse course on a conference call with Celeste, Savin, and their counsel and pull out of a deal at the eleventh hour, which was extremely unusual.

How could I have let this slip my mind? Someone hacking into our systems is not to be ignored. And why hasn't Savin mentioned it? For that matter, why hasn't Rani noticed a breach entirely in her remit—or has she? Celeste put on a game face. "Thanks, Lorraine, for raising your concerns again. Does Brett share them?"

Lorraine blushed at the mention of his name, then recovered. "Yes. He's the one who encouraged me to talk to you once more."

"Do you have any idea who it could be?"

"Well, that's why I wanted to speak with you privately. We aren't entirely sure who we can trust other than you."

Celeste understood the unspoken implication—that Savin, among others on the executive team, could be compromised. Could her longtime friend and business partner, the best man from her wedding, actually be working against her? Trust was a funny thing. It was earned over years and years but could be lost so quickly, regained, and then lost once more.

"Hmm. Interesting speculation. Well, do take all precautions. I agree we shouldn't rule anyone out. I imagine you've already thought of this, but please don't put any of this in writing. We have many people combing our files—"

"Including our newly ordained CTO—"

"Yes, she does have full access, as do Ace and a few other hackers."

They developed a plan that they hoped would entrap the person behind the leaks, and Lorraine promised to be discreet, even with Brett. Celeste dismissed Lorraine to get back to work and admitted to herself that Lorraine was the one person in the office she trusted completely.

LATER, Celeste and Savin were seated in their newly redesigned penthouse conference room when Roberto, their favorite client, strolled in. They exchanged glances. *Roberto's definitely had a glow-up.* Clad in a pinstripe periwinkle Brunello Cucinelli suit, complete with a violet tie with magenta polka dots and matching pocket square, he looked the part of debonair financier. He had even dyed his hair black and had some well-placed matching hair plugs he hadn't had in Italy only weeks before. It was hard not to stare.

He whistled in admiration as he looked around at the elegant, modern aesthetic. "So this is where all my money is going," he said with a laugh.

The partners stood to greet him.

"No, no, sit. Give me a minute to take this in." He walked directly to the floor-to-ceiling windows on the far wall and took in the panoramic view of the city. "Wow—just wow. You can see for miles. That's the Brooklyn Bridge and... and, oh, you can see the Manhattan Bridge too!"

Turning away from the windows, he scanned the space. "Was this from your safari?" He nodded toward the enormous reprint of an African leopard that appeared to be eyeing the photographer behind the camera as its next meal, crouched and ready to pounce. Theodore had captured the epic shot when he and Celeste were in the Masai Mara in East Africa during the annual great migration of over one million wildebeest. Of all the beautiful animals she'd seen on safari, that image had stuck with her over time. Only moments after the photo, they'd watched the leopard kill a wildebeest more than twice its size and then maneuver it up a tall tree in mere minutes. Celeste had been captivated (and also a little nauseated) by the scene, perhaps because she often felt like the solitary predator, carrying the burden by herself. When the designer had suggested that they hang something meaningful in the boardroom, Celeste immediately decided on that photo. It symbolized strength, resilience, cunning, sure, but it also contained a melancholy that she carried around beneath the surface. *It's lonely at the top, as they say.*

"Yes, my husband, the multihyphenate, snapped it in the Mara. Award-winning photographer, sailor, chef, pilot. He's never met an activity he didn't excel at," Celeste said, laughing. "Meanwhile, I couldn't unlock my iPhone fast enough to get a photo of a goofy warthog."

"My mate is quite the well-rounded gentleman, but don't tell him I said so," Savin joked.

"What opulence!" Roberto fingered the textured metallic gold wallpaper. "Sam is absolutely going to love what you've done." Sam was Roberto's longtime girlfriend, mother of his child, and Celeste's close friend. It was the highest compliment—Sam's taste was exquisite. She was also the most independent woman Celeste knew and had refused Roberto's many proposals, saying she had no desire to be the fourth Mrs. Roberto Barbosa.

Celeste beamed proudly. "I brought in the best," she said, referencing an exclusive designer who usually worked only with celebrities. "We needed to revamp the vibe."

"I'd say rebranding is in order since you joined the club." He was referring to her and Savin's recent success in crossing over from extremely wealthy to ultrawealthy after having unsurpassed market gains during an economic downturn. "Nice work." He came over to the conference table and sat at the head, with Celeste and Savin flanking him.

"You look well!" Celeste commented, noting Roberto's svelte frame and refreshed appearance.

"Yes, lookin' good, my man," Savin said.

"I jumped on the Ozempic train. Sam deserves to have a healthy life partner who will be around for a while." He dove into an explanation of the joys of parenthood and how having a child with his soulmate was one of the most incredible blessings he'd experienced in life.

"Of course I love my other kids—"

"Your *many* other kids—with *several* different women," Celeste joked.

Roberto laughed heartily, his belly no longer jiggling.

"Yes, there are lots more. It was so different with them because I didn't love their mothers in the same way. Are you and Theodore next, Celeste?"

"Oh, no, no, children aren't part of our journey," Celeste answered quickly.

Savin chimed in, "I want Rani barefoot and pregnant within months of our wedding."

How fun for me to have the already flustered Savin pulled in more directions with fatherhood responsibilities added to his to-do list.

After a bit more chitchat, Roberto was ready to get down to business. He pulled his reading glasses out of an interior pocket and put them on. Savin handed him a bound copy of their most recent proposal.

"Thanks. My wife and I read the updated market insights and refined investment strategy last night. We like how you two are thinking about diversifying into more profitable sectors, and given increasing downward pressures on... well, on every sector, in every market, directionally, we're aligned. More importantly, we need to discuss your most exciting brainchild yet..." He looked at the table of contents and opened to a particular page, tapping his index finger on the title, *Wellness for All: Empowering Women-Owned Community Health Centers in LMICs*, for emphasis.

"This, this is where you always set yourselves apart. Seamlessly blending philanthropy with profit through venture capital investments in healthcare. We all know the microfinancing model never provided enough for small businessowners to shift from just getting by to getting ahead in a sector. Celeste, Sam and I love the focus on women-owned startups in LMICs," he said, referring to countries defined as low- and middle-income.

"Hey, that was all my—" Savin protested.

"This was all Savin's team," Celeste interrupted. "You know we always try to amplify the best talent, which, if I do say so myself, often comes from women. But lover boy here has become an *ally* now that he's fallen in love with a strong woman who doesn't tolerate his shit."

"This is true, but in all fairness, Rani's mom worked as a nurse in a small Ukrainian village, raising four kids alone, and my lovely future wife grew up wishing that her mother had had the option of raising capital to finance the free clinic she'd always dreamed of opening. It was Rani's passion driving this."

"I love it. We can truly make a difference. The lockup period is reasonable, but do you think ten or even fifteen years would make more sense for a project of this magnitude? We want to ensure success. Some food for thought, but consider us on board.

"And a bit more on the tech sector... I believe there's going to be a different type of boom in that industry—and many years to make money—before it becomes extremely regulated and subsequently bottoms out. Even with the heavy policy losses in Europe, their lobby is much too powerful and will be successful in fighting your Congress's establishment of oversight for many more years. Revenue will remain stable in the meantime, with the American market maintaining the profit margin."

Roberto wasn't wrong. Celeste's and Savin's eyes met, and they nodded in agreement. *Go time.* They had a new proposal for Roberto —a significant capital raise—and they weren't entirely sure how he would react.

"So why did you really invite me here? Surely not merely to show off the new digs?" Roberto was nothing if not shrewd. He had provided the seed financing for D&C many years earlier and had watched them gain more and more confidence—and make him more and more money. They were now at the pinnacle of their careers and were the envy of rival hedge funds around the world, based on their unparalleled success in recent years.

Savin began greasing the wheels, as always, so Celeste could go in for the kill. "We want to spring something else on you." He paused for effect to pique their client's curiosity. "With a pretty hefty price tag."

Roberto was undeterred. He was a wealthy man. "How much are we talking?"

"We envision your contribution at eleven billion," Celeste said, deadpan.

"We believe investing in utilities such as Wi-Fi, electricity, and water to move developing countries' infrastructure from state-run institutions to privately owned companies is the only way for these companies to remain competitive and let people lift their families out of poverty. Our multiyear strategy will require lobbying in some key markets to buy up and repackage essential services. Think clean water and Wi-Fi for all. We aren't the first to imagine this—but we may be the first capable of delivering," Savin explained.

"Our vision would require significant up-front investment. We want to send a message—that D&C is nimble, ready to take on real societal issues and be part of the solution," Celeste finished.

Celeste and Savin were like-minded in that regard, but for different reasons. Sav believed that developing LMICs was a way to make the world a better place for children growing up in poverty- and war-stricken countries, as he had, while Celeste hoped the good would balance out some of the decisions she'd made.

They watched Roberto weigh their proposal as he appeared to be lost in thought. "You two are evolving. It's not just about money for you anymore, and I love this. I'll discuss it with Sam, but I'm guessing you can count us in. You know it may make a lot of your other clients skittish, though. Not everyone wants to invest in the greater good; not everyone sees it as good business," he cautioned, then pivoted. "OK, let's speak a bit about the illuminati. I'm assuming that things are smooth sailing with the Feds since you've signed the agreement, Celeste? And things are going well with Ace?"

Celeste nodded. "We haven't had anything come up since before the wedding—or at least, I haven't."

"Me neither. Is there something we should expect?" Savin asked.

"No, not necessarily. Continue taking advantage of the intel they're handing over, making the world a better place, and making us richer in the process—that works for me. But what are we going to do about Omar?"

"What do you mean, *do* about him? Omar shouldn't be a problem any longer. He's—he's gone. Forever," she added. *And I should know.*

"Yeah, yeah, he killed himself, that's what they said." Roberto screwed up his face in distaste. "A hideous overdose, from what I hear, although I wouldn't doubt if his life choices made someone off him. A sad excuse for a Brazilian." Roberto always expressed pride in his country—and disgust for his fellow citizen, Omar. "But what are we going to do about his organization? We don't know who he was working for in the US, what they know, what they're after. Maybe they were even the ones who killed him to get closer to you and other powerful financiers around the globe. Have you experienced any breaches to suggest they'll seek retribution?"

"Retribution? For what?"

Roberto looked plainly at Celeste. *Does he know something?*

He continued, "You don't think there's any possibility anyone will think the illuminati is behind his death?"

"It was an open-and-shut case, from what the Feds shared. He died the way he lived—with no dignity and soaked in his own shit. Hopefully," she added.

"I haven't spent a lot of time thinking about who else is in Omar's organization. Why would they have us on their radar?" Sav broke in. "Plus, our security is airtight and impossible to compromise, thanks to my fiancée. What do you think, Celly?"

Oh, Sav. You and your rose-colored glasses.

"That's a fool's attitude, no offense," said Roberto. "You need to have Ace run more regular checks. The last thing we want is them compromising our portfolios—don't think they haven't learned from what you guys have been up to."

Roberto had a point. She and Savin had nearly bankrupted Omar —twice. It wouldn't have gone unnoticed by people who skimmed off his profits—and felt his losses.

"Noted. Never fear—we'll take care of it. Ace will certainly find any vulnerabilities," Savin said.

Ever deepening our dependence on someone I don't know if I can trust. With Lorraine suspecting anyone and everyone in my close circle, this life will become harder and harder to navigate.

After the meeting, Sav congratulated Celeste and himself for getting positive feedback from Roberto, then turned serious.

"Do you really think Omar's guys could be after us?" he asked, furrowing his brows in concern.

"I'm not sure," Celeste answered honestly.

2

BURNED

"Here we are, Miss Celeste," her driver Monty said as they pulled up in front of the elegant Baccarat Hotel on Manhattan's Upper East Side on Saturday afternoon. "What time shall I retrieve you?"

"Oh, don't worry about me. I'll head home with one of the girls. Take the missus out for date night," Celeste replied. Monty had been working with her and Savin for many years and now had a fleet of drivers under him. Even though he could certainly afford to retire, he insisted on personally carting her and Savin around as often as possible.

"Well, I suppose she'll appreciate me coming home a bit early tonight. Our grandkids are spending the weekend with us. We can take them out to our favorite Italian place." Monty was salt of the earth.

"Wonderful! Life should be enjoyed, and why live among all these excellent restaurants with incredible foods if not to savor them like a hedonist?"

"Exactly. I'll have one of the guys pick you up. I insist." They played this game often, so Celeste knew well enough that she'd have to relent eventually. What they left unsaid was that there was good reason for vigilance.

Her head of security and personal bodyguard, Angelo, was a former NFL linebacker who had suffered from a career-ending knee injury, and had worked with Celeste for many years. Standing at least six feet, eight inches, a foreboding figure of solid muscle, Angelo wasn't exactly easy to slip into Bergdorf for an afternoon of light shopping and brunch. While it was practical for her to have a trusted escort, she wasn't always in the mood to have him in plain sight.

He'd made only one bad judgment call in all the years they'd worked together—he'd hired a driver in Europe who had been compromised. A day didn't pass when Angelo didn't regret the oversight.

So while the breach wasn't her team's fault, everyone had been exercising extreme caution since then. Depending on Celeste's mood, she was either appreciative or, more often, annoyed, mostly because Omar still controlled so much of her life, even from beyond the grave.

Celeste agreed to let Monty have one of his drivers transport her around, knowing it would be easier for her in the long run if he didn't report to Savin—and Savin to her husband—that she was sidestepping safeguards again. *It would be helpful if any of the men in my life could ever forget anything.* "Sounds great; thanks for arranging my pickup with one of the others," she said warmly. Monty opened her door, and she slid gracefully out of the black Maybach. "Now go have some fun with your family," she said.

The Baccarat Hotel was a sleek fifty-story skyscraper that pierced the skyline with its striking modern glass facade. Inside, it gave Celeste the feeling of being transported out of the city into a luxurious, serene escape, the hustle and bustle of the streets instantly disappearing as the main entrance automatic doors closed behind her. She walked to the elevator, nodding appreciatively at the seasonal flowers and accoutrements that adorned the lobby. Upstairs in the enormous Grand Salon, the hostess greeted her warmly.

"Hello, reservation for Donovan, please."

"Your guests have arrived. Right this way," the hostess said and escorted her to the table.

The muted taupe textured walls and floor-to-ceiling windows were the perfect backdrop to the namesake Baccarat chandeliers situated throughout the room, providing a soothing glow. Huge spherical bouquets containing hundreds of red roses decorated the tables. It was one of Celeste's favorite places, with the quiet ambience exuding an air of exclusivity and sophistication. The smart dress code was enforced, to her delight—she was always looking for occasions to wear her favorite outfits. Today she had chosen a new Oscar de la Renta floral minidress, with strappy metallic heels and a Barbie-pink Fendi baguette. The world was in desperate need of more decorum, and Celeste felt this place was the embodiment of it. Each sitting area, with luxe velvet couches and cozy armchairs, felt entirely private despite the openness of the room.

Sam and Meredith were deep in conversation and well into a bottle of Cristal chilling nearby when Celeste arrived. Her heart warmed as they stood to hug her.

"Darlings, I'm so glad this worked out," she said.

"Celly, this dress! Oh my God, it looks even better in the daylight," Meredith exclaimed. "Another look of perfection by yours truly," she said, pointing to herself with both index fingers and laughing.

"Your taste *is* exquisite, but what is most impressive is your humility," Celeste teased. It was true—Mere's sense of style was unmatched. Celeste left nearly all her wardrobe decisions—and many other critical life decisions—to Meredith, who was on the cutting edge of how chic was defined at any given moment, how celebrities were aging flawlessly, and where the jet-set elite traveled. Meredith also made everything *feel* like a special and monumental occasion, so her clients felt beautiful and well-kept. She radiated polish and sophistication. She was truly one of a kind.

Celeste turned to Sam. "You look amazing! Positively radiant. I can't wait to hear how it's going with the baby because motherhood certainly suits you. And Roberto's glow-up—we saw him today at the office—were you behind this?" The three sat, and Celeste nodded when the server gestured to ask if she wanted a Champagne flute. He handed her a full glass of bubbles and left.

"It was all Meredith! She pulled him aside at your reception in Tuscany and sold him on a health overhaul and a complete makeover. When we got back to São Paulo, he sat me down and said it was time for him to take better care of himself. In true Mere form, she had him in New York and booked with appointments for a week straight. He's now working with a trainer and going to acupuncture too. Mind blown."

"Whoa, that's a long way from the porterhouse-and-Scotch Roberto I met long ago. You do love a project, don't you, my dear Mere?" Celeste said. "You keep Manhattan and Beverly Hills plastic surgeons and med spas in business with your client roster." Meredith's commitment to her clients, especially to Celeste, wasn't only on the superficial level—she had ushered Celeste through some of the darkest times of her life. It had taken several surgeries to repair Celeste's broken body in Nice. Unfortunately, her psychological injuries were even more difficult to repair.

Back in New York, Celeste's soul was in pieces. Meredith was one of the people in her small circle who had helped her put herself back together again. It was quite remarkable how "look good, feel good" had helped Celeste heal from post-traumatic stress disorder after Omar's violence. Now Celeste was fully embedded in her sparkly Manhattan life once again. She thought briefly of Michel's warnings. *That's for another day.*

In fact, Celeste was riding high on the $15 billion capital raise for the LMIC health clinics and infrastructure projects that she and Savin had closed by the end of the week, and she was determined to enjoy it with her two best friends.

"OK, ladies, I know I was a nightmare during wedding season, but I'm back. You must catch me up on everything, Sam. And Mere— even though I see you all the time, it's all business. I need to hear what's going on with you."

Sam both complained and gushed about motherhood. "While breastfeeding is a natural miracle—I mean, my body manufactures food, what the fuck?—it is taxing the hell out of my body. My boobs hurt all the time, and I'm leaking through my bras at the office if I don't pump every two hours. Imagine working in a man's world and squirting milk into my bra as if I'm a cow!

"But truly, it is incredibly rewarding, and Roberto does the bulk of the work. I pump, he does the night feedings. Valentina is cute as a button, and every day, she does something amazing or hilarious. We're obsessed!"

"I'm so happy for you, Sam."

Sam pulled out her iPhone and shared a photo album with Celeste and Meredith. They cooed over the daily glimpses into Valentina's growth, videos of her first steps and words.

"I, for one, am dying to be a mother," Meredith said. "Even at a young age, I always knew I'd have several kids. Speaking of, I may have found the father for them." She took a long swig of her Champagne to pause for effect.

"OK, what? You can't drop this on us and give us no details!" Celeste urged.

"I thought you'd never ask," Mere joked and then dove into a story of how she'd met a man at Bemelmans Bar, a swanky cocktail lounge inside the Carlyle Hotel, right after she'd gotten back from Italy. "There was a lot of buildup and stress leading to your wedding —no offense—and I intended to enjoy a little NYC date night with myself, a Negroni, and a jazz band, then turn in early." Lo and behold, a handsome stranger had approached her and bought another round, and before she knew it, they were laughing over black truffle burgers at the renowned Mark Hotel at midnight. "Seth and I walked for hours, talking into the early morning, and by the time he'd escorted me to my apartment, I felt like I'd known this handsome man all my life."

I know what that's like. Celeste had been a smitten kitten after spending the first night out with Theodore. "Oh, this is fantastic!" Celeste said, burying the more truthful thought she wanted to share: *Wait until you're married, sweet Mere, when the secrets mount, and you fear you've become total strangers.*

"We're going to Paris together soon."

"It's the perfect city to explore together when you're first falling in love," Sam offered.

"Exactly, and in fact, I was hoping to tack it on to the trip you have planned in a few weeks, Celly, because I have a huge surprise for you!" She downed her Champagne and refilled it from the bottle next to their table, savoring the opportunity to have another moment of suspense. It wasn't often she could surprise the always vigilant Celeste.

"Quite a flair for the dramatic today. You have my attention. What is waiting for us on our business trip?"

"We have an appointment at the Dior atelier. Can you even believe it? We can plan it perfectly so you'll have bespoke outfits for your Moroccan holiday with Theodore. Isn't this a dream?"

"Oh, wow! Now this sounds fun. And honestly, it's exactly what I've needed in my life." Morphing from a somewhat normal human into a femme fatale with an appetite for murder in a matter of weeks could leave one feeling rather empty. Glitz and glamour would transform her and remove the heaviness she carried. She should know—she'd used this coping mechanism quite often.

"And of course, Sam, you're welcome to join," Mere said with sincerity. The two women had mutual respect for each other and had become quite close after Celeste's introductions.

"I'd love to. Roberto and I will be back in São Paulo by then, but I'm definitely joining you next time!"

With a grand flourish, their server dropped off the first course of the Le Petit Prince afternoon snack, part of the indulgent afternoon tea—a colorful array of savory finger foods presented on a tiered tower. He set their teas in front of them, each fine china cup with its own matching pot. As the tea steeped, the women sampled the sandwiches.

"I love these tiny chicken waffles!" Meredith exclaimed.

Celeste preferred the mini lobster roll but had to admit that the entire spread was delectable.

"OK, I don't want to ruin the vibe, but I wouldn't be a good friend if I wasn't here for a real talk," Sam said, wearing a somber expression. "You've just had one thing after the other, Celly. I mean, juggling the acquisitions and the wedding and then dealing with your brother and Omar dying around the same time. How are you holding up?"

A day apart, to be exact. Omar took his last breath the day before my wedding, and Keith couldn't wait to tarnish my special day with my husband as the anniversary of his death for all eternity.

Out loud, she replied, "I'm OK. I was telling Savin the other day, while Keith was taken from this world much too early, it's almost surprising he lived to be in his forties.

"He was so reckless for so long and hurt so many people along the way. I'm only sad Dawn and little Evelyn had to be brought into his dark world of addiction. I'm sure he was high and drunk when he wrecked—which was midmorning. And turning my and Theodore's happy day into a horrible memory of him—so typical." The heat rose in her cheeks, as the familiar anger toward her brother boiled up. "I know I sound cold, but it's been a lifetime of this. Ever since my parents died, he's made his problems mine. Then there was the nightmare of the embassy refusing to ship their remains."

"Wait, what was that about?" Sam asked.

"They said they had to wait for the *polizia* to rule out foul play, though to me, it seemed unnecessary. Keith was so impulsive and careless—driving off a cliff was on brand."

Meredith's cell phone vibrated from the table. "Oh, I need to take this," she said, excusing herself.

Once she was out of range, Sam probed more on the issue they couldn't discuss in front of Meredith.

"And Omar? I haven't heard a lot of updates. Can we assume his organization's reach ended with his death? How are you taking all of it?"

Celeste focused on the first question. "I haven't really thought much about it, but I'm sure his... death... has destabilized his syndicate. I'm not concerned," she lied, as she so often did these days. The truth was, her apprehension was growing with Michel's recent unraveling—which wouldn't be without good cause—and the Feds snooping around in Rome. She didn't feel guilt—she hated Omar with every inch of her existence and knew the world was better off without him. Nico, too, and all the men like them. The men who took whatever they wanted—people's lives, dignity, sense of safety—and destroyed anything and anyone in their path. No, she had no regrets.

What gave her pause was loose ends, and they seemed to keep popping up. Maybe she needed to find a way to be useful to the Feds so they would stop digging and, moreover, inadvertently help her with her cover-up. *Nothing wrong with a little quid pro quo.* She would expose what Gabe and Chet needed and serve it up to them on a silver platter.

"Well, I thought you should know Johnny sat me down this week," Sam said. Johnny Carolo was D&C's attorney. He also worked with Sam to protect D&C and other clients from SEC or DOJ inquiries. He'd always maintained an appropriate attorney-client relationship with Celeste. *Until now.* Sam continued, "He asked if I knew if anyone in the illuminati might be... involved with Omar's death. Said the Feds were asking a few questions and that he wanted to be prepared."

Celeste frowned. "I don't love that he's having conversations that could implicate my friends, and he never should've put you in that position."

"Don't worry, I said no. But please pass along to the others—we shouldn't raise any suspicions right now. Given our... arrangement with them, we are vulnerable to any change of heart the Feds may have."

My concern from the beginning. Celeste's friends and colleagues had essentially forced her into a loose alliance with two counterterrorism agents, despite her protests that it was not a partnership. No, she had argued many times, it was a lopsided deal. The Feds used her, Savin, their firm's resources, their clients and expected their gratitude for looking the other way on some of D&C's business tactics where they operated in the gray zones of the law. Celeste was no fool—the two parties were not benefiting equally in the arrangement when the Feds could renegotiate on their terms at any given time.

Why did Johnny's nosing around make her so uneasy? He often worked with Sam to keep abreast of what the SEC and DOJ were up to, to ensure Roberto and D&C were not investigation targets. Johnny had been with Celeste and Savin for a long time, a stereotypical Italian New Yorker through and through. She wanted to assume he had good intentions and was looking out for them. But she wasn't so sure.

Meredith came back to the table then, and the conversation returned to their upcoming Paris trip. It had been Celeste's idea to extend the trip and bring her husband along to Marrakech. It was such an intense, beautiful city, and she could get some business done too without raising suspicion from her husband.

Another bottle of Cristal appeared as if out of nowhere, along with another tiered tower, this time with an assortment of desserts: scones, cookies, and doughnuts.

"I am in heaven," Sam exclaimed after sampling an apple cider doughnut. "I think it melted in my mouth."

"Same. Each one is better than the last. Great recommendation, Celly," Meredith agreed.

Until the recent past with Mere, Sam, and Rani, Celeste had never had many female friends. She was an iconic beauty blessed with a mathematician's mind, comfortable in her own skin despite—or perhaps because of—the hatred and jealousy regularly directed at her by other women. As a tween, Celeste sprouted up to her five-foot, ten-inch height, towering over the other kids at that awkward time before the boys went through puberty, and was often the punchline of the school jokes. Excelling in math and the sciences also didn't help her gain acceptance into the cool middle school and high school crowds.

Her parents, both professors at Washington University in St. Louis, had drilled into her, and to some extent her brother, at a young age the importance of education and the pursuit of knowledge. She was a straight-A student, staying up late even as a child to ensure she received excellent grades. As she grew older, she discovered an additional, and more potent, motivating lesson—that knowledge could make her very rich and that money was power, power she could wield over men once she had it. She kept up her studies and made no attempt to fit in with what she then thought of as the "silly children."

Her parents, however, were unequipped to deal with her ambitions. They had chosen anonymity, a comfortable life with excitement reserved for the presentation of research at an academic conference or acceptance of a publication in a peer-reviewed journal as their career highlights. Not her. No, thank you. She wanted knowledge, and in turn to lead a powerful life, and she pursued these things with such tenacity that they became inevitable. After all, wasn't power at the root of every transaction?

Now she would find a way to regain that resolve, to reclaim control in a situation that was spiraling. She would start by finding out how she could distract or placate the federal agents she'd come to resent.

"Earth to Celly. Would you like another glass?"

She emerged from her reverie. "Yes, that would be fabulous. What a decadent feast. I always love coming here!" she said.

"Nowadays, changing out of my sweats that have baby spit-up on them is an accomplishment, so I've appreciated a bit of glamour in my day. Thanks for arranging."

The women chatted a bit more, teasing each other and making plans for a spa getaway sometime soon.

"If I can entice you to step out of your comfort zone a bit, South America is becoming quite the hot spot for relaxing travel. Uruguay, especially, Celeste, would be your vibe."

"Wait, I actually love this idea." For Meredith's benefit, she summarized the infrastructure project Sam and Roberto had invested in. "What if we planned it for a few months from now? October is what—spring?"

"Yes!"

"Meredith, are you in? I can tend to a little business and then we can explore a bit."

"It sounds incredible. I've been eyeing a yoga retreat there for a while—maybe I'll make it happen now."

Celeste slipped her black card to the server and took care of the bill. As they left their table and made their way to the elevator, Sam groaned. "Oh, no, my milk has come in. For fuck's sake." She gestured sheepishly at the two round wet spots sprouting on her blouse.

"Oh, honey, I'm so sorry."

"Ladies, you'll have to excuse me while I go *manually express myself* in the restroom." Sam sighed, suddenly looking exhausted.

"I'll come with you. I happen to have a cardigan you can borrow —and a trick to keep the milk from ruining your silk," Meredith offered. The three laughed at the inadvertent rhyme.

"Thank you so much, Mere. Celly, I won't torture you to stay and endure my mommy crisis."

"I appreciate that. I am *completely* out of my element here, so I'll let you two take care of this." Maybe it was just the Champagne, but she was suddenly overcome with emotion. "This has been wonderful, truly. Thanks for getting me out of work mode." *And away from the darkness.*

"I'll call you tomorrow," Sam said and then Celeste's two friends rushed away to handle the milk crisis.

The tenth time today I am happy to be childless, Celeste mused as she got into the waiting car outside.

"Honey, I'm home," Celeste said in a singsong voice. She was tipsy and horny. After placing her handbag on the foyer console table, she walked down the hall into the living room. Theodore wasn't in there, but she heard him clanging pans in the kitchen. Relaxing ambient music played on the Sonos speakers, and the table in the dining room was set with their new wedding china. Tapered candles burned in the crystal candelabra, shadows bouncing in the corners.

"Is that my beautiful wife I hear?" Theodore called out.

"Yes, handsome." She walked into their massive kitchen. The focal point was a single-slab marble island with large windows over-looking the city. She'd always loved the peace while living in her penthouse above the city, able to see for miles across the boroughs. The apartment had panoramic views and was one of the only luxury high-rises in the West Village.

Theodore faced away from her, in front of their Gaggenau cook-top, stirring the contents of a large saucepan. He loved to cook, so they'd upgraded the appliances and made the kitchen easier to navigate, with a new island and cabinet design. True to his word, he'd made good use of everything. She admired his back view and took him in with as much hunger as on the day she'd met him. He wore jeans and a light-blue polo shirt she'd bought him at the beginning of the season, his bare feet exposed. She ran over and hugged him from behind, squeezing his pec muscles. He laughed.

"To what do I owe this wonderful greeting?" He laid the wooden spoon down on the utensil crock and turned to her. She kissed him, enthusiastically thrusting her tongue into his mouth. He reciprocated, and they shared a heated embrace.

With his arms around her waist, he held her away from him to look at her face. "Had a little Champagne at brunch with the girls, huh?" he said, enjoying every minute. It wasn't often that Celeste let her guard down.

I've missed this, us, your carefree laughter so much. "What gave it away?" she said and giggled. "What's on the menu for tonight, my wonderful husband?"

"*Cacio e pepe*, my love. Your favorite."

He was right, and his was the best in town. Her mouth watered, even though she'd just eaten. "Is there anything I can do to help?"

"Yes, you can have some of the lovely Vermentino from Sardinia that I chose especially for tonight and keep me company while I finish up."

She noticed a bottle of white wine sitting in an insulated wine chiller. He handed her a glass and gave her a healthy pour.

"How are Sam and Mere?"

Celeste chattered away about Mere's new boyfriend and poor Sam's leaky breast milk. "And the food, of course, was perfection as always, which you know." It was never a hard sell to get Theodore to afternoon tea, given his English heritage, so he'd been with Celeste before to the Baccarat. They'd even taken his parents, Teddy and Poppy, there once. Her in-laws had found it delightful.

Theodore put the finishing touches on the pasta and then, to Celeste's surprise, pulled an entire branzino seasoned with herbs and sliced lemons out of the oven. He expertly filleted the fish and plated their meals.

"I'll never understand how you can make these meals look so effortless, dear."

"Lots of practice and a wife I love to feed," he said. "Can you grab the wine? I'll bring the food."

Seated with Theodore in the candlelight glow, Celeste was overwhelmed with happiness. *How did I get so lucky?*

"Babe, this is incredible," she exclaimed. "You've outdone yourself. I just…" Tears welled in her eyes. "I'm so grateful for you, honey."

Theodore beamed. "You're the best thing that's ever happened to me." He reached for her hand and squeezed it. "I don't know what I'd do if I ever lost you. The thought of it makes me crazy."

She changed the subject. "I'm excited for our Marrakech trip. What do you think about joining me in Paris the week before? I have to work and Mere has a few things planned."

"I've taken care of the details for Morocco, but the Paris dates conflict with a commitment I have in Zurich. I'll meet you in the Red City."

"But you've spent hardly any time at our new apartment," she protested, instantly regretting her childish tone. It was true, though. She couldn't even remember if he'd been there since the renovation was complete.

"Oh, you're upset, baby." He massaged her neck. "That's, of course, not my intent. I'll see if I can move some things around tomorrow and join you."

"I want you to see the place. It's turned out so beautiful."

Later, after they cleaned up, they made love. The slow, rhythmic sex was a contrast to their sometimes fast and furious fucking. Celeste liked it all with Theodore, and to her surprise, she was not yet growing tired of monogamy. He mixed things up enough that she never got bored and had the stamina of a much younger man, which she thoroughly enjoyed. That night, though, she came quickly, with Theodore following right after. As she lay in his arms, she dozed off, the many glasses of wine she had imbibed throughout the day contributing to her exhaustion.

Once Theodore was sure she was sleeping, he caressed her cheek and gazed at her adoringly. "Baby, what is it you're running from?" he whispered.

THE EX-MARINE TOWERED OVER CELESTE, whom he had handily knocked to the ground with one sweep. She braced herself as he brought his leg forward to land a kick to her rib cage. And then her mind pulled her back to the past, to another beating, on the sundeck of a yacht Omar had named after her, the two of them isolated in the middle of the Mediterranean with only his staff around. The sound of every hit she endured had reverberated off the water, creating an echo across the glasslike sea. She could smell the coastal breeze and see the glittering stars from that night, and almost as quickly, there it was—the fear, that split second of clarity when she was certain her life was over.

No, not again!

She jerked herself to the present, and at the last millisecond, she rolled out of the way, dodging the blow. She hopped to her feet and, once upright, instantly raised her fists up to protect her face and front body. The lub-dub of her heart pounded in her ears, and she felt the familiar panic rise again. He continued on the offensive, a barrage of fists and feet aimed at subduing her.

I am safe now, she repeated as she had practiced. *I am safe and strong and powerful. I am trained to know what to do next. I am safe now. I am safe and strong and powerful.* To her surprise, the mantras worked. Her mind became clear again, so much so that she began to sense his next moves by watching his tells, where his eyes averted, how he carried his weight between his feet. She managed to dodge most of the attack by ducking and even landed a few hits of her own.

"Not too bad, Mia," Zed told her, removing his boxing gloves and tossing them to the side. It was a grand compliment from him. Not only had he been Special Forces while a marine, but he was also an eighth-degree black belt. "Overall, your speed is improving. But you're still getting stuck; you'd have a few broken ribs right now if you hadn't pulled yourself out of it just in time. Your mind is hindering your progress."

If you only knew. She and her trainer were alone in his Brooklyn martial arts studio for her regular hand-to-hand combat training session. Sweat dripped from every pore in her body, but although it had been a strenuous workout, it seemed she could walk out unscathed. The fewer bruises to hide from Theodore, the better.

"Yeah, I know. I'm working on it; truly I am. Thanks, Zed."

"Go get cleaned up and then we'll recap."

The lactic acid soreness was already beginning to set in, slowing her pace as she walked to the tiny women's locker room, constructed only after Zed began training her, the sole woman on his schedule. She quickly rinsed off and changed back into her street clothes, a matching Alo tank top and capri set with sneakers and a jacket.

"What happened in that split second when you almost failed to respond?"

"I—" She sighed. It wasn't as though she could share much. "I had a flashback to a... a bad situation."

"But you did snap out of it, which is progress. How'd you do it?"

She blushed, embarrassed that she needed assistance. "By reciting a mantra, telling myself I am safe, strong. After a few times, it was almost as if my mind became a blank canvas, and I could anticipate your next moves."

"This is what we have been training so hard for all this time, Mia. To prepare you for what is next."

For the hundredth time in a month, she wished she could read what the future held for her.

"I am getting stronger, more strategic. I can feel it," she said honestly.

They chatted a bit more, and he gave her homework for the following week—sprints, weightlifting. He impressed on her the importance of continuing to get stronger and chided her that she must not let the business of life get in the way of her training.

"You can never anticipate when the attack you've been training for will come. And Mia? I won't tolerate tardiness again."

THAT SESSION HAD BEEN her strangest with Zed yet, but it was because of what happened before, rather than during, her session to throw her off her game. It had started off like any other Sunday morning. Celeste had awoken at 5 a.m. Theodore, still asleep, had his body wrapped around hers, spooning her. Careful not to disturb him, she turned to watch him sleep. He looked so peaceful. She often asked him what he dreamed about, and he always replied with a little grin that she had visited him in his dreams. She imagined his inner world was filled with light and happiness, puppies and ice cream, and felt a tiny twinge of jealousy. To go back to her old life, to sleep soundly at night, to walk down the street without looking over her shoulder—a return to living on such simple terms was her aspiration.

She wasn't normally late to meet Zed. He expected her promptly at 7 on Sunday mornings and was not happy with the recent demands on her personal life that were interrupting her dedication. "You must be more committed to your practice. You are lazy and undisciplined," he would say when she infrequently arrived a few minutes late.

Taking time off for her wedding resulted in another lecture. But she tolerated him mainly because his nontraditional training methods worked—she'd never be taken anywhere against her will again, of that she was confident. And he never questioned her identity—he only knew her as Mia, and she only trained in full disguise—or her true motivation. He accepted her explanation that she was in danger and never pried any deeper. He trained her—hard—so she could escape if someone ever tried to kill her again.

Poor Theodore believed she attended hot Pilates every weekend and then had a relaxing morning stroll at the Abingdon Square Greenmarket. To the contrary, she rushed to her secret sublevel basement apartment when the street CCTVs were rotating away from the entrance, changed into Mia, and dashed to Zed's martial arts studio, then rushed back, showered, and picked up a loaf of San Francisco sourdough and some locally grown vegetables.

That morning was supposed to be the same as all the others. She wore a matching set of leggings and a sports bra under a hoodie, topped off with a ball cap and sunglasses. "Good morning, Jonah," she said to her favorite front-desk concierge. "I'm off to work out."

"And what a beautiful morning it is, Miss Celeste," he replied, always greeting her with something similar. Jonah, who had watched a decade of her life unfold as a resident in the building and had witnessed a revolving door of men before Theodore, was always the consummate professional.

It was a short distance from their luxe high-rise to her other place, and by now, it was second nature for her to dodge the street cameras. She was on autopilot that morning, readying herself to get back into her practice with Zed, and when she ducked down into the dumpy basement apartment she used for cover, she didn't notice anything out of the ordinary. Inside, she headed straight to the tiny, poorly lit bathroom with fluorescent tube lighting. The checkered tile on the floor and walls was yellowing, and a water bug felt around the shower with its long antennae and then circled the drain. She shivered and made a mental note to bring bug spray next time.

Work faster. She tucked her hair into the wig cap. Satisfied, she went to the bedroom big enough for only a twin-size bed and a tiny end table. Her wigs were hanging on the wall in sealed bags. She selected the wig she used for Mia and secured it in place in front of the bathroom mirror. She added her colored contacts and rushed through her makeup to get into character.

Out on the street again, she did a quick perusal and confirmed she was alone. She set out toward the subway. *Wait.* A movement, a person, out of the corner of her eye. She looked left and right, trying to discern where it had come from. *There!* A black-clad figure began running north up Hudson Street, now about a block away. She closed her eyes to slow down her memory of what she had noticed, trying to remember if she saw their face. No, they'd had a black hoodie up, and it had shadowed their face. But the person had been pointing a phone camera toward her when she emerged onto the street. She itched to spring to action. Should she run after them? Then what? Destroy their phone? Zed had taught her that her training was to help her get *out* of a dangerous situation and not to give her the confidence to *walk into* one. Because what if they had a weapon? What if they were running from something else entirely unrelated?

But, conversely, what if they'd been following her? Had seen her go in as Celeste and come out as Mia? She'd been so careful for so long. She had to know if it was time to make new arrangements. She waffled back and forth a bit more. If she caught the person, then what? Start pummeling them until they relinquished their camera and calmly explained why they were following Celeste? Were they even following her? No. She decided it was too risky to attempt to confront the person. Either way, she would still have to take proper precautions and relocate her safe house. *I'm burned. And late for my session. Fuck.*

After her session with Zed, she walked out of his studio and onto the sunny Brooklyn street. Celeste normally didn't pay much attention to the neighborhood because she didn't make a habit of connecting with people while she was in disguise. The street was not immune to gentrification, a few two-parent families juggling co-op groceries, children, and doodles on the way to their $10 million renovated brownstones. Today she was skittish. She kept her head down as she made her way to a different train than she usually took.

She considered abandoning the apartment altogether because someone had discovered she was there but realized there was no way around it—she would have to go back there before she went home. *Ugh!*

She shot off a text to Theodore, explaining that she had a few errands to run, and then took the subway stairs two at a time, feeling an urgency to understand what, if anything, had happened earlier.

She arrived at the safe house around 10, having taken several detours to ensure she wasn't followed. This time, mindful as always of the angle of the rotating CCTV cameras, she went to the back side of the building to make sure no one had broken the small window before going around to the front and entering. She quickly locked the door behind her and confirmed no one was there. No, she was alone inside. She ripped off the wig and stuffed it into its bag, returning it to its wall hook. The bathroom was as she had left it. She removed her colored contacts and freshened up. One more quick run through and then she was out.

Oh, fuck! She did a double take when she noticed one thing awry. The cockroach was still in the shower—except now it was dead, having been smashed by a shoe while she was at Zed's, from the looks of it. *Change of plans.* She gathered all her things, only the wigs and a few articles of clothing she'd stored there, and stuffed them in a gym bag. The safe house being compromised had always been a possibility, so she was prepared to pack up on a moment's notice. As the final step, she hastily scrubbed the place down, hoping to remove any traces of her. *Goodbye, little apartment.* She secured the lock, discreetly wiped down the doorknobs, and stepped onto the street, being mindful that the CCTV did not pick her up. When she put enough distance between her and the apartment, she started toward the Greenmarket with her head held high, once again Celeste Donovan.

3

CHAOS BRINGS OPPORTUNITY TO THOSE WHO ARE PAYING ATTENTION

Celeste sat on her overstuffed Rimowa trunk in an effort to snap the latches and lock it. *This is precisely why I do not pack myself—I don't have the temperament for such tedious tasks.* Normally, Mere took care of trip prep for her. As Celeste had amassed more wealth and Meredith had become more accustomed to catering to the ultrarich, packing began to look different. Celeste would suggest a few outfits she liked and then Meredith would plan every ensemble down to the accessories, have everything wrapped in tissue paper and shipped to Celeste's destination, and ensure that it was unpacked by a butler before Celeste's arrival. But today was different.

Mere was running herself ragged with Savin's engagement party coming up, and lately, Celeste, though entirely uncomfortable with the unwelcome emotions, was feeling more empathy for her staff and guilty about piling on too much work. *I'm becoming a softie.* She'd considered hiring more staff, but bringing new people into her home seemed like overkill when she was perfectly capable of packing on her own.

Perhaps the real reason Celeste wanted to tackle it was that she had nervous energy she needed to burn off. It was Sunday afternoon, and she was still lost in thought about the potential—no, *likely*—compromise of one of her most-used aliases and the break-in at her safe house. Was there footage after all from the hotel in Rome? How could she have been so arrogant, so reckless to keep using the same disguise? She could have just as easily used any number of her others, including Brinn Horvath, which she'd successfully used in the Caymans. *Idiot.*

Normally, she would rush to tell Michel and seek his counsel. He'd berate her a bit for her carelessness and then they'd hash out a course of action. But he wasn't himself. In fact, she was concerned she'd have to cut him out entirely after his St. Louis episode. It was wholly unexpected that he seemed less equipped to handle Omar's death than she was.

Thus she needed to keep busy and had the brilliant idea to pack herself, even forgoing her custom Hermès luggage for her old Rimowa trunks, stored in one of the extra bedroom closets. She'd kept the trunks for many years, unable to part with her first luxury luggage set she'd purchased when her career had taken off. It seemed apropos to use it for this trip with all the navel-gazing and reminiscing about the past she'd been doing. She cursed Keith once more for his selfishness. The past would have stayed where it belonged if he'd been able to get a handle on his vices. *And, oh, I don't know, perhaps refrained from driving his wife and child off a cliff on my wedding day. Asshole.*

The generous walk-in where she sat had formerly been a spare bedroom. When they'd renovated the kitchen, she'd had contractors knock down the wall to build her dream dressing room, bigger and grander than her closet. Haute couture hung neatly on rods along the periphery, and an island in the center of the room was made of luxurious custom cabinetry with a white lacquer finish. A glamorous chandelier released an ambient glow that allowed her jewels in the central compartment to sparkle. At the very end was a dressing area, complete with the Hollywood vanity and three-way mirror with platform from her previous setup. It was exactly as she'd always wanted, but even more spectacular than she'd imagined.

There were two light knocks at the boudoir door. "I hear someone grunting... what in the world is going on in there?" Her husband walked in and tried to hold back a laugh. Clothes were strewn about, and Celeste was now standing on the suitcase.

"It... won't... close. Argh!" she shouted, then collapsed on the floor in a heap. She recognized that her stress level was disproportionate to a leisurely Sunday before a Paris trip, but he didn't seem to notice—or perhaps he'd grown used to how unstable she was lately.

Theodore strode over to her. "Here, let me try." He leaned over, pressed the trunk top down, and closed it with minimal effort.

"There, see? A little teamwork, and the two of us can take on the world." He lifted her in an embrace and spun her around in what she knew was an attempt to make her laugh. When she didn't, he set her on her feet and looked at her with concern.

"OK, what's going on? Where's Mere, and why are you so frazzled, babe?"

Celeste collapsed onto the floor and sank into the plush ivory carpeting. The walls she carefully constructed so that no one, not even her husband, could get inside felt as though they were on the verge of crumbling. She burst into tears. If Theodore was shocked at the rare occurrence, he hid it well.

"Honey, I was just in the other room. Let me know next time you need me." He situated himself next to her with an arm around her shoulder. The tears fell more freely then—*Why does it always seem to happen like this?*—and she pressed her face into his shoulder, embarrassed.

"I'm sorry, I don't know what's gotten into me."

The heaviness of the deaths? The secrecy and sneaking around? Or maybe it was the family memories of a road trip out West to Santa Barbara that she, her brother, and her parents had gone on when she was young—some of the only happy ones she had of her childhood —that had surfaced moments before. Her brother was really gone. Her parents were gone. The thought that continually resonated, though, was that her carefree former self was gone. And someone, or maybe many people, including the FBI and NYPD, were still after her. Getting rid of Omar hadn't changed any of it—she was still consumed by fear and tied up in legal troubles. It was devastating to realize that she may never get out of this mess.

That last fact was what she was really mourning. Her calculation of "the world isn't big enough for both of us—it's him or me, and I'm not going anywhere" had failed to account for other complexities. If the Feds discovered she had murdered a US asset, what then? How could she clear her name without Michel's help? Would he collapse with guilt and go rogue? Confess? Or worse, turn her in? Did Omar's henchman reveal to one of his superiors that she had orchestrated Omar's multiple takedowns? She hadn't yet uncovered who headed up the crime syndicate Omar worked for. She'd mistakenly assumed Omar was at the top, but she should have known he was a pawn for something bigger. He always was a bottom feeder.

She could share none of this with her husband, so other words tumbled out. "What a mess. I... I don't know what's gotten into me. It's just... all this travel and... so much to catch up on after the wedding. We're in the middle of the acquisitions, and... everything is falling through the cracks. And the packing. You know how I hate packing. Especially when Mere is so good at it. She makes everything fun and exciting. I need a break, not a work trip. We've been back only a couple of weeks, and I... don't feel like I can keep going on like this."

She sobbed an authentic ugly cry, but not for the reasons her husband believed. She longed for those first few months with Theodore before he'd disappeared, before Omar returned, before the deaths, before the aliases and the spying—before it all. They'd laughed and traveled and made love, and life was simple. The comparison with her current life was almost laughable. Almost.

Theodore exhaled heavily. "I've been wondering how you were holding it together. Your brother and his family died suddenly, baby. You got married, acquired two multinational investment firms, and learned that the man who traumatized you so many times over the years is finally gone—all this in a few short months. No one would fault you if you wanted to cancel this trip altogether and stay at Miraval or The Ranch for a month. You're allowed to have a moment to feel the enormity of life occasionally." He brushed away a tear and kissed her softly.

Was she mistaken? Were those really the things eating at her? A shitty ex who lingered from the grave, a dead selfish brother, and a few business deals? Was she more upset about her brother than she realized? She didn't know.

She inhaled deeply, annoyed with the self-pity path her mind had taken her down. *Pull it together, Donovan.* Her plan wasn't clear yet, but one thing was certain—she was more than capable of managing whatever life threw at her. She would fix it this time. For good. No more loose ends. She wasn't one to run away when things got a little difficult or someone tried to intimidate her—that wasn't her style. She fought back, she *always* fought back—and won.

Life had been a little tumultuous, sure, but that didn't mean she was going to give it all up. She loved her life. She loved her husband and her friends. Life would be empty without them. No, it would take more than yet another creepy person snapping her photo or breaking into her bare-bones safe house to scare her. The pep talk worked; the metaphorical armor was back in place. She was Celeste Fucking Donovan after all. If anyone could take care of business, she could. And she would.

"Well, that was unnecessary." Celeste sniffled and straightened up.

Unfortunately, Theodore hadn't been privy to her inner dialogue, so he was still playing the supportive partner. "I'm not going anywhere, my dear. I'm in this for the long haul. I'll stop at nothing to protect you and our life together." He lifted her chin so that their eyes were level. The look on his face was somber. "I won't let *anything* or *anyone* get in the way of our life together."

Oh, sweet husband of mine. You're going to have to leave this to me, I'm afraid.

"Gosh, I don't know what got into me. Sorry for all that, and thank you for closing my bag, which is going to explode when I open it at the Paris apartment." She gestured to the three other suitcases lined up. "Well, all of them will, really. You didn't think I was bringing only one bag, did you?"

"Packing light is for the simpleminded, and my wife is anything but," Theodore teased. Celeste laughed along with him. Then he continued, "Honey, I really think you should take some time off. You've never really had a chance to grieve. You're the only thing I care about in this world. Let me take care of you for once. Let me help you heal."

She pretended to mull over his comments for a moment.

"Oh, you're the best, darling," she said, patting his chest. "Thank you. That all sounds so wonderful, having you take care of me—truly, it does—but what's best for me is to keep moving forward. Wallowing at home is not my vibe."

"Are you sure? I can cancel my trip."

She shook her head firmly. "No, there's no need for you to do that. Besides, I need to be out in the world, wearing the most glamorous of outfits and kicking ass."

Theodore looked disappointed at her attempt to deflect the intimacy of the moment. He let it go, though, regaining his British stiff upper lip with a brisk and businesslike tone. "OK, so Savin and Mere will be with you in Paris while I'm in Switzerland, and we're meeting in Marrakech next Monday, right?"

She nodded.

"Great. Our assistants can coordinate the rest."

LATER THAT EVENING, Theodore left for his trip. Celeste, wanting nothing more than to turn her mind off, had just settled onto the sofa with a novel and a weighted blanket when her iPhone vibrated.

Jack's in town! His text was to her and Savin, suggesting they have an impromptu dinner. Who was he kidding? Everything was impromptu with Jack. She confirmed that she'd be there, and they decided to meet an hour later at a nearby hot spot.

Jack was one of Celeste's and Savin's best friends, along with

Mark, who lived overseas with his wife, Jin, and their daughter. The foursome had been close for two decades through many different life stages, and their bond had only strengthened over time.

Jack cashed out of the working world before age thirty and had been living off seemingly unlimited profits from an organic grocery store deal since then. He rarely spoke about the specifics of his adventures, but Celeste gathered it involved a lot of illicit substances and women in every corner of the world where he could find a party. With his blond hair, dark eyes, and lithe physique so similar to Celeste's, Jack was quite handsome and looked more like her family member than her biological brother had. In many ways, Jack *was* more like family than anyone else in her life. He helped her out of a very dangerous situation when Omar had first begun abusing her and had kept many of her secrets through the years. She adored him, and whenever he popped in (almost always unannounced), she and Savin made every effort to see him.

Now the three were seated outside at Anton's, a prime West Village spot at the iconic corner of West Eleventh and Hudson, known for its European-American cuisine and celebrity sightings. The patio was suffused with a soft glow, and while the tables were dressed in white linen and fine china with delicate patterns, the vibe was intimate and casual.

"What brings you to town, mate?" Savin inquired after they'd ordered a round of drinks.

"The usual—lookin' for some hot deals and hot women," Jake said. "How're you holding up, Celly? What a tragedy about your brother. I couldn't get to St. Louis in time, but I've been thinking of you."

Celeste sighed heavily. "Yes. A horrible tragedy. You should've seen Evelyn's tiny casket, and Dawn's family was sobbing the entire service. Felt a lot like when my parents passed." She paused, the familiar emotions associated with her brother bubbling up.

"Except this time, I was angry. My brother is, er, was so careless, so selfish. I'm glad they weren't here to see what he'd become." *Well, I'm not sure they'd approve of me either, to be fair*, she thought wryly. "My parents were simple people. Believed in family, getting an education, working hard, and democracy. Keith would've been such a disappointment."

The server, an Italian man who spoke rough English, dropped off their drinks then, white wine for Celeste and Scotch neat for the men. She took a sip and continued.

"I've been thinking about my family a lot, actually." She summarized her earlier breakdown after a rogue childhood memory surfaced. "My childhood wasn't terrible, but I don't remember much. Mom and Dad were academics, so they were around for breakfast and dinner most days. They would stay up late at night at the kitchen table, speaking excitedly in hushed whispers, probably about whatever boring conference they were attending next.

"They were good parents, but our lives didn't have the worldliness and excitement I craved. I grew up and went to college and then they were gone. I spent most of my adult life without them. It feels wrong to say, but they've been gone for so long, and my brother and I were so distant, that I didn't think of them or him much in the past few years. Even when my wedding was approaching, I wasn't as wistful as I would've imagined other brides to be."

"Well, from what I can tell, you probably weren't a typical bride in more ways than one. You've never exactly been *typical*," Savin said.

"Obviously. Being ordinary is one of my biggest fears. Maybe family isn't a priority for me—because I certainly wasn't sobbing like Dawn's parents."

"We're your family, Celly, and I can attest that it means a great deal to you. Look at all you've done in your life to protect us, to protect Theodore. You"—Savin choked up a bit before continuing—"well, that's what's meant by family, that's all."

"Also, there really isn't a right or a wrong way to grieve, is there?" Jack offered.

"I suppose not."

They placed their entrée orders when the server dropped off their starters, Pâté Grandmère, and East Coast oysters.

Jack added a touch of lemon squeeze to the dozen, then brought one to his lips. "Ooh, you can almost smell the brine."

He slurped it and swallowed so theatrically that Celeste lightly slapped his shoulder, rolling her eyes. "You're so embarrassing," she said, though she laughed along with the guys.

"Yum, yum," he said.

Celeste smeared a piece of crusty bread with the pâté, a savory pork liver mixture with a velvety texture. She noted the garlic and thyme flavors coming through.

"OK, enough about me. What's going on with you lately?"

"Oh, you know, a little here, a little there," Jack replied. "We were in Tuscany, what, like a month and a half ago? I played around a bit in Sardinia and then Capri. Had to stop over in Switzerland for a bit."

"Theodore is there a lot lately. You two should coordinate sometime."

"No disrespect to your choice of husbands, but I'm not sure sappy Theodore is my vibe. Doesn't seem like he'd appreciate my, uh, extracurriculars."

Celeste rolled her eyes and laughed. "You do have a point. I can't imagine that husband of mine frequenting Thai sex clubs and snorting rails off of dancers with the likes of you." While Savin was close to both her and Theodore, she considered Jack *her* friend. *So maybe I shouldn't encourage them to hang out after all.*

"I also visited Mark for a few days in Shanghai," Jack said, "which is why I couldn't get back in time for your brother's wake. Now I'm here to check on you before I hop on a plane again."

"I didn't realize you'd been to visit Mark so recently, man," Savin responded. "I was just talking to him the other night. He says Jin is expecting another baby."

"Wait, what? I mean, the first kid is cute, but she's still so small," Celeste said. "Is it a good idea to have another one so soon? Isn't that, like, bad for a woman's health? Or at least frowned upon? Has she even lost the weight from baby number one?"

Savin and Jack burst out laughing, as they always did whenever

Celeste tried to act as if she knew virtually anything about birthing a child, parenting, or saying the right thing at the right time.

"Actually, it's quite common outside of communist China to have more than one child. In fact, I think evolution hopes for that to ensure the proliferation of the species," Savin teased.

She thought back to Sam's milk coming in over brunch. "Oh, whatever, it's all fun and games until we never see Mark anymore because he's driving around a van full of children!"

"Mark in a minivan—now that I would like to see," Jack said.

"Oh, my fiancée is calling. Excuse me," Savin said, walking away to take the call.

Alone now with Jack, Celeste said, "Hey, I've been meaning to ask you something."

"Shoot."

"Did you invite someone to the villa after the wedding? I thought I saw…" She tried to conjure the memory exactly. She and Theodore had left in the wee hours of the morning at his urging. She'd looked back at Jack's house while they were in a golf cart en route to the heliport and noticed a light on in Jack's room. He'd been arguing with a dark-haired Caucasian woman. "Well, when Theodore and I left quite early to head out to Capri, I could've sworn I saw you with a woman in your room."

Jack looked at her quizzically. "It sounds like a case of mistaken identity! I was flirting with one of the staff—a gorgeous Italian woman, if I recall—but sadly, she rebuffed my advances. Pretty sure I was in bed alone that night, though the nights—and the women—are a bit of a blur, what with so many of them coming and going from my beds all over the world."

"Oh, Jesus, here we go," she said, laughing at his silliness. He did love women, so it wouldn't have been a surprise if he had shacked up for the night—but it wasn't like him to withhold the truth. "Hmm, my eyes must've been playing tricks on me."

"Probably. Or maybe it was Mark and Jin?"

Oh, right. Because you two are so easily mixed up. Mark was taller and more muscular than Jack, with dark chocolate skin and black hair versus Jack's fair coloring and blond hair. Jin was Chinese, with golden skin and a petite frame, whereas the woman Celeste had seen was equally stunning but appeared to be Jack's height. The two couples looked completely different.

Savin came back then, frowning.

"What's wrong, Sav?"

"Rani thinks our servers have been breached," he said. "She's working through it with one of our tech teams and is connecting with Ace in the background as well."

"Everyone's getting hacked these days. It's fine," Jack said. "Let's not ruin a perfectly nice buzz on boring work talk."

She thought back to the hooded figure running away from her safe house only a few hours earlier. *Even my glasses aren't so rose-colored, my friend.*

"Do you want me to skip Paris tomorrow and help you navigate this?" she asked Savin. It wasn't the first time they'd been hacked. Celeste felt a sense of dread.

He weighed the idea, his nervous energy palpable. "No, no, we've got this. At any rate, it'll probably be helpful to have you over there where you can assess impact to our satellite office."

Rani and the team hoped that their system was still secure, Savin explained, but it looked as though it was going to be a late night.

"I'm going to the office. I'll keep you posted." He rebuffed Celeste's offer to join him and told them to enjoy dinner. Then he flagged down a taxi and was off.

"Well, that's a huge bummer. Never a dull moment," Celeste said to Jack.

"You're taking it all in stride—or at least, better than Savin."

"Everyone handles things better than Savin—you know this," she said, laughing. Jack considered and joined in. Then she continued, "Yeah, I've learned not to sweat the small stuff. There's a new crisis every day, and somehow it all gets sorted."

"So, are you going to tell me what went down with Omar?" Jack asked, abruptly shifting the topic, worry coming over his face.

"Well, he's dead, so that's a good thing. For real this time. There was a body and everything."

"Do they know who did it?"

Celeste shrugged. "The official cause of death was a drug overdose, as far as I know."

"Yeah, right. He was on a lot of shit lists. That wouldn't have been too hard to stage."

Celeste laughed. "You make a good point."

"I wonder if it was someone in his circle."

"You know how reckless he was, and it sounded like he was only becoming more and more unhinged. An overdose seems quite possible."

Jack grinned devilishly. "I prefer to think it's something unsavory. I can see it now," he said, making a gesture of an arc as though presenting a show in lights. "Rapist junkie meets horribly violent death staged as an overdose, and not a single person mourns his death."

Perhaps we weren't as innovative as we thought. "Now, there's a sellout show."

"Seriously, though, how're you holding up? A lot of shit has gone down recently."

Why does everyone keep asking me that?

"The truth is, I'm more than OK. I'm free. Everyone asks me how I feel about my brother dying, and I'm relieved that I don't have to watch him ruin his life anymore. I'm relieved that I'm not faced with the disappointment and pain he would've caused my parents and has caused me every day for twenty years. I'm relieved because the call I was always waiting for—that he hurt himself or someone else—well, that call is behind me now.

"It probably goes without saying that I'm ecstatic that Omar is gone. And I hope you're right—that his death was unsavory, that he suffered every second before he died. I hope he felt all the pain he inflicted on me and on so many others. I hope he was tortured and that he's rotting in hell for all the damage he's caused." She paused and took a long pull of her wine.

The server, who must have sensed they did not want to be interrupted, made eye contact from a few tables away, and Jack signaled another round.

"I feel lighter than I have in years, knowing I'll never have to see him again."

"You know my thoughts on men who are predators. I watched my mom suffer for so many years at the hands of whatever man she'd decided she loved in that moment," Jack shared. "You're justified to feel this way. Omar nearly killed you, Celly. Seeing you all black and blue, the machines keeping you alive, barely hanging on—it's one of my worst memories, worse than anything my mom ever went through."

She realized that she'd rarely discussed that time period with Jack —and also that Omar's violence, while having such a physical impact her, had also affected those closest to her, perhaps more than they normally shared.

"You saw me? You came to the hospital in Nice? I guess I knew that. But my memories are so hazy."

"Of course, Celly, we were all there. Theodore barely left your bedside, but we tried to give him some relief. You were mostly unconscious, so it's no surprise you don't remember."

Could Jack give her some answers?

"That was really kind of all of you. So who else was there?" she probed, attempting nonchalance.

"Well, Savin, Mark, and I all flew out. We were so worried."

"Was—" She stopped herself. A question remained on her mind since more memories had been coming back to her. *It's Jack. Just ask.*

"Were there any other people there? It's so weird, but I have this memory that surfaced recently... waking up and seeing a guy who seemed vaguely familiar but wasn't any of you. Maybe it was a dream, but it felt so real."

Jack considered it, then shook his head. "No, it was only our small circle. I don't recall anyone else."

Celeste narrowed her eyes. He seemed to be telling the truth.

"That was such a terrible time. Not that anyone needs to, but you've earned the right to be happy," Jack said. He sighed.

"Do you worry about our situation with the illuminati? We've gotten so mixed up with all these criminals and now have been set up by the Feds to be so embedded in their investigations. Roberto asked me the other day if I thought Omar's organization would be after me."

"Has something happened to make you concerned?" he asked. "Do *you* think there's truth in what Roberto said?"

Maybe it was the wine, maybe her resolve had been wearing down the more the question was asked, or maybe she felt as though she were going to burst from all the secrets tucked down deep. But she had to say something honest. Jack had always had her back, and the beauty of Jack was his simplicity. He wouldn't gossip. She took a deep breath, and like a river after a dam was breached, the words were flowing out too fast before she could stop herself.

"I caught someone following me today. Taking photos. It's not the first time, of course, but it was always Omar behind it—or so I thought. Now that he's gone, it makes me wary of everyone."

"Really? What happened?" He was now wearing his big brother facial expression.

Shit. She wished she could take it back. She guzzled the rest of her glass of wine. *Liquid courage.* She badly needed to tell someone, and he was the lowest stakes. "I was... coming from my workout. I usually stop at Abingdon Square for the Greenmarket on the weekends, and I'm near certain it was me he was photographing. I mean, I assume it was a he. They had a hoodie on, shadowing their face. They ran away when they saw that I realized what was going on.

"I'm fast enough to chase them. I wanted so badly to catch them and smash their phone and find out why—why no one can seem to let me live my life in peace. But I—"

"Who knows what kind of person was behind it or whether they were armed?" His demeanor changed from concern to anger. "Are you trying to get yourself killed, Celly? We can't lose you. You must stop being so reckless—"

"Chillll, Jack. I didn't do anything stupid after all because I thought all these same things you're saying. I'm not self-destructive." *Not anymore.*

Jack was visibly relieved. He downed the remainder of his Scotch, lost in thought. "Have you told anyone else? The police?"

"No and no." *All things considered, I'd like to stay off the radar with NYPD.*

"Well, you should at least tell Theo—"

"No! And I will kill you if you do! My husband's an alarmist. He's already worried enough about me, pretty much all the time. Savin's a basket case, so there's no need to alert him either. I finally got everyone to agree that I didn't need armed guards with me all the time."

"Celly, it comes with the territory of the lives we lead." He looked her over. "I'd guess your jewelry and handbag for a casual evening out add up to a hot mill."

"So what? That's not the point. This isn't London or Mexico City! I'm not going to get robbed walking to hot yoga."

"C'mon, Celly, this isn't rocket science. You need security, period. We all do. We're public figures. How many of them wander around New York alone? And *especially* now, now that you've confirmed someone has potentially been following you again—well, you need it more than ever."

On an intellectual level, she understood. But he didn't know what it was like, how trapped she felt with someone always lurking around. She was a powerful, independent woman who could run a five-minute mile and hold her own in a shoot-out. Why did she need some guy watching over her?

"What about Angelo? You love him, and you've welcomed having him around in the past. He can tighten things up a bit. Simple."

She shook her head.

"Cell, Angelo is your bodyguard, for fuck's sake. Omar was obsessed with you for decades. As far as you know, he informed people high up in his organization that you were behind the sabotage, the trades, nearly bankrupting him... twice."

Celeste frowned. *Of course Jack knows about all the trades—how could I have forgotten?* Jack couldn't be an impartial friend lending an ear when he knew the stakes. She regretted spilling the information about the snooper. "OK, sure."

Jack looked at her doubtfully.

"I'm serious! I'll tell Angelo. Tomorrow. I promise."

"And you, uh..."

She knew what he was going to say. *My penance—having Omar creep into every conversation I have for the rest of my fucking life.*

"...have better security in Paris nowadays, I assume?"

"Yes, yes, of course."

"Good. Please don't forget to tell Angelo about today."

"Done. First thing when I wake up."

Jack seemed satisfied because he changed the subject and recounted a hilarious attempt to land one of his planes in St. Barth on its extremely short runway. He always knew how to put her in a better mood. After another glass of wine, her troubles were far away, albeit temporarily.

Though I will never allow Jack to pilot me anywhere.

"EMERGENCY ILLUMINATI MEETING AT MINE!!!!!" screamed the text from Savin. Celeste had just walked into her apartment from dinner. *Sigh.* She called Monty right away.

"Darling, could you send someone to drop me off at Sav's? I'll be ready in ten."

She changed into a casual jeans-and-blazer look, and half an hour later, she was seated in Savin's Tribeca penthouse with him, Sam, Roberto, Johnny, and Fred Warren. Celeste wanted to hear more about D&C tech issues, but she'd need Sav in private for that. Since no one knew why they'd been summoned, they made small talk until the front door opened again, and the men who'd convened them— Chet and Gabe, the awkward Feeb and the stuffy spook—walked in. They were escorted by Angelo, who remained in the hallway during the illuminati meetings to ensure there were no interruptions. Even with Savin's apartment occupying the entire floor, someone could still find a way to slip in, and they couldn't risk it.

"Please, everyone, have a seat. We don't have a lot of time," Gabe said, taking command. He worked in the CIA's counterterrorism unit, and Chet was his FBI counterpart.

The chatter tapered off. "Look, we've brought you in before when we were afraid that people inside the US government were behind a conspiracy to destabilize the country's infrastructure." Gabe sighed and continued.

"While it may sound strange, the intel you've provided from your deals and research—which oligarchs are behind different banks and funds, where the money can be traced back to, et cetera—has been the most valuable we've received. You in this room have saved the US from more disasters than we are at liberty to share in an astonishingly short amount of time." He gave each of them a meaningful glance. Celeste resisted the temptation to roll her eyes or snap a sarcastic remark.

"We're close to unveiling the perpetrators behind the latest threat, a massive cyberattack, but as you can imagine, it's no easy task," Chet jumped in. "We know that someone high up in the administration is either being blackmailed or taking bribes in exchange for information and access to our systems to carry out the attack—but we haven't zeroed in on who this is. The transaction trails are nonexistent, agency files are sealed, no one is talking—we continue to run into dead ends."

"My guys are on the ground all over the world," Gabe explained. "They provided two contacts who are part of Omar's organization and are believed to be leading whatever operation is unfolding. But we still can't figure out what their end goal is."

Well, well, well, an opportunity presents itself. If she could get them what they needed, maybe she could buy herself some goodwill—and a way out of the illuminati.

She waited for someone else to ask the first questions. Appearing too eager would raise the agents' suspicions.

"Of course we'll help in whatever way we can," Savin said. "But if you haven't been able to crack into this one, why do you think we can? Do you want more access to our hackers?"

"No offense, but the guys you employ, while useful to accomplish your goals, can't breach the US government's firewalls, at least not without raising alarms," Chet replied.

"We need you to trace the money. Use your connections on the dark web to zero in on where the money is flowing. A bonus would be if you could figure out what kind of attack we're preparing for. A virus? A Trojan horse? Botnet? A straightforward worm? Ransomware? I'd imagine the guys you normally work with would know if there was any chatter," Gabe said.

A nefarious black hat hacker, organization, or government could cripple a nation in myriad ways. A Trojan was malware disguised as legitimate software. Ransomware, as the name suggested, involved shutting down a system by holding it hostage until the victim did or didn't do something the person responsible demanded. Worms and botnets were the most common, over-whelming and confusing a system, essentially freezing all activity. The US could be vulnerable to any cyberattack if done well. The recent past had plenty of examples from which a sophisticated hacker could learn.

Celeste possessed only passable knowledge of how a virus could cause the US to collapse, but she did know one thing—a well-resourced nemesis with access to cabinet-level information could devastate the US with the tap of a mouse.

"This is Ace's territory. Have you shared with him... ahem, *them*... the prospect of the threat growing imminent?" she asked. In the beginning, Celeste and Savin had assumed that Ace was a man because the voice changer that Ace used sounded masculine. As time went on and Ace's identity remained hidden, Celeste wondered if she'd been too hasty—perhaps her assumptions about Ace had been wrong all along.

"Yes, we've been in contact. Ace's reach is broad, as you well know. But it's mostly international. They've never dabbled in US politics in a way that would grant them access to top-secret files," Gabe explained.

A sophisticated hacker, Ace was largely responsible for D&C's success. Ace had approached Celeste and Savin several years prior with a business model: leverage insider knowledge about geopolitical events that were about to happen, such as an uprising of rebel forces in a developing country or a default on a loan that would cause ripples in the stock market, and tip off Celeste and Savin in real time. The heads-up allowed D&C to develop strategies anticipating the outcomes—trades that made them and their clients quite rich in a very short time. Ace would then flood the targets' media markets with real and fabricated news stories, ensuring they had the desired effect to manipulate investor behavior in their favor.

Celeste and Savin came off as savants, and no one was the wiser —until Chet and Gabe discovered what they were up to. But the agents had no interest in putting a stop to D&C's activities by turning them in to the SEC, the oversight agency for the securities industry. No, Chet and Gabe were too cunning for that. They knew how white-collar criminals were treated in the US. Even if Celeste and Savin had been found guilty of insider trading or other fraudulent behavior, they would've been slapped with fines that wouldn't bankrupt them or, worst-case scenario, they'd spend a little time at a Club Fed, the slang for a white-collar, minimum-security prison. The founders would be free to go back to their old practices in a matter of months.

Instead of turning them in, Chet and Gabe had instead coerced the D&C duo to enter into a sort of loose partnership with their friends and the two federal agents, with a unified goal of taking down crime syndicates across the globe. After their meteoric rise into the highest realms of the finance world, Celeste and Savin were reliant on Ace and not interested in abandoning their success—so they had little choice but to work with the Feds. *Well, Savin says he volunteered so that he could save me. I, on the other hand, was forced.*

Ace remained an enigma after several years. Even with so much history between them, Celeste and Savin still knew very little about them, never having met in person, never seeing them on video. Ace never forgot to use the voice changer. Because Ace was so embedded in D&C business and also liaised between D&C and the Feds these days, the partners had to work with Ace. After Ace had several big misses that cost her a lot, Celeste began losing trust in the mysterious person who had been so integral to D&C's success over the years. She begrudgingly continued to work with Ace and the Feds when Savin disagreed with her change of heart, a source of rare tension between them.

"You don't think that I, as a Brazilian, have any ability to obtain the sort of information you need, I presume?" Roberto asked.

Chet shook his head. "We don't expect any of you to build the case for us—you'd never gain access. We need your resources to track down financial records of the transactions because we can hardly call up Chase or Charles Schwab without a warrant. Plus, as I'm sure you're aware, most of this would be taking place with crypto. What we need to know is who is paying whom? Are payments happening with any sort of regularity? Are other governments involved? Oligarchs? The dark web chatter is deafening; something is coming, dollars are flowing, and whatever it is, it is indeed imminent. We've sounded alarms all the way up the chain, but as we feared, *no one* is motivated to act. Which means one of two things—they're either involved... or they're afraid to speak up. It feels like the months leading up to nine-eleven all over again."

Gabe took the handoff without missing a beat. They'd clearly practiced their delivery. "What's even worse is that we've been ordered to stand down. Our only recourse is something that's almost impossible to pull off—we must build an ironclad case and get evidence directly to the president so that he can stop whatever is coming."

Celeste imagined for a moment what they must be going through, deeply committed to protecting the country they called home, but receiving a directive to look the other way. How desperate they must feel, day in and day out, nearly collapsing under the heaviness of the top-secret information they couldn't share with their friends or families. They'd do almost anything if someone could assist with their predicament, give them the proof they needed, to save the country to which they pledged their allegiance from the impending catastrophe. Celeste could empathize. *And use it to my advantage.* Because even if their cause was noble, Celeste wanted out of the illuminati.

The Feds seemed relieved to have shared the damning information with an audience. They finally sat down, almost in unison.

"The next part cannot be shared outside of this room. You can use it to guide your investigations, but please leave no trail of anything from this point forward."

This wasn't the first time the Feds had given the illuminati this spiel. They'd been extensively trained on the parameters of their relationship with the agents and the information shared. Celeste and her friends weren't government employees, and they did not have security clearance. As far as the US government beyond the two Feds was concerned, they were private citizens, and if their agreement was ever uncovered, Celeste did not know what would happen. But the fact that Chet and Gabe were willing to go to such lengths... well, they were either insane or reckless... or they were really in need of help. She looked around at her friends, all wearing the same somber expression.

This isn't a drill this time. Even she could feel it. The accusations the agents were making—that at least one cabinet member was a foreign agent—could not only end their careers but also place their lives and those of their loved ones in jeopardy. Celeste was smart enough to know that the mere possession of the information that Chet and Gabe were about to share put her and her friends in enormous danger as well. No one spoke of it, but the air crackled with a recognition of the severity of the situation. There would be no turning back.

"We have a list—a short list—of names. Members of Congress, agency heads, cabinet members. No one else has seen this, and it can never be leaked that we were investigating these specific people," Chet explained.

"I'll give you a quick refresher to fully apprise you of the stakes,"

Gabe added. "The US does not surveil its citizens without a warrant, except under specific circumstances."

Celeste laughed. Having been on the receiving end of a few SEC and DOJ investigations of her own, she knew the interpretation of "specific circumstances" was broad. "Oh, come on, fellas, we know a thing or two about surveillance."

Ignoring her, Gabe continued, "My agency, the CIA, is responsible for protecting US national security in basically two ways: by obtaining information from people who may be foreign agents, spies, and the like, and by monitoring US cybersecurity to prevent cyberterrorism and hacking. The CIA is not a law enforcement agency, whereas the FBI has law enforcement—in other words, arrest powers.

"But neither of us has carte blanche to initiate what we're asking you to do. While the Patriot Act expanded the government's ability to retrieve phone, email or financial records of US citizens, there are still boundaries within which the NSA and our agencies must operate."

The National Security Agency had been criticized lately for exceeding its authority. *Forgive my cynicism, but someone's always watching.*

"The guardrails are generally good," Gabe said, "and the commitment to live without the mass surveillance that other countries employ is a privilege. It should go without saying that digging around in financial records is highly illegal in this instance."

He handed off to Chet, who concluded, "I'm sure you're asking yourselves what's in it for you. Right now, nothing much beyond our original agreement—we look the other way while you cash in. But once we uncover the plan and put a stop to it, you'll know you did the right thing when your country needed you most."

She half expected them to take a bow after that performance.

"The magnitude of this—it can't be understated," Gabe said. And then in hushed tones, the two agents rattled off names that would have shocked any civilian.

The director of national intelligence could be a foreign agent. The chair of the Senate Finance Committee. Speaker of the House. Secretary of Homeland Security. That was only the beginning. Her friends were as hardened by life as she was in many ways. But hearing it out loud. Processing the impact. *Unprecedented times.*

"How quickly can you work?" Gabe asked brusquely. "We expect that we'll be hearing about a congressional inquiry soon—one that would dramatically increase the scrutiny on us, making meetings like this impossible."

Hadid had tracked down Matthew's RH Global transactions with the COO's laptop in a matter of hours. Celeste envisioned some sort of remote access being most effective, but she didn't share this with the group.

"Look, I agree with Savin," she said. "We're more than willing to help, and we have people who can move quickly. But I have to say— it's quite disturbing to me that it has come to this.

"As you know, I've long been skittish about our involvement when it's official government business. Forgive my bluntness, but if you two are canned because you've uncovered something you weren't supposed to, how do we know that these nefarious policymakers won't come after us? If a Russian hacker is planning an attack and the cabinet is complacent—"

Gabe looked at her pointedly. "You've all spent some time operating in the gray—this shouldn't feel any different." It was the same accusatory tone he'd taken with her when he'd barged in on her during her honeymoon to alert her that Omar had died—and to gauge whether she was behind it. No one in the room knew about that imposition, though, so it didn't raise alarm bells for anyone else. "And frankly, if we can't stop whatever this is, that will be the least of your worries."

Fuck you, Gabe. Your veiled threats will be no more than that when I'm in the driver's seat.

Chet jumped in to assuage his partner's suggestion. "What Agent Gutiérrez means to say is that we can't do this without you and your resources. There is no way we, as bureaucrats, can snoop around in the financials of such high-profile people without raising flags. We need people we can trust—and that list is dwindling. We trust you. You've built a solid network of hackers who can manage this. We need you. The world needs you."

Gabe muttered something under his breath. Celeste could've sworn that he said, "At least for the time being."

Just wait, asshole. Just wait. She was looking forward to the day when she could tell Gabe what she really thought of him and their arrangement.

"We'll put our heads together and deploy a plan," Savin assured the men. "Since it is only a handful of names, it shouldn't be that difficult."

"Time is of the essence. Let us know if you need to bring in others. There are two Silicon Valley types we've been thinking of vetting, but more on that later. We'll reach out midweek."

With that, the agents seemed in a rush to leave, so they hurried through their goodbyes. Once they were gone, Sam was the first to break the ice. "What the actual fuck?"

"This isn't the first time they've come to us with one of these doomsday scenarios," Celeste reminded everyone.

"No, but this feels different," Savin said. "They shared names. The director of national intelligence. A Manchurian candidate? C'mon, that's a pretty substantial accusation. They wouldn't share without some level of certainty."

"Roberto, you're unusually quiet. And Johnny? Fred? You've never been ones to hold back," Celeste prodded.

"This *request*—if you can call it that—has 'bad idea' written all over it," Roberto stressed. "Breaching financial records of cabinet members? The chair of the Senate Finance Committee? Even in Brazil, I wouldn't risk it, and I've been able to pull off a lot there."

Fred stood and walked over to the windows. A longtime rival of D&C, he'd more recently become an ally after also being a target of Omar's organization. He was around Roberto's age but had not recently had a glow-up. He was bald, and when he turned back to the group, his face looked older than usual and haggard. He was worried. Afraid, even. After a moment, he cleared his throat, then spoke.

"Look, we all know we could track down the information. The few of us in this room could prevent a catastrophic cyberattack on our country. We talk about legacy and being king—"

Celeste opened her mouth to protest.

"And *queen*-makers if you would've let me finish, Celeste. We pride ourselves on what we've accomplished, the fortunes we've amassed. But *this*—this would be a true legacy. An anonymous legacy, but lasting nonetheless. Even with the upside, though, I don't know if I have the appetite for the risk. We aren't talking about skirting a few SEC investigators. This—well, I don't have to explain to any of you. I'm not saying no. I'm just not an enthusiastic yes."

"Candidly, I'm not sure where I stand on it," Johnny replied, never stepping out of his role as their lawyer. "You raised a good point earlier, Celeste, and one that we've discussed often. If someone... disposes of Chet and Gabriel because they uncovered something that was supposed to stay buried, for instance, does the illuminati immunity also go away? Especially if you're all then in the crosshairs with an attorney general who wants to make an example of rich vigilante assholes who think they're above the law. And what if the AG is also a foreign agent?"

"You've summed us up well, counselor," Celeste said. "Vigilantes —I like it." Her mood was buoyant in spite of the doomsday scenario they were facing—her emotional turbulence was bound to give her whiplash by day's end. "On that note, who's going to make me a dirty Belvedere martini?"

"Yes, cocktails. We're in desperate need of cocktails," Savin said nonchalantly. "Let's move this to the terrace and change the subject for a bit. I could really use some air. Celly, help me with the drinks." He gestured to everyone else to head outside. From his tone, Celeste knew something was up. She followed him so that they were out of earshot.

Sav's place was spectacular. The grand ballroom had marble columns throughout, giving it an old Hollywood air of opulence. He had a full bar spanning the massive width of the entertaining area, and the walls were floor-to-ceiling windows overlooking the twinkling lights of lower Manhattan, Brooklyn, and New Jersey. He had hosted many a black-tie event there, even having a full orchestra once.

As he began shaking and stirring their drinks, he whispered, "Well, it's confirmed—our servers have been breached. We're assessing the damage."

"OK. I fly out tomorrow night; I can work with the IT team in Paris Tuesday."

"How do other people live? Is it like this for them?"

"Like what?"

"Constant chaos?"

Oh, darling, this isn't all bad news. For chaos brings opportunity to those who are paying attention. "I don't know how others live, Savin. But it seems as though it would get rather dull."

4

"FASHION IS THE ARMOR TO SURVIVE"

Celeste awoke from her Ambien-induced slumber when the jet slowed to a stop at the private hangar at Charles de Gaulle Airport in Paris. She had planned to fly alone on Monday night, fully intending to spend the time working out the details she'd mulled over the previous night. Instead, Angelo insisted on joining her because he'd magically learned that Celeste had potentially been followed before she could tell him. *I could kill Jack.*

Even on the plane, Angelo was by her side despite all the empty seats, acting as though she might disappear into danger right out from under him. He wasn't taking any threat to her safety lightly, he said, and if she wasn't amenable to having him around, he couldn't in good conscience keep the fact that someone had been following her a secret. *Great.* It couldn't be worse timing to have Angelo tagging along everywhere, and the headache would be compounded by the fact that everyone was already on edge when she was in Paris because of the past kidnapping.

Normally, she wouldn't tolerate being coerced into submission by an employee—or anyone, for that matter—but after the previous night's revelations, even she had to admit that maybe Angelo and Jack were right to take extra precautions. Having her bodyguard glued to her side was not the right solution for myriad reasons, however, and she could probably overpower Angelo herself because of her extensive hand-to-hand combat training with Zed. She could hardly share that with Angelo, though.

Only a few short years before, Celeste had welcomed having him around. With her stature, traveling alone made her a target, and she never seemed to be quite in the mood to be robbed or kidnapped. But that was before—before Omar made her a victim; before everyone, even her husband, began looking at her with pity; before they all treated her like a delicate flower. Most importantly, it was before she began training with Zed, before she owned and could use a firearm, before she'd taken matters into her own hands and proven to herself that she was a formidable opponent. Alas, she couldn't share with anyone what she was capable of, so she had to be somewhat amenable to the oversight to prevent her chosen family from staging some sort of intervention.

Allowing him to join did not mean, however, that the two of them would be chitchatting the entire evening. In fact, to prevent any further discussion of his concerns from annoying her for the duration of the seven-hour flight, she'd given in to her exhaustion and excused herself to the bedroom. She placed a silk eye mask over her eyes and fell into a deep rest until they arrived.

When she awoke upon landing, she quickly freshened up and joined Angelo in the main cabin.

After they exchanged pleasantries with the pilot and flight attendant, Angelo escorted her to the waiting BMW X5. She counted three firearms on the driver: on his ankle, at his hip, and in the small of his back. They were well concealed, but Zed had trained her to spot them. *OK, three is a bit of overkill.* Whatever. As long as she could sneak away when she needed to, she would appease Angelo and Jack. By some miracle, her many, many suitcases fit in the *coffre*, the car's trunk.

The driver was nearly as tall as Angelo and much more severe looking in an all-black suit. He appeared to be of Persian or Spanish descent, she thought, yet he had the swagger of a mafioso. Instead of smiling or offering his hand, he simply nodded when she walked to the open passenger-side back door and closed it after she slid in.

"What's your name?" Celeste asked once he was settled in the front seat. "I like to know who's driving me around."

"Julien," he said, signaling the end of the conversation by rolling up the security partition.

Rude. Celeste frowned. *Also, Julien? Would've pegged him as something other than French.* But the accent was undeniable.

"I'll explain later," Angelo said in a low voice.

Paris was Celeste's second favorite city and home away from home. She had spent time there in college studying French and bought her first Parisian pied-à-terre a decade prior. And D&C had opened its first European satellite office there after acquiring the Rome-based Ricci Fund from brothers Enzo and Nico, as well as the Dubai-based TA Capital, under the guise of deepening their global influence.

Only Celeste knew that her true motives to buy the firms had been driven by Nico's and Matthew's connections to Omar's malevolent network and not by good business sense. Because she wanted that part to remain a secret, she now had to make the deals successful, lest someone become the wiser. Luckily, she could still carry out her own plans while doing so.

To that end, she intended to summon Matthew while she was in town, but she had to be a bit more careful with Angelo watching her and a potential stalker lurking around. She knew Matthew was a horrible man, and she couldn't shake the feeling that the fortune he had amassed from RH Global was somehow connected to her or D&C. *Or Theodore?* She hadn't considered until that moment that it could perhaps even be connected to her husband. *Hmm, interesting.* Whatever the tie to her, it was in her best interest to uncover what Matthew was up to. Then she'd rid the world of him the way she had the others.

But first things first. She needed a plan to help Chet and Gabe— and in turn, herself. Celeste watched Paris whiz by. It was such a lively city, its bustling streets lined with charming cafés and boutiques. Once upon a time, she had walked them with reckless abandon, but that was in her previous life. When she had told Theodore a few months prior that she wanted to sell her old place, which carried a karmic heaviness along with significant security vulnerabilities, and buy a new one for a fresh start, he'd been concerned that even being in Paris would trigger her.

"Darling, what about London or Madrid?" he had suggested. "There are so many world-class cities, and what more do we need out of France? We've seen and done it all." But Celeste remained steadfast that she didn't feel the least bit triggered by the city itself. Sure, she probably wouldn't love being back in her old apartment any more than she would love a long stay in a Nice hospital. But it wasn't Paris's fault that Omar had kidnapped her there. She refused to let Omar win. She wasn't running away from Paris, and she couldn't always give in to the men in her life. To that end, she made a mental note to ask her therapist, Anne Marie, how she could manage her overprotective husband.

After she held firm that their new pied-à-terre would indeed be in the City of Lights, Celeste found a beautiful $17 million steal that had been fully gutted and renovated by the previous owners. The place instantly felt like home to her, and since Theodore spent so little time there, she could conduct her undercover work more freely than in New York. *Until now.* She sighed inwardly. Angelo's vigilance wouldn't be easy to divert, but she'd done it before.

"What's on your agenda for the week, Celly?"

Even with Rani's new responsibilities as D&C's CTO, she always provided Celeste with both hard and digital copies of the travel itinerary. Celeste reached into her bag, opened her Louis Vuitton folio, and pulled out a fresh copy. Her agenda included enough detail to keep Angelo busy checking security at the restaurants and such, as well as alone time disguised as spa and museum trips, where she could sneak away. She would have to take precautions, ensuring no one could geolocate her on her phone, and planned to mix up her looks as well.

Now that her Mia disguise was burned, she'd unveil a new alias on the trip. She'd bought new gear at the wig shop close to Zed's studio. Since she always left Zed's in disguise, it had been simple to walk in undetected and buy a few new ones. *Better safe than sorry.* From now on, she'd use Mia only during her sessions with Zed. The other implications would have to wait to get sorted until she was back in New York.

She walked Angelo through her agenda and overrode his objections that he needed to accompany her everywhere.

"Theodore and I actually have a second apartment in the building next door for his parents when they want to visit. I had my house-keeper make all the arrangements for you to stay there. You'll be very comfortable—we got so lucky with the spaces. Wait until you see!"

"OK. I'm sure it's great, but I'll need to regularly check that your windows are locked and such to make sure your apartment is secure."

I guess there'll be no enjoying a nice evening breeze while I sleep. Air-conditioning wasn't a necessity in Europe, as it was in most parts of America, but luckily her building had upgraded to central air, a plus given that she was going to be locked in.

Julien turned onto the Avenue de Champs-Élysées and the magnificence of the Arc de Triomphe loomed on the horizon. They drove past the iconic Chanel fashion house, and Celeste allowed herself to be immersed in the happiness she felt around the beauty and opulence of Paris. She squealed with excitement when the Dior atelier came into view, ignoring Angelo's surprise. *Or was it annoyance?* It was a reminder that the old her was still inside somewhere.

"I cannot *wait* to go to the atelier with Mere. I've never needed a day filled with couture and Champagne more than I do now."

"You have always loved style."

"It's not all superficial, you know. The way you show up in the world determines how people view you, and it also affects your confidence in yourself. One of my favorite quotes is a line from Bill Cunningham, who once said, 'Fashion is the armor to survive the reality of everyday life.' Isn't that great?" *And the universe and all the goddesses and gods must know I need as much armor as possible for what I'm up against.*

Angelo nodded, then turned back to what he was doing—poring over her schedule and reconciling it with something on his phone.

Despite her appreciation for high-end fashion, she had never taken the time to visit an atelier, let alone have the team dress her in haute couture for an entire holiday. Meredith's support was a godsend. She had almost a sixth sense about what would shift Celeste's thoughts to enjoying the present moment. Spending the day with the Dior team was exactly what she needed.

"You're welcome to join me and Mere for dinner tonight," Celeste offered to Angelo.

As much as Celeste resisted the thought of having Angelo around as a bodyguard, she enjoyed his company. He had made her feel safe and grounded through many scary times, and she now considered him a friend in addition to her head of security. Her inner critic jabbed: *Could you be inviting him because, deep down, you know that you need the protection after you froze in Zed's studio? That maybe you're not as healed and invincible as you thought?* She shook it off and continued.

"The Ritz Paris has finally moved into the twenty-first century and has its first woman as chef of Espadon." Eugénie Béziat had recently taken the helm, and from what Celeste heard, she had leveled up the cuisine and it was not to be missed. Celeste always enjoyed the Parisian food scene, but most importantly, she loved supporting women who were breaking through the centuries-old boys' club in male-dominated professions.

"Thanks for the invite. I'll get you settled at home and then go check out the restaurant," he responded. "But I must decline the dinner invite because I plan to watch soccer in the lobby now that the season has opened!"

And I'll be using your absence to my advantage, that's for sure. At the very least, she could steal away to a dark corner and call Hadid. Hopefully, she could sneak in one more phone call as well. Mere wouldn't notice.

Julien pulled up in front of Celeste's new-to-her-but-built-in-the-nineteenth-century Haussmannian-style townhome. From the street, an observer could see the wraparound terraces on each of the four stories, all adorned with red geraniums. The iconic limestone facade and wrought-iron railings had been well preserved, and the windows had been renovated to span the height of each floor. The real estate agent had marketed it as a private mansion, and it was: a stand-alone home, complete with an elevator and luxuries such as a fully equipped gym, yoga studio, and her favorite—an intricately tiled, terra-cotta-hued sauna right out of a five-star hotel spa or exclusive longevity institute. The previous owners had left the best aspects of the original layout intact, including the expansive floor plan and original wine cellar. It wasn't her usual vibe—she normally would've gravitated toward a luxury high-rise.

But change could be good. The sophistication and elegance of the place invoked classic Paris, making her feel instantly at home upon entering. Celeste also liked the additional layer of privacy that came with owning the entire building, given her previous Parisian experiences with building concierge staff being compromised. She had all the contemporary upgrades of a newer building that made it livable, while the renovation had maintained the bones of the house that made it unique. And the views! The rooftop terrace had a panorama of nearly every historic and renowned landmark in Paris.

Julien and Angelo got out of the car and retrieved her suitcases from the trunk. It took a while for them to carry everything up the exterior entry steps. Packing on her own and not having Mere ship everything in advance was supposed to give Mere a reprieve while in the throes of party planning for Savin and Rani. But it was simply too much hassle for Celeste to regularly manage trip prep on her own, so next time she would need Meredith to find her someone to help in her absence.

As she unlocked and then opened the front door, Celeste noticed each man retrieve a handgun. If it wasn't so sad that she needed a pair of armed bodyguards to enter her home, it would've been funny that they had concealed their weapons so poorly. At least Zed would've appreciated her ability to spot them so quickly.

"We're going to check the place out. You stay right here and shout if anything is awry," Angelo said in his stern "I'm working on something very serious" tone. The two men went inside.

I'm not waiting on the patio, guys.

She viewed her home security camera app to confirm they were alone, then she went inside. It wasn't even worth sharing the camera data because she knew Angelo would still want to sweep for hidden cameras, unlocked windows, assassins hiding in the basement, and the like.

The ground floor had a two-story foyer, an enormous crystal chandelier, and a winding staircase that had a black wrought-iron railing with an intricate floral pattern. The staircase stopped at each of the four floors and managed to strike the difficult balance between modern glam and traditional Parisian style. One of her favorite renovations from the previous owners was hardwood chestnut chevron flooring throughout. It was warm and captivating.

There were two living rooms, each with a modernized fireplace where the originals had been, a formal dining room, and a commercial-worthy kitchen on the main level. Celeste had done most of the decorating herself, but for the finishing touches, she'd hired a designer to work with Meredith.

She walked to the back of the house to see the new decor and final renovations in the largest of the living rooms, where party guests would gather. The late morning sun shone through the four fifteen-foot arched windows and gave the room a warm glow. On each of the two side walls were enormous paintings she'd commissioned from an artist whose powerful works represented the tension between modern feminism and the unfortunate reinvention of the patriarchy. Celeste was no stranger to what was happening around the world—a significant push by policymakers to chip away at women's rights and take everyone back to the past. Back to a time when women couldn't choose what happened to their bodies or choose careers like heading up one of the world's largest hedge funds. *Not on my watch.* She was something of an activist, at least with her dollars and voting. *Besides, I'm much too chic to live in a world that isn't run by women.*

Abstract sculptures sat on the adjacent shelves that framed each painting, adding an interesting elemental vibe and creating a stunning backdrop to the powerful art. She had selected three beautiful curved sectionals, upholstered in ivory velvet with a luxe sheen. A low-profile coffee table finished with iridescent pearl lacquer was in the center of the three. The rugs were plush taupe, which coordinated well with the neutral throw pillows strategically placed across the couches. She smiled, instantly at home with the aesthetic.

She pulled her iPhone out of her pocket and dialed Meredith on FaceTime. Her friend answered right away.

"Mere! You won't believe how gorgeous the place looks!"

"Let me see. I'm dying to see!"

Celeste scanned the enormous room with her phone camera, calling out the new additions and providing her own commentary.

"Overall, it's incredible. I can't thank you enough for pulling this together. It truly feels like home."

"Oh my God!" Meredith shrieked, unable to contain her excitement. "It looks magnificent, Celly. You deserve a fabulous pied-à-terre, especially…"

Don't say it—don't pity me.

"…after you searched for so long to find the perfect spot!"

Celeste exhaled, scolding herself for her defensiveness. "If your friends are thinking of your trauma, it's only because they care, Celeste," her therapist would say whenever she complained of them tiptoeing around her. "It may be hard to fathom, but what happened to you probably isn't the only thing they're thinking about, despite what you imagine."

Meredith shared that she had arrived in Paris a little while earlier and that she and her new man were checked in at their hotel. They were staying at the Ritz Paris, where the two women had dinner reservations later that evening. The two-bedroom suite overlooked Place Vendôme, and Mere claimed it was one of the most opulent hotel rooms she'd ever stayed in while she gave Celeste a virtual tour.

"I'm glad this guy understands the caliber of woman he is courting. Will he be joining us for dinner?"

"He'll stop by for drinks," Mere explained, "and then he has some business to attend to."

They firmed up their plans. They'd meet at the exclusive Bar Hemingway for introductions. Celeste and Meredith would have dinner as planned at Espadon.

"Kisses. See you in a few hours!" Mere said and ended the call.

Excited to see how the rest of the place had come together, Celeste went back toward the grand staircase at the same time the guys were descending.

"So, are we all set?" she asked. She was anxious to have some time to herself. After a long flight, Celeste liked to recover with exercise, protein, and hydration, followed by a nice, long shower. She had other things to do as well—it was still office hours on the East Coast, so there was work to be done, and she needed to figure out how to deal with Michel. She hadn't told him about the recent incident at her safe house yet and had been dodging his calls, which was uncharacteristic of her. She couldn't hold him off much longer. *Wouldn't want him to show up unannounced again, drunk out of his mind.* There was nothing Celeste hated more than a sloppy drunk, especially when it was her primary confidant.

"Everything looks good upstairs," Angelo assured her. "Please keep the windows and doors closed and locked. Your bags are in your room. We'll check out the ground floor and basement."

"Great, thanks," Celeste said warmly. She had to admit it was nice to have an extra layer of confidence that their home was safe—she wasn't used to large, multistory homes. "Ange, I can show you to your apartment when you're finished."

He nodded, and she ascended the stairs to her bedroom.

Oh, wow! The primary suite, which was now the entire floor, looked much the way she had left it—only better. She'd chosen an ivory tufted silk headboard that was nearly as tall as the twelve-foot ceilings. The walls behind it were now paneled, with a rich mushroom hue, and framing the bed were crystal sconces that coordinated well with the chandelier. She recognized the bedding Meredith had upgraded as the new Frette linens, a cotton silk blend with a luxurious sheen. Everything had come together beautifully to create a sexy and inviting vibe. As tempting as it was to curl up and nap in the cozy bed, she knew better, lest she have jet lag.

The terrace beckoned. She remembered Angelo's comment and scowled. *I can at least enjoy my own patio for a few minutes.* She walked through the double doors and turned her face to the sun. Geraniums were on full display, popping brightly against the uniform creamy limestone siding of her home and the adjacent ones. She smiled when she noticed the Mediterranean fan palms in every corner—she'd asked Meredith if there was an appropriate tree hardy enough to survive her long absences and appropriate for an urban garden. As always, her friend had delivered precisely what Celeste had envisioned. She snapped a photo with her iPhone and shot it off to Mere with a text: "It's like you can read my mind!"

The panoramic view of the city was the best of any of the apartments she had viewed while she was searching. She had pictured an outdoor candlelit dinner with Theodore if they could ever coordinate their schedules to be there at the same time. Paris was beyond romantic. *And then make our way into a* baignoire *for a little sexy time.* She and her husband had enjoyed many a frisky bubble bath in their time together, but the Paris bathroom may be the most opulent yet.

Back inside, she groaned when she looked at the evidence of her overpacking. The trunks imposed on the ample space in her boudoir. She was accustomed to staying in luxury five-star hotels, with Mere managing all the details, and the butler would've already taken care of the unpacking. Here at home, with no Meredith or butler, it was up to her. First things first—she had to ensure her weapons remained secure.

She went to the top of the stairwell. It sounded as though Angelo and Julien were still checking windows and the like. She walked quietly back to her bedroom, closing the door so that she'd hear if anyone entered. In the old apartment, she'd had a safe. Theodore had discovered it and ultimately figured out how to get inside. This time, she wanted to be sure she had a few hiding places. Easier in Paris than in New York. *What's a marriage without secrets, I always say.* Anne Marie hated that Celeste felt this way.

Her clothing displays were divided equally and lined the walls. They had secret compartments, hidden to the naked eye, that could not be opened without taking many steps to unlock. She set out to open a particular one by removing the liner in the top drawer of the marble island. Beneath it was a concealed access panel, where she had to clear her fingerprints and then select which section she was opening. Two more complex steps involved clearing a biometric scan and entering a twelve-digit code that changed weekly, and then she would be in.

Voilà! It worked exactly as she'd hoped. It had been nearly impossible to find someone who could build what she'd envisioned. Michel was always very resourceful, though, and managed to come through with a private security company that had the capability to create it.

Now she walked to the open one and evaluated its contents. While Zed knew little about her, he was aware that she was training to protect herself against future attacks. She—or rather, her alias, Mia—had shared that she was a survivor of domestic violence, omitting other details, like the fact that her abuser was now dead. Zed had given her recommendations for self-defense weapons. She had a handgun nearby whenever possible and had stocked stun guns, pepper gel, and expandable batons. On her own, she'd found some stylish self-defense rings. They were disguised as jewelry, worn on the middle finger. Each ring had a bauble on top hiding a miniature blade that could make a punch close to the eye deadly. It could also cut through zip ties and collect DNA. Perhaps the vendetta against her had died with Omar, but all signs pointed to more fun times ahead. She was ready. Choosing the simple silver ring, she slid it onto her right middle finger.

Outside of the United States, gun laws weren't so lax. France, in particular, had stringent laws requiring permitting and background checks, and not surprisingly, it had one of the lowest rates of gun violence in the world. Her carrying wasn't a political statement; she had no desire or need to use a weapon for any reason other than self-defense. But it did provide comfort when she remembered what Omar and his cronies were capable of. Would she have used a gun if the person who'd been inside her safe house had attacked her? *Yes.* She was certain she had it in her.

She sifted through her extra passports, credit cards, and currency before the final step in her inventory check.

Her thoughts were interrupted by a knock at the door. She quickly closed the compartment, ensured nothing was out of place, and went to answer the suite door.

Angelo stood there with an enormous Dolce & Gabbana shopping bag and a huge bouquet of blush-pink roses. "A courier stopped by with two packages." He handed her the flowers. "One from your husband."

She grinned widely. "These are gorgeous, and I know the perfect spot for them!" She turned toward the sitting room, then remembered Angelo standing awkwardly at the door.

"Come in."

He followed her with the bag in tow to the other end of the suite.

She placed the vase of flowers on the coffee table. It was such a massive arrangement that she could see it from almost every part of the room. "Perfect."

"Celeste," he scolded with a sigh, "we just discussed this—"

She turned to see him noticing she'd left the terrace doors open. He was frowning. *I'm going to kill Jack for setting this babysitter shit into motion.* "I know, I know, I wanted to feel the sunshine and enjoy the greenery for a minute. I'll lock it up tight, I promise."

"Maybe I should stay here tonight. You have room for guests, correct?"

"I'm fine. What's that?" she said, nodding to the bag.

"This one is from Meredith. She texted me and said she knew you hadn't had time to unpack yet."

Celeste shrugged. "She's not wrong." She took the bag from him and set it by the closet. "All is well downstairs, I presume?"

"Yes, we didn't find anything out of the ordinary."

"Guess it was money well spent, then, to have the high-tech security team come in. Is Julien still here? And who is he?"

"I didn't want to take any chances—"

"He's not an assassin, is he?" She laughed but stopped when she realized it could be true.

"No, but he was formerly DGSE."

Celeste looked at him quizzically.

"The Direction Générale de la Sécurité Extérieure. Basically, the French CIA."

So he is an assassin. I suppose it could come in handy.

"OK, I'll allow it."

"He's the best of the best," Angelo explained. "Yes, he's a little arrogant and probably feels this private security is beneath him. But we need someone who knows how to navigate Paris, knows how to secure a vehicle, and can help me secure a restaurant."

Her fury creeped in like an untamed monster. Her shadow side that fueled her to do the things she had done, the things her parents would not have been proud of, remained close to the surface, easily triggered. Meditation would help, she knew. But if she was being honest with herself, she needed that fire to carry out what she needed to do. *Fuck you, Omar. How dare you taint the city I love so much? I'd happily make you suffer all over again.*

It had become clear, though, that she had merely cut off one, maybe two, of the tentacles—now it was time to go for the head of the beast. Not only was she going to prevent the cyberattack but she would also destroy Omar's entire organization. Yes, she was doing it to protect those she loved and stop these evildoers before they could commit more crimes.

Michel. His fact-finding skills always came in handy—he had an uncanny ability to track down information. She needed to make that phone call to determine whether he could still be trusted.

Angelo cleared his throat, and she remembered she wasn't alone.

"Ah, yes, we need to get back to unpacking. Let's get you settled in the apartment quickly," she said resolutely, preventing further debate over whether he would stay at her home.

LATER THAT EVENING, Julien and Angelo were parked outside, waiting for her. After Angelo had left her alone, she had managed to squeeze in a workout and sauna session and placed a few calls, including one to her husband. He reported a full week of meetings in Switzerland but made time for a little FaceTime sex.

After a long shower with the luxurious waterfall showerhead, surrounded by marble walls, Celeste followed her usual thoughtful regimen, slathering on her skincare products, the abdominal scars a constant reminder. She then examined her face in the magnifying mirror. Though she had a longevity-promoting team who ensured she had the latest technological advances to age gracefully, a facelift was in her near future.

A woman should do whatever makes her feel her best, especially when a man has made her feel her worst. Perhaps she would make a two-week trip out to Beverly Hills for some A-list treatments. She deserved to splurge on some beauty procedures—especially after all the invasive surgeries she'd had in Nice and back at home.

Most people in her life were unaware of the abuse she'd endured. It was a woman's decision whether to share, and she didn't want to give those experiences any more power. But if the past two months had taught her anything, it took more than death to be rid of her ghosts. Being back in Paris with armed bodyguards only confirmed that her life was no longer what it had been before. Alas, there was no time machine to remedy the past, to save the woman she'd once been. All she could do was focus on her healing and try to prevent future wrongs to other women.

Whew, OK, Celeste, shake it off for now and enjoy the evening. She smoothed her long, golden waves and pinned her sides back. Her makeup was simple yet dramatic, with a smoky eye and clear lip gloss. After styling her hair and applying her makeup, she went in to see what Meredith had sent her. It was a Dolce & Gabbana number, black, body-hugging with a sweetheart neckline and three-quarter sleeves. Despite the midi hem, it was anything but demure. Perfect for a night out in Paris with Meredith to dine on gourmet fare from one of the hottest new chefs in town.

She chose one of her bigger, more structured bags—a Birkin that was a gift from her friend Nasrin—in which to hide some of her toys. The taser and foldable baton easily fit. With those in addition to the self-defense ring on her finger, she would be prepared for anything, even with Angelo and Julien lurking. Ultimately, she'd always had to rely on herself when it mattered most.

Nasrin. Celeste didn't carry the bag often because it reminded her of Zari's lifeless face, the two small children he wouldn't see grow up, left behind with only their widowed mother. She had always felt his death was her fault.

No, remember what Nasrin said. Her friend had said that Zari wasn't killed because he was protecting Celeste; he died for a cause greater than himself. The couple had chosen a life committed to stopping organized crime, Nasrin explained, confirming that Celeste had nothing to do with his murder. Nasrin in fact wasn't even upset with Celeste and had reiterated that time and again.

Another life that had been rocked by Omar's crew. Celeste promised herself she'd try to reach out to Nasrin to say hello to her friend in person while in Morocco, where Nasrin traveled often. Perhaps they could meet for tea or a drink.

After locking up, she went out to the car. Julien jumped out to open the door for her. She didn't need to be addressed formally, but she did want those she hired to look her in the eye and exhibit something other than disdain. To his credit, Julien seemed to have had a change of heart. *Angelo must've scolded him.*

She didn't talk much on the way. Angelo filled her in on the precautions taken at the restaurant and assured her he would be close by.

Hopefully, not too close.

～

NESTLED at the cozy Bar Hemingway in the Ritz with its signature cocktail, a Clean Dirty Martini, in hand, Celeste felt more relaxed than she had all day. Many places claimed to have the best or most well-crafted martini, but none compared to the Hemingway's take on the classic dirty martini with the polish, sophistication, and presentation of an artisanal cocktail, complete with a red rose. The Ritz had been occupied by Nazis in World War II, and it was the exuberance after Paris was liberated and the war was over that made the Bar Hemingway so special. It evoked a sense of nostalgia for the decorum of those days of glamour, like Christian Dior's New Look, rejecting the austerity of the war. Patrons could still feel it—the electricity in the air, the taste of freedom.

Celeste used to know what freedom felt like. Before. Now, though, she knew more, something different—maybe better? The jury was still out. She had discovered power—power over the man who had compromised her spirit again and again, power that came with wealth, power that came with knowing she could do anything she put her mind to. She was in a better place; she'd sacrificed a lot to get there. After all, wasn't freedom just another word for nothing left to lose? But power, as Queen Bey was quoted, was not given to you. You had to take it.

The place was sexy yet accessible, with low lighting and tufted bar stools in green leather. The bar was lined with bitters and garnishes, and atop it were silver serving bowls of snacks. Hanging on the wood-paneled walls, framing the display of liquors and liqueurs, were photographs of the bar's namesake, Ernest Hemingway, and famous guests who had visited. The room was full of people laughing or in deep conversation, many of whom were seated in the leather armchairs in warm coordinating tones. Soft jazz played over the speakers. Her nervous system was balanced—the anger had dissipated. A night out here was exactly what she needed to remind her that life was to be enjoyed, no matter what had happened in one's past. Paris was hers, not anyone else's; she would regain it on this trip by making new memories.

Meredith walked up then. "Hiii. Oh my God, you are stunning!"

she gushed, scrutinizing with an expert eye. "You did your hair and makeup yourself?" Celeste nodded. Meredith's face read impressed. "OK, stand up and show me. I mean, I'm sure you look incredible because I have incredible taste, but I need to see."

Celeste did a theatrical twirl and instantly regretted it when Meredith did her usual squeal that meant something made her happy. *She loves to make a scene, our Mere.*

Meredith's light-brown hair tumbled over her shoulders in soft curls, and her dewy makeup perfectly complemented her radiant glow. She was wearing a black silk slip dress with a hemline above her knees and sky-high, black mesh Saint Laurent heels.

"Where is your new guy?" Celeste had forgotten his name. Was it the fact that she'd slammed the martini and was sipping a second one? Or had she ever known it?

"Seth. He sends his regrets, but he's tied up in a work meeting."

"I guess that happens to the best of us."

The two ladies settled in to catch up, but not before Celeste nodded in Angelo's direction to alert Mere that he was lurking in the lobby and peeking into the exclusive, tiny bar from time to time—*as though I could be snatched from right under his nose.* Meredith indicated she saw him and then dove into the backstory of why she had flown with Seth instead of on the newly acquired D&C jet. *Seth. Now I won't forget.*

"You know I'll never approve of you flying pedestrian class, but I will say, love suits you because you are glowing."

They laughed.

"Wait, why is he flying commercial anyway? Is he poor?"

"Celly, you're terrible. He's fantastic, and he's quite successful. A bit older, never been married. Super smart. You'll love him."

Doubt it. Celeste found most people to be insufferable; they were only to be tolerated as a means to an end. The odds that she would like someone she'd never met who missed introductory drinks with one of Mere's best friends when Mere was so excited for them to meet were close to nil.

AFTER THE WOMEN were buzzed and ebullient, they were escorted to the dining room. It was elegant simplicity with an ambience deserving of one of the world's leading hotels and arguably the most luxurious hotel in Europe—cobalt-blue armchairs with white table-cloths, white scalloped dinnerware, and moquette, wall-to-wall carpeting, with burnt orange, earthy khaki, and complementary blue hues. It was at once soothing and vibrant. The gold paneling added an extra dose of luxury without seeming inaccessible. In the center of the dining room, frosted-glass light fixtures provided a soft glow.

Once they were seated, Celeste, forgetting whom she was with, began explaining the history of Espadon and its new era under one of the world's few female chefs with a Michelin star.

"Celly, darling, you do know that I'm the one who told you all this and scored the resy, right?"

Celeste giggled along with Meredith, realizing then that she may be a little drunk.

"Martinis are like boobs: One's not enough, and three's too many!" Meredith said, and the two howled.

Their server, a woman of medium height with light-brown, shoulder-length hair felt like an extension of the understated elegance of the decor. She introduced herself as Elsa and dove into a memorable story about the restaurant's garden and the philosophies under which Chef operated.

"I read a feature on Chef and told Celeste that we must eat here right away. We're so excited. I love the focus on sustainability—it's so *now*," Meredith said.

They ordered the extensive eight-course chef's tasting menu and wine pairing, and Elsa promised them a memorable experience.

"How is it? Being back in Paris again?" Meredith asked.

Celeste sighed. "Well, I've been back several times since..."

"I know. But this will be the first time in the new place since its renovation. You lived in your old place for a long time—"

"Over a decade. And the memories, the beauty of it were desecrated. I don't have to tell you because you were there, but by the end, I didn't even want to be inside. Then you helped me create another home to make new memories in, as beautiful as the last, with a clean slate.

"I was enjoying the terrace this afternoon and pictured Theodore and me dining alfresco under the moonlight or having a small cocktail party. I hope he can come soon."

"Is he ever in Paris with you?"

"Hardly. We're rarely in the same place at the same time in Europe, with my office in Paris and his in Zurich. We'll make it work soon. OK, enough about me. Tell me about Seth." *Who has a lot of redeeming to get off my shit list for skipping out on drinks.*

"He's different from anyone I've ever dated. Mature. He calls when he says he will, plans things for us."

Hmm. "Not to play devil's advocate—but this is pretty much the bare minimum a man should do when they're with *any* woman, but especially with a high-value woman like you."

"Fair, but you've dated in New York. You must admit that it's nice when a man shows you he appreciates you. And the sex is great, but it's more than that. I love talking to him."

"Uh-oh, you know who you're beginning to sound like."

"You! Oh, Celly, it's like night and day seeing you now versus... then. Well, before then, you came alive when you met Theodore. Patrick, Ty, and I had so much fun dressing you up for your dates that you always denied were special. But we knew what was going on. You had a glow—the glow that only comes with being in love."

Like Mere, Patrick and Ty, Celeste's makeup artist and hair stylist, had a front-row seat to her courtship with Theodore. They had also witnessed her fall apart, washing down Xanax bars with swigs of Macallan 25, to numb the pain when Theodore was believed to be dead.

Meredith seemed to intuit that a trip down memory lane would most definitely put a damper on the buoyant mood of the evening and changed the subject. "I cannot *wait* for the atelier, Celly. It's only a day away. To be dressed by the Dior team before your magical Moroccan escape."

As usual, Mere's enthusiasm was infectious. Celeste relaxed, allowing herself to contemplate all the possibilities. She didn't want to lose the ability to enjoy life, because otherwise, wasn't everyone just racing to the grave?

"I can't thank you enough for arranging. What a treat!"

The amuse-bouche, a miniature crab cake with a delicate sauce, arrived then. Elsa poured each of them a glass of blanc de blancs Champagne and quietly disappeared. The effervescence of the bubbly brought out the complexity of the sweet crab. Celeste closed her eyes, savoring the perfect balance of flavors, and a contented grin spread across her face.

Meredith giggled. "You look like you've never tasted good food before, and we know that's not the case," she said.

The courses kept coming, and each was better than the last.

"The artistry and attention to detail are amazing," said Celeste. "The pork is presented like a *plaisir sucré*."

"Ooh, that reminds me—maybe we should stop by Pierre Hermé after our little shopping expedition Thursday!" Meredith suggested. Recognized as the world's best pastry chef, Pierre Hermé was renowned for his pastries and had mastered the art of the macaroon. He was known for inventing the *plaisir sucré*, literally a sweet pleasure, a small, elegant rectangular dessert. His boutique was one of Celeste's favorite stops when she was in town.

"I'll never say no to that," Celeste said. "Excuse me while I escape to the ladies' room before the next course, darling," she added, putting her handbag over her shoulder and scurrying off.

She suddenly realized her few hours without Angelo leaning over her shoulder were coming to a close. At that point, she knew he'd be deep into his soccer game, so it likely would go unnoticed if she lingered a little longer in the *toilette*, as it was called nearly everywhere in the world except America. Once inside a stall, she pulled out her burner. After two rings, she got a generic message that the mailbox had not been set up. *Damn.* She shot off a text to her contact reading "RAK," which was the Marrakech Menara Airport code, so he would know which city to meet her in. Not the most complex encryption, but she was desperate to do outreach away from home in case her place was bugged. An incoming text notification vibrated her bag. The man replied right away with a colon and a closing parenthesis to make a smiley face. *I guess that's as good as I can do right now.*

She then made the call she'd been putting off.

Michel answered on the first ring. "Where have you been?"

Avoiding your drunk ass. "Had a travel day and a few crises to deal with, but all is well. I'm in Paris now," she whispered so as to not be overheard in case she'd missed someone coming in.

"I'm one step closer to finding out who is heading up Omar's organization."

"Are you also one step closer to finding sobriety? You can't show up like that—imagine if Theodore had seen. What the hell was that about? All the talk of letting someone down?"

"Just a bad day. I was talking nonsense. Forget about it—it won't happen again." He sighed. "Look, you must take extra precautions until we figure out how much the guys at the top know."

"I'm one step ahead of you. Angelo has a French spook tagging along. A bit of overkill, if you ask me, but hey, we've been compromised before, so maybe it's better safe than sorry."

"We've crippled their organization more than once. I'll stay under the radar, but you won't, Celeste. I'm hearing they are out for blood and will stop at nothing. They want revenge and retribution."

No reason to ruin a $200 buzz with more of this.

"Look, I'm at dinner. We can talk more tomorrow. I wanted to check in so you wouldn't worry."

"Make sure you keep scrambling your numbers, and mix up the SIM cards too. Sometimes the scramblers aren't one hundred percent reliable."

Click.

She exited the stall, smoothed her hair, and refreshed her lip gloss. *Now go back and enjoy the decadent meal Mere arranged.*

As soon as Celeste sat down, Elsa returned with an explanation of the lobster course. Besides the creativity she appreciated, one of the reasons Celeste loved a Michelin experience is that she could taste such a wide variety of complex, indulgent flavors and not leave feeling too gluttonous. *Everything in moderation—except perhaps our wine consumption.*

Celeste applauded their experience. "The service is immaculate, and the food is even better than I expected," she gushed. "I must bring my husband here next time. He'll love the food, but more importantly, the immaculate presentation will appeal to his English sensibilities for formality."

Elsa laughed. "Chef will love to hear it. Enjoy," she said and then left.

Meredith seemed to have something on her mind. "What's up?" Celeste asked.

"Celly, you're the most powerful businesswoman I know, and I need your business acumen."

"You know I always love a good idea. Shoot."

Meredith dove into a pitch for a new venture. She had developed a plan to capitalize on the shift that was happening in fashion and make it more accessible to the average woman.

Celeste was impressed.

"I want to develop a styling assistant powered by AI, with an algorithm designed to help women manage their wardrobes, choose outfits for events based on body shape, style, budget. The revenue stream will come from their purchases and designer sponsorships. Basically bringing what I do for you to scale."

Artificial intelligence was changing the way services were delivered, and any savvy entrepreneur was capitalizing. "I *love* this, and scaling is the most important aspect for creating a sustainable business model. I want in on the ground floor. Let's pull in Lorraine to help build your business plan and pitch. While her main focus is our philanthropic arm, she's become quite the fashion aficionado. In fact, if I had to guess, you may have had something to do with that beyond those original makeovers I basically forced her into."

Meredith grinned sheepishly. "Yes, I've been styling her for ages, but she asked me not to tell anyone."

"Get a glass or two of wine in you—"

"Or two martinis and eight glasses of wine—"

"Fair. Two martinis and eight glasses of wine, and you'll reveal any secret," Celeste said, laughing.

Meredith was suddenly earnest. "I would never, ever betray you, Celly."

Celeste believed her.

5

A MEAL WITHOUT WINE IS LIKE A DAY WITHOUT SUNSHINE

Celeste awoke to the morning sun filtering in through the blinds. She groaned, wishing to be magically hydrated and a lot less hungover. *A meal without wine is like a day without sunshine, as Jean Anthelme Brillat-Savarin so brilliantly acknowledged.* She'd never regret any part of the previous night—the chef delivered one of the best meals she'd ever had, and Mere was always great company.

Elated, the two had wrapped up the excellent dinner feeling satiated and more than a little buzzed, and Elsa had sent the chef over to greet them. "No notes," Celeste had said. "It was incredible, and there is no room for improvement." They had a great chat about the chef's vision, and Celeste promised to return.

Angelo and Julien, to their credit, had tried to be discreet, waiting for the women in the lobby. *Anyone with eyes could see they're heavily armed, though.* Oh well, Celeste had decided to choose her battles. It would cause too much of a stir with Jack potentially tattling to Savin and Savin to her husband if she ditched Angelo entirely on the trip. So she acquiesced for now so she'd be able to move freely when she needed later.

Julien escorted Meredith to her hotel room, and when he

returned, Celeste and Angelo went with him to the car. Although the end of the night was a bit hazy, Celeste recalled that both men seemed somber on the ride home.

Now she rolled over to find her phone. It was sitting on the nightstand, plugged into the charger, next to a full glass of water and an electrolyte powder packet. *Thank you, past me, for being prepared.* After stirring the powder into the water, she drank the mixture in one gulp. She reached for her phone, then decided against it.

Outside on the terrace, she sat on a meditation cushion facing the sun. It could have been the placebo effect, but she was already feeling better. *Do the hardest thing first.* She had been building the habit of starting the day alone with her thoughts. Her eyes gently closed, she assessed her body, merely observing first. The gentle rise and fall of her diaphragm, the rhythmic whisper of her breath. *I trust myself to navigate whatever comes my way.* Celeste released any expectations she had and let her imagination guide her.

An image of her higher goddess beckoned to her with an outstretched hand, as if taking her on a journey. Suddenly, seemingly unrelated events were thrust together in a soundless montage: images from childhood evenings around the kitchen table with her parents and brother, the almost imperceptible panicked energy she felt for only a moment during her wedding reception, the call about Keith's passing interrupting the languid pace of her post-nuptial retreat, Gabe the Fed sniffing around, the hooded figure leaving her safehouse apartment, Fred Warren's warnings that someone was after her. Then a carousel of images of her friends, her husband, everyone trying to urgently communicate with her, reveal something that was just beyond her mind's grasp.

Her body stiffened, the lighthearted spirit of the night before gone. But she couldn't pull herself away; she was captivated—she had to seek what her shadow self knew, what her higher goddess was trying to reveal in that moment. She allowed herself to acknowledge that deep down, she had known—known that there was something more at play than she consciously understood. The images came faster now, a blur of faces whizzing by. She squeezed her eyes shut, trying to concentrate. *Please, a clue; I need something to go on.* More people, with the heightened sense of urgency that she had to put the pieces together quickly. Zari, alive in her mind, urged her to act fast, and then Nasrin and their children popped up. *Please*, they said, *help us.* She wanted so badly to protect them. They had lost their father while he was protecting her—it was the least she could do now. *Tell me how; reveal what I have to do*, she silently pleaded.

Her parents were there then, standing together. Her mother's face was pained, her father's fearful. Her inner voice was very strong, as clear as if it had been spoken aloud right next to her. *There's no more time. Act now before something terrible happens.*

Her eyes snapped open, and she was jolted out of her trance and back onto the sunny terrace. Instead of her usual calm and grounded feeling after meditation, she was agitated with an erect spine and a racing heart. Tears dampened her cheeks, and she felt shaky. *What the fuck was that?* Was it real? Her parents' presence was tangible, as though they were communicating with her directly for the first time in decades.

She walked down to her office. Its decor was a continuation of that in the other parts of her home, with an indulgent shag rug, a modern round crystal chandelier over the alabaster wood desk, and textured ivory wallpaper that gave the feeling of the clay wall of a cave. Together, the pieces were meant to invoke the serenity of a spa, though Celeste felt anything but peaceful. After turning on her computer (*Is it always so slow?*), she logged in and pulled up the encrypted murder board file. *I'll be the female Hercule Poirot*, she thought, referring to a meticulous detective featured in many of Agatha Christie's novels. She could leave no stone unturned as she tried to narrow down who was behind the looming danger and what they were planning. She decided to evaluate everyone on the grid with fresh eyes.

In her vision, so many people she loved appeared frantic—but she had to remember that someone's presence in her vision, no matter how concerned they seemed, did not automatically exonerate them. Only proving they were not framing Celeste would establish their innocence. She wished she could find someone who could help her, but based on her instinct and experience, she realized it would be too difficult to enlist most everyone she knew, even if they had good intentions. *Savin, Mark, Jack?* No. None of them brought any helpful skills, and they would just get in the way, like Jack had by insisting Angelo babysit her.

She couldn't go to the police for help either because she could be a named suspect in any number of crimes. Also, she couldn't ignore that the Feds, despite needing her expertise, had their own agenda, which could plausibly include taking her down. If Gabe's attitude the night before was any indication, they might be working with local police anyway. She'd never trusted them in the first place, so partnering with Gabe and Chet now seemed foolish. She wondered what lengths the Feds would go to if they intended to entrap her and whether they had plans to do so. She didn't want to wait to find out; she wanted to prevent the cyberattack, learn who Omar's boss was, and negotiate a way out of the illuminati. She had to act fast.

Her husband didn't know of her double life, and under such exigent circumstances, it wasn't the right time to bare her soul. *I'll tell him. Someday.* But she did need to speak with someone objective. *Maybe Fred?* Over time, Fred Warren had become a kindred spirit since he'd also been a target of Omar's organization. Maybe it would be a good idea to have a hypothetical conversation with him when she was back in New York. She was reminded of their last conversation, when he had asked her if she had a death wish and stormed off. He'd also been standoffish at Savin's. *OK, maybe not Fred.*

Hadid had helped her in countless ways in the past, proving himself trustworthy. *Let's hope our meeting will happen in Marrakech.*

She still wasn't sure about coming clean to Michel. What if his unstable behavior at the funeral was his new normal? Was he consumed by guilt that he hadn't prevented an attack on his daughter or remorse over what he and Celeste had done to Omar? After all, the two of them had witnessed Omar die a violent death. That didn't seem right, though. It was clear from the outset that day that Michel had tortured, probably even murdered, someone before, and he had been cool and calm in the moment. *But now?* His behavior in St. Louis was completely at odds with his normal demeanor, which was concerning to say the least. But she couldn't write Michel off yet. *It's not as if I have a deep bench of allies.* She'd go to him once she'd worked out a plan with more details and feel out his state of mind.

If she took anything away from her vision, it was that more lives were at stake. Her intuition confirmed that the danger hadn't died with Omar. Despite all the crimes he'd committed, all the pain he'd caused, the powers that be had still protected him. Whatever useful information he had provided was more important to someone with extraordinary power within the US government than seeing that Celeste and all the other women and girls brutalized by Omar and his organization received justice. The illuminati had provided a solid case for putting Omar and his entire operation behind bars when she was on her whirlwind tour to avenge Theodore's disappearance. And yet no convictions had resulted. In fact, Omar's behavior had been condemned only to later be protected by the US government, and there was an explicit reticence to implicate anyone else. The fact that Gabe and Chet hadn't known many details indicated that Omar's protection was well above their pay grade, further evidence that Omar's boss really could be a senior US official as the Feds believed.

The mystery she'd never solved was to whom Omar was providing such valuable information that law enforcement protected him instead of women like her. That person or organization was the key to finding out what had already been set into motion. Her resolve was reconfirmed then—she would uncover the identity of the head of Omar's organization and also prevent the cyberattack. And she knew someone who could assist.

But the reality was that she was mostly on her own. No more taking chances, no more reckless behavior. She needed to show up as her best self. She'd be more careful, make sure she wasn't followed to places like her safe house, ensure she didn't let anything slip. It was time to take better precautions: unveil new aliases in her rotation, secure more destinations around the world where she had flight funds in case of an emergency evacuation.

Stopping the cyberattack would give her the advantage she needed with the Feds. She couldn't end the madness until she gained a deeper understanding of the hierarchy of the crime syndicate with which Omar had been associated. *Sorry, Mom and Dad, I'm doing the best I can.* But Celeste feared it may never be enough to prevent whatever catastrophe lurked in the shadows.

Gabe and Chet, as points for counterterrorism, would have some of the information she needed—they always knew more than they let on—but she couldn't risk bringing them in too close. The rest of the information she needed was probably top secret, the highest level of classified in government intel, locked away in server rooms that couldn't be hacked. *I'll find a way—I always do.*

She took stock of recent events and where there were still question marks. She felt fairly certain that the mystery person she'd seen when leaving her safe-house apartment in New York had been following her, perhaps trailing her since she and Theodore had returned from the funeral. She'd have to find new routes. But those were problems for another day. She wouldn't be back in New York for a few weeks.

What about Ace? At one point in time, Celeste couldn't imagine conducting her business without them. But now she tried to keep them out whenever she could sway Savin. Yet they had been integral to Savin and Celeste's success in scaling D&C; Savin always reminded Celeste of this when she expressed any doubts about Ace's allegiance. She'd also never live down that Ace had arranged her extraction from Riyadh, Saudi Arabia, and orchestrated an arrangement with the US government to prevent her from being held accountable for her actions while there.

Vivienne. The only one Celeste could trust to deliver what she needed.

She acknowledged some outstanding issues. D&C's servers had been hacked, and Lorraine and Brett had evidence to back it up. Now it had come to fruition. *Going to have to face the music about that today.* She thought about Lorraine's implication—that Savin or someone else in D&C leadership could have orchestrated the breach. Savin could have granted access to whomever he wanted, she supposed, but she'd never been able to find a motive for him to betray her. Besides, he was a horrible liar, and he was without question shaken up from the whole ordeal. She couldn't rule out Rani entirely, but it seemed so unlikely. *Don't forget what you overheard, Celeste.* There wasn't anyone else at heritage D&C who had their level of unfettered access necessary to pull off a software overhaul.

The first security breaches had occurred around the time D&C had acquired TA Capital and the Ricci Fund. TA was managed by Tarek Abdullah. She ranked his potential for betrayal as low, since she had successfully blackmailed him. *Beneficently, of course.* She hadn't ever trusted Kaya, his right-hand woman. Within the first thirty minutes of meeting her, it was clear Kaya would do whatever it took to get ahead. However, Celeste didn't think Kaya was in cahoots with Matthew or anyone else to hack the servers. It didn't seem like Kaya's style. That brought Celeste to good old Matthew. She'd put nothing past him. *Tsk, tsk, Matthew. You should be more careful the next time you try to cross me.*

Details. One of the reasons she was so successful was her attention to detail. What was she missing? Where could she dig deeper? *The timeline. I wonder when the payments began.* She quickly navigated to another folder that held Matthew's financials. The deposits, handsome sums growing bigger each time, began—she frowned, though only slightly because her Botox regimen from her plastic surgeon Dr. Smythe kept her face nearly impassive—the payments began shortly after Riyadh. *Hmm.*

She thought back to her honeymoon. Angelo had seemed concerned that Theodore was whisking Celeste off to Capri so suddenly—and without telling anyone else. Angelo didn't seem to trust anyone, and every time she sat down to examine the grid she regularly updated with new developments, she understood why. Michel made it no secret that he didn't trust Angelo, although he hadn't found any dirt on her security guard. The fact remained—someone was compromised. Perhaps several in her circle were.

Time for work. She sighed as she went back to her bedroom, knowing she had to maintain a semblance of normalcy for anyone observing her. She despised living under a microscope. As if he were reading her mind, Angelo texted her at that moment.

"We're outside. LMK when you're ready. All looks secure."

"Give me 30," she responded.

In the bathroom, she started the water and put a few drops of eucalyptus essential oil on the shower floor, then waited for the steam to fill the room. She would use every tool at her disposal to remain calm.

After a long shower to clear her head, she went to her expansive wardrobe. *Ugh!* She groaned, remembering she hadn't unpacked at all. Her iPhone rang in the bathroom. She ran in to retrieve it.

"Hi, babe," she said to Theodore over FaceTime while carrying the phone back to the walk-in. She propped it up on the island. "How's your day?"

Theodore whistled. "I didn't expect you to answer naked. My day just got a lot better."

She laughed. It never failed—he could always bring humor when she needed it. "Honey, remember those giant trunks you helped me with?"

"Yes."

"I have to find a respectable outfit to wear to the office, but I haven't even opened them yet. Last night, I was a little drunk."

His baritone laugh aroused her. "From what I saw, there were a few presentable things in there. Though I'd prefer to spend the day in bed with both of us wearing nothing at all."

"How's your trip?"

"My mate took me out on Lake Zurich in his sailboat yesterday. The weather was gorgeous, though I got a bit of a sunburn."

"Husband! I know you have sunscreen with you because I put it in your Dopp kit."

"I can barely function without you—don't you see?"

"Aww. I miss you too, honey. But wear sunscreen. People will start thinking I'm your pretty young thing if you age faster than I do."

They chuckled together. "They already think that. We're going out again this afternoon. I'll do better this time."

"Hey! I thought the reason you couldn't come stay in our fabulous pied-à-terre was because you had so much work in Switzerland! Turns out you were only booze-cruising around."

"Darling, the Paris place is hardly a pied-à-terre. It's a good-sized villa from what I've seen."

"Touché. Ooh, you should see it now—it's so beautiful now after the final touches. I hope you can come next time. *C'est très romantique.*"

"Absolutely." Theodore's face turned serious. "How are you holding up? Is there anything you want to talk about?"

She wondered if word had gotten to him about someone following her. Was this a test? She sighed. One way or the other, it was probably a good time to come clean. "Well, you'll be happy to know that Angelo has accompanied me here and is staying in the guest apartment. It's merely a precaution... because I thought I saw someone following me this weekend in New York."

Either he was good at acting or he was truly surprised. "What do you mean, someone was following you? When? Was it after I left? Why didn't you feel like you could tell me? I need to know when you're in danger; how else can I protect you? Married people share things, Celeste. What the hell?"

She shrugged, uncomfortable.

Theodore's face softened. "Oh, honey, I'm sorry. I didn't mean to attack you." He sighed and shook his head. "There's no excuse for it. I would've come with you if I'd known. Nothing here was that important."

I don't need everyone to rescue me. That was the crux of it all. *I want to move on from what happened,* she wanted to say, *and breathing life into all of it by talking it to death is quite the opposite.* She didn't want to sit with Theodore and Savin and Angelo and the Feds and Ace and talk, talk, talk about the who/what/when/where/why. She wanted to stop the danger, and the less people involved, the better.

Instead, she shared, "Babe, we spent millions on this security system, and Angelo is thirty feet away. He even hired a former French intelligence officer to shepherd me around with him. It hardly seemed worth calling off your trip."

"Ten meters away or not, he's not your husband. It's my job—"

She thought of how hard she'd worked with Zed, the kicks and bruises that came with learning how to truly defend herself in hand-to-hand combat. She recalled what a perfect shot she'd become through regular shooting lessons at the range. The nights she'd sat at a neighborhood pub as Mia listening to Petey, the retired NYPD detective, tell her the tricks of the trade, which ultimately helped her get away with murdering Nico. The many days in the gym, sweating her ass off, running and lifting, so she'd be strong and able if ever attacked again. *I don't need your protection. Not anymore.* But her husband didn't know about any of these things, these extracurriculars that she'd been hiding so well. She felt like a female Clark Kent some days—financier by day, Wonder Woman by night—especially when she landed a kick to Zed's rib cage or a right hook to his jaw. Omar's henchmen could never take her down now.

"OK, I hear what you're saying. I'll try to tell you these things sooner. But I must get to the office. You know I like to start promptly at eight so I can shame anyone who arrives late."

His English tendency to sweep things under the rug kicked in, as he allowed the conversation to move along. "Go get 'em, boss," Theodore said. "Love you."

"Love you too," she said, relieved.

"Wait, can I have one more look at you?"

She loved her husband, and he loved her, of that she was sure. They'd moved heaven and earth, each going through their own sort of hell and sacrifice, to be together. What he was asking for—a little transparency from her—wasn't unreasonable. Besides, even with all the nonsense floating around in her life, she didn't want a marriage with no laughter or play. *Relax a little; he's your life partner, not the enemy.* She jiggled her naked breasts playfully in a mock shimmy.

He growled huskily. "You're killing me, woman! Now I'll have to attend my breakfast meeting with a hard-on."

"Have a lovely day, dear," she said, blowing a kiss while ending the video call. Theodore had managed to lighten her mood, so much so that her breathing was back to normal.

She opened the largest of the trunks, praying that she remembered correctly where her glittered tweed Chanel blazer was. *Yes!* The ivory shift dress and nude mules to pair it with were also right on top. She sifted through another bag and found some appropriate lingerie. After dressing, she went to the platform with a three-way mirror at the end of the room. She'd had one for years in New York and found a similar one in Paris.

See, I can still pull everything together by myself. It wasn't her zone of genius, though. Mere was simply better at it, and at managing all sorts of other aspects of Celeste's life, than she was.

ANGELO AND JULIEN were waiting outside when she was ready to go. Julien thrust a takeaway coffee cup into her hands with a grunt. "It's not easy to find a matcha latte in Paris," he said. She hated him.

"Thanks, I appreciate it."

The three walked to the car, and Angelo got in back with her. Julien immediately rolled up the privacy window, and they were on their way.

"Julien and I took shifts last night watching your place. We'll remain extra vigilant. Once you're safely in the office, do you mind if I do another sweep?"

"No, that's fine. I also have my security systems in order, so hopefully, we won't have any breaches."

She took a sip of the tea, unsure what to expect. "Mmm, it's surprisingly good. Though I bet the Parisian cafés gave him shit when he asked for an American-style beverage."

"I think he can handle the shame," Angelo said, laughing.

"You're in a good mood today," Celeste observed.

"Because today is a good day."

Speak and it becomes, my friend. She hoped for a breakthrough in her sleuthing, given that Matthew and Kaya were meant to show up at the office after her email summons. She already knew that Matthew had ties to Omar's gang; maybe he'd let something slip about the higher-ups. And who knew what Kaya had up her sleeve?

Her iPhone vibrated with a text notification. "Hey, can you talk?" read a text from Lorraine.

She's up late. It was nearly midnight in New York.

So much for starting the morning meeting on time. But Celeste knew Lorraine well—if she was asking for a chat, it was important. "Sure. I'll be in the war room in the Paris office in 20 and will dial you from there," she wrote back. Lorraine replied with a thumbs-up emoji.

She scrolled through her inbox, which contained several emails from Rani to Celeste and Savin, sent a few hours before, confirming investor meeting dates, two business dinners, and a conference. *No mention of the breach, and no hysterical calls from Sav.* Perhaps it had sorted itself out. Celeste laughed. *Not a chance of that being true. But a woman can dream, can't she?*

Then she turned to Angelo. "Apologies. Getting caught up before a busy day."

"No worries. You had a bit of a rough start after last night's dirties, I'd imagine," he teased. She didn't drink to excess often, but she never regretted a good time with Mere.

Celeste feigned surprise. "Well, I never!" she said, laughing. "In all honesty, it was a bit dicey when I woke up, but I'm back in the land of the living after some meditation and my matcha." *If you could call that meditation.*

Angelo cleared his throat and looked serious. "Celly, if you had to guess, who do you think was following you the other day? I'm trying to look at this from every angle, but I keep coming up with question marks."

They rolled up to her office, a high-rise building where D&C occupied the top two floors.

"I've been racking my brain, and I honestly don't know." *And I'm not sharing my suspicions with you or anyone else, lest you lock me up in a tower "for my safety" and throw away the key.*

"OK, we'll discuss it later. I'll let you know how it goes at home."

"Sounds good," she said. Julien had rushed over to open the door for her. *Angelo is definitely keeping him in line, though I'm sure I'm paying this guy an arm and a leg to tolerate the likes of me.* She thanked him and walked inside.

Upstairs, Celeste looked at the office foyer with pride. They'd kept the branding fairly consistent with the New York office, with a similar Donovan & Clarke Capital sign in the lobby, but they had taken some liberties to make it less subdued. Paris interior designers used a lot of vibrant colors, and theirs had done well to incorporate them throughout. Even the three-foot-tall bouquet at the front desk was bright and colorful. The office manager, a no-nonsense Frenchman in his thirties who ran a tight ship like Rani did, was working the phones (*Do people still use front-desk landlines?*), so Celeste simply nodded in greeting, then walked back to the office.

It had an open floor plan with rows of desks topped with large monitors. In front of them were seated analysts wearing headsets, who were evaluating deals, making calls, developing reports and recommendations, while the traders were at the trading desk. D&C was engaged in a variety of trading, including equity, forex, arbitrage, and quantitative trading/high-frequency trades, or HFTs.

She cleared her throat to call attention to everyone. "Good morning! I had hoped we could begin promptly at eight, but I have an emergency in the New York office I must tend to. Let's plan to begin at eight thirty."

The team had grown to twenty or so. They were spread out, each with a relatively spacious desk area. All nodded in agreement. She noticed that Kaya and Matthew had just walked in at the other end of the large room. "Please show our TA Capital friends some D&C hospitality and enjoy breakfast, which should now be available in the large conference room." She glanced at her watch. Lorraine would be expecting her at any minute.

"Hello," she said to the two TA executives who were now at her side. They were an unlikely pair, and Celeste was curious as to how they got on. Kaya was even taller than Celeste, at six feet, a fashionable South African woman with flawless ebony skin and elegant bone structure. She was refined and shrewd. Matthew was quite the opposite, a sloppy Irishman with rosacea and a gut from one too many porterhouses, and was, from what Celeste had seen, mostly drunk. *I can't wait to bury you, you fuck. But I catch more flies with honey, so you won't see it coming.*

She smiled sweetly. "I have a quick issue to attend to, so feel free to mingle with the team. We'll begin in about thirty minutes. As we discussed, you'll be first on the agenda to walk us through your newly launched commodities strategy. We're excited!" As she turned to walk away, she heard Matthew mutter something under his breath.

He was volatile and would take any public reprimand as humiliating, resulting in a dramatic encounter for which she had neither time nor energy. Conversely, she understood that while she didn't care if Kaya or Matthew liked her, she needed to quash any sort of rebellion these unlikely bedfellows could be scheming. Alas, she had to confront the situation head-on to remind them who was in charge.

"What was that, Matthew? I didn't catch it."

He puffed up his chest, as though mustering up the courage to say something to her face. "I *said* I still can't believe Tarek agreed to this bullshit."

Celeste took a deep breath. *OK, honey isn't the right approach with this one.* She needed him to get in line. Fast. *Count to ten before you respond.* She kept her face neutral, for her staff was always watching. When she spoke, her voice was quiet but menacing.

"You'll want to listen up, *Matthew*, because I'll only say this once. You are TA's weakest link, a pathetic man who's only risen to such heights because of plain old nepotism. However, you came with what is otherwise a well-oiled, successful—exceptional, really—machine, and Tarek only agreed to a package deal."

Not true but what's he gonna do—ask Tarek? "So I agreed to tolerate you, despite how difficult it has been to date. But my patience is wearing thin. I have the best lawyers in the fucking business, and if you are insubordinate one more time, I. Will. Destroy. You. I'm talking scorched earth here. Accounts drained, no one willing to work with you. Your wife and children will know what a pig you are. Public humiliation, and all your scumbag friends will be getting as far away from you as they can. Are we clear?" She resisted the urge to spit in his face.

He had the audacity to stand there plainly, looking bored.

"I said, are we *fucking clear?*"

Kaya hid it well, but Celeste could tell she was a bit shocked.

Matthew pursed his lips, pained that he had to kowtow to someone—and to a woman, no less, which she was certain bothered him all the more. "Crystal."

Celeste smiled broadly, her dimples puckered. "Well, now that we've gotten the unpleasantness out of the way, let's have a nice day, shall we? If you'll excuse me, I still have that call to make before we begin." She nodded to the two, picked up her handbag and tea from a nearby desk, and walked toward the war room, careful not to seem as though she were stalking away angry. But her heart was pounding, and she wanted to physically harm Matthew. He wasn't aware that she knew what kind of person he was, as evil and vile as Omar himself. His days were limited once she got to the bottom of who was paying his bribes.

She closed the door tightly behind her, waiting to hear the automatic lock seal off the room.

Click.

She went to the center of the table and dialed the secure New York office line Lorraine would be on.

"Darling, I'm so sorry. I had to take care of a little insect problem. A cockroach in the office."

"Ugh, terrible. Can the super help? Maybe an exterminator can come today."

"I'm afraid that won't treat this type of infestation. You see, it's a particularly horrible species named Matthew."

Lorraine laughed. "I forgot those two were coming today. It's the big unveiling of their strategy, right?"

"You got it. So what's going on?"

Lorraine sighed. "Celeste, honestly, I'm not really sure. I

continued my due diligence on the security compromise. In light of the breach Savin and Rani are looking into, I also asked Ace to run the routine check you arranged a bit earlier this month."

Oh, great. "And?" Celeste prodded.

"It looks like—" Lorraine searched for the right explanation. "Unbeknownst to us, someone has doctored our records of executed trades. Made material changes to at least two significant analyses in our files, changes that would undermine the legitimacy of the trades. Big ones. Ace didn't want to speculate too much, but it appears that—"

"Someone is trying to set us up for insider trading."

Lorraine shifted in her seat, visibly uncomfortable. "Celeste, it's two trades that you signed off on. Trades you executed right around the time you gave public comments on commodities like oil and gold having a moment. None in Savin's portfolio were disturbed."

Bravo, motherfuckers, bravo.

One of those trades was too big to be ignored, Lorraine explained, sizable to the tune of $75 million. Celeste wondered if something like this would be her downfall. After all she'd done, would it boil down to a couple of falsified trades triggering an SEC investigation? If the SEC found evidence of criminal activity, it could refer to DOJ to prosecute.

Could a parallel investigation into the murders trigger a RICO investigation? Looking at the situation from all angles revealed what was now obvious—there was a larger effort to frame her for being involved in organized crime. She could be in serious trouble. *The irony.* Her mind ran through the steps she had to take to assess the damage. She'd need a forensics IT specialist, maybe several. The illuminati would be tangentially implicated, so she would have to convene her friends and potentially the Feds. Wasn't this exactly what her immunity deal was supposed to prevent?

Her phone buzzed with a notification. She noticed that she had several missed calls, likely from Ace. "Well, my mind is racing a mile a minute, but before I spring into action, I should probably get more information. Did Ace find anything else out of the ordinary?"

"Funny you should ask. Our emails about the South American infrastructure programs were all compromised, downloaded to some untraceable remote device. Any idea who would care about programs we've barely even started?"

"Wow, that's random. No clue."

The two speculated a bit more, and Celeste promised to call Lorraine back later, after she spoke with Ace.

"Wait. Do you need me to come to Paris?"

"No, no, you stay in New York. We'll get to the bottom of this."

KAYA AND MATTHEW delivered their presentation without any hiccups. Matthew was pleasant, deferential even, to Celeste, but she knew better than to be fooled into thinking she'd neutralized him. Even with his invincibility complex, she knew she'd instilled a healthy dose of fear in him, which would be beneficial until she could figure out how to get rid of him.

First things first. After her staff meeting, she bade farewell to Kaya and Matthew, who both claimed they had meetings in Dubai the following day. It was fine with her; she'd succeeded in getting what she needed.

For the next few hours, she had meetings with her team. The Paris office was full of nameless, faceless people who were competent enough, but few were exceptional. Her hope was that she'd given each enough one-on-one attention that they'd continue to work hard on the integration of TA Capital and Ricci, though she had more important concerns to address.

After the revolving door of traders and analysts, she finally had her office to herself. She closed the door and drew the blinds so she could make some calls without an audience.

She dialed Michel on her burner Nokia.

"What?" he said by way of greeting, but without his usual annoyance.

"Have you now fully recovered from your St. Louis hangover?"

To her surprise, Michel laughed. "I've had better days, I can tell you that." He sounded strong, back to himself.

"You've never explained the strange things you were saying. That you didn't protect—"

"Oh, who knows? I was drunk out of my mind," he interrupted, brushing her off as he had when she was at the Ritz. "How can I help you today?"

"Well, you were right."

"As usual."

She summarized what Lorraine had shared about the doctored trades. "So if you pair this with the other stuff, this really could be the Feds setting me up?"

Michel clicked his tongue. "Sounds about right."

"It's on brand, I suppose. I love helping women break glass ceilings. So few women have gone to prison for insider trading or been successfully prosecuted under RICO laws," she said sardonically.

"You're not going to prison. But I do expect the hits to keep coming—and more frequently—for a while. Whoever is behind this wants you off your game and out of the way. This is them turning up the heat."

She suddenly realized that was what it had always been about. The chaos of the last few years had been to keep her so disoriented that she couldn't possibly have the ability to uncover who was after her and put a stop to them. Michel sounded like himself again, the strong partner he'd been in the past. "Who do you think it is?"

He sighed heavily. Then he replied, "You know where I stand on the issue. I don't think anyone you've surrounded yourself with is trustworthy. They should all go down, including the illuminati. As for who, specifically, is after you at this very moment, Occam's razor points to the Feds. They could have some theories that aren't in our favor about Rome. Perhaps about Nico too. They'd have the capabilities to set you up, I'm sure. But not a lot of motive for those two.

"That's where I always struggle when I point fingers at them. They may not be competent, but I do believe they want to do good in the world, from all that you say. And they know you've been wronged by the same man who's caused them pain, so I think they'd give us latitude," he reasoned.

"What about the agent who was running Omar off book? How could we find out who that was?"

"We can't. They keep that kind of information locked up tight. Even if they're investigating his murder, there'll be no way into those files other than actually being in the file vault at the FBI Building or sneaking into Langley."

"Not impossible."

"That's a grandiose idea, even for you, Celeste," he replied sternly. "Not to mention a death sentence. Trust me."

She let it go. "So what should I do instead? Sit tight and wait for the FBI to show up at my door with an arrest warrant?"

"Just keep your powder dry. And for the love of Christ, don't do anything stupid. I'll be back in touch."

Click.

She worked her way down her mental list of calls to make. "Hey, Siri, call Savin," she instructed.

"Celly!"

"Hi, Sav. What's up?"

"Am I on speaker?"

"Hang on." She put her earbuds in. "Now you're not."

She heard him slam his office door, then shuffle back to the phone.

"What the actual fuck, Celeste?" She hated when he used her full name—it always meant he was going to lecture her.

"Could you be a little more specific?" *It's been quite a day so far, and it's what?* She checked the time. *Four p.m.* The only sustenance she recalled ingesting was the matcha latte in the morning. Her stomach growled, as if on command.

"You sat with me at dinner and *forgot* to mention that someone had been following you that day?"

Fucking Jack. She added him to her list of people to call for the sole purpose of bitching him out. How dare he tell anyone what she'd told him in confidence. And how dare Savin tell Theodore.

"So *you're* the one who ratted me out to my husband, huh? *Allegedly* following me, first of all. We don't have any confirmation. Furthermore, you know I hate when you treat me like a fragile doll."

"Celly!"

"Savin!"

"You can't shut us out again. Do you know—"

"No, no, no. Don't start this shit. I'm tired of hearing how hard it was on everyone else while I had to undergo... what was it... seven surgeries? Nightmares? Thinking my husband was dead? You're right, I'm sorry to have put you through all that." *And those are only the traumas you know of, Sav.*

He was silent. It wasn't the first time they'd exchanged heated words on the topic.

"Thanks to Jack, Angelo is following me around all day and has twenty-four-hour security outside my home. I'm fine, Savin."

"You've spoken with Ace, then?"

"Lorraine told me. I'd like to keep the information on a need-to-know basis until we figure out what's going on. OK?" Silence. "Savin? Seriously."

He sighed heavily. "Celly, it feels like something is happening again. I thought... well, I just..."

"You thought the trouble was over when Omar... died."

"Yes."

She couldn't be his support, not this time. "Well, we don't know exactly what's going on, but it doesn't seem like you—or D&C more generally—are a target."

"Celly, someone's setting you up. I know those trades were legit. Let's convene the illuminati and talk it through. Chet and Gabe will know exactly what to do."

"I absolutely, in no uncertain terms, do not want you to involve the Feds. Not yet." She'd have to give him more than that to talk him off a ledge. "Look, I'll have Johnny and Sam look into it, and Angelo has a sophisticated security outfit here who I can talk to." She exhaled sharply. She couldn't risk Savin going rogue. "We'll figure it out—we always do. Do you pinkie promise me you won't say anything to anyone this time?" she asked, referring to their college-age ritual when one was telling the other a secret. They only invoked it when something was dire.

"OK, I'll stand down, but I have to know that you're safe," he said gravely.

"Listen, I must get out of this office. I haven't eaten, and it's been a trying day, to say the least. I need you to give me peace of mind that you won't alert the illuminati—please."

"OK, we'll talk later."

She hung up without saying goodbye.

The burner vibrated. *Ace.*

"Yes?"

"So you heard."

"Yep."

"Doesn't look too good," Ace said in the deep monotone distorted by the voice changer.

Who are you? Can I trust you? Out loud, she asked, "So what do you suggest?"

"I'll figure out where the breach originated, but it may take a few days."

"And then what?"

"I guess that depends on who's responsible."

"Fair enough."

"Listen, I know this is difficult, but we'll get to the bottom of it."

Celeste had considered that her past could catch up with her. She couldn't let on that she had a plan, so she had to appear alarmed. "Hopefully, before I'm in prison."

"I won't let that happen."

"I appreciate that."

"I aim to please."

Click.

After sorting through a few emails from her team that needed approvals, Celeste messaged Angelo that she was ready to go. She shut down her desktop and gathered her things. Her stomach rumbled again.

She wasn't in the mood to talk, so she said, "Have a good evening, everyone," over her shoulder as she walked through the office. *I'll connect with them when things calm down.* She couldn't remember the name of a single person she'd met since she got to the office. *That's on them for being ordinary.*

Downstairs at the car, Angelo and Julien stood talking. They both wore all-black suits and sunglasses, standing out among the tourists strolling happily with shopping bags. She fumed. *So inconspicuous, guys.*

Celeste plastered a smile on her face for onlookers. When she got to the men, she spoke through clenched teeth. "What happened to staying in the shadows?"

"We need to talk," Angelo said somberly.

6

CELESTE DÉSENCHANTÉE

"I don't know what I'm supposed to be looking at. Is that a tick? Or...?" she said, exasperated, referring to the round black object that Angelo was holding. It was no bigger than a pea, so small that she almost couldn't see it in his pro-football-player-sized hands.

She, Angelo, and Julien were on the patio at Les Fines Gueules, a casual French bistro in a building *au coin*, situated at the corner of a three-way intersection, in the 1st arrondissement. They sat in wicker chairs with metal bases around a bare rectangular faux maple table. The place was much too casual for Celeste's attire, with most of the other patrons wearing jeans or shorts, and much too vibrant for her mood. She had wanted to go home, order in, and do some more sleuthing. But the bistro was rumored to be fantastic, offering a modern twist on French comfort food, and Angelo had insisted that he and Julien had something she "needed to see to believe." Looking at her somberly, he told her she'd want to discuss it at length, but it couldn't be discussed at home.

"We have evidence that someone broke into your place and planted things," he said now as he held up the pea-sized device they'd found. "Julien discovered a sophisticated audio listening device that doubles as a complete hacking system. Inside it is a microscopic chip that can pick up anything transferred over any internet or cell tower—including text messages, voice and digital calls, internet activity, and even burners. It detects biometrics of people nearby—body temperature, heart rate—and has voice recognition software that can be independently verified, and it is admissible in court."

Julien added, "We also found another device that looks identical to this in a drawer in your desk."

"What is it?"

"The other device is an explosive," Angelo said gravely.

"What the fuck?" She jerked her head around to Angelo. "You buried the lede there a bit, huh?"

Angelo blushed.

"It's military or intelligence agency grade and nearly impossible to buy on the black market," Julien explained. "In my experience, only the most sophisticated intelligence agencies can get their hands on this kind of explosive because its manufacturing is extremely limited."

"In your professional opin—"

"Wait, there's one more thing," Julien interrupted Celeste. Angelo shot him a dirty look, but he seemed determined to carry on. "There's one critical detail you must understand."

"She doesn't need to be bothered with this—" Angelo interjected.

I don't have time for a pissing contest. Celeste frowned and cut him off. "Well, carry on, then, Julien."

Angelo's eyes widened, but Julien was undeterred.

"We had to leave it where it was. We disarmed it, of course, but I don't want to move it. They'll have it geotagged. I have a device that will prevent the perpetrator from knowing the explosive is offline but won't override the location."

Celeste's jaw dropped. *Didn't have "find a bomb in the Parisian apartment" on this year's vision board.* "Is it advisable to leave an explosive—allegedly detonated, but how can one really be sure—at the desk where I sat this morning? Just hanging out there in the drawer? And how can you be sure there are no more?" *Essentially, a live bomb in my home. Fabulous.*

"We are sure. I brought in a K-9 unit and lots of equipment."

"The homeowners' association loved that, I'd imagine. A bomb-sniffing dog."

"I didn't want to scare you, Celly," Angelo said quickly, "but Julien is right—moving it would take away any element of surprise that we have. But I want to be clear—you *cannot* go back there."

She wanted to kill him. How dare he try to keep something of this magnitude from her?

There were so many holes in their plan. Her mind raced with questions, and she felt her anger rising—but it wasn't the time to let her emotions best her. She needed facts. "Is it safe to say that we can we rule out that these... devices... were placed by a government official in an official capacity?"

Julien seemed resolute in his knowledge but appeared to be weighing how much to share. "In Europe, I can't imagine any scenario where an explosive would be placed in a civilian's home like this by anyone in the government." He paused, frowning. "It's possible a terrorist organization could have access. But like I said, governments across the world hold the technology close.

"Russia and the US, for instance, are each racing to get the latest technology, but within the bounds and limitations of mutually assured destruction. They want to control its distribution, not to disrupt the careful balance of power. Neither wants it in the hands of everyday citizens, let alone nongovernmental bad actors."

Angelo jumped in, uncomfortable. "Celly, are you listening? He said it could be a terrorist organization. This isn't a small issue like someone taking your photograph. We need to report this to the police and let the Feds know." *The very people who could have planted it in the first place.* Bringing in law enforcement would make it real, put it on the record, and she could forget about any privacy to carry out her mission. The scrutiny focused on her, not allowing her to move freely, would completely compromise her ability to stop the cyberattack and shut down Omar's organization.

Pulling in the Feds would similarly result in her isolation. The alarm and chaos that would ensue... *No.* She was racing against the clock; she couldn't be sidelined for an official investigation where she'd have no inside influence. Besides, Michel believed that someone within the illuminati was a traitor. She didn't want them to know that she knew or to have all the information about what was going on.

"Hang on. Let's not do anything rash," she said calmly. She took a deep breath, outwardly containing her emotions. *Not this place too. Not another home compromised before I've even had a chance to enjoy it.* She had to remember what she'd realized earlier: This was all a game to someone. To keep her so distracted that she couldn't go on the offensive. *Two can play this game.* No one was telling anyone anything until she said when.

"Let's think through the different scenarios. We can rule out that this was legally placed—without question—yes?"

Both men nodded.

"So there's really only one option—a well-connected, well-resourced terrorist group. Omar's crew would fit that description, and it's no surprise they've begin ramping up now that they have my attention."

"I guess," Angelo said, shrugging. He seemed to be exerting enormous effort to stay calm.

Julien's energy was electric. He was much more approachable when discussing his intelligence expertise. "To be clear, as a former government official, I'd recommend reporting it *immediately*, evacuating the house, fleeing back to the US. As a private citizen and member of your security team... well, I have the equipment and tools to ensure no one else gets in. I think we should use this situation to our advantage."

"How so?"

"You must have some idea why a 'well-connected, well-resourced terrorist group,' as you say, would want to listen in on you and to have the ability to... ahem... detonate an explosive. What do they hope to hear you discussing? What could be so damning that they'd want the option to kill you then and there?"

She stared at him blankly—innocently, she hoped.

"Madame, I've been in this business a long time. You've got secrets, or you wouldn't need me and Angelo. So let's all save ourselves some time and come up with a plan. What could you say or do that would throw them off your trail? You have an advantage— they don't necessarily know that *you know* they're listening."

Hmm. He was right.

Angelo sighed. "Celly, I can't support you using yourself as bait; not again. You can't go back home. Your place is huge, with dozens of nooks and crannies. Yes, we've done several thorough sweeps, but this device is minuscule—several more could be hiding in between the caulk and the marble of your bathtub."

"No, no, a hotel has more variables that we can't control than my home does, and you know it."

"We could make it work, though."

"How so? With me sitting in a hotel room while the two of you stand outside with your guns and your mean mugs? Sitting in the dark room with the curtains drawn, not seeing sunshine because opening them could jeopardize my safety? Having meals brought to the room? Working out there because the gym is too dangerous? No. Fuck no. I have a life to live, and I'm not doing this shit again."

"C'mon, Celly, it wouldn't have to be that extreme. But being home—hell, the entire house is made of windows, where any number of people could surveil you."

She kept her face neutral as she internally processed her emotions. She tried to name them as she'd practiced with her therapist. Fear and surprise were there, of course, but most prominent was her old friend anger. Running was not the answer. It never had been. She would channel her anger, transform it into the power she needed.

"I appreciate your concern. But I'm not staying in a hotel, and neither of you is going to tell anyone, not a single fucking soul, what you found. We'll play off your bringing a *bomb dog* into my pristine neighborhood as a precaution against a gas leak, and no one will be the wiser. Or you will face my wrath, the likes of which the world has never seen."

Just then, a server walked up. Celeste smiled demurely and ordered the baked Camembert and beef tartare with a Burgundy Chardonnay she thought would complement both. *Don't wait for the storm to pass; learn to dance in the rain!*

"*Très bon choix de vin,*" the server said, impressed, nodding appreciatively at her wine pairing.

Julien ordered the roasted sea bass and a Sancerre, and Angelo went with the crab roll and a pilsner. The server left.

"As I was saying, I won't be staying in a hotel," Celeste said simply. "What I need from you now is to advise me on the pros and cons of keeping the device in place, give me your thoughts on how we can trace it back to the person or organization who planted it, and figure out how to let me out of your sight without anything terrible happening. Then you'll implement any necessary changes."

"Celly, that's my whole point," Angelo responded. "You can't be safe there. We don't know who this is, and we need to bring others in to protect you. We are out of our league."

"Then level up and rise to the occasion, Angelo. It's you, me, and Julien mitigating this. You're not here in Paris with me to book me into a hotel or set off a five-alarm shitstorm, resulting in my being locked away under a watchful eye for the next year. You're here to help me stay safe in my own home."

"I can't support this."

He is relentless. Finally, her outrage could not be contained. "It's my *home!*" she erupted, slamming a fist on the table. She looked around, sheepish, her lack of decorum shocking the other diners, who turned to stare. She lowered her voice.

"This is *not* your decision, Angelo. I sign your paycheck, and it is *my* life and *my* call. I won't go through life looking over my shoulder, lurking in the shadows." *But that's exactly what you've been doing for years, Celeste, and you know it.* She ignored the internal taunting and continued.

"I need your word that you won't share this."

Julien nodded. "Of course," he said firmly. "You are the client, and I believe we can handle this."

"Angelo? Your word."

"I will not tell a soul. For now. But it is totally against my better judgment and entirely under duress."

"I could've done without the commentary. OK, now let's be real. How the fuck did they get in there anyway, whoever *they* is? The alarm system is state-of-the-art, and I've heard of no time when the cameras were offline."

"That's just it," Julien said. "There are no signs of forced entry anywhere. It could be an inside job—"

An inside job? "That's impossible. I'm the only one who's ever there besides the designer and housekeeper."

"My guess is that the devices were shipped with your desk," Angelo interrupted. "The chain of custody is hardly airtight. Tracking down your shipments would have—"

Meredith would've had all the communications about the furniture orders, not Celeste. *Mere would never be involved.*

"Tracking *should* have been nearly impossible because our servers are *allegedly* monitored twenty-four seven." She hadn't told the men about the modified trades yet, so she stopped herself.

Her desk was one of the first pieces of furniture delivered after she'd bought the home. *So the devices could've been there for a while.* She decided the best way to remain focused was to put the explosive out of her mind.

She wasn't in Paris often, but she had stayed at the new place a few times. She tried to recall if she'd had any particular conversations revealing sensitive information and instantly knew the answer was yes. And then there was the fact that the listening device seemed able to trace her digital footprint. She'd scoured the grid that morning. Was it really an airtight encryption, as she'd been told?

Oh, what the hell does it matter anyway? I don't have a time machine, so I can't undo anything they've already seen now. Using techniques she'd learned from working with her therapist, Anne Marie, she talked herself back off the ledge. Shouting at Angelo was doing nothing to solve the problem; she'd reserve her anger for her next phone call with Chet or Gabe.

"I had hoped you and D&C would be in less danger of being infiltrated now that we have Rani in place as the CTO, along with the teams she has built," Angelo said, now on the defense.

Rani. Celeste made a mental note to check in with her for an update on how the systems were running. *And also to tease out where her head is at.*

He continued, "Let's look forward, not back. I can't speculate on how this sort of device got inside the house, but I can say this—I don't think it was an inside job."

Despite having concerns about her own group, she agreed with Angelo—it felt more likely that it was someone on the outside. *Probably Omar's crew. Wait until I get my hands on those assholes.*

Julien, the consummate professional, promised, "We'll get to the bottom of it, and in the meantime, we'll help you take reasonable precautions."

"I'm not moving to a hotel, period. So make it work." She took a sip of the chilled wine that had been dropped off. "OK, now that we've gotten that unpleasantness out of the way, I suggest we all enjoy this wonderful dinner at this cozy bistro on this spotless summer evening." And just like that, she set all her worry aside. *The only thing that can ruin a good meal is a bad attitude.*

Celeste asked Julien innocuous questions about his previous career, knowing his replies would be brief, as she primed him to ask what she really wanted to know. The server interrupted only to drop off their *entrées* and then after, their *plats*, and to occasionally refill their wine. She drank quickly, knowing the other two would keep her pace. An entrée was the starter in French, rather than the main dish as in American English; the latter was plat in French. Though she was fluent in French, she could acknowledge that it might be difficult for a native English speaker to learn.

For dessert, Celeste ordered a cheese plate and passion fruit tart for the table. As they all shared how incredible they thought the meal was, staying away from difficult topics, Celeste decided to go in for the kill. "It must have been so exciting working as part of a clandestine operation," she said to Julien. "Did you ever... what is it they say in the movies? Did you ever have any informants? They have those on the TV shows I watch." She feigned embarrassment. "*Law & Order* reruns—my guilty American pleasure."

Julien was loosened up a bit, his cheeks flushed. *Finally!* They'd had about a bottle of wine each. *He's probably out of practice holding his liquor now that he's a private citizen—or maybe he was a bad spy.*

He leaned his head in conspiratorially. "Honestly, that was one of the most fun parts of the job. *Gérer un agent*—that is, running an agent...that's what we called it—allowed me to use all my training to keep them motivated and dedicated. Persuasion, manipulation, the ability to blend in like—how do you say...a chameleon?"

Celeste nodded.

"Yes, we must blend in well. We are assigned to agents whose cultures we're familiar with and whose languages we're proficient in."

"So you were"—she paused as though struggling for the word—"Do they call it 'counterterrorist unit'?" She laughed. "I'm probably messing it up. But I recently watched an L and O episode where they mentioned it."

Julien looked eager to clarify. *Men are all the same, really. Give them a chance to mansplain anything to a woman, and it's hook, line, and sinker.*

"You are almost correct. I was 'counterintelligence,' charged with protecting the French from espionage. So my agents, as you say, were foreign nationals, *désenchanté*, discouraged with, their own governments—to say the least—and happy to protect our interests."

Angelo excused himself to go to the men's room. Celeste asked the more sensitive questions next.

"How did you keep their identities secret? I mean, it would be so dangerous for them if they were—what's the word? Compromised? I'm trying to remember from my show," she said sheepishly, feigning the look of a curious doe. She took a swig of wine and signaled to an onlooking server to bring another round. *Helpful for my cause.* The guys hadn't noticed she'd let them lap her twice so she could stay clearheaded. *Or at least slightly clearheaded.* Admittedly, she was buzzed. To absorb some of the wine, she spread some warm Brie de Meaux, considered the "king of Bries," on a piece of bread and added some fig chutney.

"We had a special unit, closed off to nearly all employees, with a special database. You couldn't send any documents via email or other traditional means."

"But didn't you have, like, reports and stuff?"

"Yeah, but those could only be uploaded on the classified information management system. Only those with clearance could access them. And it would only happen on-site."

"Oh, wow, it sounds so complex. Did anyone ever try to breach the database while you were there?"

"Once." He reconsidered. "I suppose more than once. But they never got past security."

"Oh, that's funny! *Law & Order* makes it seem so common. How would you do it if you were writing a show?"

Julien became animated. *Maybe I, as the person he is paid to protect, should be a little concerned that it's this easy to get him to talk.*

"What a fun question to consider. First, I'd get the badge of someone who looks similar to me, and the second part may sound hard, but it's easier than you think: I'd get their fingerprints."

Well, I've figured out how to do that part at least. Hurry along, my friend. Angelo knew her well enough to pick up on the fact that she was trying to extract information, so she couldn't have him returning in the middle of her inquisition.

"Then I'd... well, you'd have to get rid of them somehow. But before that, you'd have to figure out their passwords and such, though again, not as hard as you think."

"Can you, anyone really, create fake badges and profiles? Like they do in the American movies? Have you seen *Ocean's Eleven*? They make fake hotel badges and police uniforms!"

Julien looked thoughtful and gulped the last of his wine before responding. "I suppose so, with enough IT support."

She saw Angelo walking up out of the corner of her eye. "You should watch *Law & Order* sometime—it's spectacular. I'd be interested what a real intelligence expert thought of it." *Change subject.* "One more topic to pick your brain on, and then I promise I'll stop the line of questioning."

Julien nodded once, as though to say go ahead.

"My husband and I want to go wine tasting in Burgundy. Any recommendations?"

The Frenchman spoke of wine nonstop until they had paid the check.

"OK, I hate to dampen the mood, but we need to figure out a plan before we go back to your place, Celeste," Angelo said, suddenly sober.

Final order of business. "Back to what we were saying earlier. If we remove the"—she paused and took a calming breath—"explosive, then they, whoever they are, will know that we know and will be more careful. No?" she asked.

"I believe that to be a correct assessment," said Julien sternly, his buoyant mood now subdued.

"So, we leave it for a day or so while we figure out our next move." The following day was the atelier fitting, and she'd be out all day. She shared her schedule with the two men.

"OK, if you're amenable, we'll research whether we can narrow down the origins of the planted devices," Angelo said.

"That's great."

Their plan entailed her pretending she was unaware of the bug that evening, meaning she had to act as she normally would. Calling her husband, texting her friends, responding to work emails. *If I do leave it in place, I may as well more clearly establish my alibis in case they are framing me for the murders.*

"I got this. And tomorrow evening, you'll share what you learned with your fancy equipment, and we can go from there." She took a long pull of her wine.

"Thanks for keeping this under wraps for now. I trust you both to keep me safe." She hoped she'd managed to ensure everyone who had pieces of information had an incomplete picture of all that was going on—Lorraine, Angelo, Michel, Ace, Savin, Jack—so that they wouldn't band together and loop in the Feds.

They left the bistro, and the two men escorted her home.

LATER THAT EVENING, Celeste was in bed with her laptop. Her face was freshly washed and slathered with hydrating moisturizers and actives meant to keep her skin plump and youthful. She and Meredith were discussing the following day on FaceTime.

"Celly, I cannot tell you how excited I am!" Meredith exclaimed happily.

"Thank you so much for arranging it, Mere." Shopping and drinks with one of her favorite people would be the perfect distraction while serving the dual purpose of keeping her off her devices.

They planned to have *le petit déjeuner*, breakfast, at Hôtel de Crillon, which had one of her favorite hotel cafés, and Celeste arranged a time to pick up Mere. The friends said good night.

Wonder if the person who planted the device will send someone to follow us?

One more call to go. She clicked on Theodore's number on Face-Time and waited while it rang. *No answer.* She was exhausted anyway from all the wine and the mounting stress, so she texted him good night and turned out the light.

Alone with her thoughts, Celeste allowed herself five minutes to ruminate before doing her yoga nidra sleep meditation. So many new developments had emerged in the span of a day. Someone had planted a deadly device in her Parisian home, and someone (else?) seemed to be framing her for insider trading or some other sort of securities fraud. But how were they gaining access to her? The list of protections for her homes was long. She made a practice of keeping her files encrypted. Were her files vulnerable to compromise? She supposed everyone's was. Had they already been stolen? She wasn't sure, but it was possible, maybe even probable.

The bug had come from a sophisticated opponent, whom she had nicknamed "the bugger," the asshole who left the spy device in her home. Theodore would've gotten a kick out of her using British slang properly, and if it had been under different circumstances, she would've shared this with him.

If she'd learned one thing on her journey, it was that one had to know when to push hard and when to let things be revealed in due time. Yet the urgency in her visions was palpable. It wasn't the first time she'd had visions that felt prescient. When Theodore was gone, she'd had recurring nightmares of Omar killing him. They had mostly subsided for a while but had returned in different forms after Omar and Nico passed away. Her morning vision was different, though. It wasn't a nightmare—she was certain her subconscious was trying to reveal something to her and was using images of her parents and others to beg her to dig deeper. *What am I missing?* She would have to work harder to tap into the message. *But not tonight.* The mind needed rest.

The following morning, Julien pulled to a stop in front of Hôtel de Crillon on Place de la Concorde. The driveway was lined with exotic cars. "Ooh, Theodore would love that one," she said to Meredith, pointing at a mint vintage Mercedes convertible in a metallic greige.

Julien, who had put the divider window down, smirked. "That's a 1937 Roadster. Would set you back about eight million euros." *Oh, so now he's a conversationalist.*

"It's cute!" Meredith said.

Julien shook his head, his disdain apparent.

"OK, ladies, let's get you inside," Angelo said, hopping out. He opened Celeste's door. She took his hand and slid out gracefully. She had given herself a pep talk that morning. Until she fully understood the extent of the security breaches, she needed to stay away from work and her usual sleuthing. Thus the old Celeste was going to enjoy an indulgent, elegant day in Paris with one of her best friends. Using the mindfulness skills she'd developed from years of meditating, she would compartmentalize her thoughts and "parking lot" anything that involved solving murders or tracking down terrorists.

While applying her makeup that morning, she invoked a mantra: *Take a break from your troubles, and remember that life should be enjoyed.*

It was one of those perfect temperate days sandwiched between the dog days of summer and the crisp Parisian autumn. She wore a blush-pink tulip minidress that accentuated her long, lean legs and an Amina Muaddi kitten heel. She flipped her flowing tresses over her shoulder and adjusted her sunglasses. Her goal was to feel like a lady who lunched, not a battered and bruised financier with problems spiraling out of control.

Angelo walked around the car to get Meredith's door, while Celeste practiced stillness, though admittedly her hands were itching to check the stock market or her email.

Meredith strolled over to Celeste, looking flawless as usual in a flowing ivory pantsuit. Her hair was styled in a sleek low ponytail, and her neck was adorned with a simple gold choker. As always, she had a radiant glow, her lips lined with shiny gloss framing her smile. The two women latched elbows and walked toward the grand entrance.

A *portier* stood at attention in the main doorway, prepared to greet them, exuding an air of poise and grace. He was framed by two perfectly manicured evergreen trees. Soft pattering sounds from the cascading Fontaine des Mers, or Fountain of the Seas, and birds chirping in the nearby trees provided the scene's tranquil soundtrack. She allowed the calm to wash over her. *Today is for me; tomorrow, I'll get back to saving the world—but the first order of business is keeping myself alive and out of prison.*

"This is your stop, darling," Celeste said over her shoulder to Angelo.

"Celly, I need to come inside and check it out. We—I—I won't stay."

"You cause such a stir. I want to pretend..." She remembered Meredith was listening then. "Pretend that we are chic Parisian women without a care in the world."

"Cel—" he began, then seemed to weigh his options. The last thing he wanted, she knew, was for her to hide things from him.

Pick your battles, old friend. But her more sensible side realized that having him close was for the best. An explosive device was bold. Who knew what was in store. She imagined someone attacking her in the restaurant and having to pull out her weapons. *"Page Six" would have a heyday covering that one: "Ice queen frosts Parisian hot spot in dramatic shoot-out."* Likely more newsworthy than her security guard doing a walk-through. She relented instead of continuing to give him a hard time. "In and out, then."

"I'll be discreet."

Celeste's and Meredith's eyes met, and they smiled. Angelo's sheer size and muscle mass made him conspicuous—it was impossible for him to blend in. But his intentions were good.

They walked through the grand lobby, past the many sitting areas with chandeliers and muted Persian rugs, to their brunch destination, Jardin d'Hiver. Sumptuous plush couches in deep coordinating shades of purple provided a look of opulence, while the indoor-outdoor flow gave the feeling of sitting in a colorful garden. Angelo whispered something to the black-tuxedoed maître d', who nodded his head, and her bodyguard disappeared inside.

The two women were led to a corner sofa with prime views of the garden. It was a true retreat from the bustle of city life, though Paris moved at a tad bit slower pace than New York. *This is exactly the escape I needed.*

They ordered mimosas with a combination of sweet and savory—pastries and caviar boiled eggs—balanced with their more typical, healthy choices: detox juices and avocado toasts.

"OK, you've *barely* told me how things are going with the guy. Seth, right? The first trip together is a big deal!"

A memory of one of her first getaways with Theodore at a seven-star luxury hotel that entailed sex in an Amsterdam bathtub popped into her mind. *And the bedrooms and the foyer and the staircase and and... Ugh, how do we get back to* that? She so desperately longed for simpler times. *We'll get back to our essence. As soon as I get to the bottom of whatever the hell is going on.* She silently chided herself. *Presence, Celeste, presence.*

"We're having the best time!" Mere dove into a story about her dinner with Seth at L'Avenue the previous night. "Celly, I think he wants to get serious. He's been talking about us moving in together."

"OK, whoa, whoa, whoa. Before anyone moves anywhere, I need deets. We know very little about this Seth."

"He's around your age, I think."

"So then, quite youthful!"

The two laughed. "He's hard to find online, but that's because he says Gen Xers aren't as into social media as millennials like me. Seems accurate, since you also have no social media prowess to speak of," she said, giving Celeste a pointed look. Meredith had been saying for years that Celeste needed social, if for no other reason than to make people jealous. "We laugh a lot, and he loves to hear my stories. He's dying to meet you and Theodore and the gang."

"What's he like?"

"He's chivalrous and hilarious. I can't remember the last time I had this much fun with anyone." Meredith shared a few tales of their most recent dates.

"Is he kind? Theodore is kind. One piece of relationship advice I can give—always marry someone who is a much better person than you! Well, actually, two. Make sure you like fucking him because forever is a long time!" *I scored big on both counts with my guy.*

Meredith laughed. "It's not a high bar, but Seth does definitely bring up our averages in terms of giving back. He has a family foundation that does all sorts of good. He's been in New York for a year or two. He just moved into a new place in Hudson Yards. It's spectacular; I couldn't have done a better job myself. Eighty-eighth floor, four-bedroom, and you can see for miles."

He seems to be moving awfully fast. But who was she to have an opinion? Her courtship with Theodore had definitely not progressed in a traditional way, given that he had disappeared for many months and then proposed immediately when he returned.

The mimosas and pastries arrived. *Today is a dessert-for-breakfast kind of day.* Celeste selected a *pain au chocolat* and listened as her friend shared more details.

"He has some sort of finance job, as does everyone in New York, I suppose. Obviously does well, and it's such a relief that he doesn't talk about work all the time. You know how men in the city can be."

"And you said he's never been married?"

"Nope, and no kids. He lived in Hong Kong for a while for work. I think I remember him mentioning Frankfurt and Dubai also. Of course, London also, as the finance bros do. A bit of a nomad. He says I'll love Tokyo, with all the shopping and more Michelin restaurants than any other city. Did you know a lot of them with stars are food trucks?"

"I have heard that! But I've never been. OK, last question. Is he handsome?"

Mere gave her signature squeal. "Yes, he's *so* dreamy. He looks a bit like Brad Pitt—post- not pre-facelift—chiseled jawline and all."

"Well, he sounds like he makes you happy. You deserve—"

Celeste stopped herself, surprised that she was getting a bit choked up. "You've... you've always been such a ray of sunshine in my life. No matter what's happening, I can always trust that you'll come to the rescue with exactly what I need to cheer me up or make me feel sparkly. I've had some dark days, and words can never express what your kindness has meant. Thank you."

Her eyes were misty with emotion. *Oh, for fuck's sake.* She couldn't even brunch anymore without becoming unhinged.

Mere leaned over and gave Celeste a hug. "Oh, Celly, you're one of my favorite people in the entire world! Anything I've done didn't require a thank-you—that's friendship. And you've been such a friend to me too. You have no idea how much it meant that you took a chance on a fledgling stylist and helped me build a business of this scale, where something like Sav's engagement party is a side gig."

Celeste wiped away a tear as a server breezed up with their eggs. "Let's enjoy brunch, shall we?" She looked at the server. "We'll have another round of mim— Ah, fuck it. Can we have two glasses of the Taittinger instead?"

The server nodded and left.

"The sugar is a hangover waiting to happen," Celeste said with a nurturing tone. "Best to stick with Champagne."

"Seth always says that too!"

LATER, buzzed from the bubbles at a socially acceptable level for a Parisian afternoon fitting, the two friends arrived at the Christian Dior atelier, also the brand's headquarters and flagship boutique. It was officially recognized as an haute couture house, as designated by the Fédération de la Haute Couture et de la Mode, or FHCM. The French government regulated fashion houses in the same way it regulated Champagne or Bordeaux, and only sixteen houses met the FHCM's criteria.

They were giddy with excitement as they entered the elegant building and were led up to the spacious showroom. The air was charged with sophistication and exclusivity, while still being accessible and warm. One reason Celeste had always loved the Christian Dior house was the optimism the man himself had ushered in after World War II, when he used fashion as a vehicle to inspire a new era of elegance and femininity, moving away from the austerity and utility of the war.

A handsome young man with fair skin and slicked-back, medium-brown hair stood at the elevator doors when they opened. He was dressed head to toe in black. "She's finally here—the legend you've been telling us about, Mere! Mademoiselle Donovan—welcome to our home!"

Meredith beamed.

A heart of gold. Celeste wished more women recognized the value of lifting each other up. The patriarchy would never crumble with women at each other's throats.

"Celly, he's a twink, as the boys would say," Mere whispered.

"Oh my God! Stop! I know what a twink is—I'm not a hundred years old!" Celeste protested in a hiss.

Two more beautiful Parisians wandered toward them, not in a

rush. *Never in a rush in Paris.* The woman, in her mid-twenties and with the same pale skin and emaciated vibe as their greeter, looked bored. *Do French women look any other way?* The man accompanying her, tall and lithe with clear cappuccino skin, was a bit closer to Celeste's age, mid-forties, and gave off an air of authority. He was the one in charge, and he wanted them to know it. There was no gushing from him, standing at attention as the friends approached.

"Bonjour, mademoiselles. We're so happy you could visit our little studio." He embraced each of them with *la bise*, giving them double-cheek kisses. "Oh, dressing this one will be such fun!" he said in a theatric whisper to his colleagues.

They led the two women into a large semiprivate room with three-panel mirrors and a platform, and what could only be described as a parade of couture began. Their glasses of Champagne were never empty, and the mood was vibrant.

Celeste, in between her dancing and singing numbers with Meredith, tried on a golden ethereal gown, sundresses, a bar jacket paired with a pencil skirt, sweaters, and swimwear—all of it bespoke. They set aside several outfits for her trip, and Celeste couldn't remember a day when she'd laughed so much. It was euphoric.

"OK, Celly, for the grand finale, they've created—"

"No, no, mademoiselle, you've got it all wrong. Tell her the truth. *You* designed; we simply sewed."

Meredith blushed. "Well, I suppose I did." She looked at Celeste. "Darling, this last one was a co-creation with our new friends here, a labor of love on their part. We wanted vintage, and I saw a Dior look that Charlize Theron wore to Cannes. I asked them to re-create it." Celeste was touched.

Two of the Dior associates escorted the dress into the room with them, holding it gingerly at each end. They carefully hung it on the rack.

"Oh, wow! It's so delicate. Help me into it!" They were all quite careful not to snag the delicate blush-pink silk.

Each member of the group played a role in sliding the flowy gown onto Celeste's body. It fit like a glove, with a body-hugging cut. The top was off the shoulder, and the tapered waist gave way to a midi-length, A-line skirt. The hue offset Celeste's faux golden tan.

"Just as glamorous as Charlize, Celly!"

The Dior staff seemed speechless, with matching jaws open.

Celeste twirled around on the platform, alive with happiness. The dress was perfect from any angle. She felt beautiful. Everything always fell into place when she felt good in what she was wearing.

"OK, everyone, you can pick your jaws up off the floor now," Mere said, laughing.

"It's perfect for Marrakech!" Celeste cheered. "I'll wear it for a cocktail party."

"I need photos," exclaimed the twink.

The afternoon whizzed by, with more Champagne and dancing, as they all took turns gushing over Meredith's creation.

"Am I holding you back? Should you be a designer?" Celeste asked Meredith somberly when the staff sashayed away. "Because if that's what you want, you know I'll be the first to support you."

"No, no, Celly. I love what I do. It was such a treat, though, for once to be on the design side. I'm not sure if I'd want to do it all the time, honestly. It's a lot of work!"

Because Celeste was sample size, few alterations were needed to prepare the outfits for her trip. The Dior team committed to having it ready for pickup the following day, and Meredith promised she would figure out how to ship everything to Morocco.

The two women decided to have a late-afternoon cocktail nearby to enjoy the spotless summer day before Meredith's dinner date with Seth. They were situated on the terrace at Hôtel Plaza Athénée, La Terrasse Montaigne, sipping on crisp Sancerre from the Loire Valley and snacking on the lobster salad. Although Celeste found much of Paris to be iconic, Avenue Montaigne was one of the most luxurious streets, lined with designer boutiques that epitomized the spirit of French fashion and close to the vibrant Champs-Élysées.

Celeste was serious for a moment. "Mere, I don't mean to belabor what I said earlier, but I can't tell you how much today meant to me. Things have been... a little crazy, as they always are these days. You found a way for me to clear my head for a few hours. You're a rock for me."

"Oh, Celly, you're going to make me cry!"

"It's true, though. I've been having a hard time"—*Careful!*—"balancing marriage and work and staying well and maintaining a perky ass at my *youthful* age of... twenty-nine."

Meredith giggled. "But seriously, I see you, and I could tell you were having a bit of a hard time getting back into the swing of things after the honeymoon. With your brother passing and all, it's... Celly, it's just a lot. I hope you know I'm here for whatever you need."

"Thank you. I was telling Jack and Sav the other night—my parents died when I was in college, and it sounds horrible to say, but as time passed, I hardly thought of them.

"No, that's not true. I would think of them when Keith called every few months to ask for money, stoned and in trouble again. Then I'd be pissed at them for leaving me here alone to deal with him. But since my brother's... accident, I feel them more. Like they're here with me." She shook her head. "I know I sound crazy."

"Not at all. I know you believe in the spiritual realm, with as much meditating and shadow work as you do." Meredith placed her hand on top of Celeste's and looked her in the eyes. "Maybe there's something they're trying to tell you."

"Could be. Anyway, back to our lovely day as ladies who lunch on one of the most beautiful patios in one of the most beautiful cities in the world after having spent the day around the most beautiful clothing."

"You're going to be the best-dressed woman in all of Morocco."

"I'm not so sure. Poppy and Teddy are meeting us there. My mother-in-law invariably steals the show with her impeccable style."

"That's true. Even I can't outdo her."

They laughed, and Celeste pictured her in-laws warmly. "They've been so welcoming from day one, and especially when Theodore was... gone, they treated me as one of their own. You know, Theodore says they weren't always so happy together."

"You'd never know it with how in tune they are now," Meredith observed.

"Agreed."

"It's too early for Seth to meet my family, but I think they'd really like him."

"That's wonderful, Mere. Truly, I'm so happy you've met someone who seems to care deeply for you. When do we get to meet him? You know Savin will talk his ear off, and Theodore will try to get him to do something very British."

"Let's plan something for when you get back from Marrakech."

"You own my calendar, so plan away!"

"Do you think it's too soon to bring him to Savin's engagement party?"

Celeste considered the question. "It's up to you. You'll be in event-planning mode—will it be too much to juggle? You're not exactly one to half-ass it."

"Absolutely not. I've always wanted to do an event on Gin Lane. The homes are enormous and have so many gorgeous areas to decorate, move the crowd, et cetera."

Meredith talked through her thinking a bit more. "You know, I'm not going to invite him. I'll be working, and I don't want the first time he meets all of you to be when I'm stressed about the caviar."

"No one needs stressful hors d'oeuvres, that's for sure. Speaking of no stress, next time we are in town, we must try the Dior spa here. It's so serene—and you'll love the interior."

"Done!"

When it was time to leave, Celeste texted Angelo that they were ready. "To his credit, Angelo has stayed out of sight today," she said to Meredith.

After settling the tab, the two ladies walked out to the sidewalk. "Why's he been around? Is something up?" Meredith asked, a look of concern washing over her previously jubilant face.

Celeste didn't want to bring the dark reality cloud over her day, but she didn't want to be dishonest to her friend. "You know I've had people following me before, yes?"

"Yeah. When Omar was alive."

"Well, either he's come back from the grave or someone else wants to cause some trouble for me. Nothing major has happened, but we'd rather err on the side of caution."

Tears sprang to Meredith's eyes. "Oh, gosh, Celly, yes, of course we have to keep you safe." Celeste knew Mere was imagining how broken her friend had been, both physically and mentally. *Here we go again. Why did I even say anything?* She instantly felt guilty, an ingrate resenting being loved by so many. But it reminded her of her vulnerability, of the abuse she'd endured, and the constant triggering was exhausting.

Angelo and Julien pulled up then, which ended the serious conversation for the time being. Angelo sat up front with Julien again and put the privacy divider up. The two women chatted on the way to Meredith's hotel. Their excitement returned as they began to talk through when Celeste would wear each of her new outfits.

"You know I'll never want to wear RTW again, right?" Ready-to-wear fashion, while still part of the haute couture designer lines, had nothing on the experience Celeste had just had. "The thought that the outfit is only for me, and no one else will ever have it—I'll admit the feeling of exclusivity is heady."

It was a quick ride, less than ten minutes. As they pulled up in front of the Ritz, Meredith said, "Well, on that note, have a wonderful evening, my friend, and I'm glad you enjoyed the atelier." She hugged Celeste tightly and whispered, "You stay safe and call me if you need anything at all."

"Have a lovely time with Seth and tell him he'd better treat you like the magnificent queen you are, or I will have his balls."

Meredith laughed, blew a kiss, and turned toward the hotel.

When they arrived home, Angelo was uncharacteristically chill about Celeste going in alone.

"You're not coming?" she asked.

"We checked everything out thoroughly earlier. Try to stay off your devices tonight, and we can talk through the status of everything tomorrow morning. Text once you're inside with the doors locked."

"Um, OK. I'm glad you've relaxed a little."

"Yeah, no need to make a mountain out of a molehill," Angelo said.

Celeste frowned. She went inside and did as Angelo had suggested, double-locking the front door. Since she wouldn't be spending the evening on the computer, she decided on a workout, a sauna, and then a scramble around the kitchen to piece together a meal from what was in the pantry.

First things first. She padded upstairs to put on some comfortable clothes. The motion sensor lights turned on at each landing until she arrived at her bedroom. The door was ajar. *That's strange.*

She had specifically asked Angelo to search her personal living space only while she was present and had left the door closed to reinforce that. The last thing she needed was Angelo or Julien discovering her reserves of identities, cash, and weapons. She didn't think Angelo would go in there without explicit permission, nor would he allow Julien to search it. So why was the door open? She quietly slipped off her heels and placed her handbag on a nearby accent table, debating whether she should call Angelo and have him take a look.

No, you're just spooked from all that's happened lately. She was never one to cry wolf, and besides, the guys had searched the house a few hours earlier. Hadn't they?

She looked around the minimalist hallway for something, anything that could be a weapon. There was a small abstract sculpture on a lighted display shelf. *Perfect.* Zed had drilled into her brain how to turn everyday items into weapons.

She tiptoed over to the doorway, the muted Persian rug absorbing the sound of her footsteps. A shadow caught her eye. Someone was in her bedroom, moving around. She grabbed the figure—heavier than she had assumed—and stepped into the shadow to listen. *Silence now.*

Her heartbeat thrummed in her ear as she crouched, able to spring into action at any sign of trouble.

I'm ready, she told herself. She had been practicing for a moment like this one for years now. Angelo was close by, yes, but shuffling for her phone to alert him could escalate the situation. No, she would have to discern whether there was a threat on her own. She moved soundlessly to the side of the door.

A noise. She pictured the layout of the suite and determined that the sound had come from either inside the closet or right outside of it. Someone was walking around in there. Her heart sank as she imagined them gaining access to her carefully concealed compartments containing her escape insurance plan.

The hooded figure running from her West Village safe house popped in her mind. Was it a detective? An assassin? Should she surrender herself to them, whoever "they" were? Maybe strike a plea deal, spend a few years in prison, get out early for good behavior? Martha Stewart had survived; she could too.

Another sound. More fear, more anxiety, more exhaustion.

She thought of her higher self and her child self. The women and girls that Omar and his kind had beaten, raped, marginalized. Even if her home and her business would continually be violated, she didn't regret what she had done. Even if it cost her her freedom or her life, so be it. They could keep coming after her forever, and she would keep fighting. Not only for herself, but for every woman for whom she had rid the world of a few horrible men. The first step was to figure out who was in her home; the rest she would deal with as it came. Whoever had breached her security and privacy—*yet again*— was not going to get away with it. *I did not come this far to only come this far, motherfucker.*

Poised for a fight, she stormed into the bedroom and headed directly toward the boudoir with the sculpture raised over her head. Its weight was substantial and could inflict enough injury on the perpetrator to buy her time to run down and get Angelo. An upside was that a blow to the head would lead to blood and DNA, so that if they somehow got away, Angelo could track them down.

The dressing room door was cracked. She slowly pushed it open with her toe, then ducked back into the shadows.

Empty. The intruder had been nosing around, from the looks of it. Celeste frowned. She hadn't imagined the sounds she had heard.

Oh, shit. She'd forgotten that the closet, unlike her bedroom in New York, had a double entrance. The door on the other side exited right next to the terrace.

You are not getting away with this.

After making sure the bedroom was clear, she ran outside with the sculpture over her head, ready to strike.

Where are you, asshole?

She looked all around.

Her eyes bulged in surprise.

She froze.

Oh my God.

Oh my God.

Oh my God.

She wasn't sure what she expected to find out there. But this was not it.

Heat rushed to her cheeks.

How?

"Theodore? What are you doing here?"

"Surprise, my darling. My meetings wrapped up early, so I—" There stood her gorgeous husband, pouring from a bottle of wine now suspended above one of the glasses from their new collection, as he looked her over with a quizzical expression.

A beautiful table was set with the never-been-used china and flat-ware she had loved choosing. Music played softly on the Bang & Olufsen speakers, camouflaged by the trees. Meredith had promised the sound quality was state-of-the-art for the hefty price tag—Celeste hadn't realized it also meant she wouldn't hear it fifty feet away inside her bedroom. Her brain tried to catch up with what she was seeing.

"Babe, is there a reason you look like you're going to smash that wonderful piece of art into my head?" He laughed, put down the bottle of wine, and walked over to her.

"Here, let me take that. It looks heavy." Her mouth still agape, she handed him her makeshift weapon. He walked inside, set it on a table, and returned.

"H—hi, honey," she said, letting out a nervous laugh. "I, uh, thought I heard someone up here, and I... you know... wanted to be prepared."

"Dammit, I've upset you. Here I was, trying to do something nice for you, and I end up sending you into a panic instead." That look again.

Celeste wanted to collapse with relief into his arms, but her pride kept her chin up as he hugged her. She gave him a heated French kiss to recalibrate the situation. "Oh, no, it's fine. Don't worry, I was just... being cautious."

She must have looked like a rabid animal, wild-eyed, with her racing heart and bare feet. *Let's not give our husband any reason to institutionalize us this evening, Celeste.* "What do we have here? What's all this?" She gestured to the giant bouquet of red roses and the elaborately set table.

"My meetings ended early, and I couldn't wait any longer to see you, so I coordinated with Angelo. Plus, it's been how long since this place was finished, and I haven't made it here to properly enjoy it with you?" He gestured at the patio.

"It looks incredible, by the way. The entire place is calm, sophisticated. You guys have amazing taste." He cleared his throat. "I'm afraid I didn't cook. I sent Angelo to pick up dinner. He should be back any minute."

Oh, that explains Angelo's nonchalance—he knew Theodore was here.

"On that note, I'm going to change my clothes and freshen up." She kissed Theodore's cheek and scurried inside.

Keeping an eye on both doors, she went to the island in her dressing room. Now that she knew it was her husband who'd been in there, she realized what had looked out of place earlier—he'd hung up his garment bags containing his suits on a clothes rod. It wasn't as though he'd planned to ambush her; the signs of his presence were on display. She opened the drawer with the secret compartment to check if anything had been moved around. Everything was in its place.

Wait a minute. "Passcode incorrect," the screen read. So someone had been nosing around. She frowned, then chided herself for canceling her recent Botox appointment. *Well, I've been a little distracted lately—sue me for having face muscles that move.*

She would ask Angelo first before jumping to conclusions. *But what if Theodore suspects I'm hiding something?* While the paraphernalia of her other life was well concealed, that did not mean he couldn't uncover it if he went looking.

She jumped, startled, when her husband peeked his head in. Thankfully, he didn't notice how jumpy she was. "Angelo arrived, so I'll run down to retrieve the food."

"OK, honey," she said warmly. *If you go looking for trouble, dear husband, you're bound to find it.*

She changed quickly into a blouse and jeans, adding silk slippers, then went out to the table. *Wine time.*

Theodore returned as she took her first sip. "Voilà!" he said, holding a thermal insulated delivery bag with "Septime" written on the side. Septime was regularly recognized as one of the top restaurants in the world and praised for its contemporary approach to French cuisine.

"I'm fairly certain they aren't on Grubhub. How did you swing takeaway?"

He began unloading the carefully packed meal. "You recall I'm a silent investor in Rakuen?"

"Of course, how could I forget?" They'd had their first date at Rakuen, a Michelin-starred Omakase restaurant in Manhattan, and went back occasionally for date night when they were in town.

"One of the head servers at Septime heard how great it was and wanted to bring their family on a recent trip to New York. The hospitality team at the restaurant rolled out the red carpet, and they promised our team a few favors in return. I dialed one in."

She grinned, though internally, she was still urging her heart to stop racing. *Typical Theodore.* Her husband was quite resourceful.

As usual when he returned from a trip, he shared funny stories about his time in Zurich. Apparently, the sailing hadn't ended well— he and his friend had been in the middle of the lake the previous day when a storm hit. Their safety wasn't in jeopardy, though Theodore said they were soaked to the core. He shuffled through the bags, plating the entrées and sides for each of them while he talked. Somehow the meal looked as elegantly presented and irresistible as it had when they dined there previously.

"Ooh, the roasted duck! It looks incredible."

"I told them we'd happily be guinea pigs and try any new desserts they're experimenting with," he said. Theodore was partial to sweet things, and Septime was known for having one of the best pastry menus in the world. He held up two boxes. "We have a berry parfait for you and a chocolate tartelette for me—both big enough to share."

Celeste laughed. Theodore was convinced things tasted better when they were on her plate and normally ate at least half of hers.

Someone has bugged my home, our home, and someone besides Omar wants me gone. I have no business enjoying myself. But it was no way to live—constantly on edge. It was only a fluke that she even learned about the bug, and besides, she always assumed someone was listening in.

None of this will be fixed tonight. She refreshed their wine. Yes, the problems were mounting, but it was nothing she couldn't handle.

She cut into the duck and took a bite. "Oh, wow, this is fantastic." It was tender and juicy, with a perfect balance between the crusty exterior and the creamy glaze. Alongside the entrée, there was a generous portion of grilled vegetables. She realized how hungry she was and scarfed down the meal faster than usual.

"Darling, I'm so happy you're here," she said. Life with Theodore was a grand adventure.

"We've been too busy lately. Work is important, but it's not every-thing." He took her hand and looked at her. "*You* are my number-one priority. I hope you always know that loving you... well, sometimes I think my whole purpose in life is to love you. From the moment I first saw you, you've been my North Star." His eyes were misty.

It had taken Celeste a long time to learn to allow herself to be loved. After her parents died, she'd kept everyone at arm's length for many years. What she and Omar had never resembled anything healthy, and between him and Theodore, there had only been a string of casual partners.

Not that her courtship with Theodore had been anywhere near traditional either. To fall in love for the first time and then have that person disappear as abruptly as her parents had was devastating. Celeste wasn't ashamed to admit that she almost hadn't survived it when she learned that Theodore was believed to have died in a plane crash.

Her self-destructiveness had been at an all-time high, as she medicated her heartbreak with uppers, downers, anything she could get her hands on to quiet the nightmares and the visions she had of Omar torturing Theodore. She had learned the hard way that she never wanted to live without Theodore. When he came back and proposed, she said yes without hesitation, even though she'd never considered herself the marrying kind.

"You're my favorite person, babe," she said now. "I love you too. But there's no reason to be teary-eyed, is there?"

Theodore shrugged. "Look, I know you don't like to talk much about it, but I'll level with you—I'm worried. Someone's following you again? You're obviously more concerned than you let on, with the..." He mimed as though he were holding the sculpture over his head. "And I can never trust that you're telling me everything. Who knows what you're hiding. We have the resources to put a stop—"

Celeste closed her eyes and exhaled. *The bug is picking up every word we say*, she remembered. "Not tonight, please? Who knows if anyone was even following me? I could've just been paranoid, and we're taking all the precautions." She wondered how long Angelo would keep it under wraps about the *other* device Julien found.

"We can get tighter security. I could help you get to the bottom—"

"I don't want to live like a prisoner, Theodore! I'm a New York woman; I want to walk down the street without a security detail behind me. Attend a Pilates class without someone waiting in the lobby to pick me up like I'm a child.

"Do you know how many years I've felt cooped up? Like I can't stroll into a grocery store and buy... buy—" *What do people buy there?* She couldn't remember the last time she had set foot in one, intentional on her part. *Whether I actually want to food shop is beside the point.* "A loaf of bread and a gallon of... of coconut water." *So there.* She sat back and crossed her arms in a huff.

Theodore blew out a loaded exhale. "OK, look. What I need—no, scratch that. It's not about what *I* need. You're frustrated that we're all worrying about you all the time. I get it. Can we at least find a compromise?"

"The compromise is that I'm tired of the protection and the pity, so you all must stop. All the Angelos in the world won't turn back the clock and undo the harm, Theodore. Terrible things happened to me, but I survived them. I am not those things. I am a person independent of any suffering I experienced. I need you to see that. I need you to see *me* again like you used to. Before you thought of me as a victim, a fragile cornered bird."

"That's what you think? You're my wife. You're the strongest person I know. You make everything around you, including our homes, beautiful. You're magnetic, and your laugh is my favorite sound in the entire world."

She regarded him, unconvinced.

His playful attitude returned. "Now let's go christen that enormous bed as our first dessert," he said, surprising her by scooping her up over his shoulder.

The battle had been a draw. She was certain this wasn't over—but at least she'd said what was on her mind. She remembered then the tiny explosive only a stone's throw away in her desk drawer. She couldn't believe she had persuaded Angelo to let her stay in the house with it.

I guess if they want to listen in on us, may as well give them a show.

7

SEEING RED IN THE RED CITY

The following day, Theodore said he had some business to handle in Paris, so she planned to take the opportunity to spend a few hours in the office. But first, she, Angelo, and Julien caught up over croissants and espresso at a café.

"We scoured your home from top to bottom yesterday. Julien brought in a state-of-the-art electronic detection system called TSCM in the US. It stands for…"

Technical surveillance countermeasures, yes, yes, I know. But you can't know that I know.

"Technical surveillance countermeasures. We had a few different types of equipment this time…" He continued to explain the counter-surveillance tools he used, but Celeste was interested in one particular detail. *Did they find my secret stash?*

She was torn. On the one hand, if they didn't find the money and the passports and the weapons, they weren't being thorough. But on the other hand, she didn't want her system compromised. There was no reason at that point in time for anyone to know the extent or details of her backup plans. Her husband, Jack, Savin, Angelo—they were the ones who could escalate the situation in the name of protecting her, which would cause more harm than good.

Angelo wrapped up his detailed explanation of their second, more complete sweep. No mention of finding a secret drawer or her stash. She didn't think he would withhold information from her.

"Two questions remain, then. Do they—whoever "they" is—know you two were there? And more importantly, perhaps, do we keep the bug live until Theodore and I leave tomorrow?"

"I think that's right—we keep it live, don't alert them that we are aware of it. We'll figure out the next move before you're back in Paris. Like I said, you should use it to your advantage if you think there are things they could hear that would be helpful to your cause." She would have to be strategic and drop some statements into her conversations with Theodore later.

She then asked the question to which she didn't want the answer —but needed to know. "Shall I assume our New York apartment and my offices are also bugged in some way that we've overlooked?"

"No, I don't think it would've slipped past our current setup. I will, of course, do a complete sweep when I'm back in New York, so you can sleep easy after Morocco."

She thought back to her visions from a few mornings before. The familiar feelings of urgency and panic washed over her. Who needed saving? What was going to happen if she didn't figure out the riddles fast enough? Were other lives in jeopardy, or was her subconscious only trying to communicate that she was in danger? *How do I stop it all?*

CELESTE STOOD at the front of the large conference room and cleared her throat. The D&C team chatter turned to a hush.

"Bonjour! What a lively bunch today. Let's dive into some outstanding business regarding the integrations." She pulled up a slide with the executive summary of what the team would need to do over the course of the next month to stay on track with bringing the TA Capital team and the Ricci Fund on board.

"As you recall, we established up front that TA Capital will stay independent, with Tarek as the PM." Tarek was the mastermind behind TA Capital. Since Celeste's acquisition had not been based on dismantling his current setup or increasing profitability, they had built into the agreement that TA Capital would remain independent with Tarek as the portfolio manager, or PM, as long as he was alive. Celeste believed Tarek was a good man, albeit with a few vices he wouldn't want the world to discover, and her reason for buying his firm wasn't to disrupt that. It was to take Matthew down.

"What we're still evaluating is whether it's more beneficial to our clients to keep Ricci as a wholly owned subsidiary—or whether we sell it off. Does anyone have a perspective to share?"

A nondescript man in the middle of the group seated around the table spoke up. He was in his thirties and had a Scottish accent. "I've been—"

"Sorry to interrupt. Can everyone introduce themselves and their division when they speak? The New York office is on the line, and it'll help refresh everyone's memory." Celeste nodded at him to continue.

"Clyde from the Fund of Funds team. Do you mind if I project my research for everyone?"

Celeste gestured for him to do so. After he took care of the technical side, he dove into his research. He explained the Ricci Fund's vulnerabilities. "Enzo is certainly the brains behind the operation, but Nico had the relationships. I'm concerned that deals will fall short and performance will suffer without him there after his... disappearance." By then, everyone knew that Nico was gone, though there had not been any updates for a while.

Nico's brains, hopefully half eaten by Hudson River catfish, must never resurface. Though catfish didn't normally eat animal flesh, otherwise known as carrion, they were still scavengers at times, and Celeste chose to believe Nico's fate had been undignified. She kept her face neutral.

Savin, who was plugged in via the New York office video, asked, "Have there been any further updates from Enzo's team on Nico's whereabouts?"

Celeste saw what no one else would detect—the tiny beads of

sweat on Savin's upper lip. He'd been with Nico the night of the man's disappearance. Savin was still worried that something terrible had happened to Nico and that it would be pinned on him. *Poor Savin.* But his inability to control his emotions was one of the reasons Celeste could never let him in completely. He was too unpredictable when he was panicking.

"Enzo maintains that his brother is not..." Clyde cleared his throat and reddened. "That his brother is not coming back. He's, uh, dead, I guess."

A murmur broke out in the room. Savin looked relieved.

"OK, let's stay on track," Celeste commanded. "Does anyone else want to weigh in?"

A British woman, raven-haired with porcelain-white skin like Theodore, who introduced herself as Eleanor, gave an alternative perspective—that Ricci's strength was in maintaining its presence as an Italian firm, with or without Nico. After explaining that many of the major holdings and strategies were from Enzo and his Italian team, she said, "Frankly, I found Nico to be quite a liability. He was known to be violent with women and had quite an addiction problem. His reputation was rubbish, and he did nothing to add to the Ricci bottom line. Good riddance!"

Celeste beamed. *Leave it to the woman to read the situation correctly.* "If what you're saying is true about his behavior, then I couldn't agree more." *Nico was a slob kabob and monster.* "I'd like to move on, so if anyone else has opinions to share, please connect with me and Savin. We'll then align and report back."

The full team, including the New York office, provided updates in round robin style for the next half hour. But Celeste wasn't listening. She was figuring out how to get in touch with Vivienne before flying to Morocco the following morning and when to connect with Hadid without her husband or in-laws noticing. *Ruminating about all this is taking up way too much of my brain space.* Hopefully, Hadid could provide some insights into who was surveilling her.

"OK, everyone, that was great. Eleanor and Clyde, appreciate your thoughts, and we'll connect next week. I'm off to Morocco tomorrow," she said. She was the first one to leave as the others gathered their things, escaping to her office to make some quick calls behind closed doors.

Ace first. She retrieved her burner from her locked desk drawer and dialed. "Any news?" she asked before Ace could say anything. There was no time for small talk.

"Still working on it."

"Did you keep your word to keep this to yourself?"

"Only you, Savin, Lorraine, and I know. Let's keep it that way."

"My thoughts exactly."

Click.

Conversations with Ace were nothing if not direct and concise.

Her next call was to Vivienne Hayes. The protocol was different with her. They normally communicated in person because Vivienne was suspicious of any electronic or otherwise traceable mode of communication, and rightly so. She had given Celeste a number to use only in case of an emergency. *I'd say this qualifies.*

"Le Fumoir, corner of Rue de l'Amiral de Coligny and Place du Louvre, in an hour."

Click.

Celeste glanced at her watch. *Noon.*

"Hi, honey, wrapping up work and then a few errands. See you at home for dinner?" she texted her husband.

Now to call Hadid on her burner. He answered on the first ring. "I got your note. Pearl of the South, Jemaa el-Fnaa Square. Two days. Rendez-vous à vingt et une heures." *Meet me in Marrakech at the snake charmer in the square in two days at nine p.m.*

He hung up then.

She unlocked her office drawer again, this time retrieving a mug that she hoped held Matthew's DNA. Her plan had worked quite well. She had monitored the mug Matthew was using for his coffee at the meeting earlier in the week. Once the meeting adjourned, and before anyone could notice, she had carefully snatched the mug and concealed it in a cabinet next to the conference table.

Later, she had sneaked back and put the mug in a single-use

plastic bag, careful not to disrupt whatever DNA and fingerprints remained. *His computer contents and now his DNA—we must go on the offensive.* Because one thing was for sure—he was coming for her if she didn't eliminate him.

Matthew's DNA and prints could help in many ways: to discern whether they'd been found at any crime scenes, and if so, if he had other associates that she could positively ID there; to frame him for future crimes; and to ensure it was wiped from any databases so that he could not be identified postmortem if (*when, more accurately*) she decided to rid the world of his miserable existence.

Finally, she dialed her last call. Meredith answered "Hello" on the second ring, breathless as if she had run to the phone.

"Darling, could you do me a huge favor? Could you coordinate the Dior pickup and meet me at my place around four?"

"Of course," Mere said, still winded.

"Are you in the middle of a marathon?"

"Well, a type of one, I suppose, and Seth is sort of a... training coach. Now if that's all you want, I'll get back to it so I can meet you on time at the house with the most beautiful clothes in tow."

Celeste laughed, and they said their goodbyes.

It was time to go meet Vivienne. *And time to ditch Angelo and Julien.*

Outside, Celeste got into the waiting car and motioned for Angelo to join her. He slid in and closed the door.

"Hi, Julien."

The driver nodded but didn't speak.

Listen, guys, I need to do a few things on my own without an escort. So you must make yourselves scarce, she wanted to say. But that wouldn't work.

"Theodore said there were signs of someone trying to get inside the townhouse. He wants me to stay at the office, where he knows I'll be safe, and for you two to go there."

Angelo's eyes widened. "Yes, of course."

Julien looked doubtful. "You'll promise to stay there, yes?" he said, nodding to her office building. "We can't have you walking around unaccompanied."

She stared squarely into his eyes without blinking. "Of course," she said solemnly. "I take this sort of thing extremely seriously. And my husband is very worried for my safety."

They asked no further questions after the mention of her husband. *God forbid they let me exercise my own judgment and make my own decisions. But if "my husband says," the questions stop.*

"OK, go now, please. I want to make sure everything is well." She got out of the car and hurried into the office lobby, making sure they drove away.

The Jardin des Tuileries, which ran adjacent to where Vivienne wanted to meet, was a quick walk from the office. Once she was certain the men were gone, Celeste headed in the direction of the park.

When she arrived in front of Le Fumoir, the woman had already arrived. Celeste had met her only once before, and her disguise back then had made her unrecognizable. Now she was dressed as casually as a French woman meeting for a midday espresso, in a pair of wide-leg ivory pants, a cognac Celine belt, and a navy-and-white-striped short-sleeved sweater, topped off with coordinating ballet flats. Her shoulder-length blonde hair was meant to look effortless, but Celeste could tell it had been recently blown out and styled. She was wearing that season's version of oversized sunglasses, and from what Celeste could tell, she was wearing makeup. While she was ten to fifteen years older than Celeste, she could've easily passed for Celeste's age of forty-five. Celeste had almost walked by her, looking for the nondescript woman from before. Now Vivienne had that certain je ne sais quoi that only French women could pull off.

"Celeste, darling, let's walk inside the Jardin." She intertwined her elbow with Celeste's and leaned in to whisper, "It will be harder to follow us and eavesdrop this way."

Celeste smiled broadly so that anyone who might be watching would assume they were simply two friends meeting for an afternoon stroll.

"You clean up real nice," Celeste said quietly in a silly voice. The two laughed sincerely.

"I've spent a lot of time in France throughout my career, and I love the ease of dressing as a French woman. Comfy with high-quality fabrics. They know quiet luxury. It helps that no one knows my past here."

Vivienne was masterful at monitoring whether they were being followed, her eyes watching their seven and their nine, as a true intelligence or military officer would be trained to do. She could move confidently without appearing rushed or flustered. Zed had drilled into Celeste similar habits. Celeste was certain the woman could handle any situation that came her way.

After walking in silence for several minutes, they were almost to the middle of the garden. Vivienne stopped at one of the pop-up food stands and ordered each of them a cappuccino without asking Celeste what she wanted. Following her lead, Celeste stayed quiet. The woman wanted to stay unmemorable—fine with Celeste. Once they had their drinks, they continued walking.

Finally, they were in the middle of the park, and Vivienne walked toward a specific table under an enormous old linden tree. She gestured to Celeste to sit.

"We are here precisely because this tiny spot is a dead zone," Vivienne explained. "The tree camouflages the equipment that blocks any cell phone or other towers, and it gets smaller and more discreet every year as technology advances. It's a wonderful way to have a guaranteed place I can chat any time I am in town."

Celeste realized then that she was not the only client the woman had. There were so many things she wanted to ask Vivienne, especially how she'd navigated a life full of secrets with such grace. But instead, Celeste stuck to the urgent issues.

"I need your help," she began.

"Yes, I know. Things are heating up for you, no?"

"How did—"

"I know more than you think, my dear. I have a few theories, but first, tell me what's going on to make sure I have the whole picture."

Ah, what the hell. The traitor in my circle knows.

"Someone quite sophisticated has broken into our files and

doctored some of my trades. It appears they are specifically targeting me. What I want to know is who and why."

"But that's not your only problem."

"No, I have a few others." Celeste summarized that she needed to have Matthew's DNA matched in crime databases around the world and also wanted to track down the people behind RH Global. "It's tied to something to do with me or my business or my husband—or all three."

"And there's more, I presume? You could likely hire anyone for these."

Complete chaos. Celeste sighed. She despised chaos. "I have reason to believe that there is to be a cyberattack on America, and I want to stop it."

"Ah, yes, there it is. The others wouldn't take someone of my caliber and my discretion to be successful. This one, though—you'd need me."

Celeste summarized the situation and her plan.

"Can you help me pull this off?"

"It's dangerous, extremely so."

"I'm aware."

"But I agree it may be one of the only ways. I've seen what you're capable of—you've pulled off harder things than this, believe it or not. With my help, you could be successful."

She removed her glassed and looked at Celeste somberly. "You're a rare breed, Celeste," she said, clutching her companion's hand and squeezing. "The world is lucky to have someone like you looking out."

The woman rarely used Celeste's name. Sunglasses back on and she was back to business.

"A question for you," she continued. "Of course, I knew your identity from day one. But now you aren't in disguise like you were before. Do you think the danger has passed?"

Celeste burst into a laugh, a long and hearty one, until there were tears in her eyes. "Oh, my, I'm sorry. It's been a tense couple of days, and that struck a chord." She took a deep breath and continued.

"I don't know that it's worth hiding anymore. Whoever 'they' is, whether it's one person or many... well, they always seem to find me anyway."

"Have you considered that it's someone you know causing all this trouble?"

"Yes, of course. But good luck narrowing down who it is. I've been unsuccessful to date."

"OK. I must go now. I'll be in touch with what you've requested—time is of the essence."

Vivienne stood. "And once that's taken care of, I'll figure out who's compromised. We can handle that when we're both back in New York. We'll meet at our spot. Stay safe out there."

And then she was gone.

The woman gave off "I have everything under control" vibes that Celeste didn't get from anyone else. She would pay any amount of money for that peace of mind.

CELESTE WATCHED out the window as their plane descended on the Red City, as Marrakech was known for its red sandstone buildings and city walls. Theodore had urged her to sit on the right side so that she could see the Strait of Gibraltar, which separated Europe and Africa. It was a clear morning, so he had pointed out many other sites along the way, always the well-traveled tour guide.

Noting the mountain range in the center of the country, Theodore said, "These are the Atlas Mountains, where we are *not* going."

"That's right. City and beach for me, babe." Mountain climbing wasn't a skill she was interested in honing.

"Don't forget our stop in the Agafay Desert, my love."

A luxury desert camp, complete with gourmet food and wine, was an acceptable holiday adventure for Celeste.

"You'll be happy to know that your favorite Prescotts will arrive this evening and will be joining us for all the trip's adventures," Theodore said, referring to his parents.

"Oh, yes, I've been running around like crazy and forgot to reach out to Poppy before we left. They're staying at our hotel, right?"

The Amanjena, right outside the city, had a reputation as a tranquil retreat. Her husband had promised to plan everything, with one caveat—she had to choose the hotel. There was no contest—the Aman hospitality was unparalleled, and making it even more attractive, it was remote.

They would have so many amazing things to see inside the medina, the historic section of a city in Arabic-speaking countries, surrounded by walls and with narrow, pedestrian-only streets. Celeste wanted to stay off her devices for a few days. *No point in making more of a trail for the hackers to follow.* Work would have to run on autopilot—she had confirmed with Savin what to do in case of emergency.

"They are," Theodore responded. "Mum had wanted to stay at their usual spot, La Mamounia, but when I told her about the Aman, she was sold. I did, however, book a spa day for the two of you at La Mamounia. I hope that's OK."

"Darling, have I ever complained about a spa day?"

"Not to my knowledge."

"Exactly. You know me well."

The landing was smooth, and they glided into the private hangar. The copilots came out to bid them farewell. Celeste let her husband handle the pleasantries because she was already in scheming mode, thinking of how she could make the meeting with Hadid work the next evening. A deep matte black Land Rover Defender waited for them out on the tarmac.

"Darling, why do we need this giant, conspicuous vehicle?"

"You'll see," he said, smiling and winking.

So much for staying under the radar.

"I suppose we will," she said through pursed lips.

The driver, dressed in an impeccable black suit and a white turban, was likely in his late forties or early fifties, with his full beard graying. He had kind eyes, but Celeste wasn't fooled. This man wasn't a sweet driver; Celeste would put money on his having been in some sort of Special Forces earlier in life. He was as ripped as Angelo, the definition of his muscles evident even underneath the suit, and judging from the confidence with which he carried himself, it would take a lot to scare him. A wide smile spread across his face as he greeted them.

"Hello, Mr. and Mrs. Prescott. I am Hassan, here to escort you all week in Morocco," he said with a heavy French accent. "We will see all the magnificence that Maroc, as we say it in French, has to offer."

He shook Theodore's hand and bowed to Celeste, then walked around to the rear passenger door to let them in. She slid in while Theodore walked around to the other side.

"Theodore, darling, why are we in an enormous SUV with bullet-proof windows and an armed guard as our driver?" Celeste hissed. "I thought we weren't doing this whole prisoner thing again." She was geared up for a fight, albeit a quiet, fast one, given that Hassan was almost inside.

"Honey, it only makes good sense." Her eyes bored into him with anger. He tried a different angle.

"If nothing else, people of our net worth don't travel internationally without security, Celeste. You're a high-profile American woman with blonde hair, so you stand out a bit. Name another who doesn't have round-the-clock security." What he left unsaid was his annoyance and "Why do you keep fighting everyone on this?"

The truth was, their methods had never prevented any harm to her. It made her more of a target. She recalled her solo whirlwind tour around the world, heartbroken, fueled by revenge. *I did fine on my own then, and I can handle it even better now.* Theodore had rescued her once, but that was after no one had prevented her from being kidnapped in the first place.

She wasn't going to win the fight in that moment, so she would figure out how to use it to her advantage. "Fine, I'll be a good sport, but only if we can stop in the souks before the hotel. I need to do a little shopping."

"Deal."

They told Hassan the change in plans and talked about less controversial things.

"OK, darling, our first few days will be here in Marrakech. I thought we'd enjoy our hotel today and tomorrow, venture out into the medina tomorrow night..."

Perfect. I don't even have to scheme.

"Wonderful. What divine spot did you pick for us when we venture out from the hotel?"

"Terrasse des Épices," he replied. "It's close to the square. Mum always likes to see the snake charmers and such, so we can explore a bit beforehand."

"What time? Assuming we can squeeze in a workout and spa service before we go."

"Yes, definitely. Dinner isn't until eight p.m."

"Is it close to the souks?"

"Oh, yes, it's a quick walk."

"Good, because my outfits and shoes are built for beauty, not comfort."

Theodore smiled. "Some of Poppy and Teddy's friends are having a party—no, Mum says they're too old for parties—some sort of cocktail reception in a few days. Interested? If we stay for that, we can push the desert/beach portion of the trip back a bit."

"Sure, babe. You know I love spending time with your parents. I can't imagine what their friends who live on the outskirts of Marrakech are like."

"They're a lot of fun, that's for sure."

Celeste wondered what her parents would have been like in their seventies. She could only ever picture them in their forties, as they were before they died. They were so provincial; she could hardly imagine them jet-setting around North Africa, meeting up with other international friends. She recalled them up late at night in the living room, sitting on separate couches underneath reading lights, preparing for lectures or grading papers. Maybe that was their fear in her vision—they'd never ventured anywhere; maybe they couldn't fathom it for their daughter.

Hassan pulled up to the outside of the medina. Constructed of the same red sandstone used for the predominant style of architecture, the medina, or Old Town, was home to dynamic food carts, street performers, and most notable to Celeste, the snake charmers. Unbeknownst to Theodore, she would be on the lookout for Hadid's meeting spot.

"Darling, he's not coming with us, is he? I want to shop a little, and you'll be right by my side, no?" she whispered.

"It's just you and me today, babe," he said as they exited the open car door. "Hassan, go enjoy yourself. We'll call when we're ready." Hassan nodded and was off.

Celeste hid her surprise. *That was easier than expected.*

Theodore looked at his watch while Celeste took in the Jemaa el-Fnaa, the main square in the middle of the medina. "This is quite a scene," she commented.

"Yes, yes, it is. Shall we have lunch here after shopping, honey?" He put his arm around her and kissed the top of her head.

Physical displays of affection were frowned upon, and sometimes strictly forbidden, in cities with strong Arab influences. Theodore seemed to remember that and moved his arm. "Old habits die hard," he said.

"You could've gotten us arrested, and so early in our holiday, no less!" she scolded in a lighthearted tone. Though they could find humor in it, they shared the philosophy of being respectful of local cultures when visiting. They walked side by side without touching.

One of Marrakech's most popular activities was shopping in the souks in Old Town. A souk was an open-air, outdoor marketplace with small independent shops selling spices, leather goods, handbags, textiles, body oils and soaps, and food. These markets were commonly seen in large cities, with Arabic influences embedded in the fabric of the medina.

Morocco was also known for handmade rugs, called Berber rugs after the Berber tribe. The carpets were hanging at some of the larger shops, available in nearly every color—nude tones with large geometric shapes or vibrant patterns in bright purple, magenta, and turquoise.

The Souk Semmarine, the name of the main Marrakech souk where they were browsing, was lively that afternoon, with a steady buzz of consumers heckling shop owners and vice versa, everyone in search of a bargain or sale. Men, loud and taking up space, were everywhere the eye could see. Celeste wondered where all the women were; she only saw a few locals moving around quietly. As an American, it was hard to imagine being tucked away all the time, exactly what she was always fighting against.

The air was fragrant and the mood buoyant, bright, and vibrant. The souk had so many interesting things grabbing the eye that Celeste was feeling sensory overload. Large clay pots in warm colors, with various shapes and finishes, were lined up in front of many of the shops. Jewel-toned pashminas pulled a shopper's attention toward the clothing booths, while the spice stalls had colorful, inviting displays of turmeric, paprika, and cinnamon, the aromas sparking Celeste's hunger. Her stomach growled.

"What do you think?" Theodore asked.

"We need food, and I need to spend some money. Let's find an ATM. I don't think they'll appreciate our black cards here," she said.

Theodore laughed. "Touché."

They asked around until a local French-speaking man wearing a djellaba, a traditional robe, pointed them in the direction of a bank machine. After a ten-minute walk to get cash, they made their way back to the main square and debated which small café to visit. Then Theodore seemed to have a spark and recommended Le Tobsil, in a riad tucked away on a tiny street. He explained to Celeste that a riad was a traditional villa that had a courtyard in the center, often with a pool, and rooms situated around the center. Riads usually had detailed tiling and foliage to provide an indoor-outdoor atmosphere.

As they approached the building, a wooden door with brass hardware and carvings opened. A host greeted them and escorted them inside. Celeste marveled at the decor—they had stepped into a refined candlelit room where time did not seem to exist, a respite from the liveliness outside. Shadows danced on the stucco walls, and lighted globes illuminated the ceilings. A red carpet with a gold pattern ran wall to wall. The host seated them on the ground floor, at a round table with a white linen cloth strewn with red rose petals. There were more tables upstairs, lining the perimeter of the two-story main room, and vibrant paintings pulled the eye upward. Touristy or not, it was one of a kind.

Celeste was in awe of the grandeur of the restaurant. "It's so romantic, babe. It's almost as though we've time traveled to somewhere far away from the souks. Look at the intricate carvings on the archways and the crown molding," she observed. "Imagine how long it took to perfect each one."

"I don't know, but it requires a lot more patience than I have," her husband commented.

A woman wearing a traditional silk turquoise kaftan with intricate yellow patterns approached them and introduced herself as Yasmina. She continued in perfect English, "What can I get for you to drink?"

"We'll have *thé à la menthe* and still mineral water," Theodore said. Mint tea was popular in Marrakech.

"Thank you, Monsieur and Madame Prescott. I will be back shortly," Yasmina said formally, as one did when English was not a first language. Celeste noted the French accent and was pleased that her French had come in handy in Morocco, as she knew absolutely zero Arabic.

She furrowed her brow. "Wait, why is this entire place empty? And how did she know our names?"

"Turns out Le Tobsil, my favorite touristy spot in the medina, is only open for dinner. I persuaded them to make us tajine for lunch."

Laughing, Celeste replied, "Of course you did. Since you're a pro, why don't you order for us?" Her stomach moaned again, this time loud enough for Theodore to hear.

"I certainly don't want my wife to starve. In all seriousness, you'll love the food here. I've not had a single bad meal."

"I didn't realize you'd spent so much time here."

"Isn't marriage wonderful? Always discovering new things about each other."

Don't dig too deep, babe—some things are best left unexcavated.

Theodore continued, "Well, as you know, Mum and Dad loved to travel and always had me in tow, and I come back every so often."

Hmm. Celeste had known him for years and couldn't recall mention of Morocco. *I'm not the only one with secrets.* She then scolded herself. Just because she had a secret life didn't mean her husband did as well.

Theodore, animated as always, explained what a tajine was, a dish cooked slowly in a conical pot with a hole in the top to release steam. Found throughout North Africa, it was a prominent menu item featured at authentic Marrakech restaurants.

"Honey, it's the most flavorful dish, a stew of meat, vegetables, and local spices that's equal parts savory and sweet. The meat is so tender it melts in your mouth."

Yasmina returned, and Theodore ordered what sounded like the entire menu—"So you can try everything," he told Celeste—and asked for wine to be served with the main course.

"It's good I'm hungry, then," she replied with a laugh.

As the courses arrived one after the other, the two chatted about the rest of the trip and Savin's upcoming engagement party upon their return. Safe topics.

"I love the china," Celeste commented, admiring the white plates with burgundy geometric patterns.

Then it was time for the tajine. Yasmina and a man wearing all white arrived with two large pots exactly as Theodore had described. They ceremoniously took off the tops and, at Theodore's nod, dished out both stews onto their plates.

"This is lamb, and this one is chicken," the server explained.

She tried each. Theodore was right—they were tender, juicy, and perfectly spiced, with a sweet aftertaste.

"What is the flavor at the end?"

"Apricot," he replied.

The constant flow of food kept Celeste wanting more, until finally they had savored the dessert—a poached pear and some sort of biscuit with cream inside.

"What a culinary delight," she said at the end of the meal.

They'd had only two small glasses of wine, but after the journey and the late nights in Paris, it had made Celeste a bit tipsy.

"Time to spend those hard-earned dirhams on some shopping!" she exclaimed after Theodore had taken care of the bill.

They walked back to the square, Celeste taking in all the landmarks.

"What are those men doing over there?" she said, pointing to a man sitting on a carpet and another standing and playing an instrument.

"Let's get a closer look."

As she suspected, it was a snake charmer; she hoped it was the one Hadid had referenced.

They approached, and she saw several grayish-black snakes, poised as if to attack. She moved behind Theodore.

"Are you scared of a little snake?" he asked.

"There are"—she paused to count—"five ways to die right there."

He laughed. "Don't worry, I'll protect you. I must admit, I'm not sure I've ever seen you afraid of anything before. Well, except of me on the terrace the other night." He mimicked her carrying the sculpture overhead.

She playfully punched his arm. "I was hoping we could never speak of that again." She watched over Theodore's shoulder as the snakes turned to stare at the men walking around them. "These aren't my favorite animals—that's for sure." She wondered if she could tease out the men's names.

Theodore pulled out money to tip and started chatting with the man closest to the snakes.

"Hello, how often are you here?" she asked the one who seemed to be in charge of taking money.

"I am here every day and every evening," he replied. By his measured speaking, it was apparent he wasn't entirely comfortable speaking English.

"Je m'appelle... Mia." Old habits died hard. *"Comment vous appelez-vous?"*

"Je m'appelle Ahmed."

A plan was formulating.

～

THE SHOPPING WAS SUCCESSFUL. Celeste discovered shoes that were nearly identical to authentic Hermès slides. She purchased three pairs for herself and several for her friends, for a grand total of US$80. With Theodore in tow, she also found gifts for her staff, Monty and his wife, and Savin and Rani. *I'm supporting the local economy, after all.*

"Would Dina enjoy some spices and a tajine?" Celeste wondered aloud. Her personal chef used to cook for her several times a week. Dina visited them a bit less often now that Theodore was enjoying their remodeled kitchen. Dina was also in the midst of launching a chef's empire, thanks in part to Celeste's backing.

"I'm sure she would. By the way, how is her franchise performing?"

"One of the best investments I've ever made." While she sifted through silky pashminas, she told her husband about Dina's newly launched nontoxic cookware. Celeste bought several different colors for her and her mother-in-law to wear as shoulder wraps and head-scarves while they were there.

After the two had walked nearly the entire labyrinth of the souk and through much of the medina, Celeste and Theodore met Hassan at the entrance where he had dropped them earlier.

"My wife bought up all the shops," Theodore joked.

Hassan smiled but did not speak.

Following signs for their resort, he pointed out noteworthy land-marks along the way as Celeste watched the scenic transition from bustling urban streets to a more rural, desertlike backdrop. What looked like a forest of palm trees amid the sprawling desert was called the Palmeraie area, Hassan explained.

The drive was quick. After only twenty minutes or so, there it was —the Amanjena resort, the storied wellness escape in the middle of the desert. The majestic Atlas Mountains framed the traditional Moroccan building with an arched entrance surrounded by palm trees. As their driver pulled up in front of the resort, bellmen rushed out to secure their things. Their host, a young Moroccan man with olive skin and dark hair, introduced himself as Walid. He escorted them across the breathtaking property, which was remarkably green, given the climate. Walid wore a black suit, and as he pointed out the pavilion for yoga and the outdoor pizza oven, Celeste thought of how overheated he must have been.

Finally, they stopped in front of a palatial two-story building with a traditional sandstone finish, its light jade roof flowing seamlessly into the looming palm trees.

"I have a bit of a surprise for you," Theodore said sheepishly.

"Uh-oh," Celeste said. His surprises usually involved some sort of upgrade or private tour.

"Well, let's show her around first, shall we?" he said, nodding to Walid.

The riad—more like two villas, with two primary suites—and its grounds were impressive. After Walid showed them the entire indoor space, complete with a king-size bed and fireplace—"It is over one thousand meters or twelve thousand square feet, can you believe it?" asked Walid—they ventured out the back door to a massive yard. A tiled pavilion with coral-colored sandstone columns surrounded a large seating area. The yard had two gazebos, and lush palm trees and hedges taller than Theodore lined the perimeter, adding an air of privacy and tranquility and framing an inviting heated pool.

"What do you think? Does it pass muster?"

"It's gorgeous, babe. I'd love to relax on one of those sofas for hours with a novel—or *The Wall Street Journal.*"

They turned around when they heard a shuffling noise inside the villa.

"Oh, that's the bellman with your things," Walid explained.

Celeste groaned inwardly. She'd forgotten about the trunks full of couture that she had chosen for the trip.

"So this hotel room—or enormous retreat, more accurately—was a good surprise. I love it!"

"I'm glad it—well... but that's not the surprise," he said, the uncertain look returning to his face.

"Spill it, Prescott."

"Mum and Dad will be staying here with us. I thought it would be nice."

Celeste frowned. She'd been envisioning jewelry. "Oh. Well, of course I love your parents, but are you sure this is a good idea?"

As if on cue, her mother-in-law, Poppy, said in a singsong voice from inside the other wing, "Hello, darlings! We come bearing gifts of afternoon tea and cocktails!"

"They were complaining that we haven't spent much time with them lately," Theodore explained, "and they wanted a venue to host their friends—we couldn't ask for a better one."

"Successful marriages were built on choosing one's battles," Anne Marie had once advised. Celeste exhaled and plastered a welcoming grin on her face.

"Poppy, we're out here on the terrace," Celeste said loudly so that the woman could hear.

Poppy and Teddy, drinks in hand, walked out to meet them, while Walid helped a butler manage a bar cart and a tower of hors d'oeuvres. Music began playing from invisible speakers, and the mood was instantly lifted as they chatted over wine and traditional savory pastries called *briouates*.

As the afternoon sun began to lower in the sky, tiki torches and candles provided a serene glow. Celeste's in-laws were as adept as their son at shifting the energy in any environment. They often finished each other's sentences and gazed fondly at their partner across the room when they thought no one was watching. Despite Theodore's recollection of being a lonely only child with parents who fought incessantly, Celeste was wistful for the adventurous energy he must have felt, jet-setting around the world with Poppy and Teddy.

The couple must have been vibrant back then, given that they were still the life of the party well into their seventies.

Her own parents had been focused on their academic legacies, not on developing cultured children. Celeste only took on her own cultural development after moving to New York. The dark feeling washed over her once more when she remembered her parents' faces, urging her to prevent something bad from happening. *Could you at least give me a tiny hint? I'm dodging so many bullets lately; how can I discern which is the most concerning?*

"What are you wearing to dinner tonight, dear?"

It was then that Celeste remembered the gifts. "Oh, Poppy, you just reminded me—we stopped at the souks earlier, and I got us a few things. Follow me."

Once inside the villa, Celeste located the bags from her shopping. "The nights get a bit chilly here, and since we'll be in the medina where the dress is more conservative, I thought you'd appreciate a few pashminas." She pulled out the colors she'd chosen for her mother-in-law.

Theodore had gotten his raven hair from his mom, though hers was artificial later in life, and both had ice-blue eyes. As Celeste had guessed, the soft teal looked incredible on her.

"This is perfect for dinner tonight—such a thoughtful gift," she said, hugging Celeste close and then holding her at arm's length to look at her.

"How are you, dear? Theodore says you're hanging in there after your brother's passing—I can't help but wonder how you're holding it all together. You don't even have your parents to lean on."

Tears involuntarily welled in Celeste's eyes. "It's been quite shitty, to be honest, but I'm OK. It's triggering a lot of other memories and things from when my parents died." She sighed and shrugged. *A lot of oversharing lately.*

"The silver lining is that I have a fabulous husband, an amazing therapist, and the best support group of friends and family. You're a big part of that."

"Speaking of friends, I hope you don't mind, but we'd like to have a little soiree here the day after tomorrow. We have a lot of friends between here and Casablanca."

"Of course you do!" Celeste said, laughing. "You Prescotts are better connected and better traveled than anyone I've ever met."

"True, true. I suppose we should get ready for dinner before my son comes in and scolds us."

TERRASSE DES ÉPICES, close to the medina, was charming and authentic. The two couples were seated outdoors and marveled about the twinkling city and raffia globes that lit up the rooftop terrace.

The Prescott storytelling flowed as freely as their wine. Celeste listened and laughed but was ever cognizant of the minutes inching toward 9 p.m. After hearing the itinerary Theodore had planned earlier—which did not give her a single moment to herself—she feared this evening would be her only opportunity to sneak away.

At 8:55 on the dot, she excused herself for the ladies' room. She had already scoped the back door on the first floor, where Hadid would be waiting. She'd texted him earlier that the square was too far for sneaking out of dinner quickly, and he'd confirmed that he could come to her. While she descended the stairs, she transformed her pashmina into a headscarf to cover her blonde hair among a sea of dark hair in the dining room. *Be unmemorable.*

Keeping her head down, she walked confidently down the corridor leading to the restrooms—and the hidden back door. After glancing around to make sure she was alone, she exited, propping the door open with a small rock she had found at the hotel.

There he was in the shadows. He exhaled smoke and stamped out his cigarette, then walked over to her. She carefully released the door handle to ensure her rock was well placed and met him halfway, careful to stay out of view.

As Celeste remembered, Hadid had an uncanny resemblance to Omar. Omar had been Brazilian and Hadid Egyptian, but they could have been identical twins. The fact that they were indistinguishable was the only reason she and Hadid had been successful in framing Omar in Riyadh, which felt like a lifetime ago.

"Hello, old friend," Hadid whispered. "I've been busy and have much to share. I can confirm that Omar killed our friend Zari. Your new business partner, Matthew, is quite dangerous, as we suspected. He's intertwined in Omar's organization, and he's a pawn for many very bad people."

His face was somber. "There's more. Celeste, I have reason to believe the head of Omar's organization is an American who may work in government. I'll reach out when I can confirm more. But you must be careful. Trust no one."

"Does Nasrin know for certain about Zari now?" *Does she blame me?*

"Yes, she knows. I suspect she's always known. Zari was close to exposing whoever this mystery person is, and he made a lot of people very angry."

"The mystery American, you mean?"

"Yes."

She recalled an illuminati meeting a while back where Chet and Gabriel had shared their fears that their bosses were involved in a scheme to undermine the US economy and cause a national financial crisis, with the intent of destabilizing the US to the point of collapse. Now it was confirmed with the impending cyberattack. Could it all be orchestrated by the same person? Was that the person Omar was rolling over on? If they were working within Omar's organization, the aftermath could be devastating. *But there's nothing I can change about it this minute.*

"OK, thank you for everything." She started to leave but turned back, thinking of another question she wanted to ask. "Remember what you dug up in Matthew's financials? RH Global? Have you learned anything more about it? Maybe uncovering the identities would lead us to the American."

"I haven't learned anything new, but I wouldn't assume the two are intertwined."

"It doesn't seem that far off, given Matthew would be reporting up to the American."

Hadid seemed unconvinced.

She wanted to probe a bit further, but she had to get back to her family.

They said their goodbyes, and Celeste walked hurriedly upstairs while repositioning her scarf.

She saw the three of them at the other end of the terrace, but they could not see her. They were deep in conversation, heads together and speaking quietly. Her curiosity got the better of her, so she came up from behind them to see if she could catch a bit.

"Son, she deserves to know," Teddy scolded.

Who?

"She's your *wife*," Poppy said.

Me.

"I'll tell her, Mum."

Tell me what, Theodore?

Poppy sighed and looked to her husband.

"Your mother is right. You asked us to come all the way here to babysit her; have you thought how that will make her feel?"

Theodore scoffed. "Of course I have, but she's already furious with me *without* knowing that." He ran his hands through his hair, exasperated. "I can't let anything happen to her. Not again."

"When—not if—she finds out on her own, Son," Poppy said, "you'll deserve whatever wrath she directs toward you." She pursed her lips.

"She's impetuous and impulsive on a good day, and she's not ready."

I'll show you impetuous when you're sleeping on the terrace.

"There's been too much, with the wedding and her brother and everything in the background—" he continued.

My in-laws know things that I don't; my husband confides in them over me.

"She's a grown woman, Theodore," his dad broke in. "You're not being fair—"

"I *will* tell her," Theodore interrupted. "Soon."

They still hadn't seen her coming, so she waited a few beats to walk up until the topic shifted to a discussion about Poppy's cousin who had cancer.

Keeping her face neutral, Celeste cleared her throat, sat down, and took a sip before any of them processed her return. "What did I miss?"

Internally, she was seething. Her husband was doing exactly as she suspected—keeping her busy and supervised. *While he's doing Goddess knows what.* Only half listening to Poppy describing their relative's terminal cancer diagnosis, she speculated what Theodore could be hiding.

Who am I kidding? I can't even track what I'm hiding anymore, let alone work out someone else's secrets.

Food came and went, and the conversation flowed, though Celeste didn't register any of it. Her humiliation was mounting, her anger snowballing, thinking of three of the people she loved most keeping something—potentially explosive, judging by their manner —from her. *Seeing red in the Red City. Apropos.*

"Let's walk around and enjoy the souks, shall we?" Celeste suggested when they wrapped up dinner. She was struggling to maintain her composure and hoped the fresh air would calm her down. Besides, she needed fresh air and time to sort out the information from Hadid—she couldn't let this latest development distract her.

An American—an American traitor to catch. She would need to act fast when she returned to New York to ensure Theodore didn't derail her. She was running out of time.

The Prescotts moved at a relaxed pace as they headed back to the markets. They laughed and examined pottery for their vacation homes and told stories.

To speak your fears is to give life to them. Or was the converse true— saying them out loud took away their power? What if all the things she'd feared and hadn't said aloud—what if they were true? And if so, what if it meant she had to choose sides? If it came down to herself or others, she would always choose herself. Wouldn't she? *How does one go to war with her own husband? Her friends? How do I get this back on track?*

She had never felt powerless in her life until Omar. He'd had a way of taking away her agency, disenfranchising her. But he was gone, and here she was again with so little she could control, inundated with crisis after crisis.

The best defense is a good offense.

"IT'S PARTY DAY, MY DARLING!" Theodore said, waking Celeste on their final day in Marrakech.

"Morning, babe," Celeste replied, squinting from the sunlight when he threw open the blinds, pretending she hadn't been awake all night plotting. She yawned and stretched through her fingers and her toes for effect. "It's so quiet here, isn't it? I was out cold."

"Shall we have another lazy day by the pool to prepare for the old folks' gathering?"

She laughed. "Poppy and Teddy party harder than we do, dear, so I have no doubt that the friends will be up late enough to watch the sun rise."

"Welcome to my life. It's rough when your parents are cooler than you are."

"I wouldn't know," she said, recalling hers being in bed by ten most nights.

Wrapping her robe around her, she walked over to where Theodore was preparing tea.

"With all this lounging at the villa, I've only worn two of my seven Dior outfits, darling. Do you know the blood, sweat, and tears that went into our shopping? I'll be doing several outfit changes throughout the evening."

He smiled and handed her a mug with steam coming off it. "I called and requested breakfast a few minutes ago. Shall we eat on the terrace?"

She nodded approvingly. Theodore said he'd go out and greet his parents while she dressed.

Hiding in the closet, Celeste pulled out her burner and phoned Vivienne. She didn't waste time with pleasantries.

"The DNA sample was good?"

"Yes."

"Please send the report. A friend confirmed that an American leads Omar's syndicate. See what you can find."

After hanging up, Celeste made herself a promise.

I will rain hellfire down on you, Matthew. You will rue the day you first tried to cross me. In the spirit of simplifying, her plan to get rid of him was much easier to execute this way.

Celeste made one more call, this time to a man who hid behind his computer.

She dressed in a flowy Missoni chevron cover-up, paired with a hat and sandals, then joined her husband and his parents for an alfresco breakfast. Her mother-in-law was coiffed and in full makeup, and both she and Teddy were dressed in quiet luxury linen.

"I hope we're as vibrant as you two," Celeste said pleasantly as she approached the table and sat down next to Theodore.

Her husband tossed his arm around her casually and kissed the top of her head. "We will be." He and his parents were oblivious to the fact that Celeste had overheard them.

The restaurant had prepared quite a spread for them: pastries, waffles, omelets, meats, fruits, and crudités. Celeste powered through the small talk, itching for some alone time. As soon as she found an opportunity, she excused herself.

"I'm going to squeeze in a quick workout and then soak up the sun by the pool." She leaned over to kiss Theodore and was off before anyone could protest.

In the gym, Celeste lifted heavy weights and ran for an hour, using the physical exertion to focus. Her plan was as ready as it could be while she waited for everything to fall into place. The situation demanded flawless execution. *No more distractions, Celeste,* she scolded herself. Whatever her husband was up to would have to wait. She had an attack and a traitor to stop, as well as a life to destroy.

THE AMAN STAFF had been quite busy. Upon Celeste's return, all remnants of the breakfast spread had been removed, and party prep was well underway. String lights had been draped along the outdoor foliage. A formal bar now sat in the corner of the expansive patio, and lively music played over the speakers. Half a dozen workers milled about, and she marveled at how quickly they worked.

Theodore was seated casually on the bed inside their villa when she walked in, laptop open. He was in shorts, bare-chested. His chiseled abs were apparent, and his scent, a mixture of body wash and aftershave, enveloped her. She was at once aroused and livid at the sight of him.

Perhaps a hate fuck is how I move past this for now.

She closed the double doors that led outside and put her index finger to her lips.

"Hello, darling. How was your work..." He looked up, then trailed off when he noticed her hand signal.

She smiled and motioned for him to follow her into the en suite bathroom. She closed and locked the door behind them, peeled off her workout clothes, and stepped into the shower as if in almost one swift motion. She was horny, and her husband sensed it.

Theodore dropped his shorts and joined her.

Their lips locked, their bodies each craving the other. Theodore was erect, impatient, one hand finding her G-spot almost instantly and the other firmly caressing one of her breasts.

Sandwiched between his chest and the glazed ceramic tile, she climaxed from his handiwork, and he took a step back to watch her. She stifled a moan, of clear enough mind to consider her nearby in-laws in the adjacent room, and her muscles turned to jelly as the wave tingled through her entire body.

His betrayal was far from her mind.

She needed more of him, *all of him*, and he obliged, wordlessly sliding his hard cock inside her.

His hips rocked front to back, thrusting himself deeper and deeper, just as she wanted, and then she felt his hard member pulse with his orgasm.

When she could not keep quiet any longer, she yelped with pleasure, a full, hearty expression of happiness.

"Oops," she whispered with a smile.

Theodore's expression was fierce, and as their eyes locked, she could see his were hooded with desire and full of emotion.

Hunger, lust, vulnerability.

And... something else—she wasn't quite sure—flashed and was gone as quickly.

What was it? Its intensity gave her pause, and she searched his face for an answer.

She knew his visage as well as she knew her own, the exact size of his nose, the angle of his jaw, every curve, every line etched in her memory. He had visited her night after night in her dreams when he'd left her, and since his return, she never took him for granted.

He held on to her tightly, as though he expected her to *poof!* disappear, and her breath caught in her throat.

There it was again.

Fear.

Theodore was afraid.

~

LATER, Celeste, after having applied makeup and styled her hair, walked to the boudoir, where the Dior gown beckoned. The couture hung so beautifully that she almost didn't want to disrupt it.

In one of the most exotic destinations on the planet, with a man she loved who had just pleasured her not once but three times, she was living an enviable life among all the people, luxury, and good vibes that any woman would wish for. She wanted a mental photograph of that moment when she allowed herself to feel gratitude, to know peace, to ignore her racing thoughts, even if only brief.

She fingered the blush-pink silk dress gingerly. It was silly, really, how special she felt to know that the bespoke dress had been made for her. She'd had clothes designed for her before, and the dress certainly wasn't the most expensive thing in her closet. What made her feel special was being part of a legacy. *Thank you, Meredith. Thank you for always making me feel like I'm worth it.*

The vibe at the Dior workshop had been distinct from what she'd experienced when visiting a dressmaker in Italy or India. Much more than a tailor following a pattern, the dressmakers at Dior were creating wearable art, an invitation for how the world should view a person, connected to a fashion house of people dedicated to creating. She was the canvas for someone's hopes, dreams, and creativity to be on display for the world to consume, which was such a privilege. Suddenly, she couldn't wait to wear the couture designed specifically for her.

She slid the flowy dress on, careful not to disrupt her makeup or hair, and was surprised that she was able to zip it on her own.

Her strappy sandals had been placed directly below on the floor. She stepped into them, feeling proud that she'd chosen a sensible heel height for mingling all night, and went into the bathroom for one last glance in the mirror.

Life is for the living. So go, go now and live, in the armor created especially for you.

After applying a touch more lip gloss, she headed to the party.

Theodore saw her straightaway and winked from across the terrace. She strode over as he was saying, "And this is my beautiful wife, Celeste Donovan, the founder and managing director of Donovan & Clarke Capital." He put his arm around her when she stood next to him. Two men and a woman around the same age as Theodore's parents shook her hand and introduced themselves in turn. She immediately forgot their names but made note of their accents. *All from England by the sound of it.*

"Now, how do you know Poppy and Teddy?" Celeste asked.

"Oh, we've known each other since we were young," said one of the men, who called himself Earl. He was a white man, bald except for a few remaining white hairs atop his head. "Teddy and I worked together at Barclay's in the sixties."

"Poppy and I were college roommates," the woman chimed in. She was a blonde version of Celeste's mother-in-law, youthful for her age and extremely well dressed. The woman sized up Celeste. "That dress is gorgeous. Dior?"

"Good eye! Yes, I was at the Paris atelier earlier this week and fell in love with it. Perfect for a summer's eve cocktail party, isn't it?"

"Oh, yes, yes indeed."

The conversation flowed easily, taking Celeste's mind off the events of the past few weeks. She quite enjoyed getting to know people close to her in-laws, people who had watched Theodore grow up.

"So you're the Donovan of the infamous Donovan and Clarke, eh?" Earl said later when he circled back to her. "Did you inherit the firm from your father? You're much too young to be so successful."

Celeste's senses were heightened; something about the man made her uncomfortable. "Well, Earl," she said, "I'm not sure if that was meant as a compliment or not, but in the spirit of this lovely little soiree, I'll assume good intent and say thank you.

"No, I did not inherit the firm; my cofounder Savin Clarke— maybe you know him because he grew up with Theodore—and I built it from the ground up. My parents were not in finance. In fact, they were academics." She sipped her Champagne. "What did you say you did at Barclay's? Are you still with a big bank?"

"Oh, poppet, it was so long ago. I've had a thousand lives since then," Earl replied.

Before he could ask her another question, she escaped.

It was dusk, and the twinkling lights cast an intimate glow over the patio. There were twelve or so guests in addition to Theodore, Poppy, and Teddy, and the conversation was vibrant and hummed with laughter.

Servers clad in all-white tuxedos, easy to spot against the backdrop, bustled about. One came toward her with a tray of Champagne, so Celeste downed the last of hers, preparing to trade it in for a fresh glass.

"Celeste, stay calm and listen up," the man carrying the tray whispered. As Celeste took a closer look, her eyes opened wide, and she nearly dropped her clutch.

"What are you doing here?" she hissed.

"I checked out everyone before they arrived. Some of these people aren't who they say they are, Celeste."

"What do you mean?" she said. She stared at her friend Hadid, who blended in well with the other staff, his wig and colored contacts concealing any resemblance to Omar. "And how did you get in here?"

"Don't worry about that; it was necessary. Some of them are family friends, and some are actors, with the exception of one person." He discreetly gestured to Poppy's blonde double, conversing one group away. "From what I can tell, she's MI6."

It took every ounce of self-control for Celeste's face to remain neutral. *Why would British intelligence be at my party in Morocco?* Many more questions raced through her mind. "The guy? The one I was just with who said he worked at Barclay's with my father-in-law?"

"Apparently, he's legitimately a friend, but the trail ran dry on his career about twenty years ago. I'd expect he's also MI6."

Celeste scanned the room, wearing a pleasant smile to see if her husband had noticed her chatting up a server. His back was to her, and her in-laws weren't paying attention either.

"Does my family know? Did they arrange this? Or is this about me?"

"I don't know, Celeste. I honestly don't know. Several of them are legitimate friends who live nearby or are traveling in the area. You need to get through this party by acting as normal as possible, and I will keep digging. I'll be in touch."

Celeste selected the fullest flute and walked toward the middle of the group without a backward glance toward her old friend.

"There you are, gorgeous. I was beginning to think you'd found a better party," Theodore said when she walked up behind him and put an arm around his waist.

"No, of course not; it's lovely. How wonderful to meet people who've known you and your parents for so long. It's like a glimpse into teenage Theodore," she fibbed, since she hadn't discussed Theodore's adolescent years with anyone.

No more delays. She was going to have a hard enough time executing her plan with the Feds watching; to think that foreign intelligence was also involved was too much to process.

At her earliest opportunity, she sneaked back to the room, confirming that the anonymous man she'd hired had done as she asked.

~

HER CELL PHONE blaring in her ear startled her awake. *Why is Savin calling me at three a.m. local time?*

"Oh my God, thank God you picked up!" he said. "I take it you haven't been watching the news. We've got a huge mess to clean up, Celly, and I need your help to think things through."

She looked over to see that her husband's side of the bed had not yet been slept in. In fact, there was no sign of him inside. She knew Savin was visibly shaken, probably pacing and running his fingers through his hair roughly.

"OK, darling, slow down and tell me what's happened."

"Celly, it started off as a normal day, but then I got a call. Well, not directly; Rani got the call and then she—"

"It's quite late, so please give me the abbreviated version."

"OK, OK, fine. Celly, they think Matthew killed Omar. They found his DNA at the scene, I guess. By total coincidence, he was arrested in the EU somewhere for being drunk and disorderly. When they ran his prints, they discovered the record of his DNA and fingerprints in Rome. He's there now in custody. And not only that, but somehow he's been named in a bunch of other crimes, including more murders and rape."

Well done, she silently communicated with the mastermind she'd sent the DNA to earlier in the trip, who—successfully it appeared—had framed Matthew. *If you can't take a life, you destroy it.*

"Oh, wow. I mean, it's not surprising that he's a bad man. But wow, that's a lot."

"And now our clients want to know what this means for the acquisition of TA Capital. Tarek and Kaya have asked that we meet with them ASAP. As you can imagine, they're up in arms."

"Oh, c'mon, Sav. They're not as distressed by this as you think. Matthew was a total prick; I'm sure his own mother wished his cancer of a personality didn't exist." She shifted focus. Defending Matthew or feigning outrage that his life was ruined wasn't going to happen.

"So, what did you tell our clients?"

"Well, Celly, the countries where he's committed crimes are calling for his extradition, and obviously, I had to terminate his employment today and block his access to our servers."

"It sounds like you've done all the right things. As long as we're making money, our clients aren't going to care about the scandal. We did our due diligence during the acquisition; if no charges had been pressed against him, how could anyone expect us to know?"

Savin's breathing was shallow.

"Do you see this impacting our bottom line, Sav? Unlikely. Tarek is the guy running their show, and I might add he's an amazing PM, not Matthew, so why would anyone pull their business?"

"Well, then there's the press. And the twenty-four-hour news cycle."

She probed him about the press release, and they talked through how the PR team had recommended they respond. Once they'd agreed on their approach, Savin continued with his litany of concerns.

"Sav, we run a hedge fund, not a nunnery. Omar was involved in all the same shit; who knows, maybe Matthew is the person Omar was rolling over on and that's why Matthew killed him. Honestly, I say we hold a presser tomorrow and then decline to comment after that. This is up to the police and country justice departments, not two financiers."

"But what if they draw some correlation—"

"Sav, we weren't involved in how Matthew spent his time. If all goes well, he'll get the death penalty somewhere, and I'll never have to see his scowling face again."

"Celly, I love you, but you really can be an ice queen, like they say."

Only when it comes to people who cross me. Or who deserve it.

After calming Savin a bit more, she ended the call. Still no Theodore. Retrieving one of her burners, she sent a confirmation and large crypto transfer as payment for services rendered to the dark web hacker who had mobilized so quickly to get Matthew out of the way.

She then found her husband on the patio with his parents, all the guests gone.

"Darling, we didn't wake you with our Prescott enthusiasm, did we?" Theodore asked with concern.

"No, no. But boy, do I have some news to share."

She'd probably still exact further revenge on Matthew, but at least he couldn't inflict anymore harm while he was in custody.

8

"MURDER STUNS A SLEEPY HAMPTONS HAMLET"

The helicopter descended onto the immaculate Southampton lawn helipad just as Celeste finished writing the last of her work emails. It was rare for her to stop working at 2 p.m. on a Friday, but she supposed Savin's party was a good enough excuse. She snapped her laptop shut and slid it into her tote.

"Ready for this, my love?" Theodore asked, removing his headset and taking hers. He turned off the engine and kissed her cheek.

"Thanks for getting us here in one piece, my knight. You know how I loathe the traffic. It's going to be a wonderful weekend. I'm ecstatic for Sav, and I can't ask for anyone better to be his life partner." Savin and Rani meant so much to Celeste. She wasn't sure whether they'd ever be cleared of suspicion, but she wished for an indisputable sign that neither of them would ever do anything to harm Celeste or Theodore.

She couldn't imagine either of them being capable of it, but the reality was, no one ever really knew what others were capable of. Until the previous year, she had certainly never envisioned that she would be capable of some of the things she'd done. Spending the weekend with her friends without other distractions would hopefully provide clarity on any number of things, but at a minimum, knowing whether Sav was on her side would be helpful.

Is my husband on my side? She didn't know, but she was operating on the assumption that he was. She'd thought back to his parents' scoldings several times since their Morocco trip. *Darling, come clean to me. Tell me what your parents meant with their "Son, she deserves to know" and "She's your wife" comments.* Of course, Celeste had other questions as well. Was it possible that Hadid was correct that Theodore's parents were friends with MI6 agents? Anne Marie was always telling her in their therapy sessions that she shouldn't jump to conclusions. If she had no plans to ask her husband directly what was going on—which she didn't intend to do—and she was already taking precautions in nearly every aspect of her life, there was no sense in wasting a perfectly nice party weekend deciphering the cryptic conversation she'd overheard. *Whatever it is, it can wait*, she resolved.

All smiles, she took Theodore's outstretched hand, and he assisted her in getting down to the lawn. A butler rushed over to retrieve their bags. They thanked him and then held hands as they walked away from the heliport toward the main house.

"Mere has done it again!" Celeste remarked, taking in the manicured gardens that were in view to anyone who pulled up to the estate. There was magnificent bold foliage as far as the eye could see, with pink, blue, and ivory hydrangeas nearly as tall as Celeste. "She can't help but make everything flawlessly beautiful."

The beach was not visible from where they stood, but it was nearby, past the hedges and down the stairs. For now, they were exploring the rest of the property. The guesthouse was to the right, near an Olympic-length pool, and a staff house was behind that. Savin had boasted that between this and the other houses on the property, there were seventeen bedrooms. The main house had balconies off every bedroom, he said, as well as an enormous terrace off the grand room and another pool, around which staff were arranging an area for an ice sculpture and stage.

Celeste and Theodore entered the house to find dozens of people milling about in catering uniforms.

"A small gathering?" Theodore said and whistled. "This is a full-fledged affair."

Celeste laughed. "In true Meredith flair." She looked around, marveling at the home. "I do love the house he's bought. It screams Sav."

"Yet all we can agree on is an apartment in a high-rise, no respite from the city," her husband complained gently.

"Maybe someday. Soon," she added when she saw his disappointment. Celeste would likely need a compound and armed guards to feel safe out in the suburbs or the country these days. She could hardly imagine Theodore's romanticized version of a country home aligning with that.

The happy couple was nowhere to be found, and a housekeeper showed Celeste and Theodore to their room.

"Whaddya say we give this bed a whirl?" he teased.

"Not a bad idea," she replied devilishly.

Knock, knock. Celeste went to open the door. The same housekeeper who had showed them their room stood outside, holding two glasses of Champagne.

"Dinner is at seven p.m., Mr. and Mrs. Prescott. Let us know if we can escort you to the beach or for a swim. Cocktail hour with hors d'oeuvres begins at five."

Celeste took the Champagne, graciously thanked her, and the woman left.

Somewhere down the hall, Celeste heard Savin. From his voice, she could tell he was angry, a rare occurrence.

"I know you're hiding something. We're meant to be married in a matter of weeks, Ran. What gives?"

Rani's reply was muffled. Celeste, feeling too voyeuristic at glimpsing a couple's private moment, closed the door.

"What was it?"

"Oh, I thought I heard someone saying my name, but it was nothing," Celeste fibbed. No need to meddle, at least not yet.

The two made love ("It's been at least a week," Theodore had complained, to which Celeste reminded him, "It's been since eight a.m. You're insatiable!") and then Celeste spent some time sorting through her clothing and toiletries.

It had been a week of important revelations. She was one step closer to tracking down who had doctored her trades in the D&C servers, thanks to Lorraine's vigilance. Angelo had brought in three security firms to ensure that Celeste's New York apartment had no signs of entry, no bugs, and most notably, no explosives. She didn't know what that suggested about her Parisian apartment, but that could wait until Angelo and Julien turned up something new. Finally, it looked as though she may be able to rest easier about Nico moving forward.

Michel had shown up in New York with great news right after she and Theodore returned from Morocco. He'd found a way to get rid of incriminating evidence he'd accessed in Nico's missing persons report in the NYPD system.

He'd also hacked into the CCTV from the day she was photographed outside her safe-house apartment and identified the perpetrator. After all her worry that it was related to her legal woes, the photographer ended up being a paparazzo for the *New York Post*, determined to uncover the identity of the hot new woman sneaking in and out of a West Village sublevel apartment. From Michel's sleuthing, he'd determined the guy had made no connection between Celeste and her Mia alias.

Michel was proving to be quite useful again. Perhaps he was back to his old self. Time would tell.

But plenty of questions were still swirling for Celeste, like the motivation behind the faux Moroccan cocktail party with the party crashers—*Why was MI6 at our villa?*—and whether her in-laws had been involved somehow. Alas, the mystery would not be solved this weekend, so she may as well enjoy herself.

"Patrick and Ty will be here shortly," she called to her husband as she walked back to the sitting room where he was. "They're doing my glam first, then Rani and Sam."

But Theodore was distracted, frowning as he typed on his ever-present iPhone. "What, honey? I'm sorry, I didn't hear what you said."

"Nothing. Finish up your work while I get ready so you can relax —we agreed no work this weekend, remember?" she scolded lightly. The truth was, she had zero leverage with her husband because she routinely stayed up well after Theodore went to sleep, so she let it go. "I'll go find my glam team. Enjoy the quiet while it lasts," she said. Theodore knew well how rambunctious Patrick and Ty were.

Celeste went down to the main floor to see if they'd arrived. The bride and groom were still nowhere to be seen. Several uniformed people milled around, focusing on their various tasks to finalize the party. *Hopefully the lucky couple is in better spirits, after what I overheard.*

Meredith stood in the giant chef's kitchen with a clipboard, giving orders and checking over people's shoulders. Celeste imagined the staff hated her because Meredith was a perfectionist and wouldn't tolerate mediocrity or mistakes. Celeste didn't blame her—mediocrity was infuriating. *Most people are just so ordinary.*

"Where are we on the ice sculpture?" Meredith barked. "It's the one thing—the *one thing*—that cannot be replaced on this short timeline."

Two staff workers murmured replies, wearing matching expressions of dread on their faces. Mere rolled her eyes, then looked up and saw Celeste entering the room. The ice sculpture was instantly forgotten.

"Celly! Hi!" she said, putting the clipboard on a table and rushing over. She gave her friend and biggest client a hug. "Sav and Rani are napping. Jack is around here somewhere. Mark and Jin are staying a few doors down from you. I haven't heard from Roberto and Sam yet. And then, of course, there's Edward and Triston and their dates. I threatened Savin—there'd better not be any randoms disrupting yet another impeccably planned and executed event by Meredith."

"Where will Fred sleep?" Like Celeste, Fred had been in Omar's crosshairs, though for entirely different reasons. Fred had had to flee the country when Omar was on a rampage. He and Celeste, after years of despising each other, had a kumbaya reconciliation because of their shared experience. She suspected she would need his counsel at some point soon; she needed an ally who wasn't too close to the situation.

"Oh, yes, I put him and his girlfriend in the guesthouse."

Elizabeth. Celeste had met her at the last D&C gala. The woman was sophisticated, chic, and warm, not to mention an impeccable dresser. Celeste had liked her instantly.

"Wonderful. Miss Kennedy is lovely, almost too lovely for Fred." Celeste giggled, having seen Fred walk in out of the corner of her eye.

"I heard that!" he exclaimed. "But 'tis true, I suppose." Celeste and Fred greeted each other with an embrace. "You keeping out of trouble?" he whispered in her ear.

"Of course. You know me—never one to color outside the lines."

He looked at her and rolled his eyes.

Celeste turned to see Elizabeth entering the room. She was wearing a vibrant silk kaftan perfect for the breezy indoor-outdoor feel of the home and quilted Bottega Veneta mules. Her frosted blonde hair was styled in a chic bob that only she could pull off.

"Hello, darling," she said, giving Celeste a delicate hug. "Fred was saying it's been a tumultuous month for you. Hopefully you'll have some time to relax now that the wedding and..." She trailed off. Apparently, even the most polished of women were uncomfortable discussing death.

"Thank you, Elizabeth, truly. Theodore and I have planned a summer full of R and R, with this event kicking it off."

A young man carrying a tray of Champagne flutes directed them to the terrace and handed each of the three of them a glass. "Please enjoy the view."

"Well, I for one won't complain about some fresh air. It's been quite a long week. We were traveling for one of Fred's work trips."

Before Celeste could inquire, Fred chimed in, "We were in Paris. It's always wonderful in the springtime."

"Looks like we found the VIP section," Celeste heard Patrick say and then he appeared with Ty in tow. The two carried their kits, large black wheeled suitcases.

"Oh, hey, handsome, you'll need to bring some of that champs my way, love," Patrick said to one of the male servers, grabbing two glasses from his tray. He looked the guy up and down. "You are *hot*. I'll come find you later." He turned to the small group. "Celly!"

Celeste was laughing along with Fred and Elizabeth. "Though they need no introduction, this is my glam squad: Patrick, whom you've witnessed sexually harassing the staff and stealing Champagne within moments of arriving, and Ty, my makeup artist extraordinaire."

Mere walked out and explained that they'd also be staying in the guesthouse, to which Fred replied, "How lucky for us," and everyone laughed.

"Do you ever sleep?" Patrick asked Celeste and then turned to Ty. "She looks haggard again, doesn't she?"

Ty nodded, then said optimistically, "Nothing the two of us can't fix."

"They're always like this, and yet somehow I keep tolerating them," Celeste said to her friends. After excusing herself, she turned to Patrick and Ty. "Let's go get ready then."

They made their way up to Celeste and Theodore's suite. Theodore's voice was low, but she heard the tail end of his phone conversation: "...has to be stopped. These messes..." He paused to listen, then said, "Yes, yes, I agree completely."

"Darling," Celeste said loudly so that he would get off the phone, "I'm back, and look who I picked up along the way."

Theodore was seated on the sofa. When he saw her enter with her friends, he quickly ended his call, and his face broke into a broad grin.

"And my lovely wife returns," he said. He walked across the room and kissed her forehead, then shook hands with Patrick and Ty. "This is my cue to disappear until you're finished. Though I think she is already beautiful, perhaps more so, before you two do your work."

He left the room, and Patrick and Ty took over the dressing area with curling irons and airbrush machines.

The three chatted while they brushed and teased and lined and bronzed Celeste, until she was transformed into the glam goddess they wanted her to be. They helped her into a Prada nude tulle dress with embedded crystals, and she slipped her feet into her Amina Muaddi glass PVC mules.

"Ugh, it hurts my eyes. You're sparkling from every angle," Patrick joked.

"You look too amazing, and it's not fair to the bride!" Ty remarked.

"We are truly talented to be able to transform her so quickly," Patrick said. "She looked like shit when we arrived."

Celeste laughed. "You always have a way of humbling me, dear," she said to Patrick. "Now get out! You must beautify everyone else, and I need to greet Savin's and Theodore's parents!"

As they left, Theodore returned. "Hey, gorgeous," he said, wrapping her in a bear hug. "You ready to party?"

"Oh, yes, though I wager we'll all be asleep by eleven. Your parents and Savin's should be arriving soon. I was going to be the good daughter-in-law and entertain them. Your outfit is hanging in the closet there." She pointed to the summer suit Meredith had chosen for Theodore, which complemented her dress.

"Thanks for taking care of Mum and Dad," he said. "The travel has been a bit hard on them. And for the record, I don't think you need any more points in the perfect-daughter column, but they always love to see you. I'm sure they'll reiterate that you were a smashing success with their friends too. Everyone continues to remind me how lucky I am, to which I always reply that I'm quite aware, thank you very much."

Celeste moved toward the door as Theodore walked to the bathroom for a shower. "Oh, darling?" she called.

"Yeah, babe?"

"Everything OK at work? I thought I heard you arguing with someone earlier."

"Never fear. All is well. Just a little mess around"—he paused and turned to look at her—"that project I have going on in Brazil."

"Ah, OK. See you in a bit," she said breezily, though she didn't recall him mentioning any South American projects lately. The continent was more her wheelhouse than his, with the D&C presence there.

As she descended the stairs, she heard Mark and Jack chatting with Poppy and Teddy.

"Now all my favorite people have arrived," she said as she walked out onto the terrace. Two cocktail servers were bustling about, tending to everyone's drinks and carrying trays of hors d'oeuvres.

After accepting a delicate caviar-and-smoked-salmon canapé and more bubbles, Celeste walked over to the group. She greeted her in-laws first and then her friends.

"I hope these degenerates aren't taking up too much of your time, Poppy," she said.

"Oh, no, of course not, dear. Jack here was telling us about his extensive travel these days. He has a pilot's license like our Theodore."

"I try not to spend more than two days at a time on one continent," Jack joked, and everyone chuckled. "I didn't realize Theodore also flew."

"You didn't?" Celeste asked. But she supposed the two hadn't spent much time together.

"I can't believe Sav is getting hitched," Jack commented. "Well, I mean, no one can believe you're married either, Celly."

Celeste rolled her eyes and turned to her in-laws. "As I said, these guys are like annoying kid brothers much of the time." *Ah, fuck, I had to mention brothers.*

Poppy and Teddy made eye contact before Poppy proceeded. "Dear, you seemed to be holding up quite well last week, but please know you can count on us if you ever need to talk about—" Teddy gave an almost imperceptible nod, and Poppy stopped herself. "Well, you're in our thoughts is all." Could such a thoughtful, empathetic woman also be capable of bringing an MI6 agent into Celeste's life?

Thankfully, Savin's mom, Ferwa, arrived at that moment, making quite an entrance in a Lebanese-inspired red ball gown. Celeste instantly recognized it as a Zuhair Murad.

Lebanon had become a breeding ground for incredible fashion.

She made a mental note to ask Ferwa who else's designs she was wearing lately. Mere had introduced Celeste to a couple of up-and-coming Lebanese designers, and Celeste loved discovering new ones to follow.

All eyes were on Ferwa as she descended the steps to the terrace.

"Poppy! Teddy! How wonderful of you to come to our little soiree," Ferwa said loudly, walking directly to them and ignoring everyone else. Celeste took this as her cue to leave after a quick hello.

She joined Savin and Theodore, who were upstairs chatting.

"I'm guessing you saw mum's dramatic entrance," Savin said. "She has an admirable talent to make Rani's and my engagement party all about her."

"Oh dear. Is poor Rani upset?"

"No, she's not. Rani isn't the sensitive one in our relationship—I am, remember?" The three laughed, knowing it was true. Savin wore his heart on his sleeve.

"Where is she?"

"She's still with Patrick and Ty, I believe."

"I'll go check on her. Be right back." Celeste walked through the enormous house to the master suite.

"Rani?" Celeste called out, knocking softly on the door. She didn't hear anyone inside. "Rani?" she repeated once she was in the room.

Suddenly, Rani appeared from the bathroom, looking more beautiful and elegant than usual, which was a high bar. Celeste admired her long, dark hair, the Hollywood waves set against her olive skin. She looked radiant in a pale-pink slip dress that draped perfectly on her frame.

"Oh, darling, congratulations!" Celeste rushed to hug her, any suspicions tossed aside and replaced with true happiness for her friend. "You look so gorgeous! We are all so happy to celebrate you and Savin." *Rani couldn't, wouldn't hurt us.*

"Thanks, Celly. We're excited too. Is my mother-in-law-to-be here yet? Has she brought all the drama and a team of handlers?"

Celeste laughed. "I haven't seen the handlers yet, but she's wearing a deep red ball gown."

"That's what she wears around the house," Rani replied.

"That's not even the least bit surprising, given Savin's general"—Celeste stopped to make a circle with her hand—"demeanor."

"Yes, my to-be husband has a flair for the dramatic."

The two women chatted as they walked through the house to the party. The backyard was visible from the many windows.

The sun was beginning to set, and Celeste could see how beautiful everything would look at night. She drew Rani's attention to what had evolved outside. "Oh, Rani, it's straight out of a fairy tale. Mere has done it again!"

"Yes, yes, I have. I can finally enjoy myself now." Mere was coiffed to perfection, having set aside making everyone and everything else beautiful for a little glam time of her own.

"It's more incredible than I ever could have imagined. Thank you, Mere," Rani gushed, the gratitude in her voice apparent.

"I'm so happy you love it," Mere replied. "Everything turned out so beautifully. And it was a much less stressful planning process than for Celly's wedding."

She pretended to ponder. "Hmm, what could be so different about the two events? Oh, wait! Maybe it's because it's a different bride—" Mere teased, then feigned guilt.

"Haha, you and everyone else can keep your bridezilla jokes going forever, and it still won't bother me."

"Only kidding, Celly! Honestly, though, it has been a breeze here. I probably could've invited Seth to join after all, but maybe he wasn't meant to be here this weekend. Next time. It's showtime, babies!"

"Let's get this party started!" Mere said in a loud voice to the group. "Make your way to the most intimate, idyllic garden you've ever dined in."

For the next ten minutes, the staff ushered the guests to their seats.

Tea lights floated in the pool, and a clear glass floor had been placed across most of it. The tables and chairs were arranged on top of the runway, and just like at Celeste's wedding, there was an explosion of flowers on the tables and anywhere else they could be attached. One could get lost in the beauty of it all. *A home out here wouldn't be so terrible. Maybe when all this stuff settles down, Theodore and I can discuss a country home again.*

Once everyone was seated, Savin stood and clinked his spoon against his Champagne flute. "We all know I could go on forever—"

"You'd better keep this quick—the kitchen is on a tight schedule," Mere said, and a chuckle rang out across the room.

"Good point." Savin had never looked happier. He was radiant. "Thank you so much to everyone for making the trip to celebrate our engagement. Some came farther than others. Mark and Jin, I think you win for longest distance traveled, all the way from Shanghai."

He turned to his mother. "Mami, I'm so glad you're here to celebrate with Rani and me, especially because her own family was unable to come."

It was almost imperceptible, but Celeste thought she saw a cloud cross Rani's face before the bride-to-be replaced it with an ear-to-ear grin.

"Poppy and Teddy too, I'm—we're just so grateful you made the trek, and right after a long holiday in North Africa, no less."

"Hey, what about me, ya prick? I came all the way from Sydney," Jack joked.

"Oh, you had no prior engagements; you're not fooling anyone!"

Rani stood and said, "On that note, darling Savin, do sit down. And bon appétit, everyone!"

The dinner was delectable, thanks to Mere, who had developed the perfect menu for a summer evening and then flew in one of Savin's favorite chefs from London. Wine and conversation flowed, and laughter from the group carried across the vast lawn. Savin and Rani beamed ear to ear and whispered sweet nothings to each other throughout the entire dinner. Whatever she'd overheard earlier must've been a minor spat, Celeste decided.

Tears streamed down Savin's face when Theodore, Celeste, and his mates Edward and Triston gave speeches. Mark regaled everyone with funny stories of their younger days, and Jack roasted Savin. Roberto made a poignant remark about having a front-row seat for one of the greatest love stories of all time. Even Celeste teared up a little, nearly bursting with happiness for her friend, who had been through such heartache in his life. *He's finally getting the partner and life he's always wanted—and deserved.*

The group stayed for several hours, laughing and talking, until finally it was time to retire.

"Are you up for a walk on the beach, darling?" Theodore asked.

"Oh, that sounds lovely," Celeste replied. It was a clear night with many stars visible.

The couple said good night to everyone and walked toward the beach. Leaving their shoes at the edge of the sand, they went out to Savin's private section of Cooper's Beach, regularly voted one of the most beautiful in the world.

They held hands and shared how happy they were for their friends. The full moon shone brightly, casting a glow on both of their faces.

Loving someone—truly being in love with someone—was one of the most fulfilling, yet contradictory, experiences in life. Juxtaposed with her capacity to love Theodore, to go to any lengths to protect their marriage, was the fact that he could make her angrier than anyone else could. She hadn't forgotten what she'd overheard him discussing with his parents, and the humiliation and anger lingered. But the opposing force that was so much more powerful allowed her to compartmentalize—to be fully present, bursting with love for her life partner, and to keep that completely separate from the resentment and growing suspicion that maybe her husband had more to hide than she did. It's as though the conflicting emotions existed on a different plane than the two lovers walking hand in hand in the moonlight. For she could fully experience the former and tuck away the latter, the brewing confrontation, for another time. She would do anything to protect their marriage, and in that moment, it meant sweeping the questions, growing more urgent by the second, under the rug and dreaming aloud of their future together.

"It's all so magical out here, isn't it?"

"Indeed," Theodore replied in a hopeful tone.

"I could see us doing this walk after dinner each night. Much different from all the summers when I've rented houses or hotel suites out here."

"Yes, having a home of one's own has its advantages," he said cautiously. She read his tone to mean he didn't want to scare her away from the idea of a home out there by pushing too hard.

"Agreed. It's just always seemed like such a commitment, you know, always feeling like we'd have to be out here, especially given how much time we spend abroad in the high season."

"It wouldn't be a terrible idea for us to slow down a bit."

"Hmm." She wasn't sure about that. "Maybe I could be persuaded into homeownership. You're trying to domesticate me, after all, aren't you, Prescott?"

"Guilty as charged," he said. He took her into his arms and gave her a heated kiss.

Marriage really was complex. Her mind was far away from any of the mounting problems, and she was fully present and as in love as she'd been when she first met Theodore.

They marveled at the full moon, batted around a few ideas for Savin's wedding gift, and then walked back.

Everyone else appeared to be in bed when they arrived; all three houses were mostly dark. Celeste would have been willing to bet that Jack had found an afterparty somewhere. The caterers and staff were quietly cleaning throughout the grounds as Celeste and Theodore went to their suite.

Hmm. Celeste was in the middle of her nightly skin ritual when she noticed a diamond stud earring that wasn't hers sitting on the vanity. *Maybe Patrick or Ty misplaced it there.* Once she was finished, she joined her husband in bed. He was frowning at his phone again.

"Darling, is everything all right? You seem preoccupied today."

"No, no, all is well." He placed his phone on the nightstand and turned to her. Just as she was scooting closer to him, they heard a loud thud outside.

"What the—" Celeste jumped out of bed to look out the window.

Before she could get there, a deafening scream rang out through the night.

She turned around to find that Theodore already had sprung into action, throwing on pants, a T-shirt, and sneakers in record time.

Celeste grabbed her robe, and the two ran down to see what had happened.

"Someone call nine-one-one!" Savin shouted for all to hear, panic evident in his voice.

They rushed to his side to see everyone gathered around.

Celeste pushed her way to the front—and then she saw what they were all gawking at, instantly regretting that she had looked.

She let out a scream of her own in a voice she didn't recognize, a sound like a fatally wounded animal.

Collapsing to her knees, she realized one of her nightmares had come to fruition, though this time it wasn't Theodore who was hurt.

"No! No! No! Someone come and help her! No!" She lowered her head and sobbed into her hands.

Theodore was at her side then, holding her, patting her back, steadying her, and soon she heard many people moving about behind her.

Sirens. Chaos. Policemen.

She couldn't unsee what—or rather, who—was in front of her.

There on the ground by the pool, where all the tea lights still twinkled and the flowers remained so lovingly arranged, lay Mere— or Mere's body, that is, as she clearly had not survived the fall. Her body was twisted in all sorts of unnatural angles, and her eyes were open and unseeing. Blood trickled from the side of her mouth.

Celeste hugged her knees and rocked back and forth, her body trembling. She couldn't breathe; the air just wasn't getting to her lungs.

She thought she heard voices all around saying her name, but they seemed far away, as in a dream. Someone suggested she move to make way for the EMTs.

But she couldn't leave Mere there by herself.

Celeste had to stay with her, had to make them save her. A

stretcher emerged; cops were milling about everywhere. Red and blue lights distorted the ambience Mere had created.

Everything was wrong. *This wasn't supposed to happen.*

Who could've done this to Mere? Where was the security detail who always accompanied them? It made no sense. None of it made any sense. Celeste's body was racked with sobs. *No, no. Not Mere. Not her*

After many minutes of persuasion, Theodore finally got Celeste to her feet. In a daze, she spoke to the EMTs, insisting that she ride in the ambulance with Mere.

"Ma'am, I'm sorry, we can't let you come. She's, well, there's no way to... She's already gone, ma'am."

"You can't stop now," she pleaded, sobs escaping in between her words. She put her face into Theodore's chest and then, with her hands balled into fists, hit him to get his attention.

"You must tell them to keep trying. I know there's something they can do. Please, Theodore, please make them keep trying. She doesn't deserve this. Who would do this? Tell them they can't give up, Theodore."

She stumbled again, and Theodore caught her.

Mere's head was at an odd angle, indicating a broken neck. Celeste could still see her whole face, though.

Why won't they close her eyes so she can rest in peace?

She walked closer and reached over. In doing so, she accidentally turned Mere's face. One of the cops was suddenly by her side and pulled her arm away. He scolded her for "tampering with evidence" and maneuvered her away from Mere. She jerked her arm and turned back to her friend's lifeless body. And then she noticed it.

Suddenly, she couldn't breathe, the familiar feeling of a panic attack hitting her with the force of a freight train. She collapsed, and everything faded to dark.

Hazy images swam in her mind. The recurring nightmare where Omar killed Theodore, the more abstract dreams of skulls and darkness that sometimes came with no warning.

The latest one, though rare, was the most frightening nightmare since Omar's death. Blood flowing like a river through her apartment, swallowing her and Theodore. Chaos, muffled voices again, the river of blood taking her breath away.

Mere's face. This couldn't be happening.

No, no, this is just one of your usual nightmares, all a bad dream. Wake up, Celeste, wake up so you can see it's not real.

She commanded her eyes to open, her lungs to breathe, but she felt like she was being strangled; she was not in control of her own body.

Her husband. Her husband was with her. She could feel his arms now.

"Celeste, Celly, baby, can you hear me? Baby, I'm right here. Please, please, baby, open your eyes." She heard Theodore crying out, and Poppy's voice was somewhere nearby.

But she still couldn't open her eyes, she couldn't answer them. She heard someone make a sound like a wild animal being harmed and then was surprised to realize it came from her. *I have to save Mere —I have to save her.*

She finally opened her eyes, suddenly aware once again of what was happening around her. The EMTs and cops were moving around with blank facial expressions, as though this was routine, that it was every night that one of Celeste's closest friends fell to her death.

Someone, perhaps her husband, had wrapped a blanket around Celeste's shoulders and now helped her over to one of the tables, where she plopped down.

"Ma'am, this is potentially a crime scene," a cop said to her, then to everyone, "You all need to go back up to your rooms and stay there. That's an order. We don't know what happened here yet, and we need everything to remain undisturbed."

Men in cheap suits now also milled about—homicide detectives, by the looks of them. Had they just given up? Written Mere off as being dead? But once Celeste's breathing slowed down, she realized it to be true—Mere was gone.

Forever. My friend is gone forever.

She saw then that her friends were around, all red-faced and teary-eyed like her. She took Theodore's outstretched hand and walked over to where they were gathered.

The cops were barking orders, asking if everyone was accounted for, but Celeste didn't care, couldn't be bothered to pay attention.

Mere was dead, and that was that. Celeste wanted to get away from them, the law enforcement who would tell her, "We're just doing our job," if she expressed how insensitive they were.

She stood numbly while everyone tried to grasp the right thing to say. And then they were all pushed inside, ordered to return to bed. Told to lock their doors until further notice, when the police had secured the premises and the evidence.

Somehow Theodore got Celeste back to their room, and once there, he tried to give her a glass of water. *No, no, I don't need water.*

She had to puke. She pushed him out of her way, running to the bathroom, holding her hand over her mouth. She locked the door and made it to the toilet just in time. Her body continued to heave until there was nothing left in her stomach, and then she began heaving bile.

When she finally stopped vomiting, she stood up clumsily and pulled herself up to wash her hands. The culprit that had caused her panic attack, the single diamond earring sparkling where it caught the light, sat there, mocking her, holding secrets she may never uncover—the story of her friend's death. Its mate was in one of Mere's ears, her other ear unadorned, as Celeste had discovered when she had accidentally turned Mere's face earlier. Someone was sending her a message.

Later, when Theodore fell asleep, she wept until there were no more tears. She got up quietly and retrieved her burner phone from one of her bags in the walk-in closet. She turned it on silent and unlocked it to find a single unread text message:

"Consider this a warning."

～

CELESTE WAS MELANCHOLY, feeling pain reminiscent of the days when Theodore was gone or after her parents died. The following morning, the detectives had questioned everyone who attended the party for what felt like hours, trying to uncover holes in their stories. But Celeste knew no one at that party would've hurt Meredith. She was one of their best friends, who had touched their lives in meaningful ways, every single one of them. She made everything special and beautiful, and when one was in her presence, she made it feel as if anything were possible. Celeste missed Mere in a way she could not verbalize. At the same time, she was overwhelmed with guilt. Mere's death was a warning. Directed at Celeste.

The murderer wasn't one of her friends—it was whoever had stolen Mere's earring, planted it in Celeste's room, and texted her later. Someone on the outside who had breached all their safety precautions.

Angelo was beside himself. He'd personally vetted the cater waiters, the housekeepers, the drivers. Many of them had worked at Mere's parties before, were employed by her company, and had never caused any trouble in the past. No one had been on the property who had not been cleared in advance—CCTV confirmed that.

Meredith's room had no cameras, so no one could say definitively what chain of events had led to her winding up dead beside the pool. But when the autopsy was completed weeks later, it allowed the detectives to create a theory. Meredith had toxic levels of a lethal substance in her bloodstream. A teacup on her terrace was laced with a substance that matched the poison in her body. When it took effect, she had been standing against the railing, they said, probably admiring the bright moon and clear sky, as Celeste and Theodore had on their beach walk. At that point, the drug had taken effect, and she had fallen over the side or perhaps had been pushed.

Celeste's heart dropped upon hearing the news that it was the same poison—strychnine—that she and Michel had used to get rid of Omar. Celeste had watched the drug take hold of Omar's body and witnessed his suffering. She shuddered at the thought, praying that somehow Meredith did not go through the same hell, that her friend had been unconscious before the poison did its work.

After Celeste and Theodore returned to the city, she stayed in bed for days, popping Xanax and Ambien and sitting alone in the dark. She ignored all phone calls and didn't want to see visitors. Theodore cared for her as though she were ill, and she let him. She didn't mind if he saw her fall apart—she was numb to everything going on around her. He helped her to the shower, washed and blow-dried her hair, and dressed her in pajamas. Because Celeste didn't want to see anyone, Dina, their chef, dropped off meals at the door. Celeste forced herself to eat when Theodore brought food to her, but then she would go back to sleep. The pain of Mere's passing was too much to bear when Celeste was awake.

Somewhere in her psyche, Celeste knew her sadness would subside and her wrath would surface again soon, making her strong enough to go after the person who had sent her the message. But that day hadn't come yet. It wasn't lost on Celeste that Mere had helped take care of her and dress her for Theodore's and Keith's funerals. Mere was behind Celeste's looks for every major event, celebratory or devastating. She'd been in Celeste's life for many years, embedded in all the monumental and character-shaping moments. Above and beyond the practical ways that Mere had made Celeste's life better, Celeste missed the woman who had become such a dear friend.

What compounded her guilt was the relief she felt, grateful that she'd thought fast enough to conceal the planted earring and that the police had never inquired about why Mere had been wearing only one. She hoped that meant they thought its mate had disappeared in the fall.

And then it was the day of the funeral. Patrick and Ty were grieving as much as Celeste was, she was sure, so she hadn't asked them to help her get ready.

However, they called Theodore when she didn't answer and insisted they wanted to come over beforehand—like old times, they said—claiming it would be therapeutic for all of them. She dragged herself out of bed two hours before they came, allowed Theodore to help her shower and feed her breakfast, and then greeted them at the door in her robe. They were uncharacteristically subdued, eyes as puffy as hers, energy dull. But at least they hadn't had to see what Celeste had seen. Memories of Mere's spirit and beauty would be tainted by those of her broken dead body, and Celeste wondered if she would ever be able to get the image out of her mind.

The night before, Celeste had searched for an outfit that would meet Mere's approval and, remembering how much Mere had loved Savin's mother's party attire, settled on a black Zuhair Murad minidress, embellished with crystal butterflies. Mere loved butterflies' symbolism and had persuaded Celeste to buy the dress at a trunk show, saying they represented transformation and rebirth—apropos for an event centered around Mere. Celeste repurposed a black fascinator she'd worn for a horse race the previous spring, an accessory that Mere would have liked. A lightweight silk cape paired with Alaïa black leather and PVC mules topped off the look.

It felt as though the guys had rushed to get Celeste ready because it was suddenly time to go. Her driver, Monty, was waiting outside for them in his Suburban. Celeste insisted on sitting in the front seat, and she stared out the car window while the others talked in low voices in the back. And then, much too quickly, they pulled up to the cathedral.

From the looks of it, they were on the Lower East Side. She recalled Mere mentioning that her parents lived downtown, so perhaps she'd grown up there.

But I never cared to take the time to ask her more about them. Our relationship revolved around my problems, my events, my wishes, my demands —and now I'll never have the chance to ask her anything ever again.

Celeste remembered then that Mere had been so excited about Seth and wondered if he would make an appearance. Maybe Celeste should introduce herself. If their connection was as meaningful as Mere had said, he was probably hurting as well.

Celeste went through the motions to get out of the car. Dodging photographers, she allowed Theodore to direct her inside. She followed him to where their friends were waving them over. There were so many people to push through, but finally, they were seated. Celeste pulled the lace veil down over her face and let the tears fall silently for the entire service. Theodore's ever-steady support helped her, but even with him there, she was barely hanging on. She knew this version of herself, having loved and lost one too many times, and couldn't reconcile the death in any way that made sense. Celeste prayed that her self-loathing and pity would turn into the strength she would need to find out who had stolen her friend from the world way too early.

The funeral was over before she knew it. Meredith's parents embraced her and told her how much she had meant to their daughter. They made her promise to keep in touch, and she thought afterward that maybe she had agreed to do that, but then again, maybe she had just stared blankly at them. She and Theodore joined a group of the guests for a late lunch somewhere in the Village— Celeste couldn't recall where or whether she'd eaten—and then she and Theodore were back at home.

She went to their bedroom, crawled into bed, still wearing her funeral outfit, and squeezed her eyes shut, praying for sleep. Maybe she'd never snap out of the trauma, the crippling guilt, the fear— maybe too much had happened, and maybe there was only so much one person could handle. Zari, her brother, Omar, Nico. But none of their deaths had hit her like Meredith's. It was almost like experiencing the loss of Theodore or her parents all over again.

Celeste's iPhone on the nightstand suddenly rang, startling her. She instinctively answered it because she couldn't think of another way to quiet it. Once she heard the voice on the other end, she wanted to throw her phone. She cleared her throat, hoping that would shake off the benzo effects and sober her up.

"Mizz Donovan, seems like there's a lot of death happening around you lately."

You motherfucker. "It's Celeste. Is this how you send your condolences for the loss of one of my best friends, Agent Gutiérrez?" But she knew doling out sympathy wasn't the purpose of his call.

"We've picked up some online chatter, and we think it's going to lead us to Omar's boss. I'm assuming you've arrived at the same conclusion I have: that your friend's death has something to do with Omar's untimely"—he paused for effect—"passing."

She didn't bite. "Look, I'm a basket case, grieving the loss of my brother and then, shortly after, a friend who felt like family. I don't have the energy for your games—I've barely gotten out of bed for a week. Omar's gone, and I'd like to keep him and his organization in the past."

"C'mon, *Celeste*," he said, sneering at the sound of her name, "you're fooling yourself if you think this battle was over the day Omar died. We've hit their network where it hurts—his holdings were wiped out—and if anyone decides to revisit Omar's cause of death... Well, you're in this as deeply as I am..." He stopped and took a deep breath, seemingly realizing how callous he had been.

"I'm sorry for your loss, but... No, no buts... I'm not the best at these kinds of situations... but we need you. *I* need you to pull it together. Your friends need you. The world needs you.

"With headlines like 'Murder Stuns a Sleepy Hamptons Hamlet' everywhere you turn, you know what this means, right? We're getting close to uncovering something because they're getting nervous, sloppy even," he continued. "They're out for revenge, but as with any criminal, they're bound to trip up, and when they do, we must be ready. Meredith's murder was meant to send a message to us."

Us? Because she had no energy to filter her thoughts, she replied the same thought out loud: "Us? What do you mean *us*?"

"The illuminati. We're all in this together whether you realize it or not, Celeste."

She was losing her patience with his suggestion that he was somehow affected as much as she was. "Gabe, why did you call?"

"We need to meet. Abingdon Square tomorrow. Seven a.m."

Click.

Rendezvous meetings in the early morning with a spook was not how she wanted to start her day.

Michel had called her many times, she was sure, but she wasn't ready to talk to anyone else. First and foremost, she had to narrow down who was coming for her or for everyone she knew and then figure out how to stop them. If Gabe was right—if Omar's crime syndicate's message meant she was getting close to bringing them down—then it was time to get out of bed. *Tomorrow, first thing tomorrow.*

Theodore rapped softly on the bedroom door and stuck his head in. "Hi, babe. Sav barged in and heard you on the phone. He's demanding to see you. Are you up for it? I can send him away..."

He crossed the room and sat next to her on the bed. She could tell he was worried. He wasn't around the last time she fell apart, and in fact, his disappearance caused it. But this was not back then.

Celeste sighed and threw off her covers. She owed it to Mere. "OK, can you tell him I'll be out after I've had a chance to freshen up?" Using all her strength, she stood up, then looked back at her husband. Theodore remained sitting; his brow was furrowed. Was he turning gray around his temples? She supposed things were taking a toll on him too. "I'll be OK, honey. Really. I just need some time."

She walked to the bathroom and stared at her reflection for a long time. Theodore eventually left the room and quietly closed the door. There she was, Celeste Donovan, looking radiant to the outsider, still fully made up from the funeral, with her hair in neat golden waves. But she knew to look beneath the facade.

She noted the familiar emptiness behind her eyes, creeping up as it had many times before, the darkness that her soul had experienced wreaking havoc. *Time to pull it together.* In her boudoir, she considered several outfits, appreciating the different fabrics, imagining Mere's excitement when she would rush in with a new find. Meredith always wanted Celeste in the latest couture with the best accessories. "Just because you aren't a movie star doesn't mean you can't show up looking like one," she'd say while they sipped Champagne and Celeste modeled the shopping trip goodies.

Celeste almost felt Mere's presence in that moment, saw her vibrant smile, heard her laughter echoing off the walls. How many nights had they tried on different outfits for a gala or a dinner, drinking and gossiping with Patrick and Ty? That trio had carried her when Theodore was gone, celebrated her more than anyone else, and helped her bounce back.

Her bedroom suite was probably the most intimate room in her apartment, and not just because she and Theodore slept there. *These walls know all my secrets.* Celeste realized it was where she'd stood with Mere while debating what to wear on her first date with Theodore, for a $10,000-a-plate fundraiser, or for a speaking engagement at a conference—minutiae on the surface but indicative of a deeper connection between the two women. Mere had been there for it all.

Suddenly, Celeste had to get out of the funeral dress. She felt as if she were suffocating. She tried the zipper, but it was stuck. An inexplicable panic washed over her.

"Theodore! Theodore!" she called loudly, frantically. "Theodore! THEODORE!" She sat down on the floor, where he found her when he came rushing in. She held back her tears with all she had.

"Oh. Hi." She looked up at him sheepishly, surprised he'd found her so quickly and embarrassed at her overreaction.

He took stock of the closet and, seeing nothing out of order or life-threatening, looked at her quizzically. "What's wrong, honey? I thought you'd fallen or something."

Fallen apart, maybe. She saw the concern lining his brow. "It's... sorry, I didn't mean to scare you... Oh, my zipper is stuck."

"Well, that's easy to fix."

A broken heart, not so much.

He helped her out of her dress and into the outfit she'd chosen— a neutral shift and some low espadrilles. She took extra care in looking put together, choosing some of her favorite accessories—a Fendi peekaboo bag, a tasteful chunk necklace, oversized Celine sunnies, and a light sweater tied around her shoulders. She had to convey as much normalcy as possible to Theodore and her friends, especially Savin. She'd seen Sav's fear when she'd broken down in the past, and she didn't want him sidelining her over what was coming at them because he was concerned she was on the verge of falling apart again.

Theodore stayed with Celeste and watched her but didn't attempt conversation—he seemed to know she wasn't up to small talk. She appreciated the silence while she practiced mindful breathing to calm herself. Once she was ready, he accompanied her to the living room, where Savin sat with a glass of Scotch in hand.

"Getting a head start on cocktail hour, I see," Celeste said casually. Savin turned to her. "You look like shit, Sav."

"So do you," he retorted, and they laughed together.

"Mere would be embarrassed to be seen with us in public, that's for sure." She sat down and turned to Theodore, who was still standing. "Babe, could you get me some cold Pellegrino with lime wedges?" He nodded and walked out of the room. "I've been a little heavy-handed on the sedatives, so I should probably wait a bit to start drinking," she explained to Savin.

"What are we going to do, Celly? This couldn't have been a random murder, and you know it," Savin hissed as soon as Theodore was out of earshot. First Gabe and now Savin implying that she *knew* things.

Celeste considered how to respond. She was in no state to comfort Savin or try to convince him that Meredith being killed in cold blood had nothing to do with her or with him or with the illuminati. Revenge for Omar's death was the only thing that made sense, but the anonymous text merely mentioned a warning. Was it from Omar's boss? And why now? Why at that event? *Why Mere?*

Theodore returned with Celeste's sparkling water and a glass of water for Savin. "Why don't you two enjoy the evening and take a walk? Grab a bite on a patio? Rani says you've been holed up just like Celeste has, Sav. Maybe fresh air will do you both some good."

"Yes, that's a great idea. Thanks, honey." It would let them get out of Theodore's earshot.

Savin also seemed relieved. "I could probably use some food. I'm not sure I've eaten a real meal since... that night," he admitted.

When they got to the foyer, Celeste hugged Theodore and whispered in his ear, "I promise I'll snap out of this before long."

"Take all the time you need."

Theodore patted Savin on the back and said he hoped everyone would start feeling better soon. Her husband retreated into the living room as she and Savin left.

The two friends walked in silence, wordlessly deciding to head to one of their favorite pubs, the Hudson Street Tavern. It was dimly lit, a place where they could be anonymous and no one would bother them, even with their photos in a *Page Six* spread of Mere's funeral.

The restaurant was sparsely populated, just a few men, each seated alone at the bar. No one looked up when they walked in except the owner/bartender, Winston. He nodded in recognition, at once somber. *He must've seen the news.* Winston had known them for many years and always made space for them.

When they sat down, Savin bombarded her with questions, many of the same ones she had, and many others to which she knew the answers but couldn't tell Sav. He kept speculating that it couldn't have been random and wanted her confirmation.

Oh, Sav. How could a murder at a Hamptons compound be a random act of violence? Her best friend's naivete was endearing under normal circumstances, but not when their friend's dead body was freshly buried.

He wanted to know why and how and all the things she did not feel like discussing.

"What about Omar? Did you, was it—"

Fuck. She looked at Savin pointedly, silently begging him not to finish his sentence.

He seemed to hear her thoughts because he shook his head and said, "Never mind."

"So I guess we just wait until we're convened by the illuminati ?"

"Yes, I think that's the right approach." She didn't need Savin going rogue at that moment. "We should let the detectives do their jobs and not get in the way," she fibbed.

"This isn't like when Theodore was gone, Celly. She's—we saw her... body and the mess and the sirens..."

Winston approached their table and dropped off their usual—

burgers, fries, and Scotch. He straightened and cleared his throat. "I saw the news... I'm so sorry." He got choked up a bit, then continued, "You're both like family to me and my staff, and we're hurting for you."

They thanked him for the condolences, and he went back behind the bar.

"We'll never see her again. How do we... just go into the office tomorrow as though nothing happened?"

I don't know, Savin, I really don't know. "It's going to take a while for me, for all of us, to recover from the loss and the shock. Most of our team knows... knew Meredith, so I guess we begin our staff meeting tomorrow acknowledging what happened, asking for all hands on deck this week and their understanding that this is personal for us and we'll need some time."

She remembered then Gabe's demand to meet at 7 a.m. "Why don't we have Rani send out a note that we'll begin a little later tomorrow? Let's say nine o'clock."

"OK." Savin took a theatrical deep breath, as though trying to muster up the courage to carry on. "OK, I'll ask her to do that."

They ate in silence, lost in their own thoughts. After paying the bill, Savin walked Celeste home, and they said their good nights. When she got upstairs, Theodore was not there. She retrieved her phone to call him, then saw four missed calls and some texts from about thirty minutes earlier, letting her know he was going out and would be back shortly.

Meredith wouldn't tolerate her falling apart again. When Theodore was gone, Mere had been the perfect combination of supportive friend and tough-love parent. Celeste heard Mere's lectures over and over in her mind, telling her to put the pills away, beautify her space, lean on her support system, move her body, commit to self-care—any forward momentum was better than wallowing in self-pity.

"Buy some flowers and open the drapes of this dungeon, for Chrissakes. You are Celeste Fucking Donovan. Act like it," Mere had once scolded.

A small smile crossed Celeste's lips at the memory. *Fine, I'll get it together. But only for you.*

She used the alone time to draw a hot bath with essential oils, light some candles, and turn on some ambient music, invoking Mere.

Celeste awoke early, wrapped in Theodore's embrace. She was asleep before he came home and would likely be leaving while he was still asleep. Removing the covers, she delicately shifted out of his arms and went into the bathroom. After a quick shower, she packed her gym bag and laptop, then rushed out the door.

When she spotted Gabe inside Abingdon Square, she strode over to where he was seated.

"Mizz Donovan," the agent said with a nod.

"Enough with the formalities. You certainly seemed fine dropping them last night when you were scolding me—on the day of my friend's funeral—that I needed to be more helpful to your investigation. What exactly is it that you're investigating, Gabe? How are you explaining this one to your bosses? Murder is a state crime, so why does the Suffolk County Police Department need the CIA meddling? Given that Chet's remit is US-focused, wouldn't it make more sense for him to manage this if it needs federal intervention?" Now it was her turn to sneer.

He looked sheepish. "Look, I'm more involved in this than my day job would suggest. This will be part of a federal and, most likely an international, investigation because it wasn't a random murder, and you know it. Spooks all over the world are charged with bringing down Omar's organization."

She remembered the MI6 agent at the party in Marrakech and wished for some inspiration on how to ask Gabe about it. He was still droning on.

"We don't want to tip off the small-town cops too early, lest they tamper with the evidence. If they think their excellent sleuthing will make the local evening news, they're more likely to be thorough than if they know they're handing the case over to the likes of me and Chet."

If Celeste had a time machine, she vowed, she'd return to the exact moment *before* the illuminati came into her life. From day one, it had been extremely stressful, with nothing to show in terms of accomplishing what she needed them to do. *A complete failure.* For them to use Mere's murder as part of their cat-and-mouse game with their bosses, Omar's organization, or whomever else—well, it was rich. Not to mention completely heartbreaking for Gabe to make her friend's death transactional.

"Why don't you cut to the chase and tell me what you really want, OK, Gabe? I need to get to work."

PART II

REDEMPTION

9

ENTER THE INSUFFERABLE PIG

Celeste felt as though she'd aged thirty years since the last time she'd walked through the D&C lobby to her office, yet only a week had passed. Many of the analysts were already at their desks, watching the overseas markets, identifying opportunities. She appreciated their commitment to arriving to work early and was relieved when none of them stopped her for a chat. In addition to preparing for a day of back-to-back meetings, Celeste and Savin had to be at the Feds' beck and call.

Gabe had confirmed that he and Chet needed the D&C founders for a "special project" and promised to share more later that morning. He had also let on, indirectly of course, that he was fairly certain he knew what had happened to Omar—and Nico—which Celeste would've been willing to put money on was the real reason for the clandestine meeting. She pretended not to notice his veiled threats. *You're bluffing—you have your suspicions, but linking Matthew's DNA and prints to Omar's death and destroying evidence tied to Nico will make it much more difficult for you to take me down.*

After their staff meeting, Celeste and Savin sat in the war room waiting for Gabe's call. Celeste knew she couldn't commit to too much before speaking with Michel, whom she'd been avoiding for days. Maybe she blamed Michel for the breach. He was the only one, after all, who'd known everything that had gone on. But he was the only one she could tell about the earring. Maybe she just wasn't ready to face his reaction because he would tell her all the things she didn't want to hear. Savin was unusually quiet, as lost in his thoughts as she was in hers.

Gabe's video call began ringing promptly at 10:30. His face popped up on the large screen, along with Chet's in a separate box, indicating they were calling from different places. Chet, the disheveled kid brother to Gabe in his polished attire, was the more likable one. He opened the call.

"Before we dive in, I am—we are so sorry for the loss of your friend Meredith." He paused and closed his eyes as though memorializing the moment. "What Agent Gutiérrez and I have been able to ascertain from the investigation is that her death was not accidental. Unfortunately, I also have lost a loved one and one too many colleagues to organized crime," he said, alluding to his wife's murder by one of Omar's deputies when she was trying to bust an arms-dealing ring in Miami. "As you've heard me say, since then I've made it my life's purpose to take down as many of these people as I can.

"Today I come with hat in hand, needing a favor, when anyone would understand that neither of you should be in any state to offer help after the loss you've recently suffered. But we are desperate. We believe that Meredith's death was a warning meant for the illuminati, for all of us."

Us? Their "we are one team" language is insulting.

"We are getting closer to uncovering who heads up Omar's organization."

Chet's bedside manner, as it were, seemed sincere and was certainly superior to Gabe's, but Celeste could not forget that the Feds were her adversaries if they continued to poke around Omar's overdose or Nico's disappearance. Despite Michel's optimism that they had no meaningful leads beyond Matthew taking the fall for Omar, Celeste didn't want to take any chances—the agents had the power to blow open one or both of the cases. And wouldn't an ambitious Southern District prosecutor love to take down the Ice Queen of Wall Street, as she'd been dubbed many times by the *Post*, for murder?

She kept her face neutral as the two federal agents explained what they needed from her and Savin to identify more leaders of the crime ring. "Omar's death has created a power vacuum. We think he was near the top of the chain but still answered to someone. That person must be stopped."

The American.

Gabe shared his screen in the video chat, and a hierarchy chart similar to Celeste's own grid popped up, but with a lot of names Celeste didn't recognize. Omar was near the top along with several others, all reporting up to a blank box. Matthew Duncan, the COO of TA Capital, now D&C's subsidiary, was below Omar.

Savin's energy was buzzing as he asked question after question to clarify what the Feds wanted them to do, and when the meeting was over and the video calls ended, he had more questions for Celeste. Or accusations, rather.

"Please tell me that our acquisition of TA Capital had nothing to do with *Matthew Duncan*, Celeste. Surely you wouldn't leave your business partner in the dark about something of this magnitude, right, Celeste?" Savin rarely lost his temper, but he appeared about to explode. "I think you need to tell me what the fuck is going on."

"It's hard to—"

"I'm sure I'll be able to understand it just fine," Savin interrupted, making a forward hand gesture, urging her to move the story along.

"I was acting on a hunch, Sav, and I didn't want to drag you into anything if it turned messy."

"So this was what was behind the wining and dining of Tarek and team in Dubai? You're going to sit here and insult me by suggesting that the acquisition *in and of itself* wasn't DRAGGING ME INTO IT? You acquired a *billion-dollar hedge fund* with *our* money on a *hunch* that the COO *might* be an associate of Omar's?"

"Well, not exactly—" She started to explain that she'd had more certainty that Matthew was connected to Omar, but Savin interrupted again.

"That's not true... you were as surprised as I was to see his name on that chart—that the Feds knew about his relationship to Omar. OK, so we did the deal. And then what, Celly? Let's play this one out."

"What was your plan? If Matthew hadn't been connected to all those hideous crimes, what were you going to do? Have him robbed in an alleyway? Set him up with an insider trade? Did you think about what that would mean for us, for our investors, for our employees? That scrutiny could have cost us everything."

But it didn't cost us anything except a couple hundred thousand dollars. Or a couple million. Whatever—it was still a bargain. Celeste figured it wasn't the right moment—and never would be—to mention that she had indeed framed Matthew with crimes that would hopefully result in serious prison time. The charges had given her the ability to terminate him without violating his employment agreement with TA Capital and D&C. She'd spared the firm from any reputational damage.

Savin's words were challenging her, combative. He was angry, understandably so, but there wasn't a fight in his tone. He fell silent, considering the situation.

"OK, look, I don't have the energy today for this verbal flogging that you fully deserve, and I can tell that you don't either. I'll turn the other way—for now—but I want your firm commitment that you'll work alongside me to help Chet and Gabe get justice for Mere—including what they just asked us to do. If anyone can pull it off, your lying, deceitful ass can—but I need to have faith that you're giving it your all. Otherwise, the acquisitions no longer have my support, and we may need to rethink our business arrangement."

Those were harsh words coming from her best friend. But some of it was deserved. While she'd been so busy trying to track down who was betraying her, she herself had been untrustworthy. She sighed.

"Yes, of course, I will do whatever it takes to avenge Mere's death.

Too many have gotten hurt by Omar and his kind. I'm in, Sav, of course I'm in."

Satisfied, the old Savin returned. "That's the spirit, Celly," he said encouragingly. He looked at his watch. "It's just about showtime."

The Feds had tasked the D&C financiers with using their leverage to sniff out which chip-processing company CEO was behind an illegal arms-dealing and human-trafficking ring in a small village in Central America. While the operation may have seemed insignificant in the grand scheme, Chet and Gabe had explained that the tech CEO was deeply embedded within Omar's organization—and perhaps reported directly to the American potentially leading the global network. The guns and trafficking survivors were making their way via Mexico to the US, where they would be sold to the highest bidder. It was thought that the profits were substantial and funded the entire North American operation of Omar's organization. But more importantly, the Feds believed the person running the ring was the culprit behind the suspected impending cyberattack.

The cyberattack. She'd hardly thought of it since Mere's death, but she resolved to go through with her plan. Vivienne needed a little more time to get everything in place for Celeste to be able to stop it.

Celeste had always known there were bad guys in the world. Her innocence had been stripped away when she suffered and survived unspeakable trauma at Omar's hand. He was a man who could only be described as pure evil, but even she hadn't expected the crime to be so widespread until she began working with the illuminati.

The geopolitical pendulum of history repeating itself again and again, as governments and wealthy oligarchs exerted influence over the vulnerable or nosed in where they didn't belong, made for a recipe of chaos and violence. She remembered the news coverage when Walter Radcliffe had been arrested for running a sex-trafficking ring out of India. Faces of the young girls who had been fortunate enough to be rescued. There were so many people like them suffering around the world, and Gabe and Chet thought they had the chance to put an end to some of it. She would do what they asked, and maybe it would give all the trauma some meaning—or at least a higher purpose. She was in too deep now—ending Omar's carnage was merely the beginning, not the end she had once dreamed it would be. Mere's murder was proof that this was Celeste's life now.

"Ready for this?" Savin asked, jerking Celeste back to the present.

"Do I have a choice?" Celeste replied, and Savin frowned. "Only kidding, Sav. Let's get this over with."

Savin logged in to the first of several video calls with tech companies' questionable CEOs on the firm's encrypted network. Drake Samuels's pockmarked face filled the massive screen. He had hit the jackpot by selling an app he had created in his twenties, and after living the past decade in cocaine-fueled excess, he looked much older than the thirty-two years the *Wall Street Journal* had reported him to be in a recent profile. He wore a smug expression and the cliché Palo Alto uniform—a gray hoodie and tee. Celeste guessed he was wearing some ironic sneakers. *"Dress for the job you want" really doesn't mean much to these tech bros unless they want a job where everyone looks unshowered, haggard, and homeless.*

Savin kept the line muted long enough to ask Celeste, "Remember when you slapped Drake—hard—and he stumbled backward, falling down a set of stairs in front of the assembled who's who in New York? He wound up having to walk on crutches for months! And all because his hand grazed your ass at that gala." He wore a huge grin, the first she'd seen since they found Meredith.

"He deserved it." *And Mere applauded it.* She smiled at the recollection.

"Well, well, well, if it isn't Celeste Donovan and Savin Clarke," Drake's voice boomed. "I'll admit, I was surprised to receive your call. After all, you two aren't in tech, or at least you weren't when I needed funding. Remember when I came knocking? A broke college student with a genius idea and a brilliance the world had never seen. You guys laughed me out of the room." He paused for effect, looking off into the distance.

He's outrageous.

"Of course, you wouldn't think I'd want to partner with you now, not after you so rudely passed on the opportunity and let me down in the cruelest way. And especially not after you caused me to fall down a flight of stairs and tear my ACL. I imagine you heard about my difficult recuperation?" Celeste smiled inwardly. *Vindicated.*

"No, that can't be why you're calling , so my curiosity is piqued." Drake stroked his sparse hipster beard, pretending to ponder. "Maybe you're in financial trouble. That's it! You need a loan," he said. "I heard about Omar Santos kicking the bucket. Maybe that pulled the plug on your funding stream. You're looking for someone to bankroll your flailing operation. Am I getting warmer?"

Celeste rolled her eyes. Savin elbowed her and jumped in.

"We're impressed with your expansion efforts in Central and South America. Chip-processing plants in highly populous cities with a reliable workforce and ease in transportation across the US border. We can admit when we're wrong—maybe you're a visionary after all."

Celeste always left the smoothing over to Savin. She took her cue to extract anything that could be useful to the illuminati.

"Walk us through your supply chain. We have a few clients itching to get back into tech, so we're evaluating opportunities."

"They're smart—it's heating up over here. Leave no stone unturned while you're looking across the competitive landscape. It won't take long, though, to see that my operation is the best. You'd be fools to pass on my empire a second time. Who knows—maybe you hate making money."

Drake rubbed his hands together excitedly, as though warming them over a fire, and continued, "My manufacturing originates in two small cities in Brazil. The plants are the main employers in areas where the oil and gas boom didn't... well, didn't boom. An ambitious workforce but high interest rates and a shitty economy, so they're willing to work for dirt cheap, grateful to have any job. Hence my admirable margin."

He would, of course, cut labor costs for a quick buck. He probably wasn't paying a living wage. *Ugh. You awful little shit.*

"You have my attention. Tell us more," Savin prodded. Minutes into the call, and they still had no reason to tie him to the ring.

"Brooo! I've got this *posh* condo in Polanco, the Beverly Hills of CDMX. The food scene is blowing up, and I can easily flit around the continent. The parties! Diving, good weather, the women." He made a hand gesture, outlining a curvy female figure. Savin shot Celeste a look before she could roll her eyes again.

"Oh, really?" Savin probed.

"They hear you have a forty-meter yacht and they'll suck you off right then and there, bro. It's nothing like Silicon Valley. Impeccable ass and no morals!"

Celeste planned to kick him in the nuts if she ever had the misfortune of breathing the same air as Drake, maybe even twist them off and shove them down his throat. *Insufferable pig.* She hoped he was the trafficker so he would get assaulted in prison.

Savin sensed that Celeste was about to erupt, barely holding back from telling Drake exactly what she thought of him. Aware that he needed to move faster so they could wrap up the conversation, he began firing questions at Drake about the company, his footprint in Central and South America, logistics, profit margins, and the like, hoping to get him to slip up. Celeste was grateful that she didn't have to speak.

And then her head jerked up at his next response.

"Bro, you *have to* come visit! I have a private fucking island in Belize for you if you're into diving. A sweet little villa on Lake Atitlán in Guatemala. The Mexico City spot. A beachfront chacra in Punta del Este. The real estate is sick, man, and I can really be myself around here, ya know? The US is just too high-profile these days. Cancel culture means someone's always ratting me out for something."

Gross, but he's given us something to work with—a lot of ties to the region. Now let's see if he'd ever commit treason.

Almost as if on cue, Drake began railing about US politics. The government couldn't keep telling him what to do, it was stealing his money, and don't get him started on foreign policy. He checked all the boxes of the type of guy the illuminati seemed to be looking for.

Maybe he'll end up in the prison infirmary after all.

But Celeste wasn't convinced. He seemed too naive to be part of a major crime ring. Instead of concealing information, he was handing it over.

The other calls throughout the day weren't nearly as eventful, but they did present some interesting investment opportunities. She and Savin agreed that Drake was the most likely of all the CEOs they'd spoken with to be involved with the crime syndicate.

Later, back in the war room, Chet was on the line, peppering them with questions about the call. He wanted them to recount every detail. What state of mind did Drake seem to be in? Was he angry? Were there any tells?

"What did he say about his ties to Belize? To Guatemala?"

"He confessed that he was running guns, drugs, women, and children through those countries in trucks. Wait, I have the warehouse addresses where he keeps the 'goods' around here somewhere."

"This is no time for jokes, Miss Donovan."

Celeste often asked the Feds why they didn't bug the fishing expeditions they sent her and Savin on. But she suspected she knew the reason: Chet and Gabe were running the D&C founders and their friends off book, with no official record of their activities—or the protections they'd been promised. Omar had also been run off book. *Too bad I got to him first.*

She was less concerned about her own protections, though, than for the Feds to stop Mere's murderer and disband Omar's network. She wanted her life to go back to its former simplicity so that no one else would have to experience the kind of losses her group had—and so that her chosen family could remain safe from now on.

Savin answered more of Chet's questions, and then Chet explained the distinction between FBI jurisdiction inside the US and how things worked for the bureau in other countries. Basically, the FBI could do investigations abroad if another country invited them to, or they could wait until someone committing serious crimes, such as the ones Drake was allegedly involved in, came back to the US and then make an arrest. Extradition was challenging.

"You've done great work. Now, we'll need you to be a little more involved than usual because this is a special case."

Celeste frowned. "What does that entail?"

"You're going to take Drake up on his invite—and the sooner, the better," Chet deadpanned. "We're running out of time, and we don't have anyone else to send."

"It means pack your bags, princess!" Savin joked, though he sounded nervous.

You've got *to be fucking kidding me.* "What do you want us to do, raid his compounds? We aren't exactly trained in combat." Well, she actually was being trained by Zed, but Celeste's annoyance was mounting anyway. She hadn't signed up for this. "We buried our friend twenty-four hours ago, and I, for one, am barely holding it together. You want me... us... to do what?"

"Good question. What *do* you want us to do?" Savin chimed in. "Will we be wearing wires? I've always wanted to wear a wire."

Jesus fucking Christ. Celeste shot Savin a dirty look.

"What, Celly? This is the first time since Mere died that I've really felt like I could *do* something good."

But they can't confirm Drake had anything to do with Meredith's murder.

Chet explained how it would play out in detail, down to the very day he wanted them to travel—they would leave the following day.

"This plan sounds a little too well conceived to be something you just came up with on the fly," Celeste accused. She was about to continue objecting, but then she recalled Michel's warnings that she should be careful. Maybe she needed to stay on the Feds' good side for a while until she knew what they were up to.

"My job, Miss Donovan, is to find opportunities like this to stop bad people. It would seem you'd want the same thing—or maybe you haven't suffered enough yet."

Now he's suggesting I didn't experience sufficient violence from Omar. She was fuming. *Unbelievable!* She stood up, on the verge of tears, and rubbed her wrist where Omar had broken it. The pain flared up at the thought of his name. "I've had enough—"

Savin broke in. "Chet, that was completely uncalled for. Celly knows more than anyone what these guys are capable of. She and I both want to help you handicap this organization that is spreading so much violence. But I won't tolerate you speaking to her or anyone else like that."

Chet started to object, then seemed to decide against it. His voice trembled as he continued, "My child will grow up without knowing his mother because of Omar. With Omar gone, I can't figure out why his organization is still so... obsessed with you two—there's something there, and we need to move quickly before—" He stopped himself. "That's enough for now. We'll be in touch."

CELESTE FINALLY HAD the time and mental space to connect with Michel before meeting her friends for dinner. He was overseas somewhere, so they agreed to a brief call. She left her phone, laptop, and handbag at the office and took a quick detour a few blocks away to a locker where she kept extra burner phones and other emergency items. She was always switching things up in the city to ensure she was never without a go bag. She inserted an untraceable SIM card into a burner phone and found a quiet storefront doorway to stand in, away from the city sounds.

"Yeah?" Michel said as a hello.

"It's me."

"What the fuck happened?"

Celeste remembered how unhinged he'd been in St. Louis at her brother's funeral. *But it's not like I can tell anyone else.* She dove into the story of Meredith's fall. She intended to omit the part about the earring but then decided she needed to be honest if she really wanted Michel's help in tracking down Mere's murderer.

"So what do you think?" Tears were running down her face, but she managed to keep the fact that she was crying out of her voice.

"I think you've spooked them."

"*We've* spooked them. They must not have realized we could infiltrate their coalition to pull off what we did with Omar. Maybe they think we're coming for them."

"Did you recognize any other names on the Feds' org chart?"

"Only Omar and Matthew, with an empty box at the top."

"Get your hands on it, and we can cross-reference it with what I have." *And with my own grid.*

"OK." She inhaled deeply, counted to five, and then exhaled in an attempt to calm herself. "Michel—this time is different. They've killed someone I love. After Theodore returned, I guess I thought we'd intervene before anyone else got hurt. First your daughter, and now this. We have to cut off the head of the beast—find out who's giving the orders and get rid of them. What if these are the first, not the last, attacks on our families?"

"It's possible Meredith was murdered as retribution for Omar, in which case no one close to us is safe if someone knows we were behind it. But I don't think that's what this is about."

"I don't know," Celeste said, not convinced that Mere's death was inevitable.

"This isn't our fault, Celeste. Do you hear me? For whatever reason, you got locked into Omar's mind over a decade ago. That wasn't your fault. You didn't choose to be victimized by him. Don't forget that. You survived unspeakable trauma."

"You sound like a dad."

"We've been telling our daughter the same thing."

Celeste's voice softened. "Has she recovered?"

"Physically, yes, the bruising has subsided... but she jumps at the slightest sound. She has a round-the-clock bodyguard now, but that's not how a coed wants to live. She's humiliated, on top of it all, that someone leaked photos taken at the hospital right after the attack. The whole thing is a mess."

"I'm so sorry. I know all too well what it can do to a woman. It sounds like you and your wife are saying all the right things, if that's any consolation."

They talked a bit about the Drake trip. Michel pressed her once more to get her hands on the Feds' org chart and then wrapped up the call with one final comment: "Meredith's death was a message to us all—we cannot grow complacent in the fight against this network or there will be more attacks, more bodies."

Celeste couldn't bear the thought.

"HOW'RE YOU TWO HOLDING UP?" Jack asked Celeste and Savin at dinner that night. They'd met at the bar at Le Bernardin, a Michelin three-star restaurant close to D&C in Midtown Manhattan and a place they frequented to catch up after work.

"It's so hard. I see her everywhere I turn." Celeste was trying to pretend everything was fine by doing something routine. But it was the day after Meredith's funeral and a week after finding her dead, so nothing was fine. Not only were the days difficult, but Celeste was barely sleeping. Her recurring nightmares about Omar hurting Theodore had been replaced with Mere's broken body.

"Rani's a mess," Savin said, "but she's holding it all inside. Her mother has apparently told her this means our marriage is cursed. She's bottled up so tightly—it can't be healthy."

"What a tragedy. Have you heard anything from the cops about the investigation?" Jack asked. "Do they have any ideas about who would poison Mere?"

"They haven't shared anything beyond what you already know," Savin answered. "The cameras don't show anyone on the property who wasn't supposed to be there. No one has said they saw anyone going into or out of her room. I guess they'll treat us all like suspects until they solve it."

"It sounds like a professional," Jack commented.

"Yeah, maybe," Celeste said. "It doesn't change the fact that she's gone. I'm devastated. I want to stay numb to hide the pain. But Mere would be furious at me for falling apart. When I was... when Theodore was gone, and I was basically catatonic—"

"Yes, we remember," Savin interrupted. "Please don't do that again."

"I hope my suffering didn't inconvenience you too much, Sav," Celeste said. "It is all about you, after all." They shared a brief laugh.

"Mere *saw* me, ya know?" Celeste continued. "She witnessed my suffering, held space for it for what she deemed was an appropriate amount of time, and then in true Mere form, she told me to get my ass up and quit feeling sorry for myself. So it seems like she would want us to keep moving forward. On that note, did Sav tell you he's making me go on a business trip?"

"Where we going? It's been a minute since I've joined the ol' D&C crew on a trip."

"*We* aren't going anywhere, Jack," Savin retorted. "This is one trip you can't buy your way onto. We have a bunch of stops in South America."

"C'mon, you know that's one of my favorite continents to bum around!" Jack exclaimed.

"You'll bum around just about anywhere," Celeste retorted.

"OK, so tell me. Where's it gonna be?"

"We're evaluating a deal," Savin said, "so likely Mexico City, then São Paulo and a couple of small towns outside the city, with a few minor stops in Belize, Punta del Este, and or Guatemala."

"Two of the best and some great minor stops. Perfect—I'll pop by at some point."

He did lighten things up. Maybe it would be fun to have him along. "OK, fine, Jack, we'll let you crash. But a day or two max," Celeste said firmly. "We always end up feeling like we're on day three of a bender when you're around, and we actually need to get some work accomplished."

"I knew you'd come around!" Jack retorted, laughing. "And I definitely won't get in the way. Besides, you two always find a way to blame your behavior on me, but have you ever considered that I myself am the true victim at your hands?"

Then he sobered. "In all seriousness, I'm so sorry about your family, Celly, and then both of you losing Meredith so soon after."

She changed the subject then to discuss some of their favorite restaurants they'd like to frequent in the CDMX, short for Ciudad De Mexico, or Mexico City.

"Once we firm the dates, I'll have Mere snag us some—" Celeste offered, then caught herself when she realized what she'd said. "Fuck, I've been doing this all week—expecting her to appear, swoop in, and take care of everything. I'm reminded of our inside jokes all day every day."

Tears fell without warning. She wiped them away and carried on. "She was so ingrained in every part of my day for years. And now she's... gone." She sipped her Sancerre and sniffled. "Anyway, you both already know all this."

"We're going to get through this, Cell," Savin said, placing his hand on hers.

Jack, always one to lighten the mood when things got too heavy, said, "Since I've proven in the past that I am integral to your healing —it's settled, then. I'm crashing your trip!"

Celeste flipped him off. "Your ability to make everything about you is unparalleled!"

CELESTE DID NOT WANT to go on the Latin America Drake-fact-finding journey. She wanted out—out of the entire organization that was disrupting the home life she was so desperate to cultivate, out of the darkness she'd carried for months and now years, out of the pain she'd been harboring, and out of the crosshairs of the dangerous people who'd taken her friend.

Given her challenges with packing, she realized she would eventually need to hire someone to step into Mere's role. But she couldn't bear the thought of it now. She'd power through the packing and hope that the memories weren't too overwhelming.

That night, Theodore poked his head cautiously into the boudoir, as though prepared for his wife to have another unexpected melt-down. Celeste was sitting on the floor, thinking through what to pack.

"Hi, hon. How's it going? Want some help?"

She smiled at her husband. "No, I'll be fine. Really."

"What's your itinerary, and how long will you be gone?"

"Ugh, it's going to be awful." Celeste weighed her words, careful to reveal only what was necessary.

"We leave tomorrow morning. We're flying into Mexico City and will be there for two or three days. The douchebag who heads up a tech firm arranged some meetings for us, and then we'll go check out some of the... facilities." *No need to let on it's manufacturing.*

"I honestly don't know why Savin sees a lot of promise in this deal," she continued. "Alas, he's always so receptive to my ideas, so I feel I have to give it a shot." *My ideas are good, though—better than this illuminati business forcing us to be around people like Drake.*

"Then we're going to visit some manufacturing sites. I've left it to Savin to arrange it all because I know very little about travel there. I'm making him take the reins for a change." *Best to keep my whereabouts vague.*

"I think we both know that Rani is planning the entire thing," Theodore remarked.

Celeste laughed dryly. "Exactly. She runs a tight ship and keeps all our lives in order. I suppose I should try to get a good night's sleep. I have a busy week or two ahead."

"Wait, two weeks? I thought you would be gone just a few days."

"I'm disappointed too. It's all so last-minute and chaotic."

"Why doesn't this feel like one of your normal trips?"

"Because it's not. I told you, Sav planned it and there's some time-line by which we need to close the deal, so he wants to be thorough." Celeste sighed. "I'm not happy about it, either."

"Celeste, I..." She knew what was coming even before he said it. "I know the guy snapping your photo was a paparazzo and ruled out as not dangerous. But Mexico City has one of the highest rates of kidnapping, what with the cartels and other organized crime. Both of us need security. Please take Angelo."

Imagine if he knew the truth about Paris. Angelo was no closer to finding out who had planted the explosive and listening devices; she hardly needed him tagging along and slowing her down on the fact-finding mission that could be the key to buying her freedom—an exit from the illuminati.

"No!" *Settle down.* She laughed to cover the reaction. "I meant, no, babe, that's totally unnecessary."

"Is there something you're not telling me?" He'd been hypervigilant since the weekend of Savin's engagement party—understandably so, she supposed. But he didn't know about the text message or the earring or any of the other unexplained things that had happened, and she had to keep him in the dark.

"No, darling. Savin's been quite cryptic about this deal. He asked me to 'please be flexible on timing because the payoff could be huge.' I've stopped asking questions."

"OK. It's not too late to change your mind."

"Care for a little send-off sexy time with your wife, Mr. Prescott?"

"I can't think of anything I'd rather be doing with my missus." He surprised her by picking her up and putting her over his shoulder as he made his way to their master bath. "My lady has the best ass I've ever seen," he said.

"I have quite a nice view of yours, and it's pretty fine too, my handsome man," Celeste teased over her shoulder, slapping his from her position.

Just like that, there was levity between the newlyweds again. For once, she obliged when Theodore asked her to take a night off from work to relax a little. There would be plenty of time to work on her trip. They filled their enormous tub with bubbles and enjoyed a candlelit bath over a glass of Champagne, avoiding any heavy topics.

They marveled at how well suited they were for each other and were both surprised that they enjoyed marriage so much. They contemplated where they would travel next for holiday, Theodore looking forward to Provence the following spring and Celeste to a luxury week in St. Barths. For the first time in a while, Celeste was able to enjoy the evening with her husband without a thought of what had happened or what was to come.

She would do all the things Mere would have wanted her to do after experiencing the loss of a friend.

10

"DEATH BECOMES HIM"

"Here goes nothing," Savin whispered to Celeste with a wink as the flight attendant gathered their bags. Celeste adjusted the ivory Chanel blazer she was wearing over a nude bodysuit with high-waisted tailored pants and black Manolo Blahnik mules. Savin, who was also always impeccably dressed, paired a linen blazer with jeans and ivory Ferragamo moccasins.

They had just landed at a private hangar at the Toluca International Airport in Mexico City. As the cofounders and managing directors of D&C, the two often sent lower-level staff on trips to evaluate deals. But this one had high stakes, and Savin had made sure Celeste did not forget it with a monologue on the ride to the airport that morning.

"Celly, I'm sorry the travel is an inconvenience, and I can't imagine how you must be feeling after losing your brother and Meredith so close together. But we have so much power and could stop some of these evil people from making communities across the Americas unsafe—and who knows, maybe even weaken Omar's organization.

"I won't remind you how I lived in fear as a child in Lebanon, except to point out that the war and chaos were made possible by guns being in the wrong hands.

"I hope you can look past our life and our immediate troubles to see what this means—the opportunity we've been handed to make the world a better place."

"OK, Saint Savin, I humbly bow to you as a more enlightened, more superior being. How can I ever live up to the example you've set?" Celeste replied.

"I'm only saying—after what happened to Mere and everything else you've been through, this should be vindicating." Celeste had been—and still was—skeptical that the illuminati would be effective in bringing anyone down. Ultimately, she'd done most of the work herself to date. But she hoped he was right.

Now Celeste and Savin said thanks to the flight crew and descended the plane stairs. A uniformed man with a luggage cart filled with her four trunks and Savin's one was racing to the awaiting luxury helicopter across the tarmac.

"Packing light these days, eh?" Savin joked.

Celeste shot him a dirty look. "I don't know how to do anything without Mere. I packed everything I own for Paris when she was busy with your party planning, and for this trip, I did basically the same because she... wasn't around to help me pack this time either." To avoid choking up, she turned her attention to the vulgar display of wealth in front of her. "Of course Drake has a Sikorsky." She was glad she was wearing pants as the wind created by the rotor blades sent her long hair flying behind her.

"Yes, that's the ten-seater model."

"Figures he'd drop millions on an aircraft he uses probably twice a year to distract people from how hideous his entire existence is."

"*Au contraire,* mademoiselle, I bet you a hundred grand that he regularly takes that thing to Whole Foods and the gym."

She giggled. "You're probably right."

They climbed into the helicopter, and the pilot greeted them. A voice came from the back: "If it isn't the elusive New York crowd gifting us lowly mortals with their presence."

"I hate him, and I hate you for making me do this," Celeste said through gritted teeth.

"Smile, be your wonderful, charming self, and think of the children you're saving," Savin retorted, then said loudly, "Drake, my man!"

As they got closer to the degenerate entrepreneur, Celeste could smell the Scotch and see his bloodshot eyes. She wrinkled her nose in distaste. Savin held out his hand, which Drake vigorously shook from his seated position. *If you can't show up sober, you can at least stand in the presence of greats, you disrespectful little shit.*

"Savin, bro, we're going to have the best time. The CDMX is sick!" Then he turned his gaze to Celeste. He looked her up and down and then did a once-over. After adjusting his crotch, he commented, "If you ever get tired of that husband of yours—"

"Stop right there," she scolded. "I'll never get tired of my husband, and if I did, you'd be the last—"

"Well, now that we've gotten that out of the way, let's have a seat, shall we, Celly?"

Drake was everything she had him pegged as—and worse. *No one calls it CDMX, douchebag.*

When they were buckled in and had their headsets on, the pilot described the weather and explained that their flight time would be about twenty minutes.

Drake then began his jabbering. *Fabulous, he's probably coked up too.*

"You'll be able to make yourselves at home. My staff can get you anything you need at a moment's notice, and you'll basically have the entire west wing of the penthouse to yourselves."

Settle down, guy. Like the rest of us who live in the penthouse of a high-rise, you put your pants on one leg at a time.

Celeste had no intention of staying at Drake's place, but she hadn't yet figured how she would wriggle her way out of it. She had to play nice if she wanted to be successful in taking him down.

"Oh, actually man," Savin interjected, "I forgot to mention... Celly, er, Celeste and I had already booked a couple of suites at the St. Regis before you extended your very generous offer to host us, and gosh, it's too late to cancel now."

When Drake wasn't looking, Celeste mouthed "Ohmygod, thank you," to Savin, though she should have been thanking Rani. She would've known Celeste wasn't into being a houseguest.

"Well, that's disappointing," Drake said, then paused and took a swig of Scotch. He seemed to be evaluating whether he should have an outburst or remain calm. "We'll make do. You must stay in my villa when we go to Belize, though. I insist. The area is still underdeveloped, and..."

Celeste zoned out and took inventory of the next couple of days. Drake was horrible; that much she knew. But she needed to make it a fruitful trip. Vivienne had found a way into the late Nico's devices that Celeste had had someone duplicate the night of his death.

The mysterious woman, known on the dark web as the most talented forensic scientist alive, had messaged Celeste shortly after the honeymoon with instructions on how to retrieve the files. But things had gotten complicated with the news of her family's tragic accident, and then it had slipped Celeste's mind with the barrage of events that had taken place to review what Vivienne had sent over.

Now that Celeste would have the privacy of her own hotel room, with no spouse lurking around, she could investigate what Nico had been hiding. Maybe that would inform her as to what RH Global was —or more importantly, the identity of the American thought to be the head of Omar's organization and the person behind the cyberattack the Feds were worried about. Nico could even have ties to MI6 for all she knew. Nico hadn't been on the Feds' grid, so he could have been a low-level soldier. *Probably a shitty bottom feeder—just like Drake.*

Other lingering problems that she'd been pushing off also needed to be addressed. Ace, D&C's day-one hacker and the person who had helped them out of many jams, had become an enigma lately. As a result, Celeste had lost trust in them. That didn't change the fact that members of the illuminati were sharing information with Ace.

Her plan was simple: She'd save the day by tracking down the

American and stopping the cyberattack, and then she'd would use the goodwill from preventing so much devastation as leverage to break free from the illuminati altogether.

"Earth to Celly," Savin teased, jerking Celeste out of her internal evaluation.

"How is this for to-your-door service?" Drake boasted. "We're on the helipad at the St. Regis hotel," he added, as if the others hadn't caught the context clues. "Isn't this the best way to travel? I guess for thirty million, it had better be, am I right?"

Does his blathering ever end?

Savin quickly jumped in. "Celly and I will take the afternoon to check in and get settled and then meet you later. How does that sound?"

"Perfecto, bro. I'll send you the details for dinner. Prepare to be wowed."

Under normal circumstances, Celeste would've been thrilled with a gastronome for a host. Her expectations were low with Drake, however. She suspected he'd take them to a hookah lounge with belly dancers or a strip club. After Drake's staff handed off their luggage to the hotel bellman, Celeste and Savin said their thank-yous and followed the bellman to the lobby.

"Mister Drake has taken the liberty to check you in and take care of your accommodations, Miss Donovan and Mister Clarke. Here are your room keys," he said. "The elevators are this way..."

Celeste's burner phone vibrated in her Birkin, but she could hardly pull it out in front of everyone in the lobby.

"Thank you, thank you, thank you," she said hurriedly, walking briskly toward the elevator. "Sav, I'll see you in a few hours," she called over her shoulder.

When she got into her room, she pulled out the flip phone. She scrambled the number often and regularly purchased new devices to ensure her communication was not compromised. That particular afternoon, any number of people could have been calling to update her on one of the many unknowns in her life. She reviewed the text and sighed. An anonymous sender wanted to meet her inside a local Chanel boutique before dinner. *Par for the course these days.*

Suddenly, her iPhone buzzed from inside her bag. She retrieved it and found a group WhatsApp chat with a message from Drake.

"Pujol at 7." Celeste was begrudgingly impressed. Pujol was consistently ranked as one of the world's best restaurants and sat at number five on the list that year. It was virtually impossible to get a table without booking several months in advance. Not even Meredith would have been able to score a reservation.

A glance at Google Maps on her encrypted iPad on an encrypted network revealed that Pujol was quite close to the Chanel store, which would be a good cover for her to meet the mystery sender.

She shot Savin a quick text. "Fashion emergency. Need to make a quick stop in Polanco before dinner. Will meet you at the restaurant."

"LOL no worries see you then" was his reply.

Now, what to wear? The four trunks seemed to be taunting her as if to say, "Let's see how long it will take you to find the perfect outfit." She set out to unpack.

After what seemed like an eternity, Celeste settled on a satin turquoise jumpsuit that hit at the ankle, placing her glass Amina Muaddi heels on display. The color contrasted nicely against her artificially bronzed skin. She refreshed her hair and makeup, finishing the look with a Bottega woven clutch.

Perfectly festive, Mere. I hope you like it.

"YOU'RE ON THE RIGHT TRACK" came a voice from behind. Celeste startled a bit, then resumed her handbag browsing in the Chanel boutique without looking back. She knew the person wouldn't want to be identified and was likely in disguise anyway.

"Is that so?"

"Gutiérrez wants you to clone Drake's phone tonight. He indicated you've successfully pulled this sort of thing off before."

Well, at least my stellar reputation precedes me.

"All evidence points to Drake as the perp. If you get us what we need, you can cut this little fact-finding mission short and get back to your husband."

There it was. That forever suggestion that the only thing a woman would have to get back to was being a wife. Other things were different too, now that she was married. Women seemed more comfortable around (or rather, less threatened by) Celeste, and men, with the exception of those like Drake, were less awful, at least overtly.

"Fine. Where's the—" She'd brought her own equipment to snoop into Drake's systems, but it was better to use the Feds' system.

"It's already in your bag. We'll be in touch tomorrow morning." The person then disappeared.

The sales associates were busy with other customers or engrossed in whatever they were watching on their phones. When Celeste was convinced that no one had paid attention to her exchange, she nonchalantly felt around in her bag. To her surprise, there was a box in there about the size of a phone. Interactions of that nature had become commonplace for Celeste, but it never ceased to amaze her how much of what was happening all around her she had missed before she was on the inside. *I'll be damned.* She hadn't even felt the stranger reach into her bag.

So Gabe had someone—or maybe several people—following her. It might have made her feel safe, but she knew better than to trust others with her safety. The best thing she had going for her was Zed's advanced hand-to-hand combat training. He took her outside her comfort zone, and sometimes she even ended up with bruising after they sparred. Since her husband didn't know about Zed, she'd gotten into the habit of concealing her bruises with makeup. It was worth it, though, to know that she wasn't defenseless, that she navigated the world as more than a little woman relying on men to protect her.

Through minimal interaction with a sales associate, she purchased a small flap bag from the new collection (black-and-white tweed with a lambskin top handle) that would make her detour believable. The restaurant was nearby, and to allay her husband's concerns about recent reports of Americans being kidnapped via taxis and Ubers in Central America, she decided to walk the twelve minutes there, since it was still light out.

She followed her phone's map directions to a quaint residential Polanco street and made her way through a lush green courtyard to the restaurant. There was a line waiting outside, but she circumvented it and went straight in. *Drake had better not think I'd be OK with standing in line.*

The Pujol lobby was posh yet accessible. Its modern, clean aesthetic and ample large windows gave it an indoor-outdoor feel, and its open space relayed a sense of calm. It reminded her of an upscale Cosme, its sister restaurant in New York (though it was much easier to score a table at the Manhattan outpost). She was the first to arrive, according to the hostess with whom she'd checked in, who was about Celeste's five-foot, ten-inch stature. A natural beauty, the woman had thick, almost-black hair, olive skin, and the collagen of a twenty-two-year-old. She was wearing a black cocktail dress and striking heels, similar to Celeste's Amina Muaddi glass ones.

Celeste smiled warmly and asked, "Could I trouble you to hold this bag in your coat closet while we dine? I couldn't help myself—had to do a little shopping."

"It is very understandable," the woman said with a laugh and a heavy Spanish accent.

Just then, like the ominous dark cloud that he was, Drake descended upon the restaurant, and immediately the carefree vibe shifted.

"Camila, my, my. You're looking delectable today."

It was clear that Camila was as turned off by Drake as Celeste was.

"Ugh, Drake, that's enough. You are *such* a pig," Celeste scoffed. "Camila, I'm so sorry about my... colleague."

"She likes the attention, don't you, Camila?"

And then what would have been unimaginable to Celeste—had she not witnessed it with her own eyes—happened.

Drake went around the hostess stand and slapped Camila on the

behind, then slung an arm around her shoulders, almost impercep-
tibly fingering one of her nipples. The young woman looked morti-
fied and increasingly uncomfortable.

Celeste erupted. "Get your hands off her, Drake," she said
through clenched teeth.

Drake made no move to step away from Camila.

Celeste looked around wildly but saw no employees close by to
intervene.

The fear and shame in Camila's eyes told Celeste that it wasn't the
first time she'd been manhandled.

Celeste grabbed Drake by the back of his shirt, dragging him
away from Camila, and pulled him off to the side in a shadowed area.

He was surprisingly light, or maybe she was simply accustomed
to a more muscled, well-built opponent.

She turned him to face her.

"What're you going to do, Celeste? Slap me for a little ass grabbing? She deserves it for dressing like the whore that she is."

He was smug, arrogant, a cancer of humanity.

Instinct took over.

Without making a conscious decision to do so, she kicked him in
the knee, distracting him from what would come next.

Grabbing a handful of his hair to pull his crouching body up to
standing, she punched him in the solar plexus in his middle
abdomen, which she recalled Zed instructing would knock the wind
out of anyone.

Finally, she brought her knee up and landed it in his crotch with
all the force she had.

The man stumbled and tripped over himself, falling onto the
ground with a thud.

It took her a moment to process the scene: Drake held his crotch
with both hands and appeared to be sobbing.

"Get up," Celeste growled.

She looked around to see if anyone was the wiser. Miraculously,
no one besides Camila seemed to have noticed.

"Get. Up. You. Bottom-feeding. Piece. Of. Shit."

"What the fuck is wrong with you? You'll never get away with acting like this, you stupid cunt," Drake snarled.

"Name-calling while you're the one on the ground is brazen even for you," Celeste said. But he knew that there wasn't much more she could do—at least not physically—without drawing attention to them.

At that moment, Savin appeared in front of them. "What's going on here?" he asked and chuckled nervously. Celeste could read the confusion—or was it shock?—on his face.

"Sav, come join our little conversation. Drake and I had a small disagreement a few minutes ago, but we've sorted it out now, haven't we, Drake?"

Savin's arrival jarred Drake out of his self-pity. He grunted softly and winced in pain as he slowly stood up. He straightened his shirt and blazer.

"Yes, yes, of course, a small misunderstanding," Drake said, nodding vigorously. "All is well now. Let's make our way to dinner, shall we?"

As they moved back toward the host stand, a wide-eyed Camila was fighting a satisfied smile that tugged at the corners of her mouth.

"Camila, could you kindly escort us to our table? Let's have a seat and taste Central America's finest, shall we?" Drake said. If he was embarrassed that Camila had seen the exchange, he did not let on.

A uniformed young man in a white dress shirt and black pants approached them then, welcoming them to dinner and informing them that their table was ready. Drake gestured for Celeste and Savin to walk in front of him. As they followed the server to a table in the middle of the room, Drake whispered smugly in Celeste's ear, "You're lucky I'm not the type to press charges."

"You're lucky I don't call the cops myself—or better yet, rip your disgusting dick off and shove it down your throat, you scumbag," Celeste murmured back while smiling pleasantly for the sake of the other diners. "Do not ever get this close to me again, and don't ever lay a hand on Camila—or *any* woman, for that matter—again. Understand?"

He pretended to be chivalrous as he pulled out Celeste's chair for her.

You can put lipstick on a pig... but it's still a pig.

Celeste didn't like resorting to violence, yet she felt vindicated because he was so repulsive—and admittedly, she had a short fuse when confronted with predatory men. It was the second time she'd put Drake in his place—and she didn't regret it one bit.

Even though dinner had begun on a rather unpleasant note, the meal at Pujol was better than the reviews promised. The amuse-bouche and elote, cleverly framed as street snacks, constituted the first course. Then came the chicatana ants that Chef Olvera was known for. She had to admit that although the idea of eating ants seemed unappetizing, they were delicious.

A fun interpretation of Mexican street food, the tlayudas, came in the form of a velvety black bean puree that was delightful. But the crescendo of the meal was the famous mole, which was actually two moles—one aged for several years and one made that day. Celeste's anger dissipated while she sipped her ginger margaritas, course after course, and let Savin lead the conversation.

He was masterful at getting Drake to talk. Drake boasted about—well, boasted about everything—and loved the audience. Celeste paid attention but didn't contribute much, though she noted he did not say anything insulting or derogatory about women.

Not that she'd needed any further convincing, but she would destroy him, and with pleasure. The world was full of too many men like him and had too few people willing to do something about it. If the Feds didn't find anything on him, she'd get creative.

She contemplated the best way to clone his phone. One method was an old-school trick she and Savin had once used: get Drake liquored up and, while he was passed out, copy the phone's data using the SIM card–cloning tool the person at Chanel had dropped into her bag. Another would require her to spend less time with him and involved her snatching his phone quickly, without raising suspicion, and installing a cloning app that would share his every keystroke with whoever received the intel.

While she was figuring out the best way to get what she wanted, Savin was extracting information about the locations of Drake's properties, his offices, who managed his firms, and where the manufacturing sites were. Drake was still giving up the information pretty freely, which would be unusual for a man hiding something as disturbing and illegal as arms or sex trafficking. *But maybe he's arrogant enough to believe he's invincible.*

It was also clear that he was not *the* American—he was not sophisticated enough to be the head of Omar's gang—but he could still lead her to the right person.

After a delectable dessert, Celeste noticed that Drake was very intoxicated. She gave Savin a look, which he correctly interpreted to mean that they needed to keep their host out a little longer.

"Whaddya say we take this party somewhere, uh, a little less sterile?" Savin suggested.

Drake signaled for the check and ceremoniously pulled out his black card. "This one's on me tonight. Despite my wounded ego, it's been amazing to hang out with legends. And I'm confident you're going to love what I've been up to."

Once he had settled the tab, the three made their way to the front of the restaurant, where Camila was still working. Celeste made eye contact with her and nodded with a smile.

"Oh, your prize! Let me get it for you." Camila briskly walked over to the coatroom and disappeared inside. She came out seconds later with the Chanel shopping bag and handed it to Celeste.

"Oh, Christ, of course you found a Chanel boutique. Tell me, have you ever returned from a trip and *not* brought home a handbag?" Savin remarked, laughing.

Celeste shrugged. Savin was spot on—she did have a rather large collection.

In a plot twist she hadn't expected, Drake approached Camila and said quietly, "I was a jerk earlier. I had time to think about it over dinner, and I didn't... I didn't mean to make you uncomfortable. I deserved what happened."

Camila, carrying herself with more confidence than earlier in the evening, didn't immediately give Drake what he wanted—to be placated and told that his bad behavior was OK.

"I hope that you never *ever* think it's OK to treat a woman like that again, and next time, I will make sure you end up in handcuffs," she said haughtily. She caught Celeste's eye and winked.

Celeste knew her little incident had empowered Camila in a way that little else would. What she would've given to have had someone like herself around when she was younger.

OUT ON THE STREET, Drake rambled on about a bar he was sure Celeste would love.

"It's ranked number six in the world. Licoreria Limantour, it's called. It's only about twenty minutes away."

Knowing there was zero chance Celeste would sign up to spend that much time with Drake in a car, Savin insisted that they go to the lounge across the street, which he said looked nice enough.

"Oh, yes, this looks perfect!" Celeste said with fake enthusiasm. She noticed Drake was limping a bit.

"I guess I have to do what she says from now on, or she'll hit me again," Drake said to no one in particular.

Savin looked at Celeste quizzically, still unsure of what had happened earlier, and she mouthed "Later" to him.

Drake began babbling about how excited he was to work with D&C and said he couldn't wait to show them "behind the curtain."

"But you gotta tell this one she can't tattle on me," Drake slurred to Savin. "I'm making loads of money just pushing the boundaries a little. Nothing major."

Celeste and Savin locked eyes. *This is going to be a long trip.* Celeste had no interest in learning what Drake kept behind anything.

Drunk locals and tourists alike milled about the lively neighborhood as the three made their way to the bar. Once inside, Savin requested a table for the group, and the host led them to a corner.

"Best seat in the house for these VIPs, thanks!" Drake exclaimed.

He retrieved his money clip, extracted a $50 bill, and handed it to the employee. *At least make it worth his while, cheap ass.*

"Shots, let's take shots," Celeste said. She waved over a server and asked for "three shots of your finest reposado tequila." She was getting tired but still had to take care of the phone, so she needed Drake to let his defenses down a little more. In no time, three full shot glasses were on the table.

"Ooh, what's that saying? Tequila is always a good idea," Drake mumbled and slammed back his shot.

Celeste encouraged him to take hers. "I insist, so that we can bury the hatchet," she claimed. He shrugged and tipped the second one back, swallowing it in one gulp.

"Invigorating, isn't it?" Drake said. Celeste was eyeing his phone on the table.

After feeding him two more shots, she waited until he was slumped over and then touched his hand. He didn't stir. She snatched the phone and used his thumb to unlock it. *It doesn't fit in my fucking clutch.* Then she remembered she had pockets and slid it in there.

"I need to use the ladies' room and freshen up a bit," Celeste said, excusing herself.

Savin took notice of the entire scene but didn't say anything. He nodded and starting scrolling on his phone.

"Watch him—you got it? Don't let him leave."

In the ladies' room, she entered the stall on the far end. It took her less than two minutes to download the app that would allow his phone to be monitored. She could move efficiently because she'd already set up the profile in her hotel room, based on the instructions from the mystery person in Chanel.

At dinner, she'd also found another app to upload his existing phone data, including emails and texts, on the dark web.

Voilà! I am a genius.

Back at the table, Drake was still out of it. Celeste discreetly removed the phone from her pocket and set it back on the table. She gave Savin a thumbs-up.

"I guess I'll be the one to get him back to his condo," Savin offered without enthusiasm.

Celeste nodded right away. She waved over one of the servers and requested an espresso and water for "our friend."

"Drake, my man, it's time to get to bed," Savin said loudly. "Come on, snap out of it."

Drake awoke as though it had been an extended slumber. "How long was I out?"

"Not long enough," Celeste remarked wryly.

"Not long *at all*, she means," Savin corrected.

Drake downed his espresso and water, then started his incessant chatter once more. *The man does not know the meaning of the word "moderation."*

He stood up and began to move, as though swaying to the music. His rhythm was terrible, and he could barely hold his weight up. She was sure he would have a bruise the next morning. But he was smiling.

Until he wasn't.

Suddenly, Drake collapsed on the floor and began seizing for a moment. His body went limp.

Celeste and Savin looked at each other, then Savin scrambled to Drake's side. He felt around on the unresponsive man's neck and grabbed his wrist, searching for a pulse.

Savin looked at Celeste and whispered, "Celly, I think he's dead."

Celeste's iPhone vibrated then. Without thinking, she retrieved it and swiped the screen to answer.

"Do you mind telling me what the fuck is going on?" an angry voice on the other end scolded.

"You're going to have to be a little more specific," Celeste replied. Her eyes wandered across the lively bar.

The crowd was oblivious to Savin kneeling on the ground, administering mouth-to-mouth to Drake, who was still unresponsive. She hoped her life never depended on Savin's CPR skills.

I guess I'm going to have to save this fucker. "Hang on, I'll call you right back."

She walked briskly to the bar and flagged over a man in a suit who was the most professional looking of all the employees. She must have looked panicked because he rushed to her side.

"How can I help you, Senorita?"

"Can you call an ambulance? That man with us collapsed and doesn't seem to be breathing."

His jaw dropped when he saw Savin pumping Drake's chest. "Yes, yes, of course." He scurried away with appropriate urgency.

Others were beginning to notice, and a woman claiming to be a physician moved in on the situation. Celeste stayed on the periphery, observing from afar while the woman began administering what looked to be a more effective version of Savin's CPR.

Within seconds, it seemed that Drake was breathing again.

Celeste took that as her cue to walk outside for some air.

Tennyson Boulevard was bustling at that hour. Giggling bargoers stepped aside as an ambulance arrived at the lounge. Two uniformed men, presumably EMTs, got out of the vehicle with a stretcher and moved quickly inside.

It was time to call Michel back, but Celeste wasn't in the mood. Her instincts had told her that the Drake trip was a bad idea, and in mere hours, it had proven so in spades.

At least I got what I came for—hopefully.

The doors opened, and the EMTs exited pushing a stretcher on which was a prone Drake wearing an oxygen mask. He still appeared to be unconscious. Savin followed close behind, carrying her shopping bag. He was visibly shaken.

"Shall I call our car to take us back to the hotel?" Celeste inquired.

"Celly, a man we spent the entire evening with almost died, and you're completely unruffled."

"Sav, one of our best friends was brutally murdered, and you expect me to care about this piece of shit?"

Does he expect me to pretend I'm sad or—?

"Perhaps death becomes him, Sav, I don't know. If you hadn't noticed, I wasn't particularly fond of the side of himself he'd chosen to reveal to us. Are you suggesting we have another drink to relax a little?"

Savin sighed. "No, let's just go back."

Celeste texted the driver they'd hired for their time in the city, who promptly arrived in his Suburban.

"Here's your stuff," Savin said, shoving the shopping bag in her direction and then walking around to the other side of the SUV to climb in.

"Gee, thanks for the gentle handoff," Celeste said and accepted the driver's outstretched hand for assistance, getting in next to Savin and buckling her seat belt.

"You completely checked out, leaving me to manage Drake. I could've used a little help back there."

She frowned. "Why is it my job to save his life? Don't forget the reason for our trip, Savin. He's suspected to be running—" She remembered the driver and found the button to put up the privacy partition. "They think he's trafficking young girls and firearms, Sav. He's hardly a good guy. Even if he's not involved in that illegal activity, he all but told us he's comfortable breaking the law. Besides, the world would be a better place without him in it. I assumed it was his karma catching up to him."

"I don't get how you can be so blasé about this, Celly. Did you... no, you wouldn't." He looked at her suspiciously, then lowered his voice to a dramatic whisper. "Did you poison him, Celeste?"

Whoa, using my full name and everything.

"No, of course not!" *Wish I would've thought of it, though.* She sighed. "I'm sorry I didn't help you back there. I don't know CPR."

A lie. *But I certainly wasn't about to save him, anyway.*

She had a realization. "If he's out of commission, we'll probably need to cut our trip short, right? It's pretty much been a doozie up until now."

Sav rolled his eyes. "Do you ever stop thinking of yourself, Celeste?"

He'd used her full name twice in as many minutes, so Celeste decided to back off a little. That meant he was serious—and seriously frustrated with her.

"OK, I'm sorry. You know how uncomfortable I get around... feelings... and emergencies." *May as well pull the card.* "With my brother's funeral and Meredith dying and all, I just... freaked out."

Savin shook his head sympathetically. "No, no, it's OK. I get it. And I don't know what happens with our, uh, investigation. I guess we wait to hear from Gutiérrez?"

"Hmm, OK. Let's get some sleep and call him in the morning."

"I'm pretty sure I have no idea how to give CPR, by the way," Savin confessed.

"Yes, I could see that. I made a mental note to never need it when you're around."

The two laughed a little.

"Drake *is* a huge asshole, even if he's not the guy Gabe is looking for. What did I miss by walking into dinner late?"

"He made some gross remark to the hostess, Camila, and then... I'm not sure if I can even say it out loud."

She replayed it in her mind and recoiled.

"It's... I was... it was just so shocking. He slapped her on the ass. Hard. In the middle of one of the most phenomenal restaurants in the world, while people were dining, he assaulted the hostess."

She shuddered. "Then it got worse. He put his arm around her and grabbed her breast. She was so uncomfortable, and my heart was breaking for her.

"So I did what any normal person would do and dragged him into the corner and kicked him in the nuts. *Hard.*" Celeste smiled in satisfaction. Zed's training was certainly worth it.

Manners and decorum were vital to both Celeste and Savin. Her best friend looked as horrified as she'd felt in the moment.

"My God, what a piece of work," Savin remarked. "What have the Feds gotten us into?"

Vindicated. At least Savin could finally see that the Feds were using the other members in the illuminati as pawns in some game where she and her friends couldn't see the entire chessboard or anticipate the next moves.

"We're supposed to be avenging Mere's death and bringing down Omar's network," he continued, "not saving scumbags from OD'ing."

Celeste nodded in agreement.

Back at the hotel, it took everything she had not to pack up and charter a flight home then and there. *I need to get the fuck out of here.* But she knew she had to stay put. It wasn't time to make waves. Too much had happened lately, and she couldn't put herself and Theodore at risk. Also, she *did* want to stop whoever was behind the trafficking.

The hotel bathroom was modern and spacious. Her skincare products and makeup were organized on the countertop in neat rows by order of application—Mere had taught her that trick for travel. "If staying in a hotel for more than one night, it's good for the mind-body to be organized," Mere would say after she'd gotten all of Celeste's things in perfect order. Mere made every situation sparkle.

Celeste put on her cloth headband and washed her face. What had happened in the bar? So many unanswered questions. Was Savin right? Had someone poisoned Drake? Did that prove his innocence—or his guilt? When was Gabe going to be in touch with further instructions?

Her phone rang from the bedroom. She went in and answered.

"Tell me what I heard isn't true," Michel barked into the phone.

"Well, I can hardly answer that without you telling me what you heard?"

"This isn't the time for jokes. Did you really assault that guy in front of a restaurant full of witnesses and then poison him?"

"Why does everyone keep asking me that?"

"Because you have been completely—"

Oh, fuck you.

"Don't you dare finish that sentence," she interrupted. "If either of us is unhinged lately, it's you. Besides, I didn't poison anyone.

"Why are you having me followed anyway? And why didn't your guy step in and beat the shit out of him? He's an asshole."

"It sounds like you took care of that just fine on your own."

"Why, thank you very much," she said sarcastically. "That may be the best compliment I've received all day... and of course, I've received *many*."

"Asshole or not, you need to keep your head down and your powder dry. For one thing, you're in danger, or did it slip your mind? And did you also forget that you and I both are connected to *two* recent newsworthy murders and you and your friends to a third?"

"Of course I didn't *forget*, Michel," Celeste replied, exasperated.

"Then why are you assaulting people in public and disappearing when they are poisoned?"

"How do you know he was poisoned? That's what Savin said too."

"Look, I'm sorry you're grieving. But please get back into the shadows. Right fucking now. I'm still trying to figure out how we get the Feds to stop hassling you about Omar. You making headlines for beating up some tech bro and being sentenced to ten years in a Mexican prison won't be helpful."

"Oh, Sav is calling. Gotta run," she fibbed. "Talk to you later." *He's so fucking moody.*

She dialed her husband.

"Hello, my beautiful wife. I wondered if I'd hear from you tonight. How's Polanco treating you?"

"It's a gorgeous neighborhood, and the food at Pujol was to die for! We must come here together someday. You'll love it."

"I'm in. Anything exciting happen today?"

"I did snag a quilted Chanel bag I haven't been able to find in the States. Does that count?"

Theodore laughed. It was her favorite sound. "What are you guys thinking about the deal? It must be pretty big if you aren't sending others for the site visits."

"We're still evaluating. There's a lot to consider," she said truthfully. "This deal is potentially game-changing—would get us squarely into tech—so it felt right to come. Plus, we have that property development company down here, and we rarely visit any of the projects."

"Darling, you're so humble. You're investing in infrastructure in destitute areas to bring desperately needed jobs and resources to communities, not building Walmarts."

"I'm certainly no saint, but thank you for your spin." What Theodore said was true, though. She and Savin *did* invest significant resources into key communities around the globe through D&C Philanthropies. Her star employee, Lorraine, was doing incredible things. The accolades D&C received in the media for the programming was priceless. "Perhaps the Only Hedge Fund with a Conscience" was Celeste's favorite headline.

"We should continue to legitimize our involvement so we stay in everyone's good favor. I love you and miss being home with you," she added. It was true. She loved their mundane day-to-day, juggling work and relationship, each night in bed together recounting what had happened that day (well, not everything—she still kept more secrets from Theodore than she cared to admit). She hadn't ever realized domestic life was for her until him.

"Miss and love you too. Dream of us," Theodore said.

After the call, Celeste changed into an ivory silk nightgown and slipped into bed. It was still hard to believe that Drake had collapsed at the bar. Something hadn't been sitting well with Celeste. It felt... orchestrated. She'd have to wait to see how the next day unfolded.

AFTER A QUICK WORKOUT the next morning, she showered, styled her hair, and applied makeup. She decided on a silk lace cami, tailored black trousers, and a black calfskin Alaïa belt. She rummaged through the shopping bag and retrieved the Chanel box. Carefully removing the ribbon, she lifted the lid and set it aside. There in the tissue paper lay the tweed flap bag. It was beautiful indeed.

Mere would've loved this bag. She unfastened the clasp and removed the tissue paper inside—to find a flash drive in the bottom of the bag. *What the fuck?*

The nameless, faceless people of the dark web moved through the world as though concealed by invisibility cloaks. She hadn't remembered anyone dropping anything in her shopping bag, but then again, she'd left it unattended for long stretches the night before.

But the box was tied with ribbon. It had to be someone at the Chanel boutique *after* she'd purchased the bag. *No one knew I was going there except... except for the people who are always lurking.* Maybe she would never know the identity of the people meddling in her life.

Curiosity got the better of her. She had only a few more minutes until she was due to meet Savin, so she scrambled to set up her secure laptop. Once it powered on, she plugged the flash drive into the external USB port and waited for what felt like twenty minutes (but was merely a few seconds) to see what was on it.

So much of her secret life was spent combing through documents never intended for her eyes. It was no different that morning. The sender had gifted her the contents of Omar's computer and cell phone, and it was just as she had suspected. She scrolled through WhatsApp messages exchanged between him and others mere days before her wedding.

Of course, most of their correspondence was in code, but some words stood out. Texts like "What's the size of the delivery?" and "Younger this time, right?" gave Celeste the chills, imagining young girls around the world mistreated, kidnapped, and sold to the highest bidder. Knowing Omar had been protected as an asset and seeing the cold, hard evidence of his wrongdoing again—Celeste was convinced he never would've been brought to justice if she hadn't dropped the hammer herself.

Omar's files had been confiscated in the past and could've been used to incriminate him for his evils. But the US government had instead protected him. Now she saw things in a new light. She no longer had to worry about Omar. She could concentrate on uncovering the identity of the head of the entire crime network and turning that person over to the Feds, and at the same time, she could prevent the cyberattack (assuming the Feds were right that the American was behind it). *And I can get away from this asshole Drake, go home, and leverage my brilliant sleuthing and luck to finally break free from the illuminati!* It was a win all the way around.

The phone numbers and email addresses from Omar's business associates would be difficult to trace because they were using burners and dummy accounts. But she had access to the best on the dark web who might be able to dig up more information—which of his contacts were still alive, where they were located, their financials. She had faith that her hackers would be able to shed some light on the identities of the hideous criminals on the other end of Omar's messages. She could save the day and then go back to some semblance of her old life.

She remembered Michel's request that she get her hands on the Feds' org chart, and now it would be even more helpful because she could cross-reference the contact information with the names Chet and Gabe had. The faster she uncovered the identity of Omar's boss, the sooner she'd be able to prevent the cyberattack.

One thing was for sure: Whoever had sneaked the flash drive into the Chanel handbag wanted her to be the person who received the credit for identifying the American. She wondered who it was. Would she also find proof that the US government had knowingly protected someone like Omar? That could be helpful in the future if the Feds ever crossed her. She could barely comprehend the magnitude of what having these files could mean.

She scoured more of the information. It didn't seem to implicate Drake in any way, and Omar was already gone, so the sole purpose must've been for her to uncover the head of Omar's organization.

Wait a minute.

And then she knew what else they'd wanted her to see. There it was. "She apparently goes by the code name 'Ace,'" taunted a text. *She?* Was this the first real evidence of Ace's identity? Celeste had long since stopped trusting Ace, but what was the overlap with Omar and his crowd?

Time to go. Damn. She shut down her laptop and shoved it and the drive into the safe. If they were stolen, it didn't matter because she'd already uploaded the contents to her online file storage.

Then she stepped into her Prada red patent leather heels, donned her black Balmain blazer, and switched her handbag contents to her new bag.

Savin sat in the hotel restaurant with a *Wall Street Journal*, an espresso, and some uneaten scrambled eggs. When he heard her approaching, he lowered the paper and looked over to confirm it was her, then folded the paper.

"Well, well, well, if it isn't the femme fatale in the flesh," Savin said with a slight grin.

"Fuck you, I didn't kill anyone." *Well, not Drake at least.* Celeste signaled the server and ordered green tea, poached eggs, toast, and fruit.

Celeste's burner phone vibrated. She pulled it out discreetly and looked at the caller ID. "Gutiérrez," she said to Savin and answered the call. "We're in a restaurant. Can I call you back?"

"No need. I'm sending an address. You and Savin will have your driver drop you there in an hour and then wait for instructions." The line went dead.

Fucking CIA Gabe. Celeste messaged their driver that they would soon be ready for pickup and looked at Savin's expectant face. Before she could speak, a food runner dropped off her breakfast and tea and scurried away.

"Wow, they're quite efficient here." She took a bite of fruit. Nothing on the trip was adding up. "So he asked us to go somewhere. Well, demanded it really," Celeste said. "Do you think he's in Mexico? I didn't even consider it, did you?"

"Nope," Savin replied.

The two lowered their heads together while they ate and tried to think through what could be going on. Why send them if he was already down there? Why risk being spotted with them? Celeste's life was nothing more than an endless list of unanswered questions.

They settled their tab and left the hotel through the front entrance, where their car waited. Their driver, a severe-looking man who wore sunglasses, a frown, and all-black attire, seemed to have no interest in getting to know them. Even though he properly held the back door open for Celeste, he had none of the warmth of Monty, their regular driver in New York. She wasn't even sure if it was the same guy from the previous day.

"Mexico City is so much more cosmopolitan than I expected," Celeste commented, as she watched the scenery whiz by outside her window. Beautiful shopping malls and high-rises turned into cathedrals and then into manicured suburban neighborhoods.

"Yeah, I'm glad we made it down here, even if it's not the most exciting of trips."

"I thought you liked this spy life," Celeste teased, though gently. She could tell Savin was still upset about Drake's collapse.

"A little too much excitement for me last night. After seeing Mere's... I mean, that still feels like yesterday, and then that asshole not responding to CPR. I talked to Rani into the wee hours. She cheered me up."

"It was strange," Celeste admitted.

The Suburban slowed into what appeared to be a warehouse parking lot. Savin looked a little concerned. "What the..." He trailed off.

"I'm sure it's fine. Gabe would never lead us astray." She laughed at her own sarcasm.

Suddenly, the driver hit the brakes and put the car in park. "They're requiring that you be blindfolded," he explained. "It's too late to get out of this now, so you'll need to cooperate."

With that, he hopped out of the vehicle and opened Savin's door. His tone left Celeste convinced there were people with guns somewhere nearby.

"Put your hands behind your back," the man ordered. Savin did as he was told. The man quickly bound Savin's hands, pulled him out, and pushed him to sit on the ground. Next, he came to Celeste's side. She held her wrists out behind her. She'd had enough training to recognize when they were beat. He tied the rope tightly enough to ensure she had burns, then roughly pulled her out of the car and walked her around the car to be seated next to Savin on the concrete. *Asshole.*

Savin was frightened. Celeste forgot sometimes that he hadn't been through all that she had.

While the driver piddled around in the back, Celeste tried to lighten the mood.

"Aw, is this your first kidnapping?" she quietly teased. "Cute!"

Her friend gave a slight smile but didn't laugh.

"It's going to be fine. Gabe has too much vested in us to lead us astray."

"Unless he means to off us, Celeste," Savin hissed.

There was the Savin she knew and loved. Always worried, often hysterical.

"And here I thought you'd switched personalities for good and were going to be happy all the time, now that Rani agreed to get hitched. So nice to see the old spaz is back."

Whatever the man was doing, he was taking an awfully long time. Celeste knew she needed to keep Savin calm. And herself as well. But she found solace in knowing that she could wriggle her way out of the rope if necessary, that she was now trained in street fighting, and that it seemed unlikely Gabe would set them up.

The man returned and pulled them to standing. He put black potato-sack-like bags over their heads. "Stay put and don't try anything stupid," he growled. The next thing they heard was the Suburban speeding away, tires squealing.

Oh, for fuck's sake.

"Celly, what now? You've surely heard about the kidnappings of Americans down here. Maybe they've been following us since we arrived. We're too flashy, with my Patek and that rock on your hand. We're obviously targets."

"Sav, settle down." Celeste was pissed that her bag had been left in the car with her voice memo recording. She was quite proud she'd thought quickly enough to activate it. *Oh well.*

Then she heard a car turn into the warehouse lot and pull up alongside them.

"Apologies for the theatrics, folks, but you'll need plausible deniability."

Chet? So Chet the FBI agent was down in Mexico. *The Feds are here after all.* She thought it strange that Gabe hadn't mentioned this.

From the sounds of it, Chet was the only one around. He led each of them to the car, a sedan it seemed, and placed them in the back seat. Once they were settled and the back doors were closed, he slid into the driver's seat and closed his door. Then they were off.

"Chet, man, I don't like this clandestine stuff. I'm just a regular guy."

"Savin, you drop three grand a week on your skin care. You're hardly *regular*," Celeste replied.

"Taking excellent care of one's skin is not a sin," Savin retorted, "and I won't apologize for it."

Chet sighed, exasperated. "It was a necessary precaution. Any time Americans travel to Mexico City, it's like someone sends out a smoke signal to mobilize all the bad guys."

"I told you we were targeted, Celly," Savin said, sounding like a petulant child.

"Chet, have you kidnapped us to hold us for ransom and steal Savin's ridiculously overpriced watch? Or—Savin, watch what I'm doing here... it's called deduction—are you taking us to a safe house?"

"The latter," Chet said. That was all he was going to give them. Savin seemed to realize that, as he stopped making comments. Chet was more closed off than he'd been the other times Celeste had interacted with him, so she figured something must be going on.

After a few minutes of silence, Chet explained, "Things are heating up in unexpected ways. We couldn't risk having you seen with us."

"Us?" Celeste asked.

"Gabriel and I. As you know, his CIA jurisdiction only allows surveilling of non-Americans and, uh, running foreign agents, while mine is solely for Americans. We make a good team when a situation is this complicated."

"I see."

After another twenty minutes or so in a silent car on what must have been an empty highway, they headed underground. *A parking garage?* Chet slowed the car dramatically, reversed into a spot, and pulled to a stop. *Must be.*

"This location is one of our safest, thanks to the precautions we take. You'll come to appreciate it. We've never lost anyone yet."

Jesus fucking Christ. Celeste's life had been in danger far too often over the past few years. It was becoming a drag. *And now it's not even my doing.* Unfortunately, Chet and Gabe knew how much she and Savin had gained from their agreement, so jeopardizing her life seemed to be fine with them.

Chet turned the engine off, then got out of the car. He opened Celeste's door first, removing her head cover. When he reached around to unbind her wrists, he found them already free.

"How did you—"

"Magic."

Celeste stood up and looked around the garage, which was medium-sized. The sedan, with nearly opaque black window tint, was the lone car parked. This wasn't like the other safe houses she'd seen. It felt too... something she couldn't put her finger on.

Once Savin was set free, he started babbling again. It was one of his many coping mechanisms to manage his anxiety.

"Was all this necessary? I mean, you could've easily met us in one of our hotel rooms instead of—" He looked around and frowned. "There's no sound in here, and there was no sound on the way over. It felt like we were climbing. Are we in the side of a fucking mountain or something?"

Ah, that's what's off. The altitude.

Chet's facial expression and slight affirmative nod confirmed. "Let's get inside. We have a lot to discuss in a short time." He walked briskly to an elevator. They stepped in, and Chet hit the 2 button. The building appeared to have five stories.

As the door opened, Agent Gutiérrez materialized in front of Savin and Celeste. They exchanged a glance, then Gabe gestured for them to follow him. Before Celeste could interject a snarky comment, Gabe dove in.

"I'm not entirely sure what happened last night with the suspect, and unfortunately, our top agent went dark mere days before you arrived. Three Americans disappeared two hours outside of Mexico City almost a week ago, and we have no leads there. Chet and I are too short-staffed down here to pull someone from another post."

"So you have agents who can't do their jobs, and you want a couple of civilians—"

"You're our best shot at finding out who's behind the trafficking, and more importantly, we're hoping Drake can lead us to Omar's boss."

"If you need us to stay, we're in," Savin volunteered, suddenly a beacon of courage.

Celest scowled. "What is this *really* about, Gabe? You're holding back something."

He continued without answering her question, seeming to be in a hurry. "Drake won't be able to help himself—he'll reach out once he's feeling better. We need you to stick with the plan. Chet and I will strap you up because you'll need to wear wires for the next few days. Our manpower situa—" Gabe cleared his throat.

"To what end are we wearing wires?" Celeste demanded loudly. "To protect us, right? You know if anyone caught us, they'd kill us, right? Drake is wanting to take us on this fuck-all trip, and from what I can tell, he's either troubled or insane—actually, I think he's both—and someone is indeed trying to kill him."

She took a deep breath and continued, "You're sending us on a tour with someone you suspect to be an extremely dangerous man, and yet you admittedly don't have anyone to send in if things go south. You know, it took years of therapy to move on from the traumas of my past, but I love my life now.

"I'm not interested in jeopardizing it for whatever dangerous game you're playing. And I don't have a death wish. I'm out." She folded her arms across her chest, realizing then that she was stuck there until the agents decided to take them somewhere. The room was sparse, with a few couches oddly placed, nothing of sentimental or aesthetic value, and no windows. A typical safe house, in her experience.

"I presume this dump has a ladies' room?"

Gutiérrez laughed dryly. "I'll show you the way. This place is larger than it seems." He grabbed her bicep and led her away from the other two down a dark hallway.

Ouch. She jerked out of his grasp.

"OK, I'm sorry," he said in a hushed tone. "Look, we're... we're desperate. I need your help on this."

Celeste kept walking. "Why me? Why us?"

"I've seen what you're capable of. You're extremely reckless, but you've got smarts. You're tough. You have the right instincts to get the job done." He sighed. "And there's something else."

Celeste gestured as if to say, "Move it along."

"Truth be told, our bosses have officially banned us from working this case. Whatever or whoever is behind Drake's operation—they don't want it to see the light of day."

"His alleged operation," Celeste corrected.

"You met the guy. You know that he's evil to his core."

There was no disputing that. But lugging naive Savin around Central and South America with an apparent sociopath while *wearing a wire*—even for her, it was too risky.

Gabe seemed to sense her hesitation. "I understand there is a cell phone record lingering in a case in New York that's causing you and your, uh, not sure what he is to you... your partner... some consternation."

Celeste stopped and looked over her shoulder at him. His glasses were spotless, as always, so she could see his eyes were pleading. "Go on."

"I'll make it disappear—*fast*—if you can see this trip through and get me the information I need."

Celeste wondered why he was so vested, even willing to risk his job, but let it go. *Pleading the fifth seems nonsensical at this point.* Gabe must've been unaware that Michel had already taken care of it. *A little certainty wouldn't hurt.* "Fine, get me confirmation that my problem no longer exists, and we are golden."

"Done. There's a lot riding on this."

"A promotion for you, I presume?"

Gabe let out an exasperated sigh. "Mizz Dono—Celeste, not everything is about personal gain. If you only knew..."

Sorry, Gabe, not buying your bullshit.

"Well, we're already here, so I'll see it through—unless things get too hairy. Savin isn't cut out for this."

"OK. Just remember, Drake's arrogance outweighs his intellect. He'll reveal what you need to know, and we'll capture it on the wire. Bathroom's down a bit further on the right." He turned and walked toward the living room.

What is this place?

AFTER A HANDOFF FROM THE FEDS, Celeste and Savin were back in the Suburban. Her bag was where she'd left it. She was excited to see if her phone voice note had captured anything the driver had said when he thought no one could overhear.

Once she was buckled in, Celeste rolled up the privacy partition with the switch. Savin's cell rang then, and he held it up for her to see the caller ID.

"Drake?" Celeste asked. "Back from the dead, as the Feds assumed. Or is he the fucking zombie I suspected he was?" *Come to think of it, he is rather ghastly.*

"Touché," Savin said, grinning. He answered, placing the call on speaker phone.

"Drake, my man, how you feeling?"

"Fucking fugu liver, bro. Can you believe it?"

Celeste and Savin looked at each other, puzzled.

"Excuse me?"

"Japanese fucking blowfish, bro. Had some for lunch yesterday.

Three grand for sashimi if you can fucking believe it. Eating the liver is, like, illegal in Japan or some shit, and someone smuggled it here. I had to get in on that, of course. It was ah-maze-ing! It makes your entire body go numb for like—well, I don't know for how long. It was a few hours. Apparently, I had some weird reaction last night, and my heart stopped. Good as new today after some IVs, though."

"Well, that's... great."

"Tell Celeste I'd appreciate it if she didn't assault my dick again, unless it's sexually. That was worse than the brief time I was dead yesterday." He laughed and continued.

"I heard you tried to save me, man. I owe you. Big-time. I'm going to give you the trip of a lifetime. We're leaving tomorrow. My driver will pick you up at eleven and bring you to the jet."

"What's our next stop?"

"Punta del Este, baby! The Hamptons of South America."

Oh, great. She couldn't wait to see what Drake's interpretation of the Hamptons was. To be fair, though, she'd heard that part of Uruguay was spectacular. *Here goes nothing.*

THE FOLLOWING DAY, the three were in Drake's jet ready for takeoff from Mexico City. As Celeste expected, his flight attendants were all female and scantily clad in uniforms she was certain he required.

No way I'm sitting through nine plus hours of this shit, even if it would help me with my little Nico problem.

"Excuse me, I need to use the ladies' room and then I'll be sitting in the back. I have a podcast I need to listen to. Savin, please deal with"—she made a hand gesture toward Drake—"all of this."

It was the perfect excuse to put on her earbuds and listen to the voice memo on repeat. After using the restroom, she sat alone and did just that. A man, presumably the driver, was speaking with a woman he'd picked up. They didn't say much because they weren't in the car long. But Celeste was certain she'd heard the woman's voice before and kept replaying her saying, "How can you be so sure she didn't recognize you?" It had to be about Celeste. They weren't discussing—*Oh my God.* Suddenly, she knew. She knew exactly when and where she'd heard both of their voices. *Oh my fucking God.*

11

PUPPETEER OR PUPPET ON A STRING?

C eleste sat alone by the infinity pool at Drake's expansive Tuscan-style villa on Manantiales Beach, one of the most renowned and exclusive on the Uruguayan coast. It was winter there, with the temperature around fifty-five degrees Fahrenheit. She was bundled in an off-white Max Mara hooded cardigan, cashmere turtleneck, and leggings, working on her laptop. Her mind was pulled in many different directions, so she tried to zero in on the most critical issues—the American's identity and who was behind RH Global.

She'd been scouring the many files she'd confiscated over the past several months, including those she'd retrieved on Nico's laptop before his untimely but necessary demise, those on Omar from the mysterious drive in her Chanel bag and from her and Lorraine's research, and Matthew's that Hadid had given her in Paris many months before. She continually flipped back and forth through the huge amount of data in case she'd missed anything that could identify the American or provide more clarity on RH Global. But she knew the information she needed wasn't there. She'd have to trace the contacts in Omar's phone. Her calculation that her chances of getting out of the illuminati would be dramatically greater if she stopped the cyberattack was the driving force behind her thoroughness. *Back to the original plan—me relying on me.*

Losing Meredith—and in such a violent, unexpected way—made it a struggle to focus. There was no time for mourning because Celeste was tasked with catching a criminal.

When they had arrived the previous day, Drake had taken her and Savin on a golf-cart tour of his twenty-seven-acre property.

Why must I spend time with him? What did I do in a past life to deserve this punishment?

The place was complete with tennis courts, a movie theater, and three wings, one for each of them. The staff moved about soundlessly and kept the house in meticulous order. It had the guise of a tranquil respite, even under the least optimal of circumstances, and she could easily understand why Drake had chosen it—especially if he was hiding a secret life. Always a sucker for posh real estate, Celeste was nonetheless much more interested in where he was conducting business in his off-the-grid compound than in the grounds themselves.

They'd dined at Drake's house and turned in early, though she didn't sleep. Her realization about the man and woman on the voice memo kept her awake. Celeste went outside at dawn to reflect.

She didn't believe in coincidences, but even if she had, this one was too strange. There was a zero percent likelihood that those two—both posing as flight attendants when Alexsandr had escorted her to Cairo and the woman having been behind Celeste's kidnapping in Zurich—were now in Latin America at the same time as Celeste, completely by chance.

What could it mean?

She recalled that day so long ago. Overwhelmed with grief when she believed Omar had killed Theodore, she'd framed Omar, staging him committing a capital crime with a woman in Riyadh. Alex, whom she hadn't known at the time, had snatched her from the chaotic scene, telling her he'd been sent to rescue her. Celeste thought she'd had no other choice but to leave with him, so they'd fled Saudi Arabia, driving through the night in the desert. She shuddered when she remembered how swiftly Alex had murdered the two Jordanian border guards he claimed had been sent to capture her. Their detour ended with Alex persuading her to go to Cairo. When she'd boarded the plane that fateful day, the flight attendants—the driver and his woman friend from the day before—had refused to share their names. She frowned. Her memory was hazy, understandably so after witnessing such brutality, but she thought one of them referred to Ace as their boss. The revelation left her scratching her head.

The situations must be somehow linked. The Feds sent her on a wild goose chase, Ace's colleagues pick her up to be kidnapped by the Feds.

As she pondered the many warnings she'd received from known and unknown sources—watch her back, don't trust people in her circle, stop digging, walk away, take the money, don't take the money, stay out of it, let the Feds handle it, get rid of the Feds—it became clear that every time she had been close to unraveling the mounting mysteries, something else happened to call her attention away. She liked to think she was in control, but was she really? *The puppeteer? Or a puppet on a string?*

She wondered who had booked the driver. Rani? *Yes, Rani.* She would reach out and probe a bit.

Her husband was calling her on FaceTime on her laptop; he too was a morning person. She put her Bluetooth earbuds in and answered.

"Hi, darling," she said cheerfully, perhaps a bit too much so.

"My love, how are you?" Theodore's deep voice inquired. The sound of him did things to her body.

"Babe, this place is incredible. The multiwing villa is modern and chic. I have my own staff, and the food was delicious last night and this morning. A lovely retreat. Maybe we should build that place you've wanted in the Hamptons or upstate after all. I can find... solitude here."

She was mastering the art of deceiving Theodore, and the best way to keep her husband from digging too deep was to dangle domesticity in front of him.

He laughed. "A lady gets hitched, and now she's all for... what was it you said to me, dear, when I suggested that we look for a place outside the city to relax? 'Theodore, just because we're married does *not* mean that we need to be constantly nesting. It's not who I am.' It sounds like a lovely place, and even more wonderful if it's influencing you to now entertain a country home."

Then his tone became serious.

"But I'm still not clear why you're staying at someone's house. Isn't that a bit unusual? Is it safe? Who even is this guy? I'm confused by it all."

You and me both, honey; you and me both. If only I'd had more choice in the matter.

"Hmm, I suppose it's a bit unorthodox, though I'm welcoming the opportunity to slow down. Plus, I have Savin here to protect me if anything goes south."

"Well, that provides no solace," he teased. They laughed, both knowing Savin was the last person anyone would want around in a tense situation. She imagined how Theodore would feel knowing that Drake was such a pig. *Best I save that story for my return.*

"We'll be here in Uruguay for a few days, so I'm using the time to catch up on some reading and meditation when we aren't working. I'm hoping we'll have the information we need after we do the site visits so I can get back home..."

It still didn't come naturally to her to be affectionate. But her therapist Anne Marie was helping her with intimacy. *No risk, no reward.* "Home to you. I miss cuddling with you at night."

"There will be lots of cuddling in our near future." He groaned. "Speaking of missing you, I'm off again tonight. Taking a late flight."

"Where to?"

"London. I have some urgent business, and if I'm able, I'll spend some time with Mum and Dad, then I may need to take care of a few more things elsewhere."

A window of opportunity. *Bingo!* Celeste was certain she and Vivienne could get the timing worked out. Now she had to get the hell out of Uruguay and back to New York.

"OK. Well, if you'll be gone when I get back, I may go to Miraval for a few days."

"That's a great idea, honey. I'm sorry I can't go, but duty calls. What are you up to the rest of the day?"

"We're going to evaluate the financials and then have dinner here. Tomorrow we're taking a day trip to some of the manufacturing sites in Brazil. It's apparently a quick flight."

"OK, baby, enjoy and keep me posted on your whereabouts and return. I have to run. Love you," her husband said.

"Love you, too, babe." She ended the call and closed her laptop.

Celeste then phoned Rani, who picked up immediately.

"Hello, darling. Can you chat? Quick question for you."

"Of course, Celly. How's the trip?"

Celeste kept her summation light. Rani was chiming in at appropriate points but seemed distracted.

"Is everything all right, Ran?"

To Celeste's surprise, her friend burst into tears and didn't reply immediately.

Sniffling, she said, "No, it's... well, it's nothing, really. I've had some... family issues. I've been fighting with my sister Lani about... family stuff. I'll be fine."

"I'm so sorry you're having a hard time." Celeste attempted to lighten Rani's mood. "Rani and Lani—that's so cute. I'd love to meet her sometime."

"What did you need, Celly?"

OK, I guess I'm not meeting the sister. "Sav said you arranged everything for our trip. I'm curious how you found the chauffeur company?" *The one that arranged for us to be kidnapped.*

Silence on the other end. And then "Well, I called our international security agency and booked the highest-rated company they recommended. You said you didn't want Angelo involved, so I thought that was the best way to handle..."

Did you know it was Ace's operatives? Or had the reservation been hijacked by Ace, who assigned their colleague as driver, unbeknownst to Rani? *A fucking security agency with God knows who managing the place.* Celeste had to determine whether Angelo could be trusted, and if not, D&C needed a new head of security. They couldn't be traveling where their arrangements could be intercepted.

"Is there a problem? Sav also had some concerns about the trip. Maybe it's a good idea to cut it short?"

Savin strolled up then. "Speak of the devil, he just arrived. I'll call you back in a few." She hung up as Savin spoke.

"You don't have to thank me. I'm taking Drake off your hands tonight—you know, so you won't try to *murder* him again."

Celeste silently cheered. Now she could snoop around to track down the evidence she needed. "Oh?"

"He and I are going to some... I don't know what it is exactly, but some secret-society-type place. I'll bring the *thing* the Feds gave us, and you can enjoy yourself here."

Don't remind me. Celeste had blocked out Gabe's request about wearing wires. If Drake indeed turned out to be involved in organized crime, getting caught with one was certain death.

Oh, Savin.

She wanted to protect him, shield him from the dark world in which she'd been navigating right under his nose for so long. Alas, he and some of her other friends and colleagues had forced them into that undesirable position of being the Feds' pawns. Now she could only do her best to prevent more of her friends from dying and avoid her own death—or prison.

A single tear fell, and she brushed it away before Savin noticed.

He sat down on the chaise beside her. "Rani asked why we came here instead of going to the manufacturing sites straightaway and demanded to know why we're even staying at his estate. It does feel kind of... odd."

Savin looked around and lowered his voice. "Especially now that we know what a dirtbag Drake is. This doesn't feel very well thought out... or safe. Rani wants me to come home. I mean, Celly, we were basically kidnapped in another country, even if it was by people we know. Should we be concerned?"

Celeste couldn't disagree with him. It was nonsensical to be in such a remote location without knowing what—or whom—they were up against. But the clock was ticking—they were apparently the only hope the Feds had in preventing the cyberattack and finally exposing Omar's boss.

"That's sweet of her to be worried. Theodore was a bit as well, but I talked him down. Who can blame them after Mere—after what happened to Meredith? Still, I think we're OK. I mean, we're in the Uruguayan Hamptons—how bad could it be?" She plastered a huge grin on her face. But Celeste knew just how bad it could get, especially if Drake—or someone worse—discovered they were wearing wires.

Please drop it, Sav. We can't go home. At least not until she'd finished snooping.

As if on cue, Drake appeared by the pool in seemingly good spirits, indicating to Celeste that he hadn't overheard their conversation. She'd assumed that he'd have the entire place bugged. She certainly would if she were in his shoes. *Although he could be as dumb as he looks.*

"I hope you've been enjoying your stay at Casa Drake. Celeste, I come bearing a peace offering." He snapped his fingers, and one of his butlers appeared with a tray of what looked to be cocktails.

"Passionfruit elderflower cocktails with adaptogens. Savin mentioned you were big into health and all that shit." Drake, pleased with himself, dismissed his staff.

I seem to have put the fear of God in him. Someone should've kicked him in the balls much earlier in life.

"He also said you'd like to stay behind tonight. I thought you'd change your mind if you heard a little more about the area. This is the Hamp—"

"Yes, I can see it's very similar to some of our little Long Island hamlets. I'm charmed." She smiled, flashing her dimples, but it didn't reach her eyes.

"It's a top food destination as well. I've arranged an exclusive meal with the region's most sought-after chef—"

"No, no, please don't worry about accommodating me. I'm not sure if you're aware, but my brother passed away on my wedding day last month. It's been quite a whirlwind. I could really use some self-reflection and R&R. The bathtub in my suite has my name written all over it. You've created such an idyllic scene here."

"That's quite a compliment coming from Celly, er, Celeste, Drake," Savin explained. "You should quit while you're ahead because no one has ever changed her mind in the twenty years I've known her."

Drake was clearly uncomfortable but seemed to realize he was beaten. "Of... of course, enjoy, and I'm, uh, sorry for your loss."

Celeste smirked inwardly. *No one can argue with "my brother passed away on my wedding day."* May as well use it to her advantage in this case to get Drake off her back.

"You'll have the best time. I can't wait to hear all about it," Celeste said.

Drake scowled. "I'll make sure you have everything you need. What do you say we head to my office and squeeze in an hour of work before lunch?"

Abso-fucking-lutely. "I thought you'd never ask," Celeste replied with a grin.

DRAKE'S COMPOUND had a fully functioning business center, complete with a behemoth boardroom overlooking the property.

"I could run my entire operation from this state-of-the-art facility. Everything is top of the line, even the network, which is unheard of in this part of the world. I invested in new Wi-Fi capabilities installed in the area to ensure I never go dark," he bragged. "I've created somewhat of a bunker in here, where I could stay indefinitely if necessary. In fact, I'm planning to—" He started to share something else, then seemed to decide against it.

Hmm. What are you planning, you prick?

"This place is great, man. Truly amazing," Savin chimed in.

"Let's dive into the financials." Drake spent the next half hour pitching the many different facets and income streams of his tech company. The numbers spoke for themselves—revenue looked to more than double in the very near future. It was a polished campaign, and it was the first time Celeste had seen him act like an adult. Under ordinary circumstances, and if he were an entirely different type of person, she might have considered a true investment by D&C.

He's hiding something, holding back. Celeste's success could be attributed in part to her ability to read a situation faster than others. She couldn't put her finger on it, and she didn't know if it necessarily meant he was involved in organized crime or something else—but he was definitely not entirely forthcoming. She wondered if Savin had picked up on it.

"Wow, man, I'm blown away," Savin said. "I know which way I'm leaning, so I can't wait to see the facilities and infrastructure you've built." His tone was much too gracious to be sincere.

Yep, he knows, and he's ready to get the fuck out of here. Celeste was relieved. Hopefully, Savin could find some evidence to close the deal —meaning incriminate Drake—over dinner. She had a plan of her own while they were out.

Celeste began clapping. "Well, you've done it, Drake. You've managed to turn things around. Sav's right—this is exactly the type of value we're looking to provide for our clients. You've built this from nothing into a conglomerate. I'm with my business partner. Assuming the rest of the trip checks out, this looks very promising."

There it was. Yes, Drake was pleased. But more than that, he seemed *relieved.* He had something more than business riding on the deal. Which could be why he was bending over backward to accommodate her.

Drake looked at his watch. "Business out of the way before ten a.m. Now we have all day to play."

SAVIN AND CELESTE met by the pool after claiming they needed to catch up on emails before lunch. They planned to take this opportunity to exchange theories about Drake's demeanor and pitch.

Seemingly out of nowhere came a feminine voice with a heavy Russian accent: "Something has come up, and the trip will be cut short. We must get you home immediately."

They turned around to see a woman a tight gray bun, matching gray pantsuit, and a severe expression. They hadn't heard her approaching.

"Not that I'm complaining, but who the hell are you? Where's Drake?" Savin inquired.

The woman pretended he hadn't spoken. "We mustn't delay—we need to leave now." The urgency in her tone was palpable.

"This is unexpected. Who is, uh, arranging our travel?" Savin asked. He seemed to be acclimating to the chaotic occurrences that now made up Celeste's life.

"The staff has already gathered as much of your stuff as time permitted and will escort you directly to the chopper."

I have to get back to my room. Celeste stood up and announced haughtily, "Well, this abrupt departure is quite an inconvenience. I still need to freshen up—"

The woman interrupted her. "That's not possible."

"What's not possible is for me to travel in this slouchy outfit." *What if my clothes are already packed?* She tried another tactic. "At least let me... wash my face."

After some back-and-forth, the woman relented but insisted that she escort Celeste to her room. As they walked through the palatial house, Celeste noticed that they were taking a different route.

"Uh, where are we going?"

"I assure you—we're going to your room, as you requested. But we must take a detour..." She paused. "There is a, uh, a water leak."

Celeste narrowed her eyes but kept silent. She couldn't risk the woman changing course and refusing to take her to her suite. Something must have happened with Drake; nothing else made sense in light of the strange morning events. She schemed as they walked through passages and down hallways she hadn't taken before. *Focus on getting out of here safely, then deal with it.*

Finally, they arrived. The woman entered first and stood in the center of the room.

"I'll only be a few minutes," Celeste said and walked quickly to the bathroom, locking the door behind her and turning on the shower.

She'd hidden five syringes and the weapons she'd brought under the sink behind the pipes. The brass knuckles, taser, and Glock—which Zed had insisted she bring with her everywhere—were where she'd left them. She felt around for the syringes, but they weren't there. Her heart pounded in her ears. *This makes no sense.*

The woman knocked several times on the door, as Celeste frantically ran her hands over every surface inside the cabinet. The syringes contained substances varying from mild sedatives to poison —one could never be too careful. But they were gone, no longer where she'd left them. Drake's brush with death, the change of plans, and now the missing substances. *Well, this escalated quickly.*

"Is everything OK in there?"

"Yes, I'll be right out," she called. *Think, Celeste.*

She exhaled when she saw that she'd left one of her toiletry bags on the counter; it would be a good place to conceal the items she'd retrieved. She stuffed everything in but the piece—her gun had to be kept in her waistband close to her body under the circumstances—and zipped the bag. *I can't delay, lest this woman becomes curious and finds the weapons.*

Of course, Celeste could have overpowered her—she was trained well enough to take down someone much bigger. But assault was tricky in other countries. Celeste couldn't risk it. Not twice in as many days.

When Celeste opened the door, the woman jumped back as though she'd had her ear to it.

"Oh, wow, I didn't realize you were so close. It's a little disconcerting to have someone listening while I powder my nose." *Best to call a spade a spade.*

"Hurry along now. We must be going."

We? Who was this woman, and why was she under the impression that she could make decisions for Celeste? *Right now, I don't know what I'm up against.*

THE STAFF RUSHED Celeste and Savin out to a golf cart that was already loaded with their luggage.

They climbed into the back and watched the woman slide into the front seat and throw the cart into gear. Celeste grabbed the nearest handlebar to avoid toppling out as they sped along. She and her best friend tried to communicate in whispers, but they realized the woman could hear them, so they'd have to wait to compare notes. They arrived at the helipad in minutes, Drake's Sikorsky and a man waiting. Celeste didn't pay much attention to him other than to watch in amazement how quickly he transferred the bags. When he was finished, he spoke in hushed tones with the woman. Then he walked over to the golf cart, got in, and drove off.

The woman was seemingly their pilot because they were otherwise alone.

"Well, don't just stand there. We must go. I promised Ace I'd get you out of here immediately."

Celeste and Savin exchanged a glance.

"Who are you, where are you taking us, and why?" Celeste asked, folding her arms across her chest in protest. "I won't be getting on that aircraft..."

"We don't have time for explanations."

When Savin adopted Celeste's defiance and also stood locked in place, the woman relented. "Drake is in the crosshairs of the head of the crime syndicate we are fighting. We believe Drake uncovered your... arrangement with your government friends, the illuminati, and brought you here as a negotiating chip, intending to redeem himself with the big boss. He planned to trap you—to offer you up as sacrificial lambs to Omar's organization." She looked pointedly at Celeste.

"Omar's boss is particularly interested in making an example of you, Celeste, and he can't do that if you're alive. We could not risk your safety. We'll regroup in Montevideo and send you off to New York." She sighed and wore a disappointed expression, as though her small children had written on the wall in permanent marker.

Fuck you.

"Now, will you please get into the fucking chopper?" The woman's tone indicated she was willing to force them in involuntarily.

Obediently, Celeste climbed into the aircraft. Savin sat down beside her, and they placed their headsets on.

The woman put hers on as well and then began moving things on the control center, as Celeste had seen Theodore do in the past.

"Who exactly are you?"

"Ace's associate. That's all you need to know."

Ace saving the day again. Extracting Celeste against her will once more. *Par for the course.*

Given Savin's fear, a potential attempt on Drake's life, the questions that remained around Meredith's mysterious death, and Celeste's own reticence about remaining on that compound any longer, she wondered if it was the right—or perhaps the only—escape plan.

Guess we'll find out soon enough.

"Has something happened to Drake?"

"We aren't sure," the woman said unconvincingly. She knew something. "Ace will explain more when you're stateside."

Then their captor turned pilot grew silent and directed her attention to the task at hand, indicating that was all they were going to get from her. The helicopter hovered and then ascended. Celeste watched as Drake's estate grew smaller and smaller.

How would she explain to the Feds that they'd left? Would Gabe still hold up his end of the deal? It wasn't hard to imagine all the ways things could still go wrong.

Meredith. Celeste imagined what it would be like coming home to the void left by her friend's absence. The apartment was haunted with echoes of her laughter, and memories of Mere were embedded in all the bespoke pieces she'd curated for Celeste's home and wardrobe.

Celeste had only a handful of women in her life, and Meredith had meant the world to her. She wondered if the Long Island police officers had made any progress on Mere's case.

Celeste put on her sunglasses to hide her closed eyes and began a meditation given to her by Swami Maharajananda. But after a moment, Savin nudged her. He had his notes app open and wanted to show her what he'd typed of his thoughts.

Oh, Sav.

He was concerned, and rightly so, for Rani's safety, worried that Drake was somehow connected to Mere's murder, afraid that they'd mobilized some sort of international crime organization against them by joining the illuminati.

Celeste didn't have the heart to tell him that the bad guys had turned against them long before. Instead, she asked him how he'd like to handle their significant others before they got back to New York. They decided they'd wait to tell Theodore and Rani anything until after they had time to come up with a story. Celeste felt lucky that Savin also wanted to protect his fiancée and Theodore from the events of the past few days. Once they agreed on their course of action, they retreated into their thoughts until the aircraft began descending and the Carrasco International Airport's private hangar came into view. The woman spoke again.

"You'll fly private from Montevideo to Brazil—a quick flight. Then a commercial red-eye out of São Paulo to New York tonight."

Commercial? Someone who was orchestrating their evacuation wanted documentation of them leaving South America. Perhaps there had been foul play with Drake?

They landed a mere thirty minutes later, and the woman turned off the aircraft. Celeste's iPhone immediately rang. *Jack.*

"Where we partying tonight?"

Savin snatched the phone from Celeste's hand. "Hey—" she

protested, but he ignored her, keeping the phone and putting it on speaker.

"Jack, buddy, where are ya?"

"You guys said you were stopping by those Brazilian factories, so I took a chance that you'd have time for little old me and got a penthouse in São Paulo. Dinner after your tours?"

"Uh, our tours wrapped up earlier than we thought. Could you meet us for lunch? Three p.m. Eastern? We're trying to leave for the city tonight."

"Sure. I'll snag us a hot resy."

Click.

Their pilot had arranged a crew to transport them and their luggage to the awaiting plane. The transfer took mere minutes, and they were off again.

IT WAS midafternoon when they met Jack at the Tangará Jean-Georges restaurant, the chef's sole location in South America, at the Palácio Tangará hotel after having the bellmen store their luggage. Jack was seated at a spacious booth in the center of the room, and from the looks of it, he was the only patron in the place.

"Darling!" Celeste said, walking briskly toward him. Wearing a wide grin, he embraced her and then exchanged a half hug with Savin. They sat down, and a female server rushed over to retrieve their drink order.

"A dirty vodka martini for me," Celeste said. Savin ordered the same. The woman nodded and scurried away.

"Getting an early start—I like it," Jack said, nodding in approval.

"Believe it or not, it's already been quite a long day," Savin said, tossing Celeste a sideways glance.

Jack looked at Celeste's tracksuit. "I've never seen you pop into an Oetker property wearing sneakers and sweats, so I had guessed."

"Touché, dickhead," Celeste replied to his jab and laughed.

Meredith would be appalled if she saw me dressed like this right now. The thought made her sad.

"Where's the weird tech guy you were visiting? And why are D&C's managing directors touring factories? Are you guys poor?"

"Oh, uh—"

Let me handle this, Sav. "Drake's financials looked too good to be true, so we had to come check it out," she interrupted. "Our teams are underwater with onboarding these acquisitions, so we decided to make the trek and let them keep working."

"OK, so here's what I really want to know—did you poison Drake?"

"You're full of questions today," Celeste said breezily. "Ugh, that guy is such a dick."

"Sav is convinced you did," Jack said, laughing.

She looked at her Judas of a friend, narrowing her eyes. "You fucker."

Turning back to Jack, she replied, "First of all, if I set out to *off* that skinny little prick, I would've succeeded on the first try. Secondly, Jack, the actual newsworthy part of that evening was watching Savin try to revive him. Note to self: Never need CPR when Savin is the only one around who can administer it."

Savin scowled as Celeste and Jack laughed.

"Take the piss out of me and make your little jokes, but I'll have you know that the paramedic said I did a great job."

Celeste howled. "Oh, babe, there is *no* possible way you helped that situation!"

She and Jack continued teasing Savin until the food arrived.

After that, they kept the chitchat lighthearted for the rest of the meal. Savin talked about the timing for his wedding, and Jack said he was thinking of buying a place in Tokyo because his trips were always too short to make a dent in the city's long list of Michelin restaurants. "Plus, there's the Japanese Alps."

"At this rate, you'll have a spot on every continent by the end of the decade," Savin observed.

"Sooner than that, I'd hope," Jack said. "You never know when you'll need to disappear," he added with a wink.

"Mysterious party boy resigns himself to ordinary life in fifty-million-dollar Tokyo penthouse after evading taxes for two decades," Celeste joked.

"Exactly!" Jack waved to one of the servers, nonverbally requesting the check.

Once the bill was settled, Celeste glanced at the time and sighed. "This has been great, but we need to get back to the airport soon. When will you be in New York again?"

Instead of answering, Jack pulled his phone out of his pocket and frowned. "I have to take this. I'll be right back." He stood up and headed toward the lobby.

"Ready to end this twilight zone of a trip, Sav?"

"I'm dying to get home to Rani. Wait here; I'll have the bellmen retrieve our luggage. We need to give them a twenty-minute head start to get all of yours."

The two laughed, and he left in the direction of the lobby.

Celeste remained seated at the table, waiting for the guys to return. *What's taking them so long?* Finally, she gathered her bag and left the restaurant. Jack was at the other end of the lobby with his back to her, but Savin was nowhere to be found. Crossing the grand room, she strained to hear Jack's side of the phone conversation.

"There's no trace of her. She got spooked, and when a spook gets spooked, she uses her flight fund to fly."

He was silent for a moment, nodding in agreement. "OK, I'll keep looking. We need to figure out what to do about Celly."

Silence and then, sounding exasperated, "She deserves to know, Rudy..."

Even from afar, Jack's body language revealed how tense he was, as he raked his fingers through his hair and then clenched a fist.

"No... no!" he said firmly. "She needs to hear it from a friend... OK, fine, we can leave that part out—for now. I'll give you until end of the week to come up with a better idea, but that's it."

He ended the call with a huff and turned around. His eyes bulged, and his cheeks turned red. His expression said it all—the call had been about her.

Busted.

"Jack? What do I deserve to know? And who's Rudy?"

Jack, never uncomfortable or caught off guard, squirmed and was visibly shaken. He quickly recovered to look quizzical. It would have been imperceptible to a stranger—but not to her.

"Rudy? I don't know anyone by that name. That was... Mark. He's... going to miss the birthday party you're throwing for Theodore, and... I wanted you to hear about it in advance. You know, with Meredith gone and all, I didn't want anything to upset you further."

She frowned. *Birthday party. For my husband. Oh, yes.* She'd forgotten all that had been planned. *Meredith took care of it... but that was before...* That's not what Jack had been discussing, though, gauging from his reaction.

At that inopportune moment, as Celeste was preparing to call Jack out on his lie, Savin walked up.

"Bags are ready, and our chariot awaits. We need to get going—apparently, they won't hold this plebeian flight for us if we're late." He groaned. "I can't believe we have to go through airport security."

He fell silent when he noticed Celeste was fuming. He looked back and forth between his friends. "Celly, you never look that pissy at anyone but me. What's going on?"

Savin being privy to yet another potential crisis would only make things more stressful for Celeste. "I'm not upset, Sav," she said with a wide grin. "Did you count and ensure all ten of my bags made it to the car?"

Easily placated, Savin seemed relieved to hear everything was fine. "There's actually eleven, but yes, they're all accounted for."

"OK, then, let's get going. Jack, walk us out?"

"Sure."

Savin walked in front of them, chattering happily about something.

"This isn't over, Jack. I want to know by the time I land what you were discussing and with whom. It wasn't about a fucking birthday party," she hissed under her breath.

Jack had the decency to look sheepish. "I'll take care of it."

"And I'm not a child. You don't need to fly halfway across the world to tell me things—regardless of how delicate—in person."

Jack looked unconvinced. "Celly, it's... I'm not sure—"

"Please stop hemming and hawing. I'm a big girl. Just get whatever information you need and tell me by"—she stopped and looked at her watch—"I'll expect to hear from you by eleven a.m. Eastern tomorrow."

"Ready to join the working folk in cattle class, Sav?" Celeste asked in a singsong voice as she climbed into the waiting SUV with him.

Hopefully, it's not being driven by one of Ace's operatives tasked with kidnapping me again.

THE RED-EYE WAS long and boring, and she occupied herself by ticking through ideas on what Jack was hiding. By the time they landed around 10 a.m. the following day, Celeste was itching for the puzzle pieces to fall into place. After she and Savin went through Global Entry at JFK, they found Monty waiting at baggage claim with two carts to transport their luggage.

"Did you tip him off to how light I was traveling?" Celeste said.

"Yep!"

Once they were settled in Monty's Mercedes, Celeste put up the privacy partition and announced, "I won't be going to the office today."

"I gathered," Savin replied. "As a matter of fact, I'm not going in either, and Rani agreed to leave work early." Referring to their junior staff, he said, "The kids will have to keep everything afloat today," and smiled.

"No matter how crazy life is right now, we're doing the best we can," he continued, grabbing her hand and squeezing gently. "Don't forget that, Celly."

The Feds and Ace were all clamoring to download with her and Savin, if the number and frequency of missed calls were any indication.

"Can we wait to talk to Ace and the Feds? Let's take some time to unwind."

"You read my mind. I'll text them to that effect," Savin offered.

"Perfect. We can meet in the war room at seven a.m. tomorrow. Once they're sorted, I'm off to Miraval for a few days."

Savin agreed to keep things afloat while she was away. Monty pulled up to Celeste's building, where Jonah was waiting for her with a luggage cart. He and her driver quickly transferred the bags, while she said goodbye to Savin and walked into the lobby.

Her iPhone was vibrating. *Sam.*

"Hello, darling!"

"You don't call, you don't write. Roberto and I are in São Paulo with the baby. We would've loved to see you. Chet told us you stopped over," she added.

So the Feds knew they were extracted. *Word travels fast, I suppose.*

"I assumed you guys were stateside and didn't think to call. Alas, we were only there for a few hours. Had to fly *commercial* back to the States." Celeste changed topics. "How are you? How's baby"—Celeste paused to try to recall her name—"Valentina and my favorite client?"

"Roberto's great. He's still grinning ear to ear, in love with his baby girl. The breastfeeding is killing me, but I refuse to quit. Enough baby talk—it has to be so dull for everyone except me and Roberto. What the hell were you guys doing in South America, and what brought you home so abruptly?"

"It's a long story. I'll tell you over a virtual glass of wine soon. Or better yet, come visit and have a real-life girls' night with me. Sign Roberto up for parenting time so you can have a well-deserved break!"

The two women made plans for the near future, and Celeste prayed that she'd have something appropriate to share about the South America trip with her friend by then. After exchanging a greeting with Jonah and urging him to take everything up without her so she could make a call, she sat on one of the lobby sofas in a far corner.

She dialed, and Jack answered on the first ring.

"OK, Celly, are you sitting down?"

Celeste rolled her eyes. "Yes, Jack. There's no danger of me faint-ing. Now spit it out—I'm going mad!"

He sighed heavily. "Here's what I can tell you right now. I have reason to believe that your brother's death was not an accident."

Of all the things she'd guessed he would say, that was not even in the top twenty. "OK, yeah, I'm glad I'm sitting. What? Why? The *polizia* didn't seem to think there was anything suspicious." *That's not true.* They had delayed transport of the bodies in Italy much longer than expected. But Jack wouldn't have known what they had told her.

"It's hard to explain, but I'll have more information for you soon."

Celeste felt a twinge of guilt. What if she'd had it all wrong?

"Who would hurt my brother and his family? In Italy? On the day of my wedding?"

"Look, I wasn't even supposed to tell you, so you have to promise me that you'll stay out of it until I give you more information. I have, uh, friends high up in the *polizia* now that I live there."

Jack was masterful at fostering useful relationships. *Money talks, as they say.*

Gabe's words rang in her ears: *"Mizz Donovan, seems like there's a lot of death happening around you lately."*

"Does this have something to do with me? Is it my fault?"

"Not particularly, no." Jack was silent for a moment, as if consid-ering how much to divulge. "In fact, I think it has nothing to do with Keith being your brother."

"I hope he and his family didn't suffer," she said, wiping away the stray tears that had fallen.

"I'm so sorry, Celly. But I didn't want you to find out later from someone else. And of course, I'll pass along anything I find out."

"OK, thanks, Jack. I... I have to go now."

What had her brother been mixed up in for someone to murder

him and his family? Apparently she wasn't the only one stirring up bad blood.

Oh, Keith, what did you do this time?

Upstairs, Celeste was relieved to be alone. *Order and control are priority number one.* She had to get focused and back on track if she wanted to uncover information that would let her obtain freedom from the Feds and crush Omar's boss. The events of the past few weeks, bomb scares and frantic escapes, couldn't be her norm.

If Jack was right that her brother's death wasn't an accident, well, she was more motivated than ever to avoid the same fate.

Anne Marie is going to get an earful in our next session.

Had her brother been having the same urgent visions from her parents? Had he been coming to warn her? Why hadn't the visions come back to reveal something, anything for her to go on? Her head began to ache.

She threw her handbag on the sofa and nearly ran into her office, intent on addressing the pressing issues—the American's identity and preventing the cyberattack—and shoving any sadness about her brother down deep.

In her husband's absence, she would stay up all night until she discovered what else was going on. She sat down and powered on her computer.

"Hello, Celeste" came a voice from behind her.

"Jesus Christ! I nearly went into cardiac arrest. You couldn't have given me a heads-up?"

"Apologies for startling you—but it was really the only way. Plans have changed."

Emerging from a rarely used closet, Vivienne came over and sat in one of the chairs in front of Celeste's desk.

Once Celeste regained her composure, she asked, "What do you have in mind?"

"We're going to find a way to get the information you need to keep everyone safe."

12

THE PERFECT RECIPE: "HEARTBREAK, RAGE, AND AUDACITY"

C eleste exhaled slowly to calm her nerves. She reminded herself that she was in control and prepared, armed with everything she needed to guarantee success.

She had traveled from New York to DC the previous day on an Amtrak Acela, using one of her aliases to book the ticket. Vivienne had arrived separately but stayed nearby, ready to step in at a moment's notice.

The last time Celeste had attempted a machination of this scale, she had been blinded by heartbreak, perhaps not fully able to comprehend the repercussions. Now she wasn't entirely sure what drove her—bravery or stupidity or maybe a combination of both—but she knew she wasn't going to sit on the sidelines, living in fear. Vivienne had summarized what she and her team had unearthed about the pending cyberattack and the potential foreign agents acting against US interests from within the government.

A seasoned hacker, Vivienne had spent weeks underground on the dark web and learned that the head of Omar's crime syndicate was indeed an American, confirming what Celeste had guessed, and that the same person was also orchestrating the impending cyberattack—but the evidence existed behind firewalls on servers that even her team could not breach remotely. The Feds had said the same thing when they'd asked the illuminati to hack financial records of cabinet members and other higher-ups as a way to track bribes and other payments from Omar's crime ring, but Vivienne disagreed with their idea that this was the best—or even an acceptable—way to take down the American ringleader.

Just as I suspected—I must get the information myself. The catch was that only a handful of people could gain access, and they had to be on-site to do so. Chet and Gabe had made clear that it was above their pay grade. Celeste waited for Vivienne to give her instructions, but they didn't come.

Vivienne explained that Chet and Gabe were on the right track with the person they thought was involved from the cabinet and Congress, but the Feds were low-level bureaucrats. No one at the highest levels of government would believe their outlandish claims, and on top of the low likelihood they'd be taken seriously, the traitor or traitors would be actively trying to discredit them. Despite their noble counterterrorism remits, the fact remained—that the agents had limited influence and no access to the information necessary to implicate the head of Omar's crime syndicate.

So that's why they needed us.

"We did our best—trust me when I say we left no stone unturned." The savant sighed and shook her head sadly. "I'm afraid I'm at the end of my journey now because we don't have the necessary people on the inside. Unless..." She trailed off.

"Unless what?" Celeste demanded, her curiosity piqued.

Having previously been a prominent US government official, Vivienne knew what they were looking for—and that there were only two ways to get it. They needed to either secure a confession from the traitor/mob boss that could be taken to the president or—the much riskier but more likely to succeed option—go to the source.

"Specifically, break into the J. Edgar Hoover Building, headquarters for the FBI. Could I pull off something of this magnitude?" she had asked Celeste rhetorically. "Absolutely, especially back in my heyday. Maybe I even did a time or two, but you didn't hear that from me." She winked, then continued.

"To do it successfully these days, though, I would need someone with my expertise and software operating in the background. And therein lies the problem. All the 'me-types' are dead and gone—or cannot be trusted. The systems are now virtually impenetrable."

Celeste smiled, connecting the dots. "You didn't say impossible to penetrate, though, so the answer is obvious—I'll go in, and you'll be the mastermind behind the scenes. We'll get it ourselves."

Vivienne looked confused. "Did you not hear what I just said? There's only one way into the system—FBI headquarters. And we—I —don't have the team or the equipment to pull it off."

"Nonsense. I've seen what you can do. With your expertise and my focus, we can put an end to all this madness."

"There is a zero to five percent chance of success. I'm an old woman, so retiring into oblivion knowing I'd prevented the collapse of America—well, there are worse ways to go out. But you—I'm afraid you're not thinking clearly, dear," Vivienne chided. Celeste knew this was all a ruse, however—Vivienne had planted the seeds and now wanted to pretend the ideas were Celeste's. Celeste would play along because she wanted the same thing, and more importantly, she would need help from someone like Vivienne.

"To the contrary. There's at least one bounty on my head, my friend was brutally murdered, and I found out my brother may have also been killed because of me. Even with my security outfit, which is the best in the business, I've been kidnapped more than once, and a bomb was recently planted in my apartment in Paris, waiting to be remotely detonated. Suffice it to say—I'd love to hasten an end to Omar's boss's reign."

Vivienne weighed Celeste's words. "If you're caught, there's a chance that I couldn't make an arrest—or a conviction—disappear."

"I won't be—you'll see to that." A wave of emotion washed over Celeste, and her voice broke when she continued.

"I've pulled off major heists and stayed off the radar. I've experienced unspeakable violence at Omar's hand, I've lost loved ones, and still, I've carried on. Because try as I may..." Tears sprang to her eyes and threatened to fall. She inhaled sharply and then exhaled through her nose.

"Try as I may, I can't shake the feeling that I survived on that boat in the Mediterranean for a reason; that perhaps I alone have the right combination of resources, heartbreak, rage, and audacity to succeed at what others before me were unable to."

Vivienne considered what Celeste was saying, a thoughtful expression on her face.

"You remind me of me at your age. OK, then. Let's hope this isn't a fool's errand. It's time to prepare you—I've rounded up what we need."

"Wait, so all that... buildup... you were already in this entire time?"

"Well, dear, I happen to agree with you—you, with my assistance of course, may be the only one who can pull this off. I've had it planned out for months. But I had to see what you were made of first."

Touché.

And so they prepared. Celeste was in awe of the woman's thoroughness. They'd stayed up all night in Celeste's apartment, going over the plan Vivienne had outlined, scouring blueprints, practicing mannerisms and replies that would be acceptable if anyone approached Celeste once she was inside. She also learned as much as she could from social media and Google about the woman she would be impersonating, Rebecca Foster.

Celeste was in her flow, receiving everything Vivienne had uncovered or was willing to share.

The next day, more drills. More information. More of Celeste refining her Plan B to activate if things went south. Vivienne didn't reveal much more about Rebecca, only that she was usually in the field and often stayed in a hotel close to the J. Edgar Hoover Building when she came in from the field.

Vivienne had somehow pulled strings to guarantee that Rebecca would not be around, removing one additional layer of risk. Her confidence had put Celeste at ease. Celeste, always the A+ student, had spent her entire train ride going over and over the information until she felt comfortable.

Finally, it was time to go. Celeste was standing in her hotel room at the Riggs, looking at herself in the mirror disguised with hair and clothing nearly identical to Rebecca's. Celeste wore a shoulder-length wig in a mousy brown color. She'd been able to track down a Banana Republic heather-gray pantsuit Rebecca wore on repeat, if her social media DC happy-hour posts were any indication, and identical accessories, including pearl earrings, sensible shoes, and a carryall tote. Her makeup was done in the same understated style, and she'd even practiced mimicking the woman's voice from videos she found online, in case anyone approached her.

It was a brilliant cover, and once Celeste was in disguise, the resemblance was remarkable.

Celeste flung the Louis Vuitton Neverfull over her shoulder. It was heavy, containing a plethora of computer surveillance equipment, but not bulging. No need to draw unwanted attention. She inserted the micro earbuds into her ears, and instantly, Vivienne's voice came alive.

"You look so similar to her, Celeste," she said calmly, reminding Celeste she had eyes into the hotel room. "What you're doing takes courage. Know that I'll be with you the entire time, walking you through what's next."

With a nod and one last glance at her reflection, Celeste walked out of the hotel room and onto the elevator.

"You'll turn right and then take another right onto Ninth Street Northwest..."

Celeste knew the way but appreciated Vivienne's directions, reminding Celeste that she wasn't alone.

It's now or never.

～

GETTING past lobby security and up to the restricted floor was uneventful, so much so that Celeste wondered briefly if everyone there could be in on the cyber heist. *Not a chance.* These people, mostly men, were by-the-book types, scowling at her, at each other, judging her.

No, these men in their hair plugs and cheap suits would love nothing more than for the FBI to revert to the good ol' days when the only positions women were allowed to hold were administrative—and sexual harassment was not only tolerated but applauded.

Celeste made noncommittal eye contact as she made her way through the halls and nodded back to the employees who nodded to her first. She had been quiet, gracious, unmemorable; just as Vivienne had said, the woman she was impersonating seemed to have no close relationships at HQ because no one approached Celeste in the manner a work friend would.

"Everything looks good so far, Celeste," came the grounding voice from the undetectable devices in her ears. Vivienne was remotely hacked into the FBI security camera system watching Celeste's every move and gauging whether there would be any danger ahead.

Purposeful pace, shoulders back, head high—appear confident but not too.

"Easy, now. This is where things get a little more complex."

Celeste was walking through a large room with rows and rows of cubicles, which she was finding empty. Everything was gray and outdated, in sharply contrast to the chic D&C offices. *No wonder no one can accomplish anything magical here.* Ambience was everything.

If memory served from the blueprint she'd reviewed, the side door Celeste needed to slip through was coming up. Then she noticed someone in the room with her, bent over his desk in his cubicle. She could see the top of his head, his thinning wiry, disheveled hair.

The moment he began to lift his head, she knew.

Chet.

Shit, shit, shit.

Don't panic. But she already was.

How was she going to explain why she was there? Her mind raced.

Their gazes locked, and she expected him to spring to his feet, call security, and chase her down. She was faster than he was, but she wouldn't be able to slip past everyone in the entire building if an alarm was sounded.

Could he hear the pounding of her heart?

She was almost to the door. Visualizing the floorplan she'd been studying the past few days, she evaluated whether she could make it to the server room and upload the files before she was caught.

She braced herself to take off running as he pushed his chair back and stood up.

He nodded once and headed toward the end of the room where she'd entered.

"Remember to breathe. He didn't recognize you. Stay focused."

The next few minutes were the most pivotal in their plan.

Inhale two, three, four. Exhale two, three, four, five...

After looking right and left, Celeste swiped her badge and entered an empty hallway with an elevator. The doors opened and she stepped in.

"Biometrics. You know the drill."

Celeste placed her right eye in the scanner's range and her right index finger on the print reader.

An uplifting beep echoed in the empty elevator, signaling approval.

"The CCTV is on a loop, and even the maintenance team can't see the elevator movement, so you're a ghost."

The doors opened onto a sublevel two floors below what most FBI employees considered as the bottom floor, and she stepped into a sterile hallway with fluorescent lighting. Without looking, she sensed there were cameras at every angle. *I hope Vivienne is doing her job; otherwise, my face is all over the security radar. Well, Rebecca's.*

"Two more checkpoints, and you're in. There doesn't appear to be anyone between you and the data center."

Celeste allowed herself a large exhale. She still had much to do, but at least she hadn't been recognized yet.

"OK, next two are biometrics. Just like last time" came Vivienne's voice out of the earbuds.

"Seems redundant if I cleared the first one, doesn't it?" Celeste said.

"It must've given someone somewhere some sense of peace knowing that anyone breaking in would have to scan their finger-prints more than once, I suppose," Vivienne said.

"Sounds like men came up with the system," Celeste muttered.

Vivienne laughed.

After Celeste had made it through the final checkpoint and into the server room, Vivienne exhaled. *I'm not the only one on edge.*

The room looked exactly as Vivienne had described it. It was filled with rows upon rows of black hard drives with flashing lights in various colors. Celeste noted the cluster of mainframes on the wall farthest from her. She shivered from the artificial chill in the air, meant to offset the heat produced from running such a high-powered network.

There it is! She rushed over to the workstation. "OK, I'm facing what appears to be the command center."

Vivienne walked her through the steps, and Celeste had to bite her lip to prevent an excited cheer from escaping when she got into the system. She set up the remote router as Vivienne had taught her, as well as a virtual server that would allow for a quick transfer.

"It will take about five minutes to identify and upload the files we need," Vivienne said, then fell silent. Celeste navigated the search engine to track down the code names that Vivienne had provided, based on dark web chatter, for the operations that included the head of Omar's organization. The files would reveal who that person was and how they fit into the impending cyberattack on America. Celeste expected at least some overlap with the list of names from the Feds.

So many files. "Cameras show you're still good—no one in the building seems to be in a rush to find an intruder—but let's not test our luck. We must get you out of there undetected." Vivienne had been telling the truth when she alluded to having broken into head-quarters, Celeste was sure of it. It was quite an adrenaline rush to be around classified information that almost no one had access to. *I bet she could fill volumes with all she's seen and done.*

When Celeste had finished the search and the file upload showed 97.0 percent complete, Vivienne's voice came through again, but with significant static.

"Oh my, this is unexpected," Vivienne said. Then in a whisper to Celeste, "I have company, dear. I logged out of the camera system just in time, but I'm afraid you're on your own now."

Someone unwelcome must have joined Vivienne. "No, now isn't good," Celeste heard her say. "You can wave that thing around all you want, but let me be clear—I'm not going anywhere with you! Get your hands off me, asshole."

Celeste had frozen mid-keystroke and strained to hear what was happening on Vivienne's side through the earbuds while she watched the files upload: 97.5 percent, 97.6 percent. *By all means, take your fucking time, computer system.*

Vivienne was not talking now, but Celeste could hear the sounds of a struggle, glass being smashed, and a man speaking in low tones. If only she could know what was happening on the other end of the audio. She frowned, her heart racing. She hoped Vivienne wasn't hurt —or worse.

Was the voice familiar?

No.

More static, more chaos.

Then the audio feed dropped.

Vivienne had gone dark, as Celeste had heard it said in spy speak.

This was not a good omen.

Get the fuck out of Dodge, Celeste.

But she was glued to the chair. What were a few more moments, while she waited for the 97.9 percent to turn to 98? She may never have another chance to access these files.

She typed her name into the search bar, bracing herself for what she would find. Several files associated with her name popped up immediately. She clicked on the first one and skimmed the contents, which caused her to nearly fall off her chair.

CONFIDENTIAL

Asset Name: Scarlet
Real Name: [Redacted]
Country: [Redacted]
Occupation: Finance executive
Recruitment Date: Asset remains unaware of her involvement; handler to identify appropriate time to broach
Motivation: Opposition to the current regime of the Obsidian Serpent; desire to protect family and friends
Reliability Rating: A (consistently reliable)
Intelligence Provided: [Redacted]
Payment: [Redacted]
Status: [Redacted]
Current Risk of Exposure: Moderate
Security Measures: [Redacted]
Extraction Plans: [Redacted]
Family: [Redacted]

Perhaps she should have felt anger or betrayal, sadness or fear. But she felt numb. Despite the Feds' promise that they were being run off book, she was very much an asset of the US government according to the memo staring back at her on the screen. *At least Scarlet is a cute name.* She smiled sadly.

The file was almost finished, at 98.7 percent. *One minute remaining.*

She looked through the memo one more time and noticed something she had missed:

Note: Asset remains in the dark about family involvement in Operation Phantom Strike

She felt as if invisible hands were wrapped around her neck as she fought to get air into her lungs. It had to be a mistake.

Family? Someone close to her had been wrapped up in a project in a secret file?

She rested her forehead against her hand and rubbed it, willing herself back in time. But to when? How would she uncover who in her family had been working with the FBI? *Especially since they're all dead.*

She was working blind, inside FBI headquarters impersonating a real live field agent, any number of government officials could be rushing to capture her, and Vivienne had been kidnapped, from what she could gather. *If I'm going to be caught, I may as well have my questions answered.* She navigated to the search menu again.

The results were voluminous, but it was obvious from the first click. Everything she thought she'd known, what she'd trusted to be good and true. *All lies.* The wind was knocked from her with such force that she looked around to see who had done it. *Betrayal to be processed in a millisecond.*

There was no time to sit there and feel sorry for herself. She needed to move.

Yet she remained frozen in place.

She had to do one more search.

It was the only one that mattered.

Zero results found.

She exhaled. While nothing about the moment was perfect or even going well, she was relieved that her husband was not listed in the database.

Find your center. She remembered these words from her sessions with Zed and Anne Marie. None of what she'd discovered had to be processed in that moment. She mustn't get distracted. She did not want to go to prison, and she did not want to get caught up in a shoot-out.

I didn't come this far to only come this far.

She pulled a flash drive from her bag and saved her research to it, then turned her attention back to the larger files she was transferring.

Finally, the upload reached 99.9 and then 100 percent.

She had everything she'd come for—and much, much more. It was time to go. Digging deep, she tried to remember the reason she'd continued down this path for so long.

Meredith's distorted body. Zari's gentle spirit taken from the world callously, his children growing up without a father. The carousel of women and children who had been abused and discarded by Omar and his kind. Maybe her parents had also been victims to a larger force, believing in something so strongly that they had been willing to give their lives for it. And her brother, Dawn, and Evelyn. She couldn't handle the sadness anymore.

This—all this risk—wasn't only to guarantee her a safer future. It was for everyone who'd sacrificed their lives to make the world better and for those who had done it to keep her alive and well. She would complete the mission—taking down Omar's boss and stopping the cyberattack as her first and second priorities, in no order of importance—because so many were counting on her to give it all meaning.

But her heart—it was shattered. Her vision in Paris reminded her of the void she felt without her parents. And now this. They had a hidden life she knew nothing about. Was her entire life based on lies?

Her Neverfull repacked, she returned the chair to its rightful place and wiped down everything she had touched.

"She's in here!" shouted a baritone voice.

As if things couldn't get any worse.

Then more voices. *And behind those voices are armed agents trained to kill trespassers.*

"Who has access?"

Going from memory now that she didn't have Vivienne to give her directions, she made her way to the back door, sticking to the original plan.

"I don't have clearance."

"Neither do I."

"Has it occurred to you that maybe *we're* the ones who aren't supposed to be here, not her?"

Well, tweedle dickheads, thank you for waffling back and forth because you just gave me enough time to get out of here and saved me from prison. No wonder the country was behind in virtually every metric. These clowns were running it. *Not my circus, not my clowns.*

She dashed out the door and raced toward an unmarked one halfway down the hall.

Please work, please work. The badge touched the reader while she held her breath.

She looked left and right for signs anyone was coming. A door to the left began to open as the reader blinked green to indicate she could enter.

Soundlessly, she moved through the door into a tunnel that had only one way in—the doorway she'd passed through—and one way out, where it exited several blocks away from the J. Edgar Hoover FBI Building.

Inside the tunnel, she ran faster than she ever had before. No one was following her, but it didn't change the fact that she didn't have eyes on the other side.

Zed's voice boomed in her mind: *"No time for self-pity now, Mia. They will hunt you and capture you. Your only shot at survival is to rely on yourself and your training. How committed are you?"*

Very. She was certain of that—she wanted to see this through.

Finally, she reached the end of the tunnel, where she slammed into the door with all her might. It opened easily, and she nearly fell over from her force.

Celeste squinted, her eyes attempting to adjust to the sunshine blazing down on her.

Run your heart out.

Only a few more blocks and then she could rest.

Her breathing was heavy, and she was aware she probably stuck out like a sore thumb, flustered and sweaty while clad in DC attire, sprinting through mobs of people during work hours. She could only hope they were all too wrapped up in their little inside-the-Beltway bubble to notice.

Putting her fate in someone else's hands had never been Celeste's style. While she trusted Vivienne, she had realized she needed a Plan

C in case their first two went belly-up. She had stashed her own flight fund and a change of clothes in an alley with no CCTV. When she arrived at the spot, she dove behind the dumpster, scrambling for her bag.

It was still there.

If the FBI put out an APB, her hair color, height, race, and outfit would be the top descriptors. She shed the gray suit and put on a casual ivory tracksuit, with baggy pants that concealed her weapons, along with sneakers. Pulling her wig back in a ponytail, she topped off the casual look with a burgundy-and-gold Commanders hat.

Everything else she might need was still in the bag.

Time to disappear for a few hours.

Walking briskly and taking a nonsensical route to ensure she wasn't followed, she headed for M Street, where there were bustling shops and crowds she could weave in and out of.

Slow down. Be unmemorable.

The visions of her parents that she'd had that Paris morning popped into her mind again, seemingly so far in the past. *Before I knew.*

Now she understood the urgency, what was at stake. Now she knew that her parents hadn't died in a freak car accident. *They were murdered.*

After several more miles, she was alone on a Georgetown side street about five minutes away from the shops and crowds. Despite a stitch in her side, she had to push on. *No rest for the weary.*

Then came the sound of heavy footsteps running about a block away. She guessed three sets.

"You're making a habit of allowing her to slip through your fingers," scolded a man whose voice she didn't recognize. "Find her and bring her to me. Move!"

The footsteps sounded as though they were heading in her direction. Fast.

That's my cue.

It wasn't a stretch to assume the men were armed. She raced off, staying on the desolate street. There had been enough casualties.

Still no word from Vivienne. Celeste could've used some eyes on CCTV to home in on the men's whereabouts and direct her path.

Stopping behind a tree, she pulled a Glock 9-millimeter from its ankle holster and tucked it into the waistband of her pants. Tears threatened to fall, and she squeezed her eyes shut for one moment.

You've got this.

A gunshot rang out.

Move!

She took off sprinting.

Another shot and then another. One bullet whizzed past her left ear.

She moved back and forth to make it more difficult for the shooters to aim, as Zed had taught her. The men were within shooting range, and there didn't appear to be any innocent bystanders around. She held her Glock behind her, aiming her index finger knuckle toward one of the men and firing. He wasn't hit, but at least they were now aware she was prepared to put up a fight.

She ran as though her life depended on it—because it did. She was down to a five-minute mile and had been embodying Zed's philosophy, "Stay ready so you don't have to get ready," as he always said during her street-fighting lessons. She was faster than they were, and try as they might, they couldn't shrink the distance between her and them.

A small smile broke out. She could keep going comfortably at that pace for some time.

Thank you, Zed, for pushing me to prioritize those boring hours on the treadmill.

More men could be waiting for her somewhere ahead. She cut over to M Street, where she hoped the large number of people would deter the men from firing, lest they call attention to themselves. Moving through the crowd, she feigned a casual afternoon jog, all the while mindful of the heavily breathing henchmen behind her. She strained to hear them through the other sounds around her.

"Let's get out of here before we're made," a gruff voice muttered.

And then they were gone, or at least that's what they'd want her to believe, expecting her to emerge when the sun went down. She circled back a few blocks away toward a behemoth Gothic church and flattened her body against the wall on the shadowed side.

She felt as though the pounding of her heart would be detectable to anyone nearby.

It'll be nightfall soon.

She waited and waited until the bustling crowds shopping on M Street had dissipated, though it still felt too dangerous to be out in the open with no backup. She had lost those men earlier, but they wouldn't let that happen twice. They'd return with more muscle and bigger guns.

Before she could go anywhere, she needed to transform her appearance a bit. She didn't have a new disguise with her, but she could at least put on different clothes—her third outfit of the day. *If they didn't keep catching up to me, things would've gone a little more smoothly.* She reached into the bag, pulled out a pair of black leggings, a matching zippered jacket, and a white T-shirt, and changed in the shadows. *Now, I need to get the fuck out of here.*

Swallowing her pride, she reached into her pocket for that week's burner phone and begrudgingly dialed the one person who could extract her. *Plan D at this point?*

"What mess have you gotten yourself into this time, Mizz Donovan?" Gabe whispered by way of greeting.

The way he pronounced "miss" as "mizz" grated on her nerves. "It's *Celeste*," she corrected him. For the thousandth time.

"I warned you that there might be a time when we couldn't protect you anymore. Have Omar's cronies come after you? You can't expect to murder a US asset and get away scot-free."

I am a US asset, dumbass. But maybe Gabe didn't know. *Could it be possible?* Could her anger toward him and Chet be misplaced?

"I didn't murder anyone," she hissed into the phone, "and now is hardly the ideal time for a lecture." She remembered then that he was her only way out.

Tread lightly.

"I have what you've been looking for," she told him. "But in exchange, I need a favor."

"What is it then?"

"I need you"—she paused and sighed heavily—"to pick me up. I'm in DC. At Thirty-Sixth and M Street Northwest."

"You're what?!" Gabe erupted. "There's a camera on every corner," he said, lowering his voice, "and the place is swarming with plain-clothes Feds. With your track record, I'm not naive enough to think that your motives are innocent."

"Well? I don't have much time here. Are you coming or not? I promise it will be worth your while."

"I'm five minutes away. Hold tight."

Exactly five minutes later, a shiny black Chevy Malibu came barreling toward the Gothic Washington National Cathedral's front lawn and screeched to a halt. The passenger door swung open. It took her mere seconds to dash across the lawn and dive into the car. She'd barely settled in with her bag when Gabe sped away.

"I can't even imagine what you were thinking, having a shoot-out in front of Georgetown Cupcake! Of all the stupid, reckless, insane stunts you've pulled in the short time I've known you, this... this tops them all! You could've been killed, but since you hardly seem concerned about that part, a civilian could've gotten hurt! And then what? Selfish, arrogant—you literally think of no one but yourself!"

Ugh, maybe calling Chet would've been the better option.

Anger rose in her throat as she read his judgmental expression. He was the same buttoned-up prick who'd accosted her with accusations during her Capri honeymoon. Sometimes, like in that moment, she wanted to smudge his eyeglasses or ruffle his hair.

"Before you jump to conclusions—" she began.

"Oh, I know all about what you've been up to. A complaint of three men waving guns around and an unidentified woman fleeing was called in... of course, it didn't occur to me that it was you until I found out you're here in DC. It wasn't a huge intellectual leap to figure out that, as usual, you were attempting to jeopardize our entire mission on some childish vigilante suicide—"

"I wasn't made, and besides, I'd have been hard to recognize." Chet had unknowingly walked right past her earlier and was none the wiser.

Her heart slowed to its normal rhythm and her breathing evened out, while she processed all that had transpired. She unzipped her jacket pocket and fingered the tiny flash drive as if to make sure it was real.

Celeste Fucking Donovan saves the day—yet again. She wasn't as buoyant as she'd anticipated. The heaviness was back, albeit for new reasons.

Gabe slowed to a stop when the traffic light changed. He turned to her and narrowed his eyes. "What did you do?" he accused.

When she didn't reply immediately, he continued his railing. "It's going to take me all night to clean up this mess, what with the coverage all over CCTV and all. Your carelessness is costing me a lot, Mizz—"

"Stop right there. You'll be thanking me if you'd only listen."

The agent shot her a withering look.

"Buckle up, Gabe, because your mind is about to be blown." She summarized what she'd been up to the past few days, omitting the details that he couldn't know, that no one could know. Pushing the sorrow down, she awaited his reaction.

"I have to say, it's not quite what I expected." He drove in silence for a moment before speaking again, this time with admiration and excitement in his voice.

"I can't believe you figured out a way to hack into the system... it's... none of it makes sense... it's impenetrable... the possibilities, though, if we could get this information to the president. Do you know what this means? We could shut down the Senate's meddling... prevent the attack... but is it enough? Are we too late?" he rambled.

What I wouldn't give to distance myself from all this.

Gabe was referring to the joint briefing of the president of the United States and the US Senate Select Committee on Intelligence scheduled for two days later. If classified information about the cyberattack got into the wrong hands, the damage would be catastrophic. Celeste shared Gabe's concern about timing and hoped the information she'd found would at least delay the hearing. *He doesn't need to know about the rest of it.*

"But how did you... there's... no, it's not possible to pull off," Gabe said, shaking his head. "You surely would've... no security breach has even been reported, though. Only the shoot-out."

"The guns and the Georgetown chaos obviously weren't part of the original plan," Celeste told him. "I still got what I needed, though." *And more than I bargained for—or could've lived a lifetime without knowing.*

It occurred to her then that it could have been a mistake to have him pick her up. "Wait, does the agency use GPS on your car?"

Gabe dismissed her concern with a shrug.

"Ohh, it's a dupe fleet car, isn't it?" She noticed the windows had a 5 percent tint—illegal nearly everywhere in the United States. Monty had them on his vehicles for complete privacy. "Hmm, not bad. Fake plates too?"

He nodded. "Chet and I have to stay two steps ahead of our bosses," he explained.

Celeste, by hacking the secure FBI servers, could now confirm that not one, but two members of the US president's cabinet plus three members of Congress had been compromised and were essentially committing treason by working for a nefarious oligarch—the double agent who, as it turned out, was Omar's boss.

"You're in for some unpleasant surprises—they've also turned a few members of Congress. But I think you have at least a day or two to put a stop to this."

Strategically leaking the information she'd obtained would be explosive and damning. It would help Gabe and Chet immensely and prevent disaster in her home country. She only hoped that bringing in Gabe wouldn't cause Vivienne's plan to backfire.

I had no choice.

She wasn't even sure Vivienne was alive.

"You're not safe. They'll be looking for you. Where are you staying?" Gabe asked. "They" could be any number of awful people, though she knew he meant the three men pursuing her earlier.

"Don't worry, I have everything backed up on the cloud, and I took your advice—no big-box hotels. I'm staying at the Riggs in Penn Quarter under an alias. I confirmed they have few to no security measures in place—and it's quite luxurious," she added, knowing it would annoy Gabe. "Maybe I have a career in espionage ahead of me."

"You're staying two blocks away from the FBI, the same agency where you just pulled a heist by yourself, with no protection? No, you absolutely did not miss your calling."

CELESTE SLIPPED INTO HER HOTEL, confident she and Gabe hadn't been followed. She'd made Gabe stop a couple of times so she could discard the getaway tracksuit and the gray work attire in two separate Georgetown dumpsters. As far as the hotel staff would be able to tell, Rebecca Foster was a guest who'd just finished an exercise class after work, with her Neverfull bag slung over her shoulder stuffed with her work clothes.

She admired the lobby. The building was originally a bank's headquarters constructed in the 1890s. Back when you could see and feel your money—not have it taken by hackers on the dark web. Off to her right was an expansive gold-plated, barrel-vaulted reception area. The long desk was L-shaped, and a uniformed woman in a black suit and collared white shirt looked at her with a hint of curiosity. Celeste gave her a small nod of recognition but nothing more. It was critical that she "be unmemorable and remain anonymous," a mantra drilled into her head by Petey's tales of his days as an NYPD detective. She'd become friendly with him, meeting regularly at a local pub to glean everything she could from him without raising suspicion. Of course, she could've hired a dirty cop—but that wasn't what she needed.

I need a drink.

The bar and its adjoining restaurant were on her left. She walked in and scoped it out. A tall, lanky bartender with blond hair, the prototype of men Celeste had enjoyed before she met and married Theodore, was drying wine glasses, a dish towel in his hand and another on his shoulder. He silently slid her a menu and didn't look up when she sat down.

The glamorous art deco restaurant, which was otherwise empty, was larger than she had anticipated and ran the length of the hotel. A cocktail lounge was set off across the bar. Massive arched windows overlooked F Street Northwest, and marbled columns throughout gave the restaurant a stately feel. Velvet, jewel-toned booths spanned the room, and massive, custom-made chandeliers and sconces were strategically placed to provide a sexy glow. An enclosed glass tower of multicolored roses stood in the corner, tying the luxe Parisian brasserie look together nicely.

Leave it to the DC crowd to let this place sit empty, preferring cookie-cutter steakhouses over glitz and ambience.

After a cursory glance at the wine list, she cleared her throat. The bartender looked up as though seeing her for the first time. "What can I get for you?"

"Dirty martini, extra olives, please," she requested simply, habitually avoiding eye contact. "Belvedere."

She should be tucked away in her room in case the gunmen reappeared. She should be tracking down what happened to Vivienne. She should be destroying her alias now that it was burned. She should be calling Michel—if he was even the right person—to share what she'd discovered. *Should, should, should.*

But she needed a beat. She hadn't seen it coming, the flood of information that had locked her breath in her throat. Truth was, she could've gone a lifetime without knowing. The betrayal swept through her body, poisoning her thoughts like a virus. Thinking back to all the times she should have known, her cheeks burned with anger or sadness or perhaps both. The past was the past, so why did it have to rear its ugly head when she was already consumed with guilt, fear, regret?

No. Not now. There's no time for this.

She had to quash her emotions and refocus on the task at hand. The events from earlier in the day replayed like a movie in her mind. On almost all counts, the heist was a success. No one had been hurt by the gun-toting thugs, she'd gotten the information needed to halt the cyberattack, and questions she hadn't consciously known she had were answered. It was the answers that plagued her.

"Here you are, ma'am." The martini glass perspired from the cool liquid. Her mouth watered, longing for it to make her forget. She took a long swig.

"Charge it to the room?"

She looked up, fully noticing the man for the first time. His ice-blue eyes, much like her husband's, pierced into hers, and she was thankful for the glasses and colored contacts. "Sure. Last name—" Not Donovan. No sense slipping up now. "Foster."

He returned to his cleaning. As she relaxed into her seat, the cold steel of her gun tucked at the small of her back made her shiver, reminding her of the earlier danger. The men had been waiting for her when she exited and chased her as she led them away from the FBI Building. She had run and run, weaving up and down the streets to stay undetected. The crowds cleared to the other side of the street faster than she'd imagined they would when one of the men fired a shot. Time stood still as the bullet sped toward her heart. As she dove out of the way, she had tried to catch anything memorable to identify them later. The shooter, standing in the middle of the three and visibly out of breath, was about her height, five feet, ten inches. The second man was about four inches shorter, and the third was a bit taller than the shooter. All were white. They had on sunglasses—matching Ray-Bans—and Washington Nationals ball caps to hide any distinguishing characteristics and were dressed in all-black clothing.

Another shot rang out then, this time from the smallest man. Instinctively, she had reached for her gun, released the safety, and was taking aim when her higher self intervened. *Have you lost your mind? Disappear*, her inner voice yelled. She shook the urge to recip-rocate and took off running again. Zed had trained her well, although he knew very little about Celeste's secret life, only that she had to protect herself in times like this. He had helped her build up her speed, and by the time she neared the backside of the church, it seemed she had lost them.

Never a dull moment, she thought now, her adrenaline pumping at the memory. *Who were they, and how did they know I was there?*

Her old life had been so simple, when her younger, vapid self would shack up with any man she pleased in between cocaine-fueled party nights and long days on the trading desk. Her success was what drove her to each next level. She had loved—and eventually became addicted to—the euphoria after scoring a massive payday at work. Purchasing her first Birkin bag and diamond earrings, buying her first apartment in cash before she was thirty—it was a privileged life she'd only dreamed of growing up. The ornate decor of the Riggs reminded her of those first moments when she'd realized that she could live however she pleased without any interference and that everything was for sale. It was reminiscent of a simpler time.

She ordered dinner from the disengaged man and turned back to her thoughts.

Now that Agent Gutiérrez knew some of what Celeste knew, all she had to do was transfer the information. She should have run straightaway to her room and uploaded it, per Gabe's instructions. But something gave her pause. As soon as she sent the files, there would be no turning back. The illuminati would convene, and there would be to-do lists, clandestine meetings, more to hide from her husband, the possible return of her panic attacks and nightmares. She wanted five more minutes of peace.

Tapping the glass, she said, "Another of the same, please."

"Nick," the man said, proffering his hand. She shook it firmly, saying, "Rebecca Foster."

While he mixed her cocktail without any further conversation, a runner brought her meal and scurried away.

"Your filet au poivre, medium rare, and a dirty martini. Anything else I can get for you, miss?"

She dismissed him politely and turned to her food. Suddenly

famished after spending hours on the run, she cut into the meat and took a bite. The tender, juicy steak melted in her mouth. It was perfectly seared, the cracked black pepper crust balanced by the creamy, cognac-infused sauce. She savored every bite, feeling as though she hadn't eaten for days. Maybe she hadn't.

Back in her room, Celeste opened her laptop and set to work transferring most of the files. She saved a few for herself alone, the ones she'd stumbled upon in those last moments, those that could never see daylight. Flooded by emotion congruent with the magnitude of what she'd learned, she fought back a sob.

Time was of the essence to get the information she had uploaded onto the cloud into the right hands. Even without Vivienne, who still hadn't resurfaced, Celeste had ways to ensure the cyberattack was stopped before it began. Though she'd never asked for the responsibility, she realized that with Vivienne unavailable, it was solely up to Celeste to save her country from these traitorous, corrupt men and women.

Yes, the plan had morphed a bit. *The bamboo that bends is stronger than the oak that resists.* She'd complete the mission no matter what it took. But in the meantime, she sent Gabe and Chet the evidence they'd need to reveal that there were traitors acting from within the administration. *I'll let them get a few brownie points from the powers that be while I handle the situation in the background.*

Logging in to the secret corners of the dark web, she found the person who could execute her plan. There was no time for panic over having to act alone—there was only time for action. As she'd learned from watching Ace over the years, strategically placing news stories in the right outlets was sometimes the most effective way to get things done. Now the most urgent of situations—stopping the cyberattack spearheaded by Omar's boss—was being handled.

Next, she texted her husband a sweet good night with a line about how relaxing the fictitious massage and facial treatments at the Miraval Berkshires spa had been and how excited she was to see him soon. Then she got to work memorializing her alibi. So that her travel could be traced, she had already purchased a ticket from the closest train station, Wassaic, back to Grand Central Station. But that didn't solve the problem that she had to get back to Wassaic Station before that train departed to New York the following day.

Getting out of DC—which she needed to do as soon as possible—was going to be a challenge without Vivienne's help. She had plenty of transportation options between DC and New York: train, plane, car, bus. The train seemed too risky; there was always ample law enforcement moving around the stations. Chartering a jet in the nation's capital or hiring a car would be dangerous, with or without a disguise, because of the high profile. Another complicating factor was that she wasn't sure she could identify the men who had been shooting at her earlier in the day, so with any of these methods, she'd potentially be unaware she was being followed.

She mulled over the possibilities and kept arriving at the most undesirable one: calling in another favor from Gabe to have him arrange her New York to Wassaic return. The very thought of giving his smug ass the satisfaction of saving her yet again was unbearable, but more importantly, it could bring unwanted attention to her if things went awry. She tried to think of other viable options. Even calling Michel or Ace, each of whom had extracted her—*correction: Ace kidnapped me*—before, was problematic. It was too soon to reach out to Michel anyway; she wanted some time to process everything before bringing him in. She could go, tail between her legs, to Ace, but she knew they would expect her to explain why she was in DC. She didn't like any of these ideas.

After weighing everything, she decided she'd leave DC from Union Station on the Megabus. The 3 a.m. bus would get her to New York at Port Authority by morning. She'd go to Miraval with an alias and then back to New York as herself to ensure she had a solid alibi. If ever pressed, her train ticket from Wassaic to Grand Central would serve as evidence she'd been at Miraval. To make her alibi airtight, she'd pay one of her dark web friends to create a fictional reservation at Miraval. *No one has burst into my hotel room looking for me yet.* Maybe she'd get away with what she'd done, even without Vivienne's intervention.

As long as Vivienne had executed at least the first part of their plan before the man burst into the room and snatched her, Celeste's biometrics would've been wiped from the FBI system immediately after they'd been scanned, and her presence in the building would've been erased. Even if she'd been caught on CCTV in Georgetown, it was unlikely they'd be able to narrow down a woman in a generic jogging suit with a Commanders hat covering her face.

She let herself feel victorious for one small moment. Dozens, if not hundreds or thousands, of people in the intelligence community across the globe had tried to do what she'd done earlier—ID the head of Omar's organization. She had delivered, without even knowing whom she was looking for beforehand. While part of her wanted to turn the information over to the authorities—and she'd already begun the process by sending it to Gabe and Chet— the other part of her, perhaps the more powerful part, wanted to keep it under wraps for fear that the investigation would never rid the world of the man who'd emboldened and financed Omar to cause as much destruction as he had. She felt the sense of dread that she'd carried with her since her visions in Paris surfaced. She was so close to bringing the person down, and she couldn't let anything jeopardize that. It was time to get back home and figure out what else needed to be taken care of.

Back in New York, she'd have to face the things that were really bothering her: the major betrayal by her parents, with their double life; her confusion upon seeing that she was officially a US asset, whom the intelligence community referred to as Scarlet; the magnitude of what she'd just done. She hoped—was gambling—that Gabe and Chet had the capabilities to cover up any lingering loose ends from her break-in since Vivienne was MIA. It was all a lot to process.

To divert her mind from going into panic mode, she thought back to her grid. One of the biggest unknowns in all her sleuthing was the identity of the people behind RH Global. While the mystery company may have seemed unrelated to the discoveries of the day, she was convinced it also had something to do with her. Was it as simple as the R and H being initials? If so, who? She believed

Matthew was either working with or shaking down someone she knew. *Roberto? Rani? Hadid?* They'd had so many opportunities to come clean—if they were involved, why had they chosen not to tell her? Was there anyone else it could have been? She then remembered Jack on the phone in Brazil with someone named Rudy. *Could Rudy be the R in RH?* Would Jack, the one she'd always trusted to be straight with her, tell her who Rudy was if knew? Was it all—RH Global, Matthew—a red herring? Was something bigger happening right beneath her nose?

She turned it over and over in her mind—the idea that someone close to her could be paying off Matthew—evaluating it from every angle she could think of. But she would have to wait until she had more information or, if one of her weaselly friends or colleagues was deceiving her, until she drew the truth out of them.

Tomorrow's problem.

~

"WELL, Miss Donovan, I've been awaiting our introductions for quite some time now. It's so nice to finally meet you, though I'd hoped it would have been under more favorable circumstances."

"Director Stephen Lockwood, I would love to say the pleasure is all mine—but that would be a lie."

She'd recognized him the moment she'd regained consciousness. *Well played, motherfucker.* He had certainly won the battle—quite a few of them, if she were being honest.

But there could only be one loser in the war. *And it won't be me.*

Celeste looked around her. Was she still in the hotel? She sat in a dining chair like those she'd seen earlier in the restaurant, her hands and feet bound to it. The room was unfamiliar and bare, with a cement floor and a single light bulb hanging down from a long cord. It was reminiscent of the room in her recurrent nightmare where Theodore was murdered by Omar. Shadows danced in the corners, perhaps full of armed men.

Her gun was no longer at the small of her back; it had been taken from her while she was unconscious. She moved her wrist ever so slightly and felt that her diamond tennis bracelet and watch that she'd put on when she'd gotten back to the hotel were still there. Even the enormous engagement ring Theodore had surprised her with so long ago and her protective bauble ring remained on her fingers. Perhaps the needle inside the bauble would come in handy.

Lockwood might have the place swarming with henchmen. But her eyes and ears were taking everything in; Zed had drilled into her how important those senses become when one is incapacitated. There were no shadowed silhouettes in the dark corners of the room breathing, whispering, or shuffling their feet.

Her instincts told her that she and the director were alone, which in many ways illustrated how arrogant—and stupid—he was. The bureaucrat turned traitor wanted to take care of her himself. She'd slithered out of his grasp one too many times, and his ego was wounded. *Use that.*

"Are you proud of yourself that you tracked down my identity—that I've been operating for so long right under everyone's nose and you alone figured out who I was?" he asked. "I must admit, I'm impressed; I underestimated you."

"So did Omar, and things didn't end well for him," Celeste said without a hint of fear in her voice.

Anger flickered in the FBI director's eyes, indicating that he was a bit rattled at the mention of what happened to his deputy. She hoped envisioning Omar after Celeste and Michel had brutally murdered him reminded Lockwood what she was capable of.

If Celeste had learned one thing in the past few years, it was that —although she'd always have amazing people along the way to help her—she ultimately had to rely on her own judgment, instinct, and skill. She was no fool; she knew she was in danger, grave danger. But she refused to let the deaths of so many people she cared about—Zari and Meredith, not to mention her parents—be in vain. Thus it didn't matter if she made it to the end of the day alive—Lockwood was going to be exposed in a matter of hours for the whole world to see.

A sham press release from the US attorney general, Lockwood's boss, would be sent out over the wire the following morning alerting the US president, cabinet members, ranking members of Congress, every government agency, and foreign heads of state that the director of the US Federal Bureau of Investigation was acting as the head of a global crime syndicate involved in cyberwarfare, arms and sex trafficking, money laundering, and racketeering. And moreover, the chair of the Senate Finance Committee, the director of national intelligence, and most notably, the vice president were acting within the government as foreign agents assisting the director.

Appearing as a legitimate communication from the AG, it would claim that the DOJ would hold each of them criminally liable to the highest extent of the law as traitors. It would be difficult to walk back the statement because redacted classified documents were attached.

It would be as effective as all the work Ace had done, and importantly, Celeste would ensure that the American public turned on the traitors quickly in case the global powers that be wanted the scandal swept under the rug. She'd learned a thing or two watching Ace navigate over the years. Planting stories moved markets, crumbled governments, started and ended civil wars. This would be similar in magnitude.

In tandem, a powerful social media campaign would bombard all Americans of voting age on every widely used platform. It would contain the stunning revelations and the evidence along with it in short- and long-form videos. The final message would encourage constituents to reach out to their members of Congress and "finally end the corruption in the swamp that is our nation's capital." She was particularly proud of that line, which she had come up with herself. The public would be angry, afraid, and looking for blood—a powerful combination in effecting social change.

It's no wonder I have a goddess complex—I'm a fucking savant.

No matter what happened with Lockwood, the public affairs campaign would expose him in a matter of hours.

If I don't get out of here soon—and I may never—I won't get to see my handiwork.

After navigating the underground world of global crime virtually alone, she found it strange to think that her sort of vigilante justice and activism was in her DNA. Her parents, those kind teachers committed to educating America's youth, had themselves been hiding behind a facade. Had her brother known? Was that why he was always so troubled? Did Vivienne know what Celeste would discover in those precious moments alone inside the secret FBI server room? That her parents, seemingly so provincial and normal, were actually some of the most powerful double agents in all of America's history? That they were so decorated and feared by enemies that they had to change their names, go underground, and move to Middle America right before Celeste and her brother were born? They were heroes, weren't they? Was it part of her legacy to follow in their footsteps? Would they be proud of what she'd done and was capable of? Or disgusted? She hoped she would have the chance to find out.

Lockwood must have been hiding in her hotel room and knocked her out with chloroform right after she'd sorted her travel.

As long as he was alone, Celeste would take her odds with Lockwood. Zed had trained her so that she could handily outperform most men, even those in intelligence or law enforcement. It was almost as if he knew what she'd be up against in that very moment. Celeste was in the best shape of her life.

"You're awfully quiet for someone on a suicide mission. Does this look familiar?"

Celeste narrowed her eyes. Lockwood was standing in front of her, holding up the syringes that had been removed from her hiding spot at Drake's villa.

"Guess which wannabe femme fatale is being framed for Drake's untimely murder as we speak?" he said. "You know he's dead, right? Imagine how happy I was when I realized you'd done all the work for me—I couldn't have done a better job at setting you up for this myself. Roughing him up at a restaurant, not trying to revive him after a failed attempt to poison him, placing yourself as the only suspect in his death. Bravo, Celeste, you're as dumb as the criminals on true crime shows."

He smiled, a wide Cheshire-cat shit-eating grin across his face. *I can't wait to wipe that grin right off your face.* She was almost done, but she had to keep him talking for a minute—he was pacing and had his back to her at times while in storytelling mode. Not that he would allow her to interrupt—he wanted to brag about his plan and was just getting started. He seemed unrushed.

So we must be somewhere secure and soundproof in the hotel because he's not worried about anyone bursting in. The basement, perhaps?

"Clever to kill him with the same poison as you used to kill Omar, wasn't it?" he gloated. "It won't be hard to paint you as the scorned amateur you are. It goes something like this: You tried to get Omar back, and when he rejected you, you took matters into your own hands. Doubly scorned by Drake, you exacted the same revenge. The world will see the pathetic, desperate woman you are and demand that you're held accountable.

"You see, I've been on to you for quite some time. Drake was a good soldier, but he was a liability and had to go. Your timing couldn't have been better, really. You did my dirty work, and in the process, you framed yourself. Your RICO prosecution will be a piece of cake— your fabricated file is this thick," he said, putting the syringes aside to make a hand gesture to indicate a file more than a foot high.

"Wow, you are cunning. But my husband is expecting me. So why don't you let me go and no one will be the wiser?"

Almost done.

"The same husband who faked his death to get away from you? So he could carry on with his secret life? That husband? Hmm. You're bluffing, and he's in Myanmar as we speak—if you can believe it."

Celeste remained stoic. "I know who you are. I recognized you straightaway from a photo Meredith had of the two of you together, Director Lockwood. Or as you're otherwise known, *Seth*," she sneered.

He slow-clapped sarcastically three times. "Well done, Donovan. What gave it away?"

She continued, ignoring him. She had to get him angry, and she had to hold it together until then. "Bold to infiltrate my friend group.

Courting my best friend to get close to me. But Seth, what I haven't been able to figure out is—why are you so obsessed with me? You've gone to such pathetic lengths to take me down, yet you've been unsuccessful time and again."

She feigned a frown and made a childlike sound indicating sadness. "I'm sure it must have been embarrassing for you in your little bad guy world to know that your deputy, your disgusting, deplorable operative Omar, was taken from you right under your own nose—by an American citizen and a woman, no less!"

His cheeks turned red. "No more painful than it must have been seeing Meredith's body so distorted from that fall she had. Did you like the strychnine, reminiscent of whatever you did to Omar in Rome? I thought it was a nice touch. I was planning to add her death to your list of crimes. I can see the headlines now. *Ice Queen, Blinded by Jealousy, Murders Her Best Friend.*"

Oh, Mere. I'm so sorry.

While she'd never knowingly have put Mere in harm's way, her friend would still be alive if she'd never been associated with Celeste. *If Mere could answer today, she'd say she wished she never met me. And the same goes for Zari. Seth and his kind are toxic, but aren't I equally so?*

The asshole was still talking. "You wouldn't imagine how much fun I had and how easily she handed over your daily and travel schedules. I knew where you were and what you were doing at all times because that dumb bitch couldn't keep her mouth shut. You should really vet your employees better next time."

Now! a voice inside her screamed. The image of her parents, with their troubled expressions, silently urging to her to run pulled her out of her inner examination and back into the present. Back into her power. The gods must have been in her favor because, in that moment, when her rage had all but taken over, she severed the rope securing her wrists with the tiny bauble needle.

Lockwood's back was to her now, as he had retreated into the shadows. Moving soundlessly, she took only seconds to slither out of the tie around her ankles.

She had to act fast, lest he discover she was free. Shoving her grief down deep, she assessed the situation as Zed had taught her to do. Lockwood was fit, but he wasn't agile like she was. Even so, her main potential weapon, the chair, would be easy for him to dodge. He came back out into the light, a small scalpel in his hand.

"It will be reported as a suicide, your death. Slit wrists after a few years living a life of crime. Your name will be smeared, disgracing your family, your husband..."

What little family remains.

"...and after a few news cycles, you'll be forgotten, just as Meredith—or Mere, as you call her—already has been."

He laughed. "What a gift she was. You should've seen how she ate up all my empty promises, opening her legs for a nice dinner without any hesitation, spilling all the inner workings of D&C and your life so freely."

Her heart ached and her temper flared as she listened to him say horrible things about Meredith. He clearly knew how close the two women were and was trying to get a rise out of Celeste. But she wouldn't take the bait. She remained outwardly stoic and calm, waiting for the absolute perfect time.

"And now your husband will be rid of you, so he can finally bring that brunette he spends a lot of time with out in public."

Celeste instantly regretted the frown that crossed her face. Theodore having secrets, yes, that she could fathom. But having a side piece? Either way, it was the least of her worries. Mere was gone, and the same man who had murdered her was moments away from killing Celeste. She zeroed in on his eye movements and body language, which she hoped would help her anticipate his next move. She'd need every advantage she could get to make it out of here.

"Oh, you didn't know? Oh, yes. Why do you think he's always in Zurich? You women are all the same, so trusting, so blind. Ironic that Meredith's biggest error in judgment was befriending you."

He moved slowly toward her, savoring the moment.

Four, three, two, one.

When he was almost close enough to harm her, she sprang into action.

The chair fell behind her with a thud, startling Lockwood.

He took a step back, nearly tripping over his feet, but kept hold of the scalpel.

She pounced.

The bauble on her ring now gone, the miniature knife on her finger was exposed.

She raised her arm, and channeling all the grief, shock, and fury she'd been carrying for as long as she could remember, she struck down on him while she had the chance, driving the tiny dagger directly into his eyeball.

Blood squirted everywhere, and the floor became slippery with the sticky goo. Her white T-shirt and black leggings were soaked, and it felt as if she were covered head to toe in his guts.

Lockwood screamed out, the sound of a wild animal under attack, crouching over and holding his eye. The scalpel hit the ground with a clang. Before he could recover, she retrieved it and sprang into action.

End him.

Celeste cut the horizon with the surgical knife, which made a whooshing sound in the air, and then made contact with his neck, slashing it from left to right.

She must have severed the carotid artery because more liquid was flying in every direction.

The screaming halted. Silence now.

What a mess.

Footsteps. Running toward the room.

Celeste grabbed one of Lockwood's firearms from his ankle and removed the safety.

She straightened up, ready to attack—a crazed predator, finally doling out the justice the situation required.

The door opened. She could make out a person's face, but the features were concealed by the shadows."

Bring it on.

She cocked the handgun, ready to fire when whoever it was walked into the open.

"It's me," said a familiar female voice.

Vivienne emerged from the shadows. She looked Celeste up and down, then took in the scene. Wearing a slight smirk, she nodded her head appreciatively.

"Well. This is certainly one way to finish the job. Nice work."

Celeste looked around the room with fresh eyes, at once realizing the enormity of what she'd done. Her hand was shaking, and she wanted the gun away from her. As if reading Celeste's mind, Vivienne gently took the piece from her and placed it next to Lockwood's body.

"My cleaner will take care of this scene."

Celeste steadied herself against Vivienne. Her teeth were chattering, and she felt clammy.

"I'd like to get home, please," she said. She longed for her bed. To bury herself under the luxurious weight of her down comforter and Frette sheets for a while before she had to face any of what had transpired in a mere twelve hours.

"You're in shock, dear." Vivienne put an arm around Celeste and led her to a doorway and stairwell. "It doesn't get much easier, no matter how many times you do it. Now, let's get you out of those clothes and showered."

Celeste could hear music, faint in the background. "Where—where are we? Underneath the hotel? Is that music coming from the Silver Lyan speakeasy?" Celeste loved sexy Prohibition-era lounges like the Lyan, though she doubted another DC visit was in her future.

"Yes. We're one level below the basement. From what we can tell, Lockwood has been blackmailing hotel management to use this empty room and was operating some sort of torture chamber out of it for some time. There are no security cameras, and it has a secret entrance that he would use to come and go."

Sick piece of shit. Good riddance. Celeste wondered briefly if the agent she'd impersonated all day had known what was going on right under her nose when she regularly stayed at the Riggs.

Celeste followed Vivienne upstairs to the secret entrance. Vivienne pushed open a heavy door into a desolate alleyway. A white florist van with The Blooming Beltway and cherry blossoms painted

on the side was waiting. Even in her trancelike state, Celeste appreciated the branding.

She suddenly realized that she couldn't simply walk outside
drenched in the FBI director's blood and that everything she'd
brought with her, including her new aliases and computers, were
upstairs.

"Wait, I have to go back inside," she said. "My things, my
disguises."

The window rolled down to reveal Michel in the driver's seat. "We
have people for that. Get in the fucking car before you're made,
Celeste."

Celeste bristled at being given orders but obeyed. She was too
drained and confused to make any sense of the day. She slid the back
door open and climbed in, while Vivienne walked around the vehicle
and got into the front passenger seat.

"Where are we going?" Celeste asked as they sped off.

"We're driving you to the Berkshires, honey," Vivienne replied.
"Given the gravity of what we had planned, Michel arranged for an
airtight alibi. Your doppelgänger, whom you met in the UAE, was
delighted to have a few days of pampering. So Celeste Donovan has
indeed enjoyed a spa getaway to anyone who inquires, verifiable by
CCTV."

"Cool. I'll send her a bottle of wine."

Michel and Vivienne exchanged a look.

"We'll make a quick stop for you to grab a shower and a change of
clothes, and then we'll drive through the night. You'll arrive in time
for breakfast," Michel said, his eyes on the road.

"What about—"

"Your press release and social media campaign?" Vivienne
interrupted.

Celeste nodded.

"Impressive. I tweaked the campaign a bit, but it'll go out in a
couple of hours just as you'd planned. We can discuss everything
once you've had some rest."

A short while later, Michel entered an unmarked parking garage.

It was entirely empty but for them. He drove around and around up to the fourth floor and parked right by the elevator.

"Who owns this building?" Celeste asked. It was in an up-and-coming, bustling part of the city and would've cost a fortune if it remained empty.

Again, her companions exchanged a look.

"I'm too depleted to shout, but one of you needs to give me some details. I haven't even begun to understand how you two are working together."

"We're going to have to tell her sometime," Vivienne said.

Michel sighed. "It's owned by the DGSE. We'll get into everything else on the road."

Julien, her Parisian handler and a former spy for the French intelligence agency DGSE, came to mind. "French foreign intelligence maintains a pied-à-terre in an empty office building in an up-and-coming neighborhood like Navy Yard?" She rolled her eyes. "Sounds like a totally normal scenario you cooked up," she said, directing the sarcasm at Michel.

"It's time to bring you into the fold. Don't worry—this will all make sense very soon," Vivienne said sympathetically.

"I'm not so sure she's going to view it that way, but I admire your optimism," Michel muttered as he opened the door into a large apartment.

Michel was right—Celeste had already connected some dots and was furious. She was no fool.

Unlike the rustic parking garage, the fourth-floor suite had been built out into an upscale home with only a few telltale signs that it was a front. Celeste noted that the blinds were drawn and covered with blackout curtains, and the art was fake. Other than that, it could've been any one of the high-rise apartments in the gentrified area.

Vivienne showed her to one of the restrooms.

Grabbing a roll of large trash bags from under the sink, Vivienne instructed, "Put your clothes and anything else you want destroyed in here. We'll incinerate them before we leave. The shower is here, as well as toiletries and a blow-dryer. Help yourself to anything you like in the closet or dresser in there."

With that, the no-nonsense woman left her alone.

Celeste peeled off the damp, bloody T-shirt and leggings. She stuffed the clothes and the wig and cap into the bag, then tied it emphatically.

No wonder I was shivering.

After her makeup and other remnants of Rebecca were gone, she ran a scalding hot shower and scrubbed every inch of her body that she could reach. On one of the shelves were a bottle of hydrogen peroxide and a nail brush, which she used to remove the blood from underneath her fingernails.

Soaked in Meredith's boyfriend's guts is not *how I envisioned the day ending.*

Some time passed as she willed the water to wash away the trauma of the day—twenty minutes or two hours, Celeste wasn't sure —and then she got out and toweled off. She dried her hair and applied some basic skincare, feeling a bit more human now.

The bedroom closet, much smaller than her sprawling Manhattan one, had been stocked with brand-new men's and women's clothing. She wondered what other sorts of people had stopped over on their way out of the city. After browsing through some of the tops on the women's side, she looked down at the shoes.

Déjà vu hit her like a freight truck, jerking her into the past, when she'd stayed at a similar apartment in Cairo with an almost identical setup and similar clothes. Even the Chloé ballet flats she'd worn that time were lined up in her size.

But Ace had arranged that safe house, so it must be a coincidence. Mustn't it?

She was still reeling that Michel and Vivienne were working together. Adding another layer of complexity would have to wait for another day.

13

A SYMBIOTIC RELATIONSHIP

Once they were back on the road, Vivienne began, "There's no good way to deliver this news besides directly, Celeste. We've been framing you—or rather, one of your aliases—for a while as the head of a rival crime syndicate with extensive reach to cartels in Central and South America, rebel militants in Africa, and terrorist organizations across the globe, pitting you and Lockwood against each other."

"Oh. Well, that's unexpected," she said nonchalantly instead of screaming, which would have fit the magnitude of the situation.

"What Vivi means to say is—"

"Don't take what I just said and mansplain it to her, Michel."

"You left out the most important part."

"By all means, if you think you can do a better job, please proceed," Vivienne replied through pursed lips.

"I wasn't saying you weren't doing—"

"Then what exactly *were* you suggesting, dear?" Vivienne said snidely.

Celeste rubbed her temples. *I can't listen to this bickering for the next six hours.*

"Children, please. I've just brutally murdered the chief law enforcement officer in the US and committed a cyberbreach to reveal significant secrets from which our country may never recover. What I need from you in this moment is the solace of knowing that your plan can withstand the next however many days, months, years so that I don't get the death penalty for treason. With all this chaos, I couldn't possibly care who explains what I need to know. The only thing I care about is that someone tells me what in the actual fuck is going on—and that whatever course of action we are taking plays."

The mood was somber inside the van as they barreled down the highway from the nation's capital en route to the Berkshire Mountains in Massachusetts in the dark of night, suggesting that the next few hours weren't going to be much fun once she learned what they had in store for her.

MICHEL AND VIVIENNE had been at it for a while, providing spurts of information that were interesting and sometimes helpful, but their storytelling wasn't painting the picture Celeste needed to fully understand the whole picture. She'd been sitting up stiffly on the long bench in the back seat of the van for much too long, and her body craved movement. *Time for me to do what I do best—take control.*

As much as she wanted to, though, her mindset was unstable. Her thoughts waffled back and forth between the Celeste Donovan who was larger than life and the Celeste who wanted to curl up on her sofa with her favorite self-pity cocktail—Xanax and a bottle of Macallan—and have them wake her when it was all over. She sighed heavily.

"Look, we're getting nowhere with these breadcrumbs you're giving me, and we don't have much time. Besides, you desperately need to replace the shocks in your abduction van. I'm feeling nauseated from bouncing around back here. Find me a ladies' room and a snack."

"Sure thing. There's a secure rest area a few exits up."

Finally, after so many years of questions, the answers were within reach—but now she wasn't sure she actually wanted them. Still, her curiosity was piqued, and she had to probe now that the floodgates had been opened.

"So let me get this straight. You both worked within the intelligence community with my parents, who, mind you, I only discovered were spies a few hours ago."

The two spies nodded in unison.

Celeste turned to Michel with an accusatory tone. "And you, after promising my parents you'd watch over me, fulfilled their promise by stalking me, a coed studying abroad in France, luring me to bed, and trying to keep me as your mistress. Do I have that right?"

"Oh, darling," Vivienne said, "you wouldn't believe the fight he and I had over that one. Our Paris townhome was in shambles. Dishes were thrown—I think neighbors even filed noise complaints, prompting a police house call for a domestic disturbance. I had slapped him so hard—and he was wearing the palm print on his cheek to match—that the officers asked him if he needed protection. The good ol' days were so exciting." Celeste could tell from her side profile that she was wearing a wistful smile, longing for her youthful passion.

"Men are idiots, dear," Vivienne added matter-of-factly without looking back at Celeste from the front seat. "They are—and always have been—the lesser sex."

"Wait, you two are married? Jesus fucking Christ, I don't have the brain space for this right now." Michel had never revealed anything to her about his wife. In fact, they'd only discussed his daughter, whom Omar had attacked. His alleged daughter.

Did Michel fabricate the entire daughter story to manipulate me into murdering Omar?

"Yes, Vivi is—how do you Americans call it—my old ball and chain." Michel said, taking his eyes off the road to blow a kiss in Vivienne's direction. "We assumed you'd figure it out sooner—maybe you're not as sharp as I thought."

"Fuck you, Michel."

"Oh, we won't keep you in suspense. I'm his beard, darling. And yes, we did worry you'd put it all together earlier and were afraid it would expedite the timelines. The good news is that everything went according to plan."

Michel had been quite pushy in getting her into the sack when they dated, so she had never gotten the vibe that he was gay. Perhaps he was bisexual. But it wasn't a top concern at that moment. Now that Celeste considered them as a married couple, they did seem to fit well together, at least in image. Sophisticated, worldly, impeccably dressed—*with an affinity for keeping secrets from me.*

"So you have a daughter together? Or it was all a ruse?"

"No, no, not a ruse," Vivienne explained. "Omar really did attack our firstborn, and I was prepared to kill him myself. But you already trusted Michel at that point and had only recently tracked me down to do a few favors for you. Getting rid of Omar right under your nose would've been poor form. You, more than anyone else, deserved to witness his last breath."

The realization that these two had been friends of her late parents—and her puppeteers for much of her adult life... well, it was a lot to process.

"What kind of risk are Theodore and I facing? Mere... Lockwood said he... well, she'd be alive today if it weren't for me. Omar said similar things about Zari. The blood of two of the kindest people I've ever met is on my hands. I can't lose anyone else."

"Unfortunately, this began long ago, before you were born. The sixties and seventies were a complicated period for America. Your parents had arrangements with the CIA. Michel was a French spy, and I... well, we can get into my career path another time.

"The CIA was tasked with ensuring the US had a reliable oil supply, among other interests, and to that end, they were bankrolling unstable militant rebel groups, overthrowing governments that didn't subscribe to Western values."

Michel chimed in. "Your parents pushed back significantly, as they witnessed firsthand how America was devastating communities in developing countries, making the war-torn regions a hotbed for Russia and China to step in and radicalize them against the West."

"Michel can better explain, but our European allies were not pleased. Your parents began working through back channels with the UK and France—namely, through Michel—to slow down and soften the blow of American imperialism."

"And then they became parents, and they had you and your brother to think of," Michel picked up. "Lockwood's predecessor, the head of Omar's organization in the late seventies and early eighties, wasn't happy that America was stepping in and exploiting his trade routes and access to raw materials in those regions, and the job grew much more dangerous. So rather than jeopardize their children's lives or risk that you and your brother would be orphaned, they retired, at least officially."

"Dear, we don't want to paint the picture that anything was easy for them. Under their cover as professors, they were communicating secretly with Michel, with me, with so many others around the world to guide us. They loved you two, more than life itself, but their spy craft and their commitment to stopping oligarchs beckoned them."

Celeste thought back to the hushed conversations she'd sometimes stumbled upon as a teen. Her parents would be sitting at the dinner table, their heads together, with some sort of radio present. She remembered making fun of them for not buying a more updated cassette or DVD player. She never consciously thought much about the radio when she was young, but right there in the van, she remembered that they'd always switched it off when she walked in.

"Did Keith know?"

Silence.

"Well, don't stop now."

"When I first began pursuing you, you were a mark."

"He means we wanted to bring you inside, as they say."

"But you were too headstrong and had too many big ideas," Michel continued. "You wouldn't have been interested in setting those grandiose dreams aside for anything. So rather than recruit you, I decided we'd watch over you, and we did always have someone monitoring, as we'd promised your parents."

Creepy, but OK.

"Michel noticed Keith had fallen in with a bad crowd. Your brother was better suited as an asset—he had no clear direction, nothing to leave behind. He became one of us within a few years of your parents passing."

"OK, c'mon. My dirtbag brother, may his soul rest in peace, who only called to beg for money, was actually—"

"He was a mastermind," Vivienne said. "We'll get into it another time, but your head would spin at how many lives he saved. He lived and died as a hero. Your parents would've been so proud. I worked with him closely for most of his adult life. His strategy of staying in occasional contact with you worked because you clearly never suspected anything.

"It's a lot to process, and there's much more. But right now, we'll wrap up this little trip down memory lane with how this relates to Omar and Stephen Lockwood—the man you know as Seth—and then to you as mob boss. Even though your parents had escaped into the shadows, Omar and Seth knew of them—and in turn, you and your brother—because the head of their crime syndicate at the time, when they were only teenage henchmen, pledged to wage war on your parents."

"So Omar and Lockwood knew—"

"Yes, Omar knew who you were and targeted you when you were old enough," Michel said. "He had planned to kill you but instead fell in... whatever his feelings could be called for you. He went to Lockwood himself and convinced him that it would be a bigger payoff to bring you inside."

Vivienne picked up: "Imagine how terrifying it was for us to watch what he was doing to you on the sidelines—we couldn't blow our cover until you were ready, but we couldn't let him hurt you either. To our pleasant surprise, you and Savin were pretty effective on your own with the Biochrome short you orchestrated in the aughts. After that, we drove him away as best we could"—she paused heavily and then continued—"though there was clearly a time or two when we failed to protect you. And then Ace took over—more on that later—so we knew you were protected and that we could bide our time before showing you our hand."

"Jesus Christ, every answer raises forty more questions."

The sun had begun to rise. Celeste knew it wouldn't be much longer before they dropped her off at the spa. "You're not off the hook for the past, but we don't have much time. Walk me through the thinking behind making me some sort of mob boss and what I need to do."

"That's what I was trying to say earlier before my lovely wife interjected," Michel replied. "It's not you, exactly. It's the aliases you've been using over the years—the brunettes."

"It wasn't our original intent," Vivienne explained, "but then we picked up chatter from some of our sources that Lockwood, Ace, and others viewed this woman as a massive threat to the stability of their own organizations."

Michel continued, "They felt that she had to have a large organization behind her to pull off all that she—you—did. They were confused, chasing their tails, trying to get a fix on this mystery woman. It bought us time."

Celeste recalled being picked up in an unmarked van in Zurich while in disguise. Whoever picked her up had threatened her, making clear that they expected Celeste—or her fake persona, rather —to stop digging.

"The mistaken identity explains my kidnapping in Zurich, right? Which reminds me—was Seth or Lockwood or whatever his name was telling the truth? Is my husband secretly fucking some Swiss woman? Omar had also alluded once to some secret life Theodore leads, but I've been a little too busy to look into it."

The couple exchanged one of their knowing glances.

"We can't spoon-feed—"

"What Michel means to say—doesn't feel so good being inter-rupted, does it, honey—what he means to say is that we can advise you, prepare next steps, ensure that someone else doesn't step in to fill the power vacuum with Lockwood and Omar out of the way. I'd rather we focus on those things before we arrive. Other matters, like those between you and your husband, aren't our domain."

Without answering, they'd given her the confirmation she needed —Theodore wasn't the picture-perfect husband. After all she'd risked to save him, after all she'd lost for him, because of him, the pain she felt from then learning, from Lockwood nonetheless, that the man she thought was an actual saint for loving her was some basic bro— she transmuted all those emotions to rage. *I won't need a weapon this time—I'll finish this one off with my bare hands.*

Her therapist, Anne Marie, the voice of reason, popped into her head. "Let's not jump to conclusions before talking to your husband," she would have advised if sitting there in that moment. *Too late.*

"Celeste, I have to admit," Vivienne continued, turning the conversation away from Theodore, "I expected a much stronger reaction from you when you'd realized what we'd done, how much danger you could potentially be in. You haven't even made us pitch you to recruit you."

"Look, I'm a pragmatist, and it's not that far off from what I was trying to do. I would've appreciated being brought in sooner, and there are still massive holes in this. But I want to do it—I just need some time to sit with it first.

"What exactly have you two propped me up as? Is this like foreign agent territory? Have I been acting as a spy for France? You wouldn't have access to a DGSE apartment in DC as CIA."

"Let's do a bathroom break, and then I'll answer anything I can," Michel said.

They pulled up to a rest stop, complete with a Taco Bell and 7-Eleven. She noticed both Michel and Vivienne retrieve firearms from various places in the front seat.

"Uh, don't forget about me. I'm the one who'd get attacked first, let's be honest."

Vivienne pulled a SIG Sauer P229 from the glove box and handed it to Celeste, who put it against her back and got out of the car.

Theodore, husband of mine. What was she going to do? Celeste had kept her iPhone off to ensure she couldn't be geolocated, so she didn't know if he'd messaged since the night before. She felt as though she'd lived seven years since she shot off that good-night text. At some point, she'd have to reach out. No need raising any suspicion by halting communication—she wanted to blindside him.

The bathroom entrances were outside, on the periphery of the gas station building. Michel and Vivienne wanted her to stay away from any cameras, so she went directly there while they got her snacks and water.

A stench enveloped her when she opened the one-stall women's restroom. She held her breath as she quickly went and then attempted to scrub her hands with the tiny dollop remaining in a hand sanitizer pump. As she groaned in disgust, Michel and Vivienne were walking back to the car, apparently unaware she was within eavesdropping range.

"I've thought it over," came Michel's voice, "and I don't want to scare her off when we've gotten her so far. Coming clean about Theodore's business could have sweeping repercussions. The fact that he's managed to hide it for so long means he doesn't want her to know—it's not our place. Believe me, I've dropped hints for years, and she doesn't bite."

"Secrets jeopardize the mission, and a mark operating blind isn't always a good thing, Michel. We could solidify her trust by being honest with her."

Oh, Theodore, darling, you've made a fool of me for the last time.

Back in the van and on the road, Celeste practiced some deep-breathing exercises until she was feeling more like herself, having transformed from apoplectic to calm. She was ready to launch into her planned diatribe and a tirade of questions. Once she was on a roll, she'd drop a few unexpected ones to fish for answers. She wanted to strike a balance of being a commanding presence without being divisive. She was running out of allies. But her instincts told her that they needed her as much as she them.

A symbiotic relationship.

"Well, I should be livid about your deceit. Shame on you for dragging me into this without full transparency. It's not like you haven't had the opportunity to come clean, bring me into the fold. You've literally known of me since I was a child. And I've been so open with both of you. I could leave this van—and you—behind.

"But try as I might to walk away, I'm in this now, and I'm not entirely turned off by your plan. As I said earlier, I'd already been operating in a similar way. And frankly, we make a good team, as you've both helped me prevent a lot of harm when I felt I couldn't trust anyone else."

She remembered Michel in that hotel room in Rome not that long ago, Omar writing in the pain they'd inflicted on him, and she now saw it clearly for what it was—Michel's way to process his help-lessness after Omar attacked his daughter. And Michel had been so broken up about Keith's death at the funeral. Similarly, Vivienne had been nothing but extremely resourceful and empathic up to that point.

"So take me through how this all plays out."

By the time Michel and Vivienne had revealed their five-point plan, Celeste's mind was blown.

"WE'VE GIVEN you a lot to think about, Celeste."

They pulled up outside a safe house, a small log cabin set back a mile from the highway, about forty minutes away from the resort. Michel dropped the women at the front door and drove around to a large, free-standing garage.

"He's switching out vehicles; let's get you changed into proper spa attire," Vivienne said, leading Celeste inside.

In a matter of hours, her entire childhood had been rewritten—she'd learned that her parents were renowned international heroes and that her brother was not a deadbeat after all and had been murdered for his commitment to the greater good. And her combat training with Zed had paid off. She was a force, and not only in the boardroom or bedroom. Her strength, her cunning, and her skill had all been tested, and she had prevailed. Two of the top spies in the world, who had survived decades in place, wanted her as their mark, as their asset, as the head of the faux crime syndicate they were building. *Omar and Seth had fucked with the wrong woman.* But she also wished to the core of her existence that she'd gotten to him before he destroyed Meredith.

In a small bedroom, she found sage-green loungewear—perfect vibes for a spa getaway—and lingerie that had been laid out for her on the bed, along with a pair of sneakers. She had an identical outfit at home, right down to the Le Mystère bra and matching thong. She stripped down while Vivienne was still standing there, taking advantage of the time to continue with her questions.

"What is the real Agent Foster coming back to?" Celeste asked about the field agent she'd impersonated when she broke into the FBI. "How do you plan to cover this up? You saw that room, and we still don't know who found me inside or who was chasing me. Wait a minute—you also haven't explained where you disappeared to while I was in the middle of a mission."

"We need to move more quickly, but I'll answer what I can now. Regarding Agent Foster, that's an easy one—she never existed, so she'll simply be impossible to find."

"I saw her social media videos, the badge... they'll track her down. What do you mean, they won't find her? Will she receive a burn notice?" Celeste asked. A burn notice was an announcement that an agent was no longer reliable. It could be used in many scenarios, such as when their cover was exposed or if they committed a crime that the intelligence agency had to distance itself from.

"No, I'm telling you she doesn't exist. Think about it, Celeste. Did you ever see her in 3D? We had to make you think she was real so that you felt confident enough to carry an air of belonging. But there is no field agent with that name—or face, for that matter. We have a team that can create an online footprint for a fake persona."

Celeste opened her mouth to ask another question.

"The videos were AI-generated. It's not a real woman."

"Wow."

"As for your instinct that the FBI would be out for blood—the agency, the administration, and the military would not want the public or our adversaries to know that a lone wolf woman broke into FBI headquarters and stole classified information, now, would they?"

That's what I initially thought! "I suppose not."

"So we'll take care of the rest. We have people who can influence what is said and investigated inside. I apologize I had to leave you alone in the last phase of the break-in, but it was necessary for me to step away to protect the mission. I knew you could handle it, even with as off script as it became."

What the woman wasn't saying had more impact than what she did say. Celeste began connecting the dots.

"Was that all a training exercise? It was, wasn't it? You never had an intruder; you weren't snatched in the middle of our heist. The sounds of the struggle—that was all staged? Did you plant the men to come after me to see how I'd respond under pressure? And you could've gotten into the FBI Building without me anyway—you said so yourself. You left me stranded—how could you take that chance?"

Evading the questions, Vivienne said, "Let's not live in the past. You made it out, and the mission was a success. You've not only managed to stop the cyberattack on our country, but you've also exposed the traitors in our government and single-handedly—and quite literally—gutted our chief law enforcement officer. Once it was in motion, you in no way needed my—or anyone else's—help to pull it off. Now you know that. And besides, we needed you to be the heroine of the day. One of us breaking in would've muddied the omnipotent leader we've painted you as."

She and Michel are perfect for one another. That sounds like some bull-shit he'd dream up.

"Listen, can you extend your Miraval trip a day?" Vivienne asked. "We've already taken care of it at the hotel. You'll just need to let your husband and Savin know."

"I suppose so."

"It's settled, then," Vivienne replied. "We want some time to scour the CCTV archives, doctor them a bit, before we delete them. You being safe and sound at Miraval ensures no one implicates you."

"What about Gabe? His first thought when Chet tells him about the breach will be to inform him that I did it."

"I'll see to it that Agent Gutiérrez won't share anything with anyone," Michel chimed in. "If he does have some idiotic idea to try, that will be his last. He's just excited to save the day. He and Chet will be credited with stopping the attack—will receive medals of honor, even. They couldn't ask for anything more."

"And don't worry—we've cleaned up the loose ends regarding Omar, Nico, and Drake," Vivienne said. "You'll have fun learning about what we did there. Well, you know I framed Matthew for Omar, but that was just the beginning. The way we've set this up allows you to walk away scot-free and go back to your old life, or you can step into the one that's waiting for you, as the woman leading a faux crime syndicate, and continue to do more good. It's important to us that you have the choice because in the past you haven't."

The woman looked Celeste in the eye, somber. "I hope it was clear earlier, but please remember that whatever you decide, you must not share anything about me, Michel, your parents, or your missions with Theodore, Savin, Jack, Mark, no one. So really think through whether you want this life—because the lies and the secrets compound with each mission."

Her parents and her brother had made it work. *Or did they? Look at the fate they met.*

"I'm not insane, so don't worry about me sharing anything with them," Celeste responded. "On top of everything else, they're all so overprotective, they'd try to make it so I could never leave home without one of them. And, yes, the secrets and the deceit are heavy to carry—but I don't feel I'll ever truly be danger-free if I stay on the outside. I have to believe Matthew isn't the only one left who is out to get me."

"You take some time to think things through." Vivienne looked at her watch. "We must get going."

THEY PULLED up to the sprawling Miraval property around seven a.m. in the Suburban for which Michel had traded the florist van. The familiar grounds with luscious greenery and uniform white clapboard cottages brought Celeste a sense of calm. *Breakfast, meditation, workout, sauna, spa.*

Her work and her training had paid off—she'd saved the day. Now she could relax and recharge. *For a day.* One day and then it was back to whatever her life had become.

They drove to a side entrance of the main arrival center building, where her carbon copy was waiting. Celeste had met the woman only one other time, when she'd helped out in Dubai. The woman hopped in when the car slowed to a stop.

"It's like looking in the mirror," Celeste said incredulously.

"We all have them—twins or body doubles—in the craft, dear," Vivienne explained. "Humans would like to believe we're each one of a kind, but we're all just little ants marching along on a common journey. Enjoy your day as best you can. All this stuff will be waiting, assuming you're ready to get back to work." Vivienne wasn't referring to running D&C.

In an uncharacteristically emotional tone, Michel said, "Celeste, we need you. You're uniquely positioned to allow us to continue this mission. Please take that into consideration. You saved thousands of lives yesterday."

"Oh God, I've walked in on the impassioned Michel recruitment," her doppelgänger said after she'd closed the door.

Celeste laughed. "On the nose!"

"I've made you several spa reservations today: a two-hour four-hands massage, a hammam scrub, infrared sauna, and time for a workout. Your first appointment is in thirty minutes."

She can even read my mind about my favorite treatments. Celeste wondered how much the woman was aware of about Lockwood and the rest of it.

"I don't even know your name."

"Dear, there will be time for that later. Go relax—and stick to the plan," Vivienne chided gently. "We need to get back—as you can imagine, there's a lot of work to do."

Celeste normally wouldn't allow herself to be brushed off, but she didn't feel much up to chitchat anyway.

Her look-alike gave her the number of their cottage, as well as a quick rundown of the past few days so Celeste wouldn't trip up with the staff or other guests. They were dressed identically, down to their Tod's suede sneakers.

"You guys managed to orchestrate everything so perfectly," Celeste said. "How did you know what I'd be wearing?"

"It's my job to be able to step in at any time," her twin said in an almost robotic tone. "Goodbye and good luck." Celeste suspected people in her line of work didn't have much of a personal identity. *How could they, if they were pretending to be someone else all the time?* But right as the thought popped into her head, Celeste realized the irony.

"Thank you. I must be going," Celeste said. "A day of pampering awaits."

Lost in thought, Celeste had four hours of focused bodywork during which to figure out her course of action, as she was massaged, scrubbed, enveloped in a heavenly cocoon of steamed towels, and slathered in luxurious moisturizer. *No chance there's any remnant of last night's trauma left on my body.*

She was certain she wanted to continue working with Michel and Vivienne. But what would it mean for her marriage, her friendships, if she was always rushing off, putting her life in danger? *And endangering the lives of people I love.* Could she continue in her leadership capacity at D&C? It was something she had always imagined would have an end date: when Omar died or when she took down Seth or Matthew.

But now she knew better. This business hadn't begun, and it

wouldn't end, with her. It was in her bloodline, and it could be her legacy, just like that of her parents and her brother.

She'd felt her parents' presence all around her on the drive, but it was gentler than before. It was as if they were telling her that the danger had subsided for now and that she needed to rest so she could then prepare for what was to come.

Wait.

In all the story sharing on the drive, Celeste hadn't had time to check the news to see how her press campaign had landed. Part of her wanted to march out of her treatment room. But a larger part was demanding that she stay put. *It will all be there tomorrow.*

It dawned on her that the reason Michel had wanted her to extend her trip was to shield her from whatever was happening in the media for as long as they could. Little did they know that she wasn't rushing to get back to real life. There was too much she had to face: the cleanup at D&C because of Matthew being associated with a life of crime, the fact that Meredith's dead faux boyfriend was potentially connected to the D&C leaders, whether the person (or people?) who had been trying to kill Celeste was now out of the way.

The unanswered questions preyed on her mind. Who were the people behind RH Global, and why were they paying off Matthew? How would Americans react upon learning about the corruption that had infiltrated the very framework on which their country was built? There were others that also needed answering. But the main issue— or person, as it were—that she would have to face when she returned to New York was Theodore. Whatever he was involved in would be at odds with her new life as mob boss, wouldn't it? Sleeping with the enemy wouldn't be feasible—or would it?

After the spa services, she enjoyed the infrared sauna and some small talk with the front-desk greeter, who sold Celeste a few products. *Always helps with the alibi to have physical evidence of being in a different location.*

Her cottage was beautiful, clean, a respite away from the noise. She had just finished wrapping herself in a plush blanket with a book and a cup of tea when her iPhone rang out, a shrill tone startling her. She hadn't even remembered turning it on.

Wait, her iPhone would've been in DC in her Riggs Hotel room, wouldn't it? She answered the call, a New York number, though she didn't have anyone's memorized. It wasn't programmed in the phone.

"Hello?" she said cautiously.

A woman's soft sobs came through. "Oh, Celly, I don't know what to do or where else to turn. I couldn't keep it a secret any longer. I don't want to ruin your spa day. But I can't do this anymore."

Rani.

Celeste's twin must've either cloned her phone or worked with the cleaner to forward calls from the abandoned phone in DC because Rani hadn't noticed.

"Hi, darling. Of course, you can tell me anything—what has you so upset?"

Her good friend Rani—who was engaged to Celeste's best friend, had been a permanent fixture in her life for many years, and had seen her through some of her darkest moments—sobbed once more, then drew in a sharp breath.

"I don't talk much about my family, Celly, and there's a reason for that. My... my sister Lani is a scam artist. She's always wrapped up in some kind of scheme that usually ends with me having to bail her out of some kind of trouble. But this, oh my God, Celly, this—you have to know that I would've never let this happen if I'd known. You have to believe me."

"Ran, I can sense you're really upset, sweetie. Why don't you take a few deep breaths while I tell you a bit about my day? How does that sound?"

Celeste could still hear occasional sobs from Rani, but she seemed to be calming down the longer they spoke.

"I just had the most incredible four-hands massage for over two hours. I'm so relaxed. I was thinking—when I get back, let's have a luxurious day of pampering, just the two of us, and get NAD plus infusions and microneedling. We'll feel like a million bucks. How does that sound?"

"OK, OK, you managed to cheer me up with that," Rani said, sniffling but with a laugh. "Celly, I began noticing that some files had been modified months ago when I first became CTO."

Yes, Lorraine told me.

"I pulled in Angelo and Ace, and they rounded up their best teams to track down what was going on."

"I remember you were very thorough." *Michel didn't think so.*

"Right around the time of your brother's funeral, Celly, I had concrete evidence that my sister had been snooping, remotely hacking into my devices and such. She denied it, of course, but I had someone monitoring my network. You see, I suspected for a long time that she'd been in with some shady cyberterror types. So a while ago, I hired my cousin, who has been in the cybersecurity world for some time, to make sure my network was ironclad, impenetrable."

So that's why Angelo and Michel couldn't gain access. Not because she was *hiding* something. *Because she was protecting our data* from *someone.*

"My cousin called me the day before we arrived in St. Louis. He was frantic. He believed that not only had my sister been reading my texts and emails, but she had nefarious intent—he thought she was either going to hold our servers hostage with the threat of making them public or release some sort of virus that would crash our entire portfolio."

"I confronted her, and she totally denied it."

That must've been the exchange I heard between Rani and someone on the other end of the line when I walked in on her in the restroom in St. Louis. Celeste's mind was buzzing, though she kept her expression soft.

"But I was getting more and more paranoid, more afraid. Savin thought I was hiding something, and you know how well he handles—"

"Oh, I know how well—or how poorly—my best friend handles just about anything out of the ordinary," Celeste replied. The two women laughed. "Anyway, go on."

"Well, I believe she's the one who doctored your trades, Celly. She denies it, tells me I'm crazy. We've been fighting for months because I know she's up to no good. That's why she and my family didn't come to the engagement party—or so she says. Either she has some vendetta against you personally or she's trying to weaken D&C. Which I'm an executive at and my future husband and one of my best friends run, mind you. She's such a bitch."

Four-seven-eight breathing seems fitting right about now. Celeste was proud she kept her calm, though she felt like running far, far away from her life. She hadn't banked on this sort of nemesis—she was only prepared for the policymaker or organized crime type.

Celeste had never put much thought into Rani's sister, but now she intended to get as much information as she could to pass along to Vivienne and Michel. "Let's talk through this, and I'm sure we can figure it out together. Tell me a bit about her."

"She lives... well, I don't know where she lives really. She's all over the place, bouncing around Europe with this guy, jetting off to Tokyo with that guy. She's never been very stable."

"So no real relationship to speak of. Is she in finance? Like why the preoccupation with D&C?"

"I don't know. I've never heard her talk about a job. She's always just mid-travel—Shanghai to Rome to Mozambique to Zurich. It's exhausting. I don't know how she even has time to concern herself with you between shopping and bedding men."

Celeste perked up at the mention of Switzerland, and she recalled what she'd overheard Theodore's parents saying. *"Son, she deserves to know"* and *"When—not if—she finds out on her own, Son, you'll deserve whatever wrath she directs toward you."*

"OK, so no job. You're Eastern European, right? Any sort of anti-America sentiment that could lead to some sort of activism?"

"No, she doesn't care enough about anyone but herself. And disrupting your life, apparently."

"Her name's Lani, right? Could you send me a photo? I can think about whether I've ever seen her." *More like check it in the Interpol database.*

"Yes. Well, Lani's a nickname. Rudrislana is her full name. A photo should be coming through."

Rudy.

Celeste nearly dropped the phone when she saw the woman's face smiling in the photo, her elbow locked with her sister Rani's in front of a palm tree on some generic beach. How had Celeste never noticed the resemblance between the two?

So many seemingly disjointed memories flooded Celeste's mind —Rani's sister Lani, a.k.a. Rudy, had been the flight attendant on the Cairo flight, the woman in the car when the Feds had snatched Celeste and Savin in Mexico, the person Jack had been arguing with in Tuscany in the early morning after Celeste's wedding, and the person on the phone whom Jack had been arguing with in São Paulo. *Who didn't want Jack to tell me that my brother may have been murdered.*

She kept her voice calm, but inside she was reeling. "Got it. She's beautiful, just like you. Well, look, I appreciate you coming clean. I have some friends who can quietly look into this for us. As long as it doesn't bring any attention to you, Savin, or D&C, do I have your permission to color outside the lines a little if necessary to get to the bottom of it all?"

Rani laughed. "Of course. Do what you need to do. I knew you'd have exactly the right plan of attack."

Oh, there will be an attack, all right.

"Now, is that everything? Can I get back to my day of bliss?"

"Yes, that's it. And again, I'm really sorry. I hope you know that."

They said their goodbyes, and Celeste ended the call.

She lay back on the luxe California king bed and closed her eyes. Maybe she should've left Omar alive. At least when he was alive, she was too distracted to notice all the other things going on around her.

There's no use trying to make sense of any of this shit. It's going to take some spy craft. And I know just who to call.

Vivienne and Michel had left her a new burner phone as well, which she found easily in the top drawer. There were three SIM cards, so she popped one in and dialed the number that would scramble to whatever phone Michel was using at that moment.

"You wouldn't be calling unless you found out something," he said, "so spill it before the line is traced. Vivienne is here with me, so I'll put the call on speaker phone."

"Well, you can say I told you so," Celeste retorted. "Rani is compromised, though not in the way you thought." She quickly explained the situation and how she had crossed paths with Rudy.

"Who is this woman?" she demanded. "What is her beef with me? I just got used to the idea of being a mob boss—I'm not going down like this, am I? Some nobody framing me for insider trading?"

"We just have to tell her, dear—you were right," Michel said in an aside to his wife.

"Thank you for acknowledging I was right, dear husband, and yes, we do have to tell her," Vivienne responded. "Celeste, Rudy's not just some opportunistic party girl—she's not officially in the intelligence community, but she runs in the same circles as we do. We believe she works for the person you know as Ace."

Although Celeste had already connected the dots when she saw Rudy's photo, hearing this now from Vivienne brought Celeste back to that Cairo flight, which seemed like a lifetime ago. She recalled that Rudy, Alex, and the other man had been sitting together when Celeste had come out to the cabin. Alex had said Ace was like a big brother to each of them . *Or something to that effect.* So it would make sense.

"In what fresh hell does the hacker I trusted for years hire someone who then hacks into my system to frame me for several insider-trading felonies?"

"I share your frustration, dear," Vivienne said, "but we need to focus on what's at hand. This Rudy woman doesn't change—"

"Wait, one more thing—do you know who Ace is?"

"Not for certain, no," Michel answered.

"But you have some ideas—"

Michel sighed. "You're asking the wrong questions, Celeste." He looked to his wife. "I told you, Viv, you can only lead a horse to water..."

"Fuck you, Michel. Then what question should I be asking?" But she already knew.

"What you want to know is how Theodore fits into all this," Vivi-enne said.

Celeste's anger turned to sadness. It was indeed what she wanted to know, what she'd always wanted to know.

"Is he a bad guy? Is he... with this Rudy woman?"

"That was two questions," Michel said sarcastically in a failed attempt to lighten the mood. "Here's what we speculate. Theodore hasn't always lied to you, but he hasn't always been truthful either. You've told me he said he was in one place, when in reality he was halfway across the globe.

"He seems to be some sort of a... freelancer, a vigilante who rolls in when the situation piques his interest. He wanted to take down Omar for years, and we know from mutual contacts that he was pleased that fucker was gone. I imagine he wondered if you had done it—killed Omar—for a minute, but then decided you were incapable of it. And no, we don't think he's cheating on you."

Celeste sighed heavily. "I guess I will have to speak with Theodore directly about this."

"Well, that's what we wanted to discuss—" Vivienne said at the same time that Michel blurted out, "No, no, we decided against—" Then they both fell silent.

They took turns telling Celeste why she could not in fact confront her husband. It was better to focus on their end goal, they explained —weakening the oligarchs' influence by destroying organizations like Omar's.

"This is actually quite an important pivot, Celeste. We need you to be one hundred percent in lockstep with us," Michel urged.

"If we have one minor slip—" Vivienne chimed in. "Let's say Theodore has his friends start digging into you and learns something we don't want him to know. He accidentally tells a client that you were actually in Rome the day Omar died or are tied to something we've done or caused to happen—you see how it could be catastrophic, right?"

My husband never accidentally says or does anything. Everything was intentional. That was what was so infuriating.

"We're positioning your aliases as the number-one bad guy—or woman, as it were—to give the crime families around the world a reason to be afraid," Vivian explained. "Of course, we could have someone else step in if you're ready to call it quits. But you have done what many others, including us, have tried and failed to do. You're better at this than we are."

Celeste laughed. "You must be pretty bad at your jobs then."

"I'll say it again—I'll beg if I must—we need you, Celeste," Michel said. "And that means your husband and your friends must believe that you're *just* a hedge fund manager who sometimes does what the illuminati asks of her to help make the world a less miserable place," Michel continued.

"Goddamn, you two are persuasive. Fine, I'll hold off on checking in with my husband—at least until we discuss this further. But I do want to know what he's up to, so maybe I'll tag along a bit more on his trips."

"That could be helpful. You really can step back from your Nancy Drew work a bit and let others handle some of it now. We have people who can do all the little errands you were doing, trying to track down the bad guys."

"That's it!" Celeste exclaimed. "Sorry, entirely unrelated, but I just put it together. Rudy and Hadid are RH Global. I don't know how they know each other or why they're paying Matthew, but I will find out. It would make sense."

"Nice work, but—" Michel began.

"This is going to take some getting used to," Vivienne said, "but if you proceed, and it sounds like you are planning to, it's our job now to find out why RH Global is bribing Matthew—or, more likely, why he's extorting them. Your time will be spent on different types of projects, solidifying your leadership and putting the fear of God in the most awful of men. Our goal is to have the heads of the rival groups so afraid of losing their profits and security that they come to you on bended knee."

Celeste had to admit, if only to herself, that being able to address crime on such a grand scale would be invigorating. But she needed time to clear her head.

"OK. Can I rest now? I've learned more in the past twenty-four hours than in the entire decade of my thirties and first few years of my forties combined. My head needs to process everything."

"Yes, enjoy yourself," Vivienne said. "Call your husband. Act normal."

"And maybe wait until tomorrow to check the news," Michel urged.

Gladly.

~

Queenpin or Lone Wolf?
Mysterious Femme Fatale Linked to
Murder of Scorned FBI Director

Washington, DC
  By Avery Quinn | August 12

The famed Riggs Hotel, reminiscent of the glamorous art deco era, was the scene of a deadly stabbing in the early morning hours, according to local police. Authorities were called to the scene around 2:30 a.m., after a hotel employee on a cigarette break saw a woman covered in blood fleeing down a back alley. During a search of the hotel premises, the body of slain FBI Director Stephen Lockwood was found in a sublevel storage room.

"There was so much blood," said the employee, who spoke on condition of anonymity. "It was everywhere—on the floors, on the walls, even on the light fixtures. Something really terrible must have happened there."

Later this morning, the US Attorney General's Office released a statement that Director Lockwood had been under investigation for his ties to vast drug-, arms-, and human-trafficking organizations, and his termination was in process.

A spokesperson for the Metropolitan Police Department confirmed that one suspect—a woman who has not yet been identified—is being actively pursued in connection with the murder. Authorities have not determined whether she acted alone or is linked to a broader network of international crimes. No arrests have been made. The incident is still being assessed, and the investigation is ongoing. This is a developing story, and more information will be provided as it becomes available.#

QUEENPIN HAS *a nice ring to it.*

The story was time-stamped early in the morning, but there had been no new updates all day. She imagined dozens of DC police and the Feds running around, trying to piece together what had happened.

Snuggled in her bed that night after the luxurious retreat day, Celeste did some further internet investigation. Her search revealed that Vivienne had let Celeste's public affairs campaign move forward, but with one significant modification. Any references to the involvement of anyone beyond Lockwood—other lawmakers, including members of the administration, the cabinet, and Congress—had been removed from the press materials and the now-viral campaign Celeste had orchestrated.

The news reported that the prevention of the cyberattack was credited to a masterful investigation led by two agents, none other than Gabriel Gutiérrez and Chet Connolly. The two had planned to arrest Director Lockwood the following day, but he was murdered by an unknown woman in an unrelated crime.

It was no wonder Lockwood had enemies, the journalists had all concluded, given that he was running one of the world's global terror organizations. This "queenpin" mob boss or lone wolf, when found, would be held accountable to the fullest extent of the law, the US attorney general said in a press conference, but there was an unspoken "good riddance" on cable news. Her handiwork was being heralded as having rid the world of another horrible man.

Go ahead, try to put me in jail. She'd disappear before it ever got to that.

Celeste understood and appreciated the tactic of omitting the other policymakers—let the Feds and the local police be able to claim the win for themselves. Rather than causing the integrity of every branch of the US government to crumble in one fell swoop, they'd take their time to set up rock-solid cases, motivate the American public to hold their represented officials accountable, and maybe eventually effect change in the corrupt DC culture.

Three more calls to make, then Celeste could enjoy her enormous tub and bubble bath she'd bought from the hotel spa. She started with the easy one.

"Mizz, er, Celeste, I... well, I know we have had our disagreements, and I haven't always condoned the way you, uh, color outside the lines. But I thank you for your service, the country thanks you for your service, even if we can't do so officially. What you've set into motion has saved thousands of lives."

"Agent Gutiérrez, I'd imagine you're having a pretty good day. Hopefully, this will cause Congress to free up some new appropriations for you and Agent Connolly to continue your work."

"And don't worry—I agree that it's best if no one knows you were in DC this week."

Celeste smiled wryly. Of course he enjoyed the accolades for himself.

Savin next.

"Celly, oh my God! I've been calling and calling today. I mean, I know I said I wouldn't bother you and that I could handle all the fallout from Matthew being implicated in so many crimes—God, he really is a prick, you were right—but there's something going on that's more important than work. It's Rani. She's hiding something, and I don't know what it is. She was crying all morning."

"Sav, I'm sure it's nothing. Maybe she's sad about losing Mere and nervous about the wedding. We're all so sad, and they had gotten closer recently with all the planning."

"Yeah, that's true. She's also had a fight with one of her sisters, which is the real reason everyone in her family boycotted our engagement party, I hear, and that must really bother her a lot."

"Just be there for her, and she'll confide in you when she's ready if there's something else."

"OK. When are you back to the city?"

"I'm leaving tomorrow midday on the train. It's such a nice ride."

"You? Metro North? Seems off-brand."

"I actually loved it on the way up. It's only a few hours, and I can unplug a little more than in a car."

"To each her own. Will I see you tomorrow?"

They planned on dinner the following evening and hung up.

Now, for the husband. Celeste didn't have her laptop, so she Face-Timed Theodore from her phone.

"Hi, honey," he said groggily. His screen was pitch black.

"Babe, I can't see your face—are you in bed?"

"It's the middle of the night here."

"Oh, yes, you're in Europe. Did you get my text? I decided to stay an extra day at Miraval for a little more relaxation."

"I just saw that and can tell that's not our bedroom at home in your background. I must've fallen asleep at like nine here while I was watching football."

"You should come here with me next time. You know how I love Miraval."

"Yes, and we need to have some serious together time very soon. I miss you like mad. What have you been up to there?"

"Oh, you know, the usual spa stuff. Reading, meditating, spa, sauna, yoga. Recharging." *Oh yeah, and I slit the FBI director's throat and volunteered to become an international mob boss.*

"That's lovely." He yawned.

"Get some sleep, OK? We'll talk tomorrow when I'm back home."

"Yes, and a little sexy time, too, please."

"Definitely."

The call ended.

So her double life meant her marriage would consist of minutiae and lies. *Maybe that's what all good marriages are made of.*

THE TRAIN RIDE from Wassaic to Grand Central was the first interruption-free time Celeste had to process, to grieve all that she'd lost, and to face the reality that the simple life she had so often longed to return to the past few years was perhaps gone forever. Pulling her Celine ball cap down over her eyes, she allowed herself a good cry, the kind that had to happen on a train or while walking down the street, a sentiment that only New Yorkers seemed to understand.

Monty retrieved her at Grand Central and took her downtown. He chattered on about his grandkids, unaware of how different Celeste's worldview had become while she was away. She had shed the childlike version of herself who had believed things would go back to normal—whatever that meant—someday. The gravity of losing Mere, the loss of the innocent version of her parents and her brother, the realization that her entire childhood had been a facade, the things she'd done to protect herself and everyone she loved—all these things had changed her, and there was no going back. She acknowledged that her marriage and her friendships would now have to come second to the mission to which she'd committed.

Hardened with resolve, she walked into her penthouse with Jonah in tow, maneuvering her luggage. Or, rather, not her bags. Those that her look-alike had brought to Miraval.

Nothing was out of place in her home, yet the energy inside it felt foreign, as though it existed on a parallel timeline to her actual apartment.

"Oh, one more thing, Miss Celeste. A delivery came for you. It's in the foyer."

"Thank you, Jonah. I'll walk you out."

He wished her a good day and left.

A leather tote was sitting on the table. She opened the bag gingerly, as though she expected Seth's head to spring out. It contained nothing out of the ordinary: her iPhone and laptop, the clothes and toiletries she'd had in DC.

Something white beside the bag caught her eye. *An envelope.*

She opened it without any investigation. Inside was a note in an unfamiliar scrawl.

I've grown tired of these sinister deliveries within deliveries.

"Celeste, darling, please join me at Sadelle's for brunch tomorrow. 10 a.m. xo, Nasrin," read the notecard with a silver-foiled *N* at the top.

It would be wonderful to catch up with Nasrin. Her widowed friend had finally taken a vacation and used the opportunity to bring her children on their dream trip to America. It was just a vacation, she told herself; there was no deeper reason for Nasrin to have traveled seven thousand miles from her Dubai home to hand deliver a card to Celeste with their code smoke signal—Celeste was sure of it.

Fiction is the lie through which we tell the truth.

EPILOGUE

Theodore

My wife walks toward me in the grand ballroom, a vision in a silky seafoam-green gown that hugs her curves, with an asymmetrical slit revealing a tanned, toned leg as she moves. Her long, golden locks are styled to one side, still elegant but more tousled than usual to reflect the relaxed island vibes. The jewels I gave her last night sparkle as the light catches them.

She hasn't noticed me yet, so I have a few extra seconds to greedily take her in from my seat in the back of the pavilion. Though there are dozens of party guests between the two of us, I see only her —all of her. From the moment I first laid eyes on her a dozen years ago, Celeste Donovan has taken my breath away every time she enters a room.

Her mouth turns up in a wide grin when she spots me. She stops to say hello to a group of our friends standing by the bar. She bores easily from small talk, so it's no surprise when her eyes find me again seconds later and she is on her way toward me once more. To this day, it is a battle to control myself around her, whether at the wedding of my best mate, Savin, as we are now, or in the bedroom. I shift in my seat as I harden at the thought of our tangled limbs last night. I can still taste her essence on my lips. I stand as she approaches.

"Whatever are you doing hiding over here in the corner, darling?" she says, in a buoyant mood.

I smell Champagne on her breath, always sweeter when it comes from her. It's unusual to see her playful these days. She suspects I know she keeps secrets, but she isn't aware of how much I've uncovered—or what I've done to intervene.

The black-and-blue bruises she covers up, how she's gone from thin and fit to chiseled and lean, how she sometimes winces when I touch her after her lessons—she must think I do not know that someone is training her in hand-to-hand combat. From my understanding, she's transformed into a deadly asset and a weapon any cause would want in its arsenal. But it was never supposed to be this way—I was supposed to save her from this life; instead, I've driven her toward it.

It was easy for someone like me to uncover the firearms she's hidden in our homes, though they were well hidden from the naked eye. At least she is proficient with them, because the fact remains that there will come a day when I can no longer protect her. If that's what I've even done up to this point.

I've had her followed enough to know that she has go bags with fake passports and cash hidden all over Manhattan and several European cities. She's prepared and has the means to disappear if necessary, but I'm doing all I can to make sure it never comes to that.

I catch her unconsciously rubbing the scar on her arthritic wrist that was shattered in Omar's almost lethal beating as she walks, part of a punishment inflicted because I didn't rescue her fast enough. I've failed her so many times, and yet she is still here. Only because she doesn't know what I am.

I want to draw her close, allow her scents to envelop me, take her far away from here. But she would never allow it. She's made it quite clear she doesn't need to be rescued by me or anyone else. Besides, once she knows the truth, fully comprehends the extent of my betrayal, she'll never want to see me again. It is why I cherish every moment with her as if it were my last—because one of these days, it will be.

"I wanted a good vantage point from which to admire your moves on the dance floor, my love," I say as I push her chair in and sit beside her. She plants a kiss on my cheek, and I pull her closer and kiss her mouth with an intensity I hadn't planned, grateful when she returns it.

"Mmm, Mr. Prescott, if you keep moving your tongue around like that, I may strip down and beg you to take me right here."

A guttural sound escapes my lips. "As much as I'd love that, Savin would never forgive us for taking attention away from him on his big day."

"He's much more bridezilla than I am, isn't he?"

"Absolutely," I reply.

"We've completed our duties as matron of honor and best man, so what would you say about heading back to our room?" she whispers in a sultry tone.

I'm ready to leave as well, but I'm waiting on confirmation of a drop. I nod anyway because I will never say no to her.

In response, she pulls me up and toward the dance floor. The secrets, the lies—all is forgotten when she laughs genuinely, as she is doing now while we wade through everyone. I don't register the song that's playing—I too am a bit tipsy—so instead, I revel in her happiness. I want to bottle up this moment and hold on to the memory forever.

Our foreheads are touching as she whispers sexy sweet nothings, and the crowd fades away.

Savin and Rani brought us all to her family's private island in the Maldives. I am certain Celeste has no idea how much danger we are in while in claustrophobic proximity to people we cannot underestimate. The security is airtight, so no one arrives on the island or departs from it without following specific procedures—essentially trapping the guests. Nothing is foolproof, though, so my own body-guard—a former MI6 sniper who'd received a burn notice—is also here, having arrived last night by swimming from a nearby island about ten kilometers away. My plane is there on standby in case we need to leave in a hurry, and my sniper hid a boat in one of the remote areas of this island. Yet my wife is blissfully unaware, pulling me closer to her so there is no space between our bodies. I am not complaining.

If I'd had the courage to bare my soul, maybe I could have convinced her that, together, we should escape. That the situation has already spiraled so far out of control that I don't even recall the original objective. Alas, I am a coward, and I have waited too long to bring her in. Besides, no one, especially not I, can coerce my wife to do anything she doesn't want to. Without understanding where her allegiance lies or what her mission is, my pleas will fall on deaf ears. At least, that's what I'm hiding behind. Mum says I'm not giving her enough credit.

Jack is across the room, gesturing in a way that would be imperceptible to anyone else that he needs to talk—and *now*. He darts out of the pavilion undetected.

"Darling, why don't you begin your farewells while I steal away for a quick smoke?" I ask. She hates my infrequent Nat Sherman habit, but tonight she doesn't lecture.

"Hurry back," she says suggestively, then turns away to join Rani and Sam.

Jack and I never acknowledge each other in public, so I take a roundabout way to our previously designated meeting spot on the resort grounds. The evening is pleasant, with a calm breeze, and the gentle lapping of the waves gives the setting an idyllic feel, although it's anything but. I follow the dimly lit winding pathway to the farthest point on the resort grounds to make sure we aren't detected.

"T, we have to get to ground quickly," Jack says from the shadows, his face illuminated as I light my cigarette. His excited energy is palpable.

"We're at our best mate's wedding in the middle of the Indian Ocean. It's going to be hard to sneak away. My wife will have a few questions." What I don't say is that I want to take her and leave this life behind.

"We've worked for this for years. We need to go *now*," Jack's girl-friend Rudy urges as she emerges from the shadows. She is a stunning brunette and looks nearly identical to my best mate's wife, Rani.

"The last time I checked, *I* call the shots here, Rudy," I remind her. "We'll stick to the plan."

"I've risked everything to make this trip, not the least of which involved breaking my sister's heart because you refused to let me tell her I'm here with her at her wedding," Rudy replied haughtily, "and *you* want to just hang out here and lose precious hours? After all we've sacrificed for this moment? Because you're too big of a pussy to answer to your diva of a wife? Got it."

I swallow my flash of anger. Rudy, though she can lash out with biting words, is a good soldier and has been invaluable over the years. She continues ranting furiously, but I interrupt when she takes a breath.

"Are you finished? I won't tolerate insults about Celeste, so I'll chalk it up to you being as stressed as we all are. We've sacrificed a lot... too much. But now is not the time to be raising red flags. We'll stay on course, meeting in Zurich three days after we return."

"She's a liability, and you know it!" Rudy spews. "She could jeopardize everything if you wait a week. And if I am detected—you know what happens."

She looks to Jack, but he remains silent.

I nod, wordlessly thanking him for not escalating the situation. This isn't the first time we've seen Rudy sound off.

"Why am I the only one concerned? Our past efforts to get your wife under control, Theodore, have been unsuccessful. You don't even know who she's working for!"

Rudy is right, but I don't acknowledge it.

"C'mon, Rudy," Jack cuts in. "We're all a little on edge. Celly is brilliant, and she wants the same things we do."

"Does she? Are you sure of that, Jack? Really?"

Jack continues as though his girlfriend hadn't spoken. "We need her on our side, and I support T's decision to—"

I smell her perfume that the breeze carries to us before I see her. This evening just went from a disagreement among coworkers to a full-on battle.

My heart plummets as my mind struggles to find a way through this. There is no satisfactory explanation.

"Well, hello," Celeste says in a chipper voice that disguises the fury I know she's barely managing to contain. She doesn't take kindly to being in the dark. About anything, ever.

She looks back and forth between the three of us, her expression thoughtful, as though she's working out a complex math problem instead of evaluating her husband's and best friend's treasonous ways.

"Cel—" I begin.

Without looking at me directly, she says, "No one speaks until I say so." She's suddenly sober and in control. I can almost see the wheels turning as she connects the dots.

"You're Rudy," Celeste says in a matter-of-fact tone. "Or shall I call you Lani, as your sister Rani does when she cries about the sibling who couldn't be bothered to attend her wedding?"

Rudy looks pissed—but ashamed. Celeste hit her where it hurt. Jack, Rudy, and I debated for weeks and determined that Rudy's official attendance as a wedding guest was too risky. Rudy was devastated.

"Imagine how upset she'd be to know you're *here*, not continents away as you'd lied, but half a mile from the reception. Skulking in the shadows with my best friend and my husband, plotting Goddess knows what. Oh yes, and by the way, I recognize you now. Our paths have crossed many times, haven't they, *Lani*?"

Rudy, similar in height to Celeste, puffs out her chest and draws in a breath, ready to do battle.

"No, no, you'll not speak yet," my wife says, wagging her index finger as though she's scolding children. The eruption is brewing just below the surface.

My face falls. Jack eyes me sympathetically, fully aware of the catastrophic implications for me if Celeste puts it all together.

"I should've realized you were related to Rani," she continues. "You share her raven-haired beauty, and on reflection, you even sound like her, with your elegant breeding and Eastern European accent. You were on Alex's little rescue mission in the Middle East to take me to Cairo. Where is Alex? I presume he is lurking somewhere."

Celeste brings her hand to her forehead, feigning a search in the distance. She's enjoying this.

"Or maybe you can tell me why you're blackmailing that scumbag, Matthew Duncan? Are you paying him to terrorize me? Tsk, tsk, I never like to mix business with pleasure, but now you've brought my business into this, haven't you? Does Rani know what you've been up to?"

Rudy's face reveals the truth. "She'll be heartbrok—"

"She already is, *Lani*," Celeste scolds. "Now, pray tell, why was it that you *kidnapped* me in Zurich months ago, with your shallow threats?"

We are all surprised that Celeste has deduced that it was Rudy, and our faces reveal it.

"Oh, yes, I remember your little stunt, and I'd never forget the voice telling me to back off. I suppose we're almost like old friends, you and I, Lani. So in the spirit of transparency, please share—was all this on my husband's orders?"

Rudy is too stunned to speak.

I try once more and am met with a venomous glare. I close my mouth.

"And you—" She turns to Jack. Her voice is eerily calm. "One of my closest friends, someone in whom I've confided my deepest, darkest secrets, over the *decades*? Am I to understand that all your stories over the years, all the adventures, the jetting off to exotic places, the women, the *friendship*, all were merely *lies* to distract me from what you were really doing? What *was* it you were doing, exactly?"

"Celly, we can explain," Jack replies. "Let's all—"

The explosion I anticipate does not come. Instead she says, "The time for explaining was *years* ago before the betrayal, the lies." She is looking at Jack, but I know from her tone that it is meant for me.

I assess the situation as she continues to berate Jack. All we can do at this point is try to bring her in, which is the best way for me to protect her now, all that I've ever wanted to do anyway. I resist the shame and self-pity, though I acknowledge it's true—I've not prevented any harm to her; I've hastened it and put her life in jeopardy more times than I care to admit. But now is not the time. I must get through to my wife before it's too late.

Having finished the first in a few anxious puffs, I light another cigarette and wait for the dopamine calm to rush over me. It does not.

The hairs on my neck stand up as I hear rustling in the greenery behind us. We are not alone, the four of us, anymore. Someone has followed us here from the wedding, and if it is who I suspect, we are outmaneuvered—and most likely dead. Jack and Rudy also notice, and we all make small movements toward our weapons.

As smoke curls in front of her face, my wife finally looks over at me, her expression guarded.

"I want a divorce, Theodore."

And then all hell breaks loose.

TO BE CONTINUED

ALSO BY RACHAEL ECKLES

Continue the Celeste Donovan Series

Trading Secrets, Book One

Risky Assets, Book Two

ACKNOWLEDGMENTS

As I write this, I still don't fully grasp the magnitude that I am (finally!) finished with the third novel in the Celeste Donovan series. I'm first and foremost grateful to my readers who continue to inspire me with your love for the series and who see yourselves in Celeste. I never would've stayed the course without your enthusiasm and support. We did it!

It's been a wild journey. In the five years since I became a published author, I've experienced all five of the significant life changes (in addition to the universal one—the pandemic). Of course so many people can say the same—these modern times are not without challenge. My wish for everyone going through change is that you have a creative outlet. Immersing myself in the Celeste Donovan world was how I fully surrendered to the present moment, worked through my own struggles, and crafted a powerful main character in Celeste who was willing to take on the bad guys for the greater good—a heroine so many of us have longed for throughout our lives. The more her story moves through me, the more I admire Celeste for her courage, resilience, and feminine ferocity—traits I try to embody every day.

I believe storytelling, whether it be through books, music, film, or some other medium, is the most effective and efficient way to ignite personal and social change. Good stories are powerful: They win over juries, influence elections, and sell products. But great stories? Their impact is truly magical. They shape how we see ourselves, others, and our place in the world, they move our hearts and minds, and they transcend all our differences by distilling complex issues into simple reflections on the human experience.

As a little girl born with big dreams and an appetite to experience the world, I immersed myself in the stories between the pages of the hundreds of books I read per year. If only we'd had Goodreads in the eighties and nineties—I'm confident I would've been among the top global performers. The stories gave me the inspiration and courage to leave my hometown and move to a big city—well, *the* big city—for the energy and diversity of thought I craved, travel to some of the most exotic places in the world, and accomplish so many things I never would've imagined possible if I hadn't had a library card. Thank you to all the authors who inspired me by bravely putting your words out in the world, providing younger me with a strong sense of self to defy the life that had been laid out for me and instead pursue my life purpose.

I'm also incredibly grateful to people I'll never meet who took tangible steps to make self-publishing more accessible because you believe, like I do, that the exchange of ideas shouldn't be limited to those books that a handful of big corporations decide to publish. The democratization of storytelling is in my view one of the greatest developments in modern times. My dream is to carry that torch with Aphrodite Books to amplify unique, fierce voices who share my vision to give back to the world through my foundation, Aphrodite Gives, and its cause partners.

Now, onto the people I *have* met who made this book possible. Claudia Carravetta, you always get first mention as my personal Wendy Rhoades performance coach. Without your steady encouragement and unwavering belief in my abilities—both storytelling and entrepreneurial—from the first time we met 15 years ago, it's hard to say whether this trilogy would've ever made it to a single bookshelf or whether Aphrodite Books would be expanding to empower more authors to share their stories. I'm forever thankful.

Roxanne, we've worked together for a decade now, and your reminders to be gentle with myself are always exactly what I need to hear to keep going. Having you remind me that I should take time to be proud of myself is also wonderful. I don't do it often, but I still appreciate the sentiment.

Joyce Bond, this last round of editing was a doozy. They say to work until you're proud, and I think you share the sentiment that we did it this time. Thank you for your commitment to Celeste's world and for all you do to polish her story. Anna Dorfman, thank you for translating what little guidance I gave you into the most beautiful, sparkly romantic suspense covers I've seen. Alex Davies, you've been invaluable in bringing polish to my platform and for spearheading the launch campaign.

Christi Dee, your friendship spans decades and for that I'm grateful, but even more meaningful is that you were the first author who took the bold step of publishing with Aphrodite Books. Thank you for believing in me and my vision and for your commitment to the work we can do together with other authors to ignite positive change through storytelling.

Throughout my 45 years on this planet, my friendships have never been more important to me—or contributed more to my well-being—than in the past two years. A thank you doesn't even scratch the surface of how grateful I am to have you in my life, but here on the page, it will have to suffice.

Jennivere Kenlon, you take the cake for helping me navigate perhaps the most difficult challenges I've ever faced. Thank you for always seeing me and recognizing what I need without my asking.

Alexandra Borchard, you have such a grounding presence in my life. Thank you for being equal parts friend and big sister who can somehow say the things to get through to me when no one else can. You always seem to know the right course of action.

Sarah Yekinni, Mike Carter, and Amanda Koziura-Quick, I'm a firm believer that law school creates friendships that never miss a beat. Thank you for your support, candor, and senses of humor. I know who I'd call if I ever needed to get out of trouble—or wanted to get into some.

Courtney Roberts, we're long overdue to celebrate the sparkly women we are becoming while enjoying a few bottles of Champagne. We have arrived.

Liz Lawson, wow, it's been a wild ride to get to where we are today. Thanks for being one of the smartest people I know (evidenced by how often we have the same opinion on complex issues) and for reliving the old days with me when we need a laugh—or a "late" night out where we're home in bed by 10 p.m. (knowing our twenty-four-year-old selves would find us extremely dull).

Kelsey Lang, you've always been one of my biggest cheerleaders. I'm thankful to for your support, your sense of humor, and your shared love of the perfect lady date night. I'm still waiting for your green light on our group project. It's time!

Amy Miller and Annie Stover—I love celebrating life with both of you, whether it's in NYC or oceans away. Let's do it again soon!

Katherine LaPointe, Peggie LaPointe, Regina Altizer, Cassaundra Saylor, and Megan Wanzo, thank you for your endless support and for cheering me on. You're the best! I can't wait to celebrate with you all very soon!

Jenni Wagoner, Francesca Danzi, Amy King, Denise Bissell—you're lumped together because while I don't get to spend nearly enough time with any of you, I always feel your positive vibes and unwavering support. I'm so grateful to have friends I can pick up with at any time and in any place without missing a beat.

Traci Medford-Rosow, thank you for being a mentor over the years as I somehow stumbled my way to finishing a third book. You're the real deal!

Kathryn Thiele, I love our conversations about the realities of entrepreneurship. Who knew when we had our little meet-cute in the Mediterranean Sea that we'd be where we are today?

Champagne dreams ladies, I'm grateful to you collectively for making daily life in NYC so much more fun and individually for being the sparkly women you are. Lauren-Saint Louis, thank you for cheering me on to become the strongest, most powerful version of myself and for your encouragement as we both continue down our entrepreneurial paths. Katie Noon, so glad that train was canceled long ago and that we met. It's wonderful having a friend who is up for nearly any adventure. Simone Mrs. Eck-less Holoman, thank you for being a kindred travel soul, for being up for our impromptu Manhattan dates, and last but certainly not least, for birthing Koda. Koda, thank you for being Sassy's biggest fan. She appreciates that you facilitate her stealing your toys, even though you realize she'll never let you near hers.

Juan Pedro Liotta and Mia, you two have pivotal roles in bringing my books to life because you're Sassy's NYC family. Thanks for bringing her along on all your clandestine outings to coffee shops across lower Manhattan—don't worry, she never reveals where you've gone; your secrets are safe with her. Keeping her company when she isn't in the mood to tolerate my nonstop working has kept both Mommy and Puppy sane.

To the Aphrodite Insiders not previously mentioned—especially Joanna Serra, Therra Wilbrandt, Dorothy Bennett Hoffman, Gary Meltz, and Caroline Langer—thank you for your enthusiasm and patience as I took *Blind Trust* from concept to bookshelves. You've been in this for the long haul!

Finally, this novel never would've happened without my family. You've all grown accustomed to my grandiose ideas (I'm going to become a lawyer! I'm going to become a yoga teacher! I'm moving to New York! I'm going to become a writer! Guess what, guys? I'm a publisher now!), and yet you automatically assume that I will succeed. Your faith in my abilities is what has gotten me this far in life.

My Grandma Ellie sadly passed away in October 2024 while I was writing this book, but I would be remiss not to credit her role in my becoming a romantic suspense writer. She recognized my love for romance novels when I was way too young and lent me books from her robust LaVyrle Spencer and Danielle Steele collections. She never let me forget how proud she was of me for how hard I worked to become a lawyer and a writer.

Sassy, my sweet fur baby, the past couple of years have been so much transition for us, and I owe you so much for bringing levity and laughter into my everyday life and for staying by my side. We're going to take many long walks on the beach (and OK, yes, we'll go to Europe again soon also) to make up for lost time.

Jessie/Saster and Jordan, I know you're my number-one fans. Thank you for always being amazing cheerleaders for me!

Mom and Daddy, you've been incredible parents. Thank you for supporting my love of reading and my insatiable thirst for books, books, and more books. You two are the ultimate storytellers. Your elaborate tales have fed my imagination since childhood and allowed me to grow up and tell stories of my own.

ABOUT THE AUTHOR

Photo Credit: Oksana Pali

An Indiana native, Rachael Eckles moved to New York City after law school. There she worked in the finance industry, her inspiration for the elusive Celeste Donovan world. She currently lives in Manhattan, where she is working on her next novel. Rachael donates a portion of her proceeds to local and global programs that empower women and girls through her foundation, Aphrodite Gives.

For more information, please follow Rachael Eckles at:
www.RachaelEckles.com

www.ingramcontent.com/pod-product-compliance
Lightning Source LLC
Chambersburg PA
CBHW030338120726
47901CB00007B/1832